The Philo Vance
Murder Cases: 5

The Philo Vance
Murder Cases: 5

The Garden Murder Case &
The Kidnap Murder Case

S. S. Van Dine

LEONAUR

The Philo Vance Murder Cases: 5—The Garden Murder Case
& The Kidnap Murder Case
by S. S. Van Dine

Published by Leonaur Ltd

ISBN: 978-0-85706-433-2 (hardcover)
ISBN: 978-0-85706-434-9 (softcover)

http://www.leonaur.com

Publisher's Notes

The views expressed in this book are not necessarily
those of the publisher.

Contents

The Garden
Murder Case

And two men ride of a horse, one must ride behind.

                   —*Much Ado About Nothing*

Characters of the Book

Philo Vance

John F.-X. Markham—*District Attorney of New York County.*

Ernest Heath—*Sergeant of the Homicide Bureau.*

Ephraim Garden—*Professor of chemistry.*

Martha Garden—*Professor Garden's wife.*

Floyd Garden—*Their son.*

Woode Swift—*Nephew of the Gardens.*

Zalia Graem—*Young sportswoman, and friend of Floyd Garden.*

Lowe Hammle—*An elderly follower of horse-racing.*

Madge Weatherby—*A woman with dramatic aspirations.*

Cecil Kroon—*Another of Floyd Garden's friends.*

Bernice Beeton—*A nurse in the Garden home.*

Doctor Miles Siefert—*The Gardens' family physician.*

Sneed—*The Garden butler.*

Hennessey—*Detective of the Homicide Bureau.*

Snitkin—*Detective of the Homicide Bureau.*

Sullivan—*Detective of the Homicide Bureau.*

Burke—*Detective of the Homicide Bureau.*

Doctor—Emanuel Doremus *Medical Examiner.*

Captain—Dubois *Finger-print expert.*

Detective—Bellamy *Finger-print expert.*

Peter Quackenbush—*Official photographer.*

Jacob Hannix—*A book-maker.*

Currie—*Vance's valet.*

Chapter 1

The Trojan Horses
Friday, April 13; 10 p.m.

There were two reasons why the terrible and, in many ways, incredible Garden murder case—which took place in the early spring following the spectacular Casino murder case[1]—was so designated. In the first place, the scene of this tragedy was the penthouse home of Professor Ephraim Garden, the great experimental chemist of Stuyvesant University; and secondly, the exact *situs criminis* was the beautiful private roof-garden over the apartment itself.

It was both a peculiar and implausible affair, and one so cleverly planned that only by the merest accident—or, perhaps I should say a fortuitous intervention—was it discovered at all. Despite the fact that the circumstances preceding the crime were entirely in Philo Vance's favour, I cannot help regarding it as one of his greatest triumphs in criminal investigation and deduction; for it was his quick uncanny judgments, his ability to read human nature, and his tremendous flair for the significant undercurrents of the so-called trivia of life, that led him to the truth.

The Garden murder case involved a curious and anomalous mixture of passion, avarice, ambition and horse-racing. There was an admixture of hate, also; but this potent and blinding element was, I imagine, an understandable outgrowth of the other factors. However, the case was amazing in its subtleties, its daring, its thought-out mechanism, and its sheer psychological excitation.

The beginning of the case came on the night of April 13. It was one of those mild evenings that we often experience in early spring following a spell of harsh dampness, when all the remaining traces of winter finally capitulate to the inevitable seasonal changes. There was

---

1. *The Casino Murder Case*, 1934.

a mellow softness in the air, a sudden perfume from the burgeoning life of nature—the kind of atmosphere that makes one lackadaisical and wistful, and, at the same time, stimulates one's imagination.

I mention this seemingly irrelevant fact because I have good reason to believe these meteorological conditions had much to do with the startling events that were imminent that night and which were to break forth, in all their horror, before another twenty-four hours had passed.

And I believe that the season, with all its subtle innuendoes, was the real explanation of the change that came over Vance himself during his investigation of the crime. Up to that time I had never considered Vance a man of any deep personal emotion, except in so far as children and animals and his intimate masculine friendships were concerned. He had always impressed me as a man so highly mentalized, so cynical and impersonal in his attitude toward life, that an irrational human weakness like romance would be alien to his nature. But in the course of his deft inquiry into the murders in Professor Garden's penthouse, I saw, for the first time, another and softer side of his character. Vance was never a happy man in the conventional sense; but after the Garden murder case there were evidences of an even deeper loneliness in his sensitive nature.

But these sentimental side-lights perhaps do not matter in the reportorial account of the astonishing history I am here setting down, and I doubt if they should have been mentioned at all but for the fact that they gave an added inspiration and impetus to the energy Vance exerted and the risks he ran in bringing the murderer to justice.

As I have said, the case opened—so far as Vance was concerned with it—on the night of April 13. John F.-X. Markham, then District Attorney of New York County, had dined with Vance at his apartment in East 38th Street. The dinner had been excellent—as all of Vance's dinners were—and at ten o'clock the three of us were sitting in the comfortable library, sipping Napoléon 1809—that famous and exquisite cognac brandy of the First Empire.[2]

Vance and Markham had been discussing crime waves in a desultory manner. There had been a mild disagreement, Vance discounting the theory that crime waves are calculable, and holding that crime is entirely personal and therefore incompatible with gener-

---

2. I realize that this statement will call forth considerable doubt, for real Napoléon brandy is practically unknown in America. But Vance had obtained a case in France; and Lawton Mackall, an exacting connoisseur, has assured me that, contrary to the existing notion among experts, there are at least eight hundred cases of this brandy in a warehouse in Cognac at the present day.

alizations or laws. The conversation had then drifted round to the bored young people of post-war decadence who had, for the sheer excitement of it, organized crime clubs whose members tried their hand at murders wherein nothing was to be gained materially. The Loeb-Leopold case naturally was mentioned, and also a more recent and equally vicious case that had just come to light in one of the leading western cities.

It was in the midst of this discussion that Currie, Vance's old English butler and major-domo, appeared at the library door. I noticed that he seemed nervous and ill at ease as he waited for Vance to finish speaking; and I think Vance, too, sensed something unusual in the man's attitude, for he stopped speaking rather abruptly and turned.

"What is it, Currie? Have you seen a ghost, or are there burglars in the house?"

"I have just had a telephone call, sir," the old man answered, endeavouring to restrain the excitement in his voice.

"Not bad news from abroad?" Vance asked sympathetically.

"Oh, no, sir; it wasn't anything for me. There was a gentleman on the phone—"

Vance lifted his eyebrows and smiled faintly. "A gentleman, Currie?"

"He spoke like a gentleman, sir. He was certainly no ordinary person. He had a cultured voice, sir, and—"

"Since your instinct has gone so far," Vance interrupted, "perhaps you can tell me the gentleman's age?"

"I should say he was middle-aged, or perhaps a little beyond," Currie ventured. "His voice sounded mature and dignified and judicial."

"Excellent!" Vance crushed out his cigarette. "And what was the object of this dignified, middle-aged gentleman's call? Did he ask to speak to me or give you his name?"

A worried look came into Currie's eyes as he shook head.

"No, sir. That's the strange part of it. He said he did not wish to speak to you personally, and he would not tell me his name. But he asked me to give you a message. He was very precise about it and made me write it down word for word and then repeat it. And the moment I had done so he hung up the receiver." Currie stepped forward. "Here's the message, sir." And he held out one of the small memorandum sheets Vance always kept at his telephone.

Vance took it and nodded a dismissal. Then he adjusted his monocle and held the slip of paper under the light of the table lamp. Markham and I both watched him closely, for the incident was unusual, to say the least. After a hasty reading of the paper he gazed off into space, and a clouded look came into his eyes. He read the message again, with more care, and sank back into his chair.

"My word!" he murmured. "Most extr'ordin'ry. It's quite intelligible, however, don't y' know. But I'm dashed if I can see the connection. . ."

Markham was annoyed. "Is it a secret?" he asked testily. "Or are you merely in one of your Delphic-oracle moods?"

Vance glanced toward him contritely.

"Forgive me, Markham. My mind automatically went off on a train of thought. Sorry—really." He held the paper again under the light. "This is the message that Currie so meticulously took down: *There is a most disturbing psychological tension at Professor Ephraim Garden's apartment, which resists diagnosis. Read up on radioactive sodium. See Book XI of the Aeneid, line 875. Equanimity is essential.'*. . .Curious—eh, what?"

"It sounds a little crazy to me," Markham grunted. "Are you troubled much with cranks?"

"Oh, this is no crank,"Vance assured him. "It's puzzlin', I admit; but it's quite lucid."

Markham sniffed sceptically.

"What, in the name of Heaven, have a professor and sodium and the *Aeneid* to do with one another?"

Vance was frowning as he reached into the humidor for one of his beloved *Régie* cigarettes with a deliberation which indicated a mental tension. Slowly he lighted the cigarette. After a deep inhalation he answered.

"Ephraim Garden, of whom you surely must have heard from time to time, is one of the best-known men in chemical research in this country. Just now, I believe, he's professor of chemistry at Stuyvesant University—that could be verified in Who's Who. But it doesn't matter. His latest researches have been directed along the lines of radioactive sodium. An amazin' discovery, Markham. Made by Doctor Ernest 0. Lawrence, of the University of California, and two of his colleagues there, Doctors Henderson and McMillan. This new radioactive sodium has opened up new fields of research in cancer therapy—indeed, it may prove some day to be the long-looked-for cure for cancer. The new gamma radiation of this sodium is more penetrating than any ever before obtained. On the other hand, radium and radioactive substances can be very dangerous if diffused into the normal tissues of the body and through the blood stream. The chief difficulty in the treatment of cancerous tissue by radiation is to find a selective carrier which will distribute the radioactive substance in the tumour alone.

But with the discovery of radioactive sodium tremendous advances have been made; and it will be but a matter of time when this new sodium will be perfected and available in sufficient quantities for extensive experimentation. . . ."[3]

"That is all very fascinating," Markham commented sarcastically. "But what has it to do with you, or with trouble in the Garden home? And what could it possibly have to do with the *Aeneid*? They didn't have radioactive sodium in the time of Aeneas."

"Markham old dear, I'm no Chaldean. I haven't the groggiest notion wherein the situation concerns either me or Aeneas, except that I happen to know the Garden family slightly. But I've a vague feeling about that particular book of the *Aeneid*. As I recall, it contains one of the greatest descriptions of battle in all ancient literature. But let's see. . ." Vance rose quickly and went to the section of his book-shelves devoted to the classics, and, after a few moments' search, took down a small red volume and began to riffle the pages. He ran his eye swiftly down a page near the end of the volume and after a minute's perusal came back to his chair with the book, nodding his head comprehensively, as if in answer to some question he had inwardly asked himself.

"The passage referred to, Markham," he said after a moment, "is not exactly what I had in mind. But it may be even more significant. It's the famous onomatopoeic *Quadrupedumque putrem cursu quatit ungula campum*—meanin', more or less literally: 'And in their galloping course the horsehoof shakes the crumbling plain.'"

Markham took the cigar from his mouth and looked at Vance with undisguised annoyance.

"You're merely working up a mystery. You'll be telling me next that the Trojans had something to do with this professor of chemistry and his radioactive sodium."

"No. Oh, no." Vance was in an unusually serious mood. "Not the Trojans. But the galloping horses perhaps."

Markham snorted. "That may make sense to you."

"Not altogether," returned Vance, critically contemplating the end of his cigarette. "There is, nevertheless, the vague outline of a pattern here. You see, young Floyd Garden, the professor's only offspring, and his cousin, a puny chap named Woode Swift—he's quite an intimate member of the Garden household, I believe—are addicted to the po-

---

3. It is interesting to note the recent announcement that a magnetic accelerator of five million volts and weighing ten tons for the manufacture of artificial radium for the treatment of malignant growths, such as cancer, is being built by the University of Rochester.

nies. Quite a prevalent disease, by the way, Markham. They're both interested in sports in general—probably the normal reaction to their professorial and ecclesiastical forebears: young Swift's father, who has now gone to his Maker, was a D.D. of sorts. I used to see both young johnnies at Kinkaid's Casino occasionally. But the galloping horses are their passion now. And they're the nucleus of a group of young aristocrats who spend their afternoons mainly in the futile attempt to guess which horses are going to come in first at the various tracks."

"You know this Floyd Garden well?"

Vance nodded. "Fairly well. He's a member of the Far Meadows Club and I've often played polo with him. He's a five-goaler and owns a couple of the best ponies in the country. I tried to buy one of them from him once—but that's beside the point.[4] The fact is, young Garden has invited me on several occasions to join him and his little group at the apartment when the out-of-town races were on. It seems he has a direct loud-speaker service from all the tracks, like many of the horse fanatics. The professor disapproves, in a mild way, but he raises no serious objections because Mrs. Garden is rather inclined to sit in and take her chances on a horse now and then."

"Have you ever accepted his invitation?" asked Markham.

"No," Vance told him. Then he glanced up with a far-away look in his eyes. "But I think it might be an excellent idea."

"Come, come, Vance!" protested Markham. "Even if you see some cryptic relationship between the disconnected items of this message you've just received, how, in the name of Heaven, can you take it seriously?"

Vance drew deeply on his cigarette and waited a moment before answering.

"You have overlooked one phrase in the message: 'Equanimity is essential,'" he said at length. "One of the great race-horses of today happens to be named Equanimity. He belongs in the company of such immortals of the turf as Man o' War, Exterminator, Gallant Fox, and Reigh Count.[5] Furthermore, Equanimity is running in the Rivermont Handicap tomorrow."

"Still I see no reason to take the matter seriously," Markham objected.

---

4. At one time Vance was a polo enthusiast and played regularly. He too had a five-goal rating.
5. When Vance read the proof of this record, he made a marginal notation: "And I might also have mentioned Sir Barton, Sysonby, Colin, Crusader, Twenty Grand, and Equipoise."

Vance ignored the comment and added: "Moreover, Doctor Miles Siefert[6] told me at the club the other day that Mrs. Garden had been quite ill for some time with a mysterious malady."

Markham shifted in his chair and broke the ashes from his cigar.

"The affair gets more muddled by the minute," he remarked irritably. "What's the connection between all these commonplace data and that precious phone message of yours?" He waved his hand contemptuously toward the paper which Vance still held.

"I happen to know," Vance answered slowly, "who sent me this message."

"Ah, yes?" Markham was obviously sceptical.

"Quite. It was Doctor Siefert."

Markham showed a sudden interest.

"Would you care to enlighten me as to how you arrived at this conclusion?" he asked in a satirical voice.

"It was not difficult," Vance answered, rising and standing before the empty hearth, with one arm resting on the mantel. "To begin with, I was not called to the telephone personally. Why? Because it was some one who feared I might recognize his voice. Ergo, it was some one I know. To continue, the language of the message bears the earmarks of the medical profession. 'Psychological tension' and 'resists diagnosis' are not phrases ordinarily used by the layman, although they consist of commonplace enough words. And there are two such identifying phrases in the message—a fact which eliminates any possibility of a coincidence. Take this example, for instance: the word uneventful is certainly a word used by every class of person; but when it is coupled with another ordin'ry word, recovery, you can rest pretty much assured that only a doctor would use the phrase. It has a pertinent medical significance—it's a cliché of the medical profession. . . To go another step: the message obviously assumes that I am more or less acquainted with the Garden household and the race-track passion of young Garden. Therefore, we get the result that the sender of the message is a doctor whom I know and one who is aware of my acquaintance with the Gardens. The only doctor who fulfils these conditions, and who, incidentally, is middle-aged and cultured and highly judicial—Currie's description, y' know,—is Miles Siefert. And, added to this simple deduction, I happen to know that Siefert is a Latin scholar—I once encountered him at the Latin Soci-

---

6. Miles Siefert was, at that time, one of the leading pathologists of New York, with an extensive practice among the fashionable element of the city.

ety club-rooms. Another point in my favour is the fact that he is the family physician of the Gardens and would have ample opportunity to know about the galloping horses—and perhaps about Equanimity in particular—in connection with the Garden household."

"That being the case," Markham protested, "why don't you phone him and find out exactly what's back of his cryptography?"

"My dear Markham—oh, my dear Markham!" Vance strolled to the table and took up his temporarily forgotten cognac glass. "Siefert would not only indignantly repudiate any knowledge of the message, but would automatically become the first obstacle in any bit of pryin' I might decide to do. The ethics of the medical profession are most fantastic; and Siefert, as becomes his unique position, is a fanatic on the subject. From the fact that he communicated with me in this roundabout way I rather suspect that some grotesque point of honour is involved. Perhaps his conscience overcame him for the moment, and he temporarily relaxed his adherence to what he considers his code of honour. . .No, no, that course wouldn't do at all. I must ferret out the matter for myself—as he undoubtedly wishes me to do."

"But what is this matter that you feel called upon to ferret out?" persisted Markham. "Granting all you say, I still don't see how you can regard the situation as in any way serious."

"One never knows, does one?" drawled Vance. "Still, I'm rather fond of the horses myself, don't know."

Markham seemed to relax and fitted his manner to Vance's change of mood.

"And what do you propose to do?" he asked good-naturedly.

Vance sipped his cognac and then set down the glass. He looked up whimsically.

"The Public Prosecutor of New York—that noble defender of the rights of the common people—to wit: the Honourable John F.-X. Markham—must grant me immunity and protection before I'll consent to answer."

Markham's eyelids drooped a little as he studied Vance. He was familiar with the serious import that often lay beneath the other's most frivolous remarks.

"Are you planning to break the law?" he asked.

Vance picked up the lotus-shaped cognac glass again and twirled it gently between thumb and forefinger.

"Oh, yes—quite," he admitted nonchalantly. "Jailable offence, I believe."

Markham studied him for another moment.

"All right," he said, without the slightest trace of lightness. "I'll do what I can for you. What's it to be?"

Vance took another sip of the Napoléon.

"Well, Markham old dear," he announced, with a half smile, "I'm going to the Gardens' penthouse tomorrow afternoon and play the horses with the younger set."

CHAPTER 2

Domestic Revelations
Saturday, April 14; noon

As soon as Markham had left us that night, Vance's mood changed. A troubled look came into his eyes, and he walked up and down the room pensively.

"I don't like it, Van," he murmured, as if talking to himself. "I don't at all like it. Siefert isn't the type to make a mysterious phone call like that, unless he has a very good reason for doing so. It's quite out of character, don't y' know. He's a dashed conservative chap, and no end ethical. There must be something worrying him deeply. But why the Gardens' apartment? The domestic atmosphere there has always struck me as at least superficially normal—and now a man as dependable as Siefert gets jittery about it to the extent of indulging in shillin'- shocker technique. It's deuced queer."

He stopped pacing the floor and looked at the clock.

"I think I'll make the arrangements. A bit of snoopin' is highly indicated."

He went into the anteroom, and a moment later I heard him dialling a number on the telephone. When he returned to the library he seemed to have thrown off his depression. His manner was almost flippant.

"We're in for an abominable lunch tomorrow, Van," he announced, pouring himself another pony of cognac. "And we must torture ourselves with the viands at a most ungodly hour—noon. What a time to ingest even good food!" He sighed. "We're lunching with young Garden at his home. Woode Swift will be there and also an insufferable creature named Lowe Hammle, a horsy gentleman from some obscure estate on Long Island. Later we'll be joined by various members of the sporting set, and together we'll indulge in that ancient and fascinatin' pastime of laying wagers on the thoroughbreds. The Rivermont Handicap tomorrow is one of the season's classics. That, at any rate, may be jolly good fun. . ."

He rang for Currie and sent him out to fetch a copy of The Morning Telegraph.

"One should be prepared. Oh, quite. It's been years since I handicapped the horses. Ah, gullible Youth! But there's something about the ponies that gets in one's blood and plays havoc with the saner admonitions of the mind. . .I think I'll change to a dressing-gown."[1]

He finished his Napoléon, lingering over it fondly, and disappeared into the bedroom.

Although I was well aware that Vance had some serious object in lunching with young Garden the following day and in participating in the gambling on the races, I had not the slightest suspicion, at the time, of the horrors that were to follow. On the afternoon of April 14 occurred the first grim act of one of the most atrocious multiple crimes of this generation. And to Doctor Siefert must go, in a large measure, the credit for the identification of the criminal, for had he not sent his cryptic and would-be anonymous message to Vance, the truth would probably never have been known.

I shall never forget that fatal Saturday afternoon. And aside from the brutal Garden murder, that afternoon will always remain memorable for me because it marked the first mature sentimental episode, so far as I had ever observed, in Vance's life. For once, the cold impersonal attitude of his analytical mind melted before the appeal of an attractive woman.

Vance was just re-entering the library in his deep-red *surah*-silk dressing-gown when Currie brought in the Telegraph. Vance took the paper and opened it before him on the desk. To all appearances, he was in a gay and inquisitive frame of mind.

"Have you ever handicapped the ponies, Van?" he asked, picking up a pencil and reaching for a small tablet. "It's as absorbin' an occupation as it is a futile one. At least a score of technical considerations enter into the computations—the class of the horse, his age, his pedigree, the weight he has to carry, the consistency of his past performances,

---

1. Vance at one time owned several excellent race-horses. His Magic Mirror, Smoke Maiden, and Aldeen were well known in their day; and Magic Mirror, as a three-year-old won two of the most important handicaps on the eastern tracks. But when, in the famous Elmswood Special, this horse broke a leg on entering the back-stretch and had to be destroyed, Vance seemed to lose all interest in racing and disposed of his entire stable. He is probably not a true horseman, any more than he is a truly great breeder of Scottish terriers, for his sentiments are constantly interfering with the stern and often ruthless demands of the game.

the time he has made in previous races, the jockey that is to ride him, the type of races he is accustomed to running, the condition of the track and whether or not the horse is a mudder, his post position, the distance of the race, the value of the purse, and a dozen other factors—which, when added up, subtracted, placed against one another, and eventually balanced through an elaborate system of mathematical checking and counter-checking, give you what is supposed to be the exact possibilities of his winning the race on which you have been working. However, it's all quite useless. Less than forty per cent. of favourites—that is, horses who, on paper, should win—verify the result of these calculations. For instance, Jim Dandy beat Gallant Fox in the Travers and paid a hundred to one; and the theoretically invincible Man o' War lost one of his races to a colt named Upset. After all your intricate computations, horse-racing still remains a matter of sheer luck, as incalculable as roulette. But no true follower of the ponies will place a bet until he has gone through the charmin' rigmarole of handicapping the entries. It's little more than abracadabra—but it's three-fourths of the sport."

He gave me a waggish look.

"And that's why I shall sit here for another hour or two at least, indulging one of my old weaknesses. I shall go to the Gardens' tomorrow with every race perfectly calculated—and you will probably make a choice and collect the rewards of innocence." He waved his hand in a pleasant gesture. "Cheerio."

I turned in with a feeling of uneasiness.

Shortly before noon the next day we arrived at Professor Garden's beautiful skyscraper apartment, and were cordially, and a little exuberantly, greeted by young Garden.

Floyd Garden was a man in his early thirties, erect and athletically built. He was about six feet tall, with powerful shoulders and a slender waist. His hair was almost black, and his complexion swarthy. His manner, while easy and casual, and with a suggestion of swagger, was in no way offensive. He was not a handsome man: his features were too rugged, his eyes set too close together, his ears protruded too much, and his lips were too thin. But he had an undeniable charm, and there was a quiet submerged competency in the way he moved and in the rapidity of his mental reactions. He was certainly not intellectual, and later, when I met his mother, I recognized at once that his hereditary traits had come down to him from her side of the family.

"There are only five of us for lunch, Vance," he remarked breezily. "The old gentleman is fussing with his test-tubes and Bunsen burners

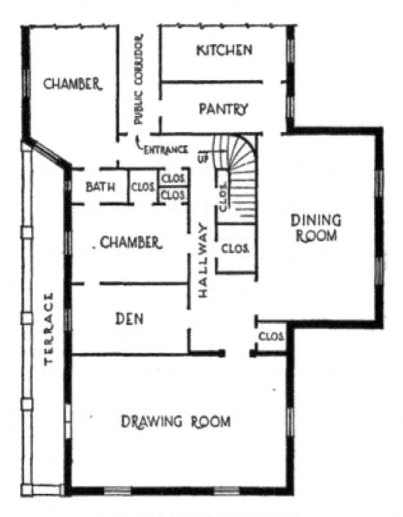

MAIN FLOOR OF GARDEN APARTMENT

at the University; the mater is having a grand time playing sick, with medicos and nurses dashing madly back and forth to arrange her pillows and light her cigarettes for her. But Pop Hammle is coming—rum old bird, but a good sport; and we'll also be burdened with beloved cousin Woode with the brow of alabaster and the heart of a chipmunk. You know Swift, I believe, Vance. As I remember, you once spent an entire evening here discussing Ming *celadons* with him. Queer crab, Woody."

He pondered a moment with a wry face.

"Can't figure out just how he fits into this household. Dad and the mater seem inordinately fond of him—sorry for him, perhaps; or maybe he's the kind of serious, sensitive guy they wish I'd turned out to be. I don't dislike Woode, but we have damned little in common except the horses. Only, he takes his betting too seriously to suit me—he hasn't much money, and his wins or losses mean a lot to him. Of course, he'll go broke in the end. But I doubt if it'll make much difference to him. My loving parents—one of 'em, at least—will stroke his brow with one hand and stuff his pockets with the other. If I went broke as a result of this horse-racing vice they'd tell me to get the hell out and go to work."

He laughed good-naturedly, but with an undertone of bitterness.

"But what the hell!" he added, snapping his fingers. "Let's scoop one down the hatch before we victual."

He pushed a button near the archway to the drawing-room, and a very correct, corpulent butler came in with a large silver tray laden with bottles and glasses and ice.

Vance had been watching Garden covertly during this rambling recital of domestic intimacies. He was, I could see, both puzzled and displeased with the confidences: they were too obviously in bad taste. When the drinks had been poured, Vance turned to him coolly.

"I say, Garden," he asked casually, "why all the family gossip? Really, y' know, it isn't being done."

"My social blunder, old man," Garden apologized readily. "But I wanted you to understand the situation, so you'd feel at ease. I know you hate mysteries, and there's apt to be some funny things happening here this afternoon. If you're familiar with the set-up beforehand, they won't bother you so much."

"Thanks awfully and all that," Vance murmured. "Perhaps I see your point."

"Woode has been acting queer for the past couple of weeks," Garden continued; "as if some secret sorrow was gnawing at his mind. He seems more bloodless than ever. He suddenly goes sulky and distracted for no apparent reason. I mean to say, he acts moonstruck. Maybe he's in love. But he's a secretive duffer. No one'll ever know, not even the object of his affections."

"Any specific psychopathic symptoms?" Vance asked lightly.

"No-o." Garden pursed his lips and frowned thoughtfully. "But he's developed a curious habit of going upstairs to the roof-garden as soon as he's placed a large bet, and he remains there alone until the result of the race has come through."

"Nothing very unusual about that." Vance made a deprecatory motion with his hand. "Many gamblers, d' ye see, are like that. The emotional element, don't y' know. Can't bear to be on view when the result comes in. Afraid of spillin' over. Prefer to pull themselves together before facing the multitude. Mere sensitiveness. Oh, quite. Especially if the result of the wager means much to them...No...no. I wouldn't say that your cousin's retiring to the roof at such tense moments is remarkable, after what you've volunteered about him. Quite logical, in fact."

"You're probably right," Garden admitted reluctantly. "But I wish he'd bet moderately, instead of plunging like a damned fool whenever he's hot for a horse."

"By the by," asked Vance, "why do you particularly look for strange occurrences this afternoon?"

Garden shrugged.

"The fact is," he replied, after a short pause, "Woody's been losing heavily of late, and today's the day of the big Rivermont Handicap. I have a feeling he's going to put every dollar he's got on Equanimity, who'll undoubtedly be the favourite...Equanimity!" He snorted with undisguised contempt. "That rail-lugger! Probably the second greatest horse of modern times—but what's the use? When he does come in he's apt to be disqualified. He's got wood on his mind—in love with fences. Put a fence across the track a mile ahead, with no rails to right or left, and he'd very likely do the distance in 1:30 flat, making James-town, Roamer and Wise Ways look like cripples.[2] He had to cede the win to Vanderveer in the Youthful Stakes. He cut in toward the rail on Persian Bard at Bellaire; and he was disqualified for the same thing in Colorado, handing the race over to Grand Score. In the Urban he tried the same rail-diving, with the result that Roving Flirt won by a nose...How's any one to know about him? And there's always the chance he'll lose, rail or no rail. He's not a young horse any more, and he's already lost eighteen races to date. He's up against some tough ba-bies today—some of the greatest routers from this country and abroad. I'd say he was a pretty bad bet; and yet I know that nut cousin of mine is going to smear him on the nose with everything he owns."

He looked up solemnly.

"And that, Vance, means trouble if Equanimity doesn't come in. It means a blow-up of some kind. I've felt it coming for over a week. It's got me worried. To tell you the truth, I'm glad you picked this day to sit in with us."

---

2. These three horses were the first to better, by fractions of a second, Jack High's 1:35 record for the mile at Belmont.

Vance, who had been listening intently and watching Garden close-ly as he talked, moved to the front window where he stood smoking meditatively and gazing out over Riverside Park twenty stories below, at the sun-sprayed water of the Hudson River.

"Very interestin' situation," he commented at length. "I agree in the main with what you say regarding Equanimity. But I think you're too harsh, and I'm not convinced that he's a rail-lugger because of any innate passion for wood. Equanimity always had shelly feet and a quarter crack or two, and as a result often lost his plates. And, in addi-tion, he had a bad off fore-ankle, which, when it began to sting at the close of a gruelling race, caused him to bear in toward the rail. But he's a great horse. He could do whatever was asked of him at any distance on any kind of track. As a two-year-old he was the leading money-winner of his age; as a three-year-old he already had foot trouble and was started only three times; but as a four-year-old he came back with a new foot and won ten important races. The remarkable thing about Equanimity is that he could either go right to the front and take it on the Bill Daly, or come from behind and win in the stretch. In the Futurity, when he was left at the post and entered the stretch in last place, he dropped two of his plates and, in spite of this, ran over Grand Score and Sublime to win going away. It was a bad foot that kept him from being the world's outstanding champion."

"Well, what of it?" retorted Garden dogmatically. "Excuses are easy to find, and if, as you say, he has a bad foot, that's all the more reason for not playing him today."

"Oh, quite," agreed Vance. "I myself wouldn't wager a farthing on him in this big Handicap. I spent some time porin' over the charts last night after I phoned you, and I decided to stay off Equanimity in to-day's feature. My method of fixing the ratings is no doubt as balmy as any other system, but I couldn't manipulate the ratios in his favour. . ."

"What horse do you like there?" Garden asked with interest.

"Azure Star."

"Azure Star!" Garden was as contemptuous as he was astonished. "Why, he's almost an outsider. He'll be twelve or fifteen to one. There's hardly a selector in the country who's given him a play. An ex-steeple-chaser from the bogs of Ireland! His legs are too weak from jumping to stand the pace today. And at a mile and a quarter! He can't do it! Personally, I'd rather put my money on Risky Lad. There's a horse with great possibilities."

"Risky Lad checks up as unreliable," said Vance. "Azure Star beat him badly at Santa Anita this year. Risky Lad entered the stretch in the lead and then tired to finish fifth. And he certainly didn't run a good mile race at the same track when he finished fifth again in a field of seven. If I remember correctly, he weakened in last year's Classic and was out of the money. His stamina is too uncertain, I should say. . ." Vance sighed and smiled. "Ah, well, *chacun à son cheval*. . . .But as you were sayin', the psychological situation hereabouts has you worried. I gather there's a super-charged atmosphere round this charmin' aerie."

"That's it, exactly," Garden answered almost eagerly. "Super-charged is right. Nearly every day the mater asks, 'How's Woody?' And when the old gentleman comes home from his lab at night he greets me with a left-handed 'Well, my boy, have you seen Woody today?'. . .But I could die of the hoof-and-mouth disease without stirring up such solicitude in my immediate ancestors."

Vance made no comment on these remarks. Instead he asked in a peculiarly flat voice: "Do you consider this recent hyper-tension in the household due entirely to your cousin's financial predicament and his determination to risk all he has on the horses?"

Garden started slightly and then settled back in his chair. After he had taken another drink he cleared his throat. "No, damn it!" he answered a little vehemently. "And that's another thing that bothers me. A lot of the golliwogs we're harbouring are due to Woode's cuckoo state of mind; but there are other queer invisible animals springing up and down the corridors. I can't figure it out. The mater's illness doesn't make sense either, and Doc Siefert acts like a pompous old Buddha whenever I broach the subject. Between you and me, I don't think he knows what to make of it himself. And there's funny business of some kind going on among the gang that drifts in here nearly every afternoon to play the races. They're all right, of course—belong to 'our set,' as the phrase goes, and spring from eminently respectable, if a trifle speedy, environments. . ."

At this moment we heard the sound of light footsteps coming up the hall, and in the archway, which constituted the entrance from the hall into the drawing-room, appeared a slight, pallid young man of perhaps thirty, his head drawn into his slightly hunched shoulders, and a melancholy, resentful look on his sensitive, sallow face. Thick-lensed pince-nez glasses emphasized the impression he gave of physical weakness.

Garden waved his hand cheerily to the newcomer.

"Greetings, Woody. Just in time for a spot before lunch. You know Vance, the eminent sleuth; and this is Mr. Van Dine, his patient and retiring chronicler."

Woode Swift acknowledged our presence in a strained but pleasant manner, and listlessly shook hands with his cousin. Then he picked up the bottle of Bourbon and poured himself a double portion, which he drank at one gulp.

"Good Heavens!" Garden exclaimed good-humouredly. "How you have changed, Woody!...Who's the lady now?"

The muscles of Swift's face twitched, as if he felt a sudden pain.

"Oh, pipe down, Floyd," he pleaded irritably.

Garden shrugged indifferently. "Sorry. What's worrying you today besides Equanimity?"

"That's enough worry for one day." Swift managed a sheepish grin; then he added aggressively: "I can't possibly lose." And he poured himself another drink. "How's Aunt Martha?"

Garden narrowed his eyes.

"She's pretty fair. Nervous as the devil this morning, and smoking one cigarette after another. But she's sitting up. She'll probably be in later to take a crack or two at the prancing steeds. . ."

At this point Lowe Hammle arrived. He was a heavy-set, short man of fifty or thereabouts, with a round ruddy face and closely cropped grey hair. He was wearing a black-and-white checked suit, a grey shirt, a brilliant green four-in-hand, a chocolate-coloured waistcoat with leather buttons, and tan blucher shoes the soles of which were inordinately thick.

"The Marster of 'Ounds, b' Gad!" Garden greeted him jovially. "Here's your Scotch-and-soda; and here also are Mr. Philo Vance and Mr. Van Dine."

"Delighted—delighted!" Hammle exclaimed heartily, coming forward. He extended his hand effusively to Vance. "Been a long time since I saw you, sir. . .Let me see. . .Ah, yes. Broadbank. You hunted with me that morning. Nasty spill you got. Warned you in advance that horse couldn't take the fences. But you were in at the kill—yes, by George! Recollect?"

"Oh, quite. Jolly affair. A good fox. Never fancied your bolting him from that drain into the jaws of the pack after the sport he showed."[3] Vance's manner was icy—obviously he did not like the man—and he turned immediately to Swift and began chatting amiably about the day's big race. Hammle busied himself with his Scotch-and-soda.

---

3. In America, where earths are not stopped, not more than one fox in twenty is actually killed in the open, and it is very unpopular—and by many considered unsportsmanlike—to force a fox out of a place in which he has taken refuge, in order to kill him. But this practice is regularly resorted to in England, for various reasons; and occasionally an American Master will ape the English to this extent in order to boast that he had killed his fox and not merely accounted for him.

In a few minutes the butler announced lunch. The meal was heavy and tasteless, and the wine of dubious vintage,—Vance had been quite right in his prognostication.

The conversation was almost entirely devoted to horses, the history of racing, the Grand National, and the possibilities of the various entrants in the afternoon's Rivermont Handicap. Garden was dogmatic in stating his opinions but eminently pleasant and informative: he had made a careful study of modern racing and had an amazing memory.

Hammle was voluble and suave, and harked back to the former glories of racing and to famous dead heats—Attila and Acrobat in the Travers, Springbok and Preakness in the Saratoga Cup, St. Gatien and Harvester in the English Derby, Pardee and Joe Cotton at Sheepshead Bay, Kingston and YumYum at Gravesend, Los Angeles and White in the Latonia Derby,[4] Domino and Dobbins at Sheepshead Bay, Domino again and Henry of Navarre at Gravesend, Arbuckle and George Kessler in the Hudson Stakes, Sysonby and Race King in the Metropolitan Handicap, Macaw and Nedana at Aqueduct, and Morshion and Mate, also at Aqueduct. He spoke of the great upsets on the track, both here and abroad—of that early winning of the Epsom Derby by an unnamed outsider known as the "Fidget colt"; of the lone success of Amato over Grey Momus, forty-one years later; of the lucky win of Aboyeur in 1913, when Craganour was disqualified; and of the recent win of April the Fifth. He discussed the Kentucky Derby—the unlooked-for success of Day Star as a result of the poor ride given Himyar, and the tragic failure to win of Proctor Knott. And he talked of the great strategy of "Snapper" Garrison in bringing Boundless home in the World's Fair Derby of 1893; of the two lucky races of Plucky Play when he won over Equipoise in the Arlington Handicap and over Faireno in the Hawthorne Gold Cup. He mentioned the fateful ride that Coltiletti gave Sun Beau at Agua Caliente, losing the race to Mike Hall. He had a fund of historic information and, despite his prejudices, knew his subject well.

Swift, nervous and somewhat peevish, had little to say, and though he assumed an outward attitude of attention, I got the impression that other and more urgent matters were occupying his mind. He ate little and drank too much wine.

Vance contented himself mainly with listening and studying the others at the table. When he spoke at all, it was to mention with regret

---

4. "Lucky" Baldwin, the owner of Los Angeles, insisted upon run-off (which was the privilege of the owners of dead-heat winners up to 1932), and Los Angeles won.

some of the great horses that had recently been destroyed because of accidents—Black Gold, Springsteel, Chase Me, Dark Secret and others. He spoke of the tragic and unexpected death of Victorian after his courageous recovery, and the accidental poisoning of the great Australian horse, Phar Lap.

We were nearing the end of the luncheon when a tall, well-built and apparently vigorous woman, who looked no more than forty (though I later learned that she was well past fifty), entered the room. She wore a tailored suit, a silver-fox scarf and a black felt toque.

"Why, mater!" exclaimed Garden. "I thought you were an invalid. Why this spurt of health and energy?"

He then presented me to his mother: both Vance and Hammle had met her on previous occasions.

"I'm tired of being kept in bed," she told her son querulously, after nodding graciously to the others. "Now you boys sit right down—I'm going shopping, and just dropped in to see if everything was going all right. . .I think I'll have a *crème de menthe frappée* while I'm here."

The butler drew up a chair for her beside Swift, and went to the pantry.

Mrs. Garden put her hand lightly on her nephew's arm.

"How goes it with you, Woody?" she asked in a spirit of camaraderie. Without waiting for his answer, she turned to Garden again. "Floyd, I want you to place a bet for me on the big race today, in case I'm not back in time."

"Name your poison," smiled Garden.

"I'm playing Grand Score to win and place—the usual hundred."

"Right-o, mater." Garden glanced sardonically at his cousin. "Less intelligent bets have been made in these diggin's full many a time and oft. . .Sure you don't want Equanimity, mater?"

"Odds are too unfavourable," returned Mrs. Garden, with a canny smile.

"He's quoted in the over-night line at five to two."

"He won't stay there." There was authority and assurance in the woman's tone and manner. "And I'll get eight or ten to one on Grand Score. He was one of the greatest in his younger days, and the old spark may still be there—if he doesn't go lame, as he did last month."

"Right you are," grinned Garden. "You're on the dog for a century win and place."

The butler brought the crème de menthe, and Mrs. Garden sipped it and stood up.

"And now I'm going," she announced pleasantly. She patted her nephew on the shoulder. "Take care of yourself, Woody. . .Good afternoon, gentlemen." And she went from the room with a firm, masculine stride.

After a soggy *Baba au Rhum*, Garden led the way back to the drawing-room and the butler followed for further instructions.

"Sneed," Garden ordered, "fix the set-up as usual."

I glanced at the electric clock on the mantel: it was exactly ten minutes after one.

CHAPTER 3

The Rivermont Races

Saturday, April 14; 1:10 p.m.

"Fixing the set-up" was a comparatively simple procedure, but a more or less mysterious operation for any one unfamiliar with the purpose it was to serve. From a small closet in the hall Sneed first wheeled out a sturdy wooden stand about two feet square. On this he placed a telephone connected to a loud speaker which resembled a midget radio set. As I learned later, it was a specially constructed amplifier to enable every one in the room to hear distinctly whatever came over the telephone.

On one side of the amplifier was attached a black metal switch box with a two-way key. In its upright position this key would cut off the voice at the other end of the line without interfering with the connection; and throwing the key forward would bring the voice on again.

"I used to have ear-phones for the gang," Garden told us, as Sneed rolled the stand back against the wall beside the archway and plugged the extension wires into jacks set in the baseboard.

The butler then brought in a well-built folding card-table and opened it beside the stand. On this table he placed another telephone of the conventional French, or hand, type. This telephone, which was grey, was plugged into an additional jack in the baseboard. The grey telephone was not connected with the one equipped with the amplifier, but was on an independent line.

When the two instruments and the amplifier had been stationed and tested, Sneed brought in four more card-tables and placed them about the drawing-room. At each table he opened up two folding chairs. Then, from a small drawer in the stand, he took out a long manila envelope which had evidently come through the mail, and, slitting the top, drew forth a number of large printed sheets approximately nine by sixteen inches. There were fifteen of these sheets—called "cards" in racing parlance—and after sorting them he spread out three on each of the card-tables. Two neatly sharpened pencils, a well-stocked cigarette box, matches and ash trays completed the equipment on each table. On the table holding the grey telephone was one additional item—a small, much-thumbed ledger.

The final, but by no means least important, duty of Sneed in "fixing the set-up" was to open the doors of a broad, low cabinet in one corner of the room, revealing a miniature bar inside.

A word about the "cards": These concentrated racing sheets were practically duplicates of the programs one gets at a race track, with the exception that, instead of having each race on a separate page, all the races at one track were printed, one after the other, across a single sheet. There were only three tracks open that month, and the cards on each table were the equivalent of the three corresponding programs. Each of the printed columns covered one race, giving the post position of the horses, the name of each entry and the weights carried.[1] At the top of each column were the number and distance of the race, and at the bottom were ruled spaces for the *pari-mutuel* prices. At the left of each column was a space for the odds; and between the names of the horses there was sufficient room to write in the jockeys' names when that information was received.

When Sneed had arranged everything he started from the room, but hesitated significantly in the archway. Garden grinned broadly and, sitting down at the table with the grey telephone, opened the small ledger before him and picked up a pencil.

"All right, Sneed," he said, "on what horse do you want to lose your easily earned money today?" Sneed coughed discreetly.

"If you don't mind, sir, I'd like to risk five dollars on Roving Flirt to show."

Garden made a notation in the ledger.

"All right, Sneed; you're on Roving Flirt for a V at third."

With an apologetic "Thank you, sir," the butler disappeared into the dining-room. When he had gone Garden glanced at the clock and reached for the black telephone connected with the amplifier.

"The first race today," he said, "is at two-thirty, and I'd better hop to it and get the line-up. Lex will be coming on in a few minutes; and

---

1. On the "cards" for New York State, however, the numbers do not correspond to the post positions, as here these positions are drawn shortly before the races begin, except in stake races.

the boys and girls will want to be knowing everything and a little bit more when they arrive with their usual high hopes and misgivings."[2]

He lifted the receiver from the hook of the telephone and dialled a number. After a pause he spoke into the transmitter:

"Hello, Lex. B-2-9-8. Waiting for the dope." And, laying the receiver down on the stand, he threw the switch key forward.

A clear-cut, *staccato* voice came through the amplifier: *"O.K., B-2 -9-8."* Then there was a click, followed by several minutes of silence. Finally the same voice began speaking: *"Everybody get ready. The exact time now is one-thirty and a quarter.—Three tracks today. The order will be Rivermont, Texas, and Cold Springs. Just as you have them on the cards. Here we go. Rivermont: weather clear and track fast. Clear and fast. First post, 2:30. And now down the line. First race: 20, Barbour; 4, Gates; 5, Lyon; 3, Shea; scratch twice; 3, Denham; 20, Z. Smythe—that's S-m-y-t-h-e; 10, Gilly; 10, Deel; 15, Carr.—And the Second race: 4, Elkind; 20, Barbour; 4, Carr; 20, Hunter; 10, Shea; scratch number 6; 20, Gedney, and make the weight 116; scratch number 8; 3 to 5, Lyon; 4, Martinson.—And the Third race: The top one is 10, with Huron; scratch twice; 20, Denham; 20, J. Briggs—that's Johnny Briggs; 20, Hunter; 4, Gedney; even money, Deel; 20, Landseer. And now race number Four. The Rivermont Handicap. The top one is 8, with Shelton; 15, Denham; 10, Redman; 6, Baroco; 20, Gates; 20, Hunter; 6, Cressy; 5, Barbour; 12, J. Briggs—that's Johnny Briggs; 5, Elkind; 4, Martinson; scratch number 12; 20, Gilly; 2 1/2, Birken.—And the Fifth: 6, Littman; 12, Huron. . ."*

The incisive voice continued with the odds and jockeys and scratches on the two remaining races at Rivermont Park. As the announcements came over, Garden attentively and rapidly filled in the data on his card. When the last entrant of the closing race at Rivermont Park had been reached there was a slight pause. Then the announcements continued:

"Now everybody go to Texas. At Texas, weather cloudy and track slow. Cloudy and slow. In the First: 4, Burden; 10, Lansing—"

Garden leaned over and threw the amplifier switch up, and there was silence in the room.

"Who cares about Texas?" he remarked negligently, rising from his chair and stretching. "No one around here plays those goats anyway. I'll pick up the Cold Springs dope later. If I don't, some one's sure to ask for it, just to be contrary." He turned to his cousin. "Why don't you take Vance and Mr. Van Dine upstairs and show them around the

---

2. Alexis Flint was the service announcer at the central news station.

garden?...They might," he added with good-natured sarcasm, "be interested in your lonely retreat on the roof, where you listen in to your fate. Sneed has probably got it arranged for you."

Swift rose with alacrity.

"Damned glad of the chance," he returned surlily. "Your manner today rather annoys me, Floyd." And he led the way down the hall and up the stairs to the roof-garden, Vance and I following. Hammle, who had settled himself in an easy chair with a Scotch-and-soda, remained below with our host.

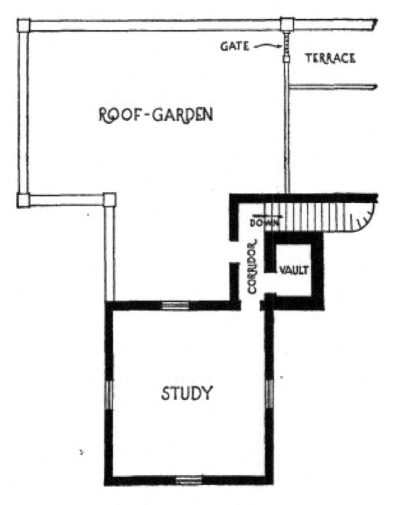

ROOF PLAN OF GARDEN APARTMENT

The stairway was narrow and semicircular, and led upward from the hallway near the front entrance. In glancing back up the hall, toward the drawing-room, I noticed that no section of that room was visible from the stair end of the hall. I made this mental note idly at the time, but I mention it here because the fact played a very definite part in the tragic events which were to follow.

At the head of this narrow stairway we turned left into a corridor, barely four feet wide, at the end of which was a door leading into a large room—the only room on the roof. This spacious and beautifully appointed study, with high windows on all four sides, was used by Professor Garden, Swift informed us, as a library and private experimental laboratory. Near the door to this room, on the left wall of the corridor, was another door, of calamine, which, I learned later, led into a small storeroom built to hold the professor's valuable papers and data.

Half-way down the corridor, on the right, was another large calamine weather door which led out to the roof. This door had been propped open, for the sun was bright and the day mild. Swift preceded us into one of the loveliest skyscraper gardens I have ever seen. It covered a space about forty feet square and was directly over the drawing-room, the den and the reception hall. In the centre was a beautiful rock pool. Along the low brick balustrade were rows of thick privet and evergreens. In front of these were boxed flowerbeds, in which the crocuses, tulips and hyacinths were already blooming in a riot of colour. That part of the garden nearest the study was overhung by a gay stationary awning, and various pieces of comfortable garden furniture were arranged in its shade.

We walked leisurely about the garden, smoking. Vance seemed deeply interested in two or three rare evergreens, and chatted casually about them. At length he turned, strolled back toward the awning, and sat down in a chair facing the river. Swift and I joined him. The conversation was desultory: Swift was a difficult man to talk to, and as the minutes went by he became more and more distrait. After a while he got up nervously and walked to the other end of the garden. Resting his elbows on the balustrade, he looked for several minutes down into Riverside Park; then, with a sudden jerky movement, almost as if he had been struck, he straightened up and came back to us. He glanced apprehensively at his wristwatch.

"We'd better be going down," he said. "They'll be coming out for the first race before long."

Vance gave him an appraising look and rose. "What about that *sanctum sanctorum* of yours which your cousin mentioned?" he asked lightly.

"Oh, that. . ." Swift forced an embarrassed smile. "It's that red chair over there against the wall, next to the small table. . .But I don't see why Floyd should spoof about it. The crowd downstairs always rags me when I lose, and it irritates me. I'd much rather be alone when I get the results."

"Quite understandable," nodded Vance with sympathy.

"You see," the man went on rather pathetically, "I frankly play the ponies for the money—the others downstairs can afford to take heavy losses, but I happen to need the cash just now. Of course, I know it's a hell of a way to try to make money. But you either make it in a hurry or lose it in a hurry. So what's the difference?"

Vance had stepped over to the little table on which stood a desk telephone which had, instead of the ordinary receiver, what is known as a head receiver—that is, a flat disk ear-phone attached to a curved metal band to go over the head.

"Your retreat is well equipped," commented Vance.

"Oh, yes. This is an extension of the news-service phone downstairs; and there's also a plug-in for a radio, and another for an electric plate. And floodlights." He pointed them out to us on the study wall. "All the comforts of a hotel," he added with a sneer.

He took the ear-phone from the hook and, adjusting the band over his head, listened for a moment.

"Nothing new yet at Rivermont," he mumbled.

He removed the earphone with nervous impatience and tossed it to the table. "Anyway we'd better get down." And he walked toward the door by which we had come out in the garden.

When we reached the drawing-room we found two newcomers—a man and a woman—seated at one of the tables, poring over the racing cards and making notations. Vance and I were casually introduced to them by Garden.

The man was Cecil Kroon, about thirty-five, immaculately attired and sleek, with smooth, regular features and a very narrow waxed moustache. He was quite blond, and his eyes were a cold steely blue. The woman, whose name was Madge Weatherby, was about the same age as Kroon, tall and slender, and with a marked tendency toward theatricalism in both her attire and her make-up. Her cheeks were heavily rouged and her lips crimson. Her eyelids were shaded with green, and her eyebrows had been plucked and replaced with fine pencilled lines. In a spectacular way she was not unattractive.

Hammle had moved from his easy chair to one of the card-tables at the end of the room nearest the entrance, and was engaged in checking over the afternoon's entries.

Swift went to the same table and, nodding to Hammle, sat down opposite him. He removed his glasses, wiped them carefully, reached for one of the cards, and glanced over the races.

Garden looked up and motioned to us—he was holding the receiver of the black telephone to his ear.

"Choose a table, Vance, and see how accurate, or otherwise, your method of handicapping is. They'll be coming to the post for the first race in about ten minutes, and we'll be getting a new line shortly."

Vance strolled over to the table nearest Garden's, and seating himself, drew from his pocket a sheet of note-paper on which were written rows of names and figures and computations—the results of his labours, the night before, with the past-performance charts of the horses in that day's races. He adjusted his monocle, lighted a fresh cigarette, and appeared to busy himself with the Rivermont race card. But I could see that he was covertly studying the occupants of the room more intently than he was the racing data.

"It won't be long now," Garden announced, the receiver still at his ear. "Lex is repeating the Cold Springs and Texas lines for some subscribers who were late calling in."

Kroon went to the small bar and mixed two drinks which he took back to his table, setting one down before Miss Weatherby.

"I say, Floyd," he called out to Garden; "Zalia coming today?"

"Absolutely," Garden told him. "She was all stirred up when she phoned this morning. Full of sure things. Bulging with red-hot tips direct from trainers and jockeys and stable-boys and all the other phoney sources of misinformation."

"Well, what about it?" came a vivacious feminine voice from down the hall; and the next moment a swaggering, pretty girl was standing in the archway, her hands on her muscular boyish hips. "I've concluded I can't pick any winners myself, so why not let the other guy pick 'em for me?...Hello, everybody," she threw in parenthetically... "But Floyd, old thing, I really have a humdinger in the First at Rivermont today. This tip didn't come from a stable-boy, either. It came from one of the stewards—a friend of dad's. And am I going to smear that hay-burner!"

"Right-o, Baby-face," grinned Garden. "Step into our parlour."

She started forward, and hesitated momentarily as she caught sight of Vance and me.

"Oh, by the way, Zalia,"—Garden put the receiver down and rose—"let me present Mr. Vance and Mr. Van Dine...Miss Graem."

The girl staggered back dramatically and lifted her hands to her head in mock panic.

"Oh, Heaven protect me!" she exclaimed. "Philo Vance, the detective! Is this a raid?"

Vance bowed graciously.

"Have no fear, Miss Graem," he smiled. "I'm merely a fellow criminal. And, as you see, I'm dragging Mr. Van Dine along the downward path with me."

The girl flashed me a whimsical glance.

"But that isn't fair to Mr. Van Dine. Where would you be without him, Mr. Vance?"

"I admit I'd be unknown and unsung," returned Vance. "But I'd be a happier man—an obscure, but free, spirit. And I'd never have unconsciously provided the inspiration for Ogden Nash's poetic masterpiece."[3]

Zalia Graem smiled broadly, and then pouted.

"It was horrid of Nash to write that jingle," she said. "Personally, I think you're adorable." She went toward the unoccupied card-table. "But, after all, Mr. Vance," she threw back over her shoulder, "you are terribly stingy with your g's."

At this moment Garden, who was again listening through the receiver, announced:

"The new line's coming. Take it down if you want it."

He pressed forward the key on the switch box, and in a moment the voice we had heard earlier was again coming through the amplifier.

"Coming out at Rivermont, and here's the new line: 20, 6, 4, 8 to 5, scratch twice, 3, 20, 15, 10, 15. . . Who was it wanted the run-down at Texas—?"

Garden cut out the amplifier.

"All right, boys and girls," he sang out, drawing the ledger to him. "What's on your mind? Be speedy. Only two minutes to post time. Any customers?. . .How about your hot tip, Zalia?"

"Oh, I'm playing it, all right," Miss Graem answered seriously. "And he's ten to one. I want fifty on Topspede to win—and. . .seventy-five on him to show."

Garden wrote rapidly in the ledger.

"So you don't quite trust your hot tip?" he gloated. "Covering, as it were. . .Who else?"

"I'm playing Sara Bellum," Hammle spoke up. "Twenty-five across the board."

"And I want Moondash—twenty on Moondash to show." This bet came from Miss Weatherby.

---

3. Vance was referring to Nash's famous couplet: "Philo Vance Needs a kick in the pance."

"Any others?" asked Garden. "It's now or never."

"Give me Miss Construe—fifty to win," said Kroon.

"How about you, Vance?" asked Garden.

"I had Fisticuffs and Black Revel down as about equal choices, so I'll take the one with the better odds—but not to win. Make it a hundred on Black Revel a place."

Garden turned to his cousin. "And you, Woody?" Swift shook his head. "Not this race."

"Saving it all for Equanimity, eh? Right-o. I'm staying off this race myself." Garden reached for the grey telephone and dialled a number. . ."Hello, Hannix.[4] This is Garden. . .Feeling fine, thanks. . .Here's the book for the First at Rivermont: Topspede, half a hundred-0-seventy-five. Sara Bellum, twenty-five across the board. Moondash, twenty to show. Miss Construe, half a hundred to win. Black Revel a hundred a place. . .Right."

He hung up the receiver and cut in the amplifier. There was a momentary silence. Then:

"I got 'em at the post at Rivermont. At the post, Rivermont. Topspede is making trouble. . .They've taken him to the outside. . .And there they go! Off at Rivermont at 2:32 and a half. . .At the quarter: it's Topspede, by a length; Sara Bellum, by a head; and Miss Construe. . .At the half: Sara Bellum, half a length; Black Revel, a length; and Topspede. . .In the stretch: Black Revel, a length; Fisticuffs, a head and gaining; and Sara Bellum. . .AND the Rivermont winner: Fisticuffs. The winner is Fisticuffs. Black Revel is second. Sara Bellum is third. The numbers are 4, 7, and 3. Winner closed at eight to five. Hold on for the official O.K. and the muts[5]. . ."

"Well, well, well!" chortled Garden. "That was a grand race for Hannix, as far as this crowd was concerned. They came in like little trained pigs. Even our two winners here didn't nick the old fox for much. Pop Hammle chiselled out a bit of show money, but he has to deduct fifty dollars. And Vance probably picked about even money at place on Black Revel. . .What, about that humdinger of yours, Zalia? Oh, trusting child, will you never learn?. . ."

"Well, anyway," protested the girl good-naturedly, "wasn't Topspede a length ahead at the quarter? And he was still in the money at the half. I had the right idea."

"Sure," returned Garden. "Topspede made a noble effort, but I suspect he's a blood-brother of Morestone and a boy-friend of Nevada

---

4. Hannix was Floyd Garden's book-maker.

5. The *pari-mutuel* prices.

Queen—the world's most eminent folder-uppers. He'd probably go big at three furlongs on the Nursery Course."[6]

"Who cares?" retorted Zalia Graem. "I'm still young and healthy..."

The voice over the amplifier came back:

"*O.K. at Rivermont. Official. They got off at 2:32 and a half. Winner: number 4, Fisticuffs; second, number 7, Black Revel; third, number 3, Sara Bellum. The running time, 1:24...And here are the mots: Fisticuffs paid $5.60—$3.10—$2.90. Black Revel paid $3.90 and $3.20. Sara Bellum paid $5.80...Post time for the second race 3:05. The line: 3, 15, 5, 20, 12, scratch, 15, scratch, 4 to 5, 6...They're coming out at Cold Springs. And here's a new line—*"

Garden cut out the amplifier again.

"Well, Vance," he said, "you're the only winner on the first race. You made ninety-five dollars—all entered up in the ledger. And you, Pop, lose two dollars and a half."[7]

Since no one present was interested in the Texas or Cold Springs meets, there was approximately a half-hour between races. During these intervals the members of the party moved from table to table, chatting, discussing horses, and indulging in pleasant, intimate give-and-take; and there was considerable traffic to and from the bar. Occasionally Garden cut in the amplifier to pick up any late scratches, changes of odds, and other flashes from the tracks.

Vance, while apparently mingling casually with the alternately gay and serious groups, was closely watching everything that went on. I

---

6. David Alexander, the entertaining turf chronicler, wrote an item about these two horses recently. "Morestone," said Mr. Alexander, "could run plenty fast—up to six furlongs. But after six furlongs he flagged the horse ambulance. Morestone could quit in track record time. Nothing like it had been seen since they tried to make Nevada Queen go more than a half-mile a few years ago. There were two mysteries about Morestone. One was how he could run so fast, and the other was how he could quit so fast."

7. *Mutuel* prices are figured on the basis of a two-dollar bet made at the track, and already paid in there. Therefore, away from the track, where the money wagered has not actually been passed over, the two dollars is subtracted from the *mutuel* price and the remainder is then divided by two to ascertain the exact odds which the horse paid on one dollar. In this particular race, Vance's horse paid $3.90 to come in second, or place. Two dollars subtracted from this leaves $1.90, and this amount divided by two gives ninety-five cents—that is, in the position in which Vance played him, Black Revel paid ninety-five cents on the dollar. Hence, Vance, having wagered $100 on the horse to place, won $95. In Hammle's case, the horse paid $5.80 in third place, so that the net odds were $1.90 to the dollar in that position. And, since he bet $25 on the horse to come in third, he won $47.50. But, from this must be deducted the $25 he played on the horse to win, and the $25 he put on the same horse to come in second—both of which bets he lost. This left him minus $2.50.

could plainly see that he was far less interested in the races than in the human and psychological relationships of those present.

Despite the superficial buoyancy of the gathering, I could detect an undercurrent of extreme tension and expectancy; and I made mental note of various little occurrences during the first hour or so. I noticed, for instance, that from time to time Zalia Graem joined Cecil Kroon and Madge Weatherby and engaged them in serious low-toned conversation. Once the three strolled out on the narrow balcony which ran along the north side of the drawing-room.

Swift was by turns hysterically gay and dejected, and he made frequent trips to the bar. His inconsistent moods impressed me unpleasantly; and several times I noticed Garden watching him with shrewd concern.

One incident connected with Swift puzzled me greatly. I had noticed that he and Zalia Graem had not spoken to each other during the entire time they had been in the drawing-room. Once they had brushed against each other near Garden's table, and each, as if instinctively, had drawn resentfully to one side. Garden had cocked his head at them irritably and said:

"Aren't you two on speaking terms yet—or is this feud to be permanent?. . .Why don't you kiss and make up and let the gaiety of the party be unanimous?"

Miss Graem had proceeded as if nothing had happened, and Swift had merely given his cousin a quick, indignant glance. Garden had then smiled sourly, shrugged his shoulders, and turned back to the ledger.

Hammle maintained his complacent, jovial manner throughout the afternoon; but even he seemed ill at ease at times, and his gaze drifted repeatedly to Kroon and Miss Weatherby. Once when Zalia Graem was at their table, he strolled over and boisterously slapped Kroon on the back. Their conversation ceased abruptly, and Hammle filled in the sudden silence with a pointless anecdote about Salvator's race against time at Monmouth Park in 1890.

Garden did not leave his seat at the telephones, and, with the exception of an occasional furtive scrutiny of his cousin, he paid little attention to his guests. . . .

The Second race at Rivermont Park, which went off at eight minutes after three, brought the group better results than the first. Only Kroon lost—he had played the odds-on favourite, Invulnerable, heavily to win; and Invulnerable, though in the lead coming into the stretch, quit badly. However, the next race—which took place a few minutes after half-past three—was a disappointment to every one.

The even-money favourite was bumped at the stretch turn and barely managed to finish third, and an outsider, Ogowan, won the race and paid $86.50. Luckily, no large amount had been placed on the race by any of those present. Swift, incidentally, made no wagers on any of the first three races.

The following race, the Fourth—the post time of which was announced as 4:10—was the Rivermont Handicap; and Garden had no more than cut out the amplifier after the third race, than I felt a curiously subdued and electrified atmosphere in the room.

CHAPTER 4

The First Tragedy
Saturday, April 14; 8 p.m.

"The great moment approaches!" Garden announced, and though he spoke with sententious gaiety, I could detect signs of strain in his manner. "Hannix's phone is going to be pretty busy during the last ten minutes of this momentous intermission, and I'd advise all of you to get your bets in before the post line comes across. There won't be any material changes, anyway; so speed the hopeful wagers."

There was silence for several moments, and then Swift, looking up from his card, said in a peculiarly flat voice:

"Get the latest run-down, Floyd. We haven't had one since the opening line, and there may be some shifts in the odds or a late scratch."

"Anything you say, dear cousin," Garden acceded in a cynical, yet troubled, tone, as he drew down the switch to cut in the amplifier and picked up the black receiver. He waited for a pause in the announcements from Texas and Cold Springs, and then spoke into the transmitter:

"Hello, Lex. Give me the run-down on the big one at Rivermont."

From the amplifier came the now familiar voice:

"I just gave the latest line there. Where've you been?. . .All right, here it is, but listen this time—6, 12, 12, 5, 20, 20, 10, 6, 10, 6, 4, scratch, 20, 2. Post, 4:10. . ."

Garden cut out the amplifier and looked down at the new row of figures he had hastily scribbled beside the earlier odds.

"Not very different from the morning line," he commented. "Heat Lightning, down two; Train Time, down three; Azure Star, up two; Roving Flirt, down one; Grand Score up from six to ten—what a picnic for the mater if he comes in! Risky Lad, up one—and that helps me. Head Start, down two; Sarah Dee, up one; and the rest as they were. Except Equanimity." He shot a quick look at his cousin. "Equanimity has gone from two-and-a-half to two, and I doubt if he'll pay even that much. Too many hopeful but misguided enthusiasts shovelling coarse money into the tote."[1]

Garden got up, mixed himself a highball, and carried it back to the table. Having disposed of it, he turned about in his chair.

"Well, aren't any of the master minds present made up?" He was a little impatient now.

Kroon rose, finished the drink which stood on the table before him, and dabbing his mouth with a neatly folded handkerchief which he took from his breast pocket, he moved toward the archway.

"My mind was made up yesterday." He spoke across the room, as if including every one. "Put me down in your fateful little book for one hundred on Hyjinx to win and two hundred on the same filly a place. And you can add two hundred on Head Start to show. Making it, all told, half a grand. That's my contribution to the afternoon's festivities."

"Head Start's a bad actor at the post," advised Garden, as he entered the bets in the ledger.

"Oh, well," sighed Kroon, "maybe he'll be a smart little boy and beat the barrier today." And he turned into the hall.

"Not deserting us, are you Cecil?" Garden called after him.

"Frightfully sorry," Kroon answered, looking back. "I'd love to stay for the race, but a legal conference at a maiden aunt's is scheduled for four-thirty, and I've got to be there. Papers to sign, and such rubbish. I'll try to get back though, if I don't have to read the bally documents." He waved his hand and, with a "Cheerio," continued down the hall.

Madge Weatherby immediately picked up her cards and moved to Zalia Graem's table, where the two women began a low, whispered conversation. Garden's inquiring glance moved from one to another of the party.

"Is that the only bet I'm to give Hannix?" he asked impatiently. "I'm warning you not to wait too long."

"Put me down for Train Time," Hammle rumbled ponderously. "I've always liked that bay colt. He's a grand stretch runner—but I don't think he'll win today. Therefore, I'm playing him place and show. Make it a hundred each."

"It's in the book," said Garden, nodding to him. "Who's next?"

---

1. Short for totalizator, an electrical, automatic betting device used at *mutuel* tracks.

At this moment a young woman of unusual attractiveness appeared in the archway—and stood there hesitantly, looking shyly at Garden. She wore a nurse's uniform of immaculate white, with white shoes and stockings, and a starched white cap set at a grotesque angle on the back of her head. She could not have been over thirty; yet there was a maturity in her calm, brown eyes, and evidence of great capability in the reserve of her expression and in the firm contour of her chin. She wore no make-up, and her chestnut hair was parted in the middle and brushed back simply over her ears. She presented a striking contrast to the two other women in the room.

"Hello, Miss Beeton," Garden greeted her pleasantly. "I thought you'd be having the afternoon off, since the mater's well enough to go shopping. . .What can I do for you? Care to join the madhouse and hear the races?"

"Oh, no. I've too many things to do." She moved her head slightly to indicate the rear of the house. "But if you don't mind, Mr. Garden," she added timidly, "I would like to bet two dollars on Azure Star to win, and to come in second, and to come in third."

Every one smiled covertly, and Garden chuckled. "For Heaven's sake, Miss Beeton," he chided her, "whatever put Azure Star in your mind?"

"Oh, nothing, really," she answered with a diffident smile. "But I was reading about the race in the paper this morning, and I thought that Azure Star was such a beautiful name. It—it appealed to me."

"Well, that's one way of picking 'em." Garden smiled indulgently. "Probably as good as any other. But I think you'd be better off if you forgot the beautiful name. The horse hasn't a chance. And besides, my book-maker doesn't take any bet less than five dollars."

Vance, who had been watching the girl with more interest than he usually showed in a woman, leaned forward.

"I say, Garden, just a moment." He spoke incisively. "I think Miss Beeton's choice is an excellent one—however she may have arrived at it." Then he nodded to the nurse. "Miss Beeton, I'll be very happy to see that your bet on Azure Star is placed." He turned again to Garden. "Will your book-maker take two hundred dollars across the board on Azure Star?"

"Will he? He'll grab it with both hands," Garden replied. "But why—?"

"Then it's settled," said Vance quickly. "That's my bet. And two dollars of it in each position belongs to Miss Beeton."

"That's perfect with me, Vance." And Garden jotted down the wager in his ledger.

I noticed that during the brief moments that Vance was speaking to the nurse and placing his wager on Azure Star, Swift was glowering at him through half-closed eyes. It was not until later that I understood the significance of that look.

The nurse cast a quick glance at Swift, and then spoke with simple directness.

"You are very kind, Mr. Vance." Then she added: "I will not pretend I don't know who you are, even if Mr. Garden had not called you by name." She stood looking straight at Vance with calm appraisal; then she turned and went back down the hall.

"Oh, my dear!" exclaimed Zalia Graem in exaggerated rapture. "The birth of Romance! Two hearts with but a single horse. How positively stunning!"

"Never mind the jealous persiflage," Garden rebuked the girl impatiently. "Choose your horse, and say how much."

"Oh, well, I can be practical, if subpoenaed," the girl returned. "I'm taking Roving Flirt to win. . .let's see—say, two hundred. And there goes my new spring suit!. . .And I might as well lose my sport coat too; so put another two hundred on him a place. . .And now I think I'll have a bit of liquid sustenance." And she went to the bar.

"How about you, Madge?" Garden asked, turning to Miss Weatherby. "Are you in on this classic?"

"Yes, I'm in on it," the woman answered with affected concern. "I want Sublimate, fifty across."

"Any more customers?" Garden asked, entering the bet. "I myself, if any one is interested, am pinning my youthful hopes on Risky Lad—one, two, and three hundred." He looked across the room apprehensively to his cousin. "What about you, Woody?"

Swift sat hunched in his chair, studying the card before him and smoking vigorously.

"Give Hannix the bets you've got," he said without raising his head. "Don't worry about me—I won't miss the race. It's only four o'clock."

Garden looked at him a moment and scowled.

"Why not get it off your chest now?" As there was no response, he drew the grey telephone toward him and dialled a number. A moment later he was relaying to the book-maker the various bets entered in his ledger.

Swift stood up and walked to the cabinet with its array of bottles. He filled a whiskey glass with Bourbon and drank it down. Then he walked slowly to the table where his cousin sat. Garden had just finished the call to Hannix.

"I'll give you my bet now, Floyd," Swift said hoarsely. He pressed one finger on the table, as if for emphasis. *"I want ten thousand dollars on Equanimity to win."*

Garden's eyes moved anxiously to the other.

"I was afraid of that, Woody," he said in a troubled tone. "But if I were you—"

"I'm not asking you for advice," Swift interrupted in a cold steady voice; "I'm asking you to place a bet."

Garden did not take his eyes from the man's face. He said merely: "I think you're a damned fool."

"Your opinion of me doesn't interest me either." Swift's eyelids drooped menacingly, and a hard look came into his set face. "All I'm interested in just now is whether you're going to place that bet. If not, say so; and I'll place it myself."

Garden capitulated.

"It's your funeral," he said, and turning his back on his cousin, he took up the grey hand set again and spun the dial with determination.

Swift walked back to the bar and poured himself another generous drink of Bourbon.

"Hello, Hannix," Garden said into the transmitter. "I'm back again, with an additional bet. Hold on to your chair or you'll lose your balance. I want ten grand on Equanimity to win. . .Yes, that's what I said: ten G-strings—ten thousand iron men. Can you handle it? Odds probably won't be over two to one. . .Right-o."

He replaced the receiver and tilted back in his chair just as Swift, headed for the hall, was passing him.

"And now, I suppose," Garden remarked, without any indication of raillery, "you're going upstairs so you can be alone when the tidings come through."

"If it won't break your heart—yes." There was a resentful note in Swift's words. "And I'd appreciate it if I was not disturbed." His eyes swept a little threateningly over the others in the room, all of whom were watching him with serious intentness. Slowly he turned and went toward the archway.

Garden, apparently deeply perturbed, kept his eyes on the retreating figure. Then, as if on sudden impulse, he stood up quickly and called out: "Just a minute, Woody. I want to say a word to you." And he stepped after him.

I saw Garden put his arm around Swift's shoulder as the two disappeared down the hall.

Garden was gone from the room for perhaps five minutes, and in his absence very little was said, aside from a few constrained conventional remarks. A tension seemed to have taken possession of every one present: there was a general feeling that some unexpected tragedy was impending—or, at least, that some momentous human factor was in the balance. We all knew that Swift could not afford his extravagant bet—that, in fact, it probably represented all he had. And we knew, too, or certainly suspected, that a serious issue depended upon the outcome of his wager. There was no gaiety now, none of the former light-hearted atmosphere. The mood of the gathering had suddenly changed to one of sombre misgiving.

When Garden returned to the room his face was a trifle pale, and his eyes were downcast. As he approached our table he shook his head dejectedly.

"I tried to argue with him," he remarked to Vance. "But it was no use; he wouldn't listen to reason. He turned nasty. . .Poor devil! If Equanimity doesn't come in he's done for." He looked directly at Vance. "I wonder if I did the right thing in placing that bet for him. But, after all, he's of age."

Vance nodded in agreement.

"Yes, quite," he murmured dryly, "—as you say. Really, y' know, you had no alternative."

Garden took a deep breath and, sitting down at his own table, picked up the black receiver and held it to his ear.

A bell rang somewhere in the apartment, and a few moments later Sneed appeared in the archway.

"Pardon me, sir," he said to Garden, "but Miss Graem is wanted on the other telephone."

Zalia Graem stood up quickly and raised one hand to her forehead in a gesture of dismay.

"Who on earth or in the waters under the earth can that be?" Her face cleared. "Oh, I know." Then she stepped up to Sneed. "I'll take the call in the den." And she hurried from the room.

Garden had paid little attention to this interruption: he was almost oblivious to everything but his telephone, waiting for the time to switch on the amplifier. A few moments later he turned in his chair and announced:

"They're coming out at Rivermont. Say your prayers, children. . .Oh, I say, Zalia," he called out in a loud voice, "tell the fascinating gentleman on the phone to call you back later. The big race is about to start."

There was no response, although the den was but a few steps down the hall.

51

Vance rose and, crossing the room, looked down the hallway, but returned immediately to his table.

"Thought I'd inform the lady," he murmured, "but the den door is closed."

"She'll probably be out—she knows what time it is," commented Garden casually, reaching forward to throw on the amplifier.

"Floyd darling," spoke up Miss Weatherby, "why not get this race on the radio? It's being broadcast by WXZ. Don't you think it'll be more exciting that way? Gil McElroy is announcing it."

"Bully suggestion," seconded Hammle. He turned to the radio, which was just behind him, and tuned in.

"Can Woody still get it upstairs?" Miss Weatherby asked Garden.

"Oh, sure," he answered. "This key on the amplifier doesn't interfere with any of the extension phones."

As the radio tubes warmed up, McElroy's well-known voice gained in volume over the loud speaker:

"...and Equanimity is now making trouble at the post. Took the cue from Head Start...Now they're both back in their stalls—it looks as if we might get a—Yes! They're off! And to a good even start. Hyjinx has dashed into the lead; Azure Star comes next; and Heat Lightning is close behind. The others are bunched. I can't tell one from the other yet. Wait a second. Here they come past us—we're up on the roof of the grandstand here, looking right down on them—and it's Hyjinx on top now, by two lengths; and behind her is Train Time; and—yes, it's Sublimate, by a head, or a nose, or a neck—it doesn't matter—it's Sublimate anyway. And there's Risky Lad creeping up on Sublimate...And now they're going round the first turn, with Hyjinx still in the lead. The relative positions of the ones out front haven't changed yet...They're in the backstretch, and Hyjinx is still ahead by half a length; Train Time has moved up and holds his second position by a length and a half ahead of Roving Flirt, who's in third place. Azure Star is a length behind Roving Flirt. Equanimity is pocketed, but he's coming around on the outside now; he's far behind but gaining; and just behind him is Grand Score, making a desperate effort to get in the clear..."

At this point in the broadcast Zalia Graem appeared suddenly in the archway and stood with her eyes fixed on the radio, her hands sunk in the pockets of her tailored jacket. She rocked a little back and forth, her head slightly to one side, wholly absorbed in the description of the race.

"...They're rounding the far turn. Equanimity has improved his position and is getting into his famous stride. Hyjinx has dropped back and Roving Flirt has taken the lead by a head, with Train Time second, by a length, in front *of Azure Star, who is running third and making a grand effort. . .And now they're in the stretch. Azure Star has come to the front and is a full length in the lead. Train Time is making a great bid for this classic and is still in second place, a length behind Azure Star. Roving Flirt is right behind him. Hyjinx has dropped back and it looks as if she was no longer a serious contender. Equanimity is pressing hard and is now in sixth place. He hasn't much time, but he's running a beautiful race and may come up front yet. Grand Score is falling by the wayside. Sublimate is far out in front of both of them but is not gaining. And I guess the rest are out of the running. . .And here they come to the finish. The leaders are straight out—there won't be much change. Just a second. Here they come. . .and. . .the winner is Azure Star by two lengths. Next is Roving Flirt. And a length behind him is Train Time. Upper Shelf finished fourth. . .Wait a minute. Here come the numbers on the board—Yes, I was right. It's 3, 4, and 2. Azure Star wins the great Rivermont Handicap. Second is Roving Flirt. And third is Train Time. . ."*

Hammle swung round in his chair and shut off the radio.

"Well," he said, releasing a long-held breath, "I was partly right, at that."

"Not such a hot race," Miss Graem remarked with a toss of her head. "I'll just about break even. Anyway, I won't have to join a nudist colony this spring. . .Now I'll go and finish my phone call." And she turned back down the hall.

Garden seemed ill at ease and, for the second time that afternoon, mixed himself a highball.

"Equanimity wasn't even in the money," he commented, as if to himself. . ." But the results aren't official yet. Don't let your hopes rise too high—and don't despair. The winners won't be official for a couple of minutes—and there's no telling what may happen. Remember the final race on the get-away day of the Saratoga meet, when all three placed horses were disqualified?. . ."[2]

Just then Mrs. Garden bustled into the room, her hat, fox scarf, and gloves still on, and two small packages tucked under her arm.

"Don't tell me I'm too late!" she pleaded excitedly. "The traffic was abominable—three-quarters of an hour from 50th Street and Fifth Avenue. . .Is the big race over?"

---

2. Garden was referring to the last race of the final day of a recent Saratoga season, when Anna V. L., Noble Spirit, and Semaphore finished in that order, and all were disqualified, Anna V. L. for swerving sharply at the start and causing other horses to take up, Noble Spirit for swerving badly at the eighth pole, and Semaphore for alleged interference with Anna V. L. The official placing, after the disqualifications, was Just Cap, first; Celiba, second; and Bahadur, third—the only other three horses in the race

"All over but the O.K., mater," Garden informed her.

"And what did I do?" The woman came forward and dropped wearily into an empty chair.

"The usual," grinned Garden. "A Grand Score? Your noble steed didn't score at all. Condolences. But it's not official yet. We'll be getting the O.K. in a minute now."

"Oh, dear!" sighed Mrs. Garden despondently. "The only foul claimed in a race I bet on is against my horse when he wins—and it's always allowed. Nothing can save me now. And I've just spent an outrageous sum on a Brussels lace luncheon set."

Garden cut in the amplifier. There were several moments of silence, and then:

"It's official at Rivermont. O.K. at Rivermont. Off at 4:16. The winner is number 3, Azure Star. Number 4, Roving Flirt, second; and number 2, Train Time, third. That's 3, 4, and 2—Azure Star, Roving Flirt, and Train Time. The running 2:02 and one-fifth—a new track record. And the mats: Azure Star paid $26.80, $9.00 and $6.60. Roving Flirt, $5.20 and $4.60. Train Time, $8.40. . .Next post at 4:40. . ."

"Well, there it is," said Garden glumly, throwing back the switch and making rapid notations in his ledger. "Sneed, our admirable Crichton, makes six and a half dollars. The absent Mr. Kroon loses five hundred, and the present Miss Weatherby loses one hundred and fifty. Our old fox hunter is ahead just two hundred and twenty dollars, with part of which he can buy me a good dinner tomorrow. And you, mater, lose your two hundred dollars—very sad. I myself was robbed of six hundred berries. Zalia—who gets her sizzling tips from the friend of a friend of a distant relative of the morganatic wife of a double-bug rider—is one hundred and twenty dollars to the good—enough to get shoes and a hat and a handbag to match her new spring outfit. And Mr. Vance, the eminent dopester of crimes and ponies, can now take a luxurious vacation. He's the possessor of thirty-six hundred and forty dollars—of which thirty-six dollars and forty cents goes to our dear nurse. . . .And Woode, of course. . ." His voice trailed off.

"What *did* Woody do?" demanded Mrs. Garden, sitting up stiffly in her chair.

"I'm frightfully sorry, mater,"—her son groped for words—"but Woody didn't use his head. I tried to dissuade him, but it was no go. . ."

"Well, what did Woody do?" persisted Mrs. Garden. "Did he lose much?"

Garden hesitated, and before he could formulate an answer, a paralyzing sound, like a pistol shot, broke the tense silence.

Vance was the first on his feet. His face was grim as he moved rapidly toward the archway. I followed him, and just behind came Garden. As I turned into the hallway I saw the others in the drawing-room get up and move forward. Had the report not been preceded by so electric an atmosphere, I doubt if it would have caused any particular perturbation; but, in the circumstances, every one, I think, had the same thought in mind when the detonation of the shot was heard.

As we hurried down the hall Zalia Graem opened the den door. "What was that?" she asked, her frightened eyes staring at us.

"We don't know yet," Vance told her.

In the bedroom door, at the lower end of the hall, stood the nurse, with a look of inquiring concern on her otherwise placid face.

"You'd better come along, Miss Beeton," Vance said, as he started up the stairs two at a time. "You may be needed."

Vance swung into the upper corridor and stopped momentarily at the door on the right, which led out upon the roof. This door was still propped open, and after a hasty preliminary survey through it, he stepped quickly out into the garden.

The sight that met our eyes was not wholly unexpected. There, in the low chair which he had pointed out to us earlier that afternoon, sat Woode Swift, slumped down, with his head thrown back at an unnatural angle against the rattan head-rest, and his legs straight out before him. He still wore the earphone. His eyes were open and staring; his lips were slightly parted; and his thick glasses were tilted forward on his nose.

In his right temple was a small ugly hole beneath which two or three drops of already coagulating blood had formed. His right arm hung limp over the side of the chair, and on the coloured tiling just under his hand lay a small pearl-handled revolver.

Vance immediately approached the motionless figure, and the rest of us crowded about him. Zalia Graem, who had forced her way forward and was now standing beside Vance, swayed suddenly and caught at his arm. Her face had gone pale, and her eyes appeared glazed. Vance turned quickly and, putting his arm about her, half led and half carried her to a large wicker divan nearby. He made a beckoning motion of his head to Miss Beeton.

"Look after her for a moment," he requested. "And keep her head down." Then he returned to Swift. "Every one please keep back," he ordered. "No one is to touch him."

He took out his monocle and adjusted it carefully. Then he leaned over the crumpled figure in the chair. He cautiously scrutinized the wound, the top of the head, and the tilted glasses. When this examination was over he knelt down on the tiling and seemed to be searching for something. Apparently he did not find what he sought, for he stood up with a discouraged frown and faced the others.

"Dead," he announced, in an unwontedly sombre tone. "I'm taking charge of things temporarily."

Zalia Graem had risen from the divan, and the nurse was supporting her with a show of tenderness. The dazed girl was apparently oblivious to this attention and stood with her eyes fixed on the dead man. Vance stepped toward her so that he shut out the sight that seemed to hold her in fascinated horror.

"Please, Miss Beeton," he said, "take the young lady downstairs immediately." Then he added, "I'm sure she'll be all right in a few minutes."

The nurse nodded, put her arm firmly about Miss Graem, and led her into the passageway.

Vance waited until the two young women were gone: then he turned to the others.

"You will all be so good as to go downstairs and remain there until further orders."

"But what are you going to do, Mr. Vance?" asked Mrs. Garden in a frightened tone. She stood rigidly against the wall, with half-closed eyes fixed in morbid fascination on the still body of her nephew. "We must keep this thing as quiet as possible. . .My poor Woody!"

"I'm afraid, madam, we shall not be able to keep it quiet at all." Vance spoke with earnest significance. "My first duty will be to telephone the District Attorney and the Homicide Bureau."

Mrs. Garden gasped, and her eyes opened wide in apprehension.

"The District Attorney? The Homicide Bureau?" she repeated distractedly. "Oh, no!. . .Why must you do that? Surely, any one can see that the poor boy took his own life."

Vance shook his head slowly and looked squarely at the distressed woman.

"I regret, madam," he said, "that this is not a case of suicide—it's murder!"

CHAPTER 5

A Search in the Vault

Saturday, April 14; 4:30 p.m.

Following Vance's unexpected announcement there was a sudden silence. Every one moved reluctantly toward the door to the passageway. Only Garden remained behind.

"I say, Vance,"—he spoke in a shocked, confidential tone—"this is really frightful. Are you sure you're not letting your imagination run away with you? Who could possibly have wanted to shoot poor Woody? He must have done it himself. He was always a weakling, and he's talked about suicide more than once."

Vance looked at the man coldly for a moment.

"Thanks awfully for the information, Garden." His voice was as cold as his glance. "But it won't get us anywhere now, don't y' know. Swift was murdered; and I want your help, not your scepticism."

"Anything I can do, of course," Garden mumbled hastily, apparently abashed by Vance's manner.

"Is there a telephone up here?" Vance asked.

"Yes, certainly. There's one in the study."

Garden brushed past us with nervous energy, as if glad of the opportunity for action. He threw open the door at the end of the passageway and stood aside for us to enter the study.

"Over there," he said, pointing to the desk at the far end of the room, on which stood a hand telephone. "That's an open line. No connection with the one we use for the ponies, though it's an extension of the phone in the den." He stepped swiftly behind the desk and threw a black key on the switch box that was attached to the side of the desk. "By leaving the key in this position, you are disconnected from the extension downstairs, so that you have complete privacy."

"Oh, quite," Vance nodded with a faint smile. "I use the same system in my own apartment. Thanks awfully for your thoughtfulness. . .And now please join the others downstairs and try to keep things balanced for a little while—there's a good fellow."

Garden took his dismissal with good grace and went toward the door.

"Oh, by the way, Garden," Vance called after him, "I'll want a little chat with you in private, before long."

Garden turned, a troubled look on his face.

"I suppose you'll be wanting me to rattle all the family skeletons for you? But that's all right. I want to be as useful as I possibly can—you believe that, I hope. I'll come back the minute you want me. I'll be down there pouring oil on the troubled waters, and when you're ready for me you've only to press that buzzer on the book-shelves there, just behind the desk." He indicated a white push-button set flush in the centre of a small square japanned box on the upright between two sections of the book-shelves. "That's part of the inter-communicating system between this room and the den. I'll see that the den door is left open, so that I can hear the buzz wherever I am."

Vance nodded curtly, and Garden, after a momentary hesitation, turned and went from the room.

As soon as Garden could be heard making his way down the stairs, Vance closed the door and went immediately to the telephone. A moment later he was speaking to Markham.

"The galloping horses, old dear," he said. "The Trojans are riding roughshod. Equanimity was needed, but came in too far behind. Result, a murder. Young Swift is dead. And it was as clever a performance as I've yet seen. . .No, Markham,"—his voice suddenly became grave—"I'm not spoofing. I think you'd better come immediately. And notify Heath,[1] if you can reach him, and the Medical Examiner. I'll carry on till you get here. . ."

He replaced the receiver slowly. Taking out his cigarette case, he lighted a *Régie* with that studied deliberation which, from long observation, I had come to recognize as the indication of a distressed and groping frame of mind.

"This is a subtle crime, Van," he meditated. "Too subtle for my peace of mind. I don't like it—I don't at all like it. And I don't like this intrusion of horse-racing. Sheer expediency. . ."

He looked about the study appraisingly. It was a room nearly

---

1. Sergeant Ernest Heath of the Homicide Bureau, who had had charge of the various criminal investigations with which Vance had been associated.

twenty-five feet square, lined with books and pamphlets and filing cabinets. On some of the shelves and in cabinets and atop every available piece of furniture were specimens of a unique collection of ancient pharmacists' paraphernalia—mortars and pestles of rare earthenware, brass, and bronze, chiselled and ornamented with baluster motives, *mascarons*, lion herms, leafage, cherub heads, Renaissance scrollings, bird figures, and *fleurs de lis*—Gothic, Spanish, French, Flemish, many of them dating back to the sixteenth century; ancient apothecary's scales of brass and ivory, with round columns on plinths, with urn finials, supporting embossed scale pans on straight and bow-shaped steel arms—many of them of late eighteenth-century French design; numerous early pharmacy jars of various shapes, cylindrical, ovoglobular, ring-moulded barrel, incurvate octagonal, ovoid, and one inverted pear, in faience, majolica, and priceless porcelains, exquisitely decorated and lettered; and various other rare and artistic pharmaceutical items—a collection bespeaking years of travel and laborious searching.[2]

Vance walked round the room, pausing here and there before some unique vase or jar.

"An amazin' collection," he murmured. "And not without significance, Van. It gives one an insight into the nature of the man who assembled it—an artist as well as a scientist—a lover of beauty and also a seeker for truth. Really, y' know, the two should be synonymous. However..."

He went thoughtfully to the north window and looked out on the garden. The rattan chair with its gruesome occupant could not be seen from the study, as it was far to the left of the window, near the west balustrade.

"The crocuses are dying," he murmured, "giving place to the hyacinths and daffodils; and the tulips are well on their way. Colour succeeds colour. A beautiful garden. But there's death every hour in a garden, Van—or else the garden itself would not live...I wonder..."

He turned from the window abruptly and came back to the desk.

"A few words with the colourless Garden are indicated, before the minions of the law arrive."

He placed his finger on the white button in the buzzer box and depressed it for a second. Then he went to the door and opened it. Several moments went by, but Garden did not appear, and Vance again

---

2. This collection was later sold at auction, and many of the items are now in the various museums of the country.

pressed the button. After a full minute or two had passed without any response to his summons, Vance started down the passageway to the stairs, beckoning me to follow.

As he came to the vault door on the right, he halted abruptly. He scrutinized the heavy calamine door for a moment or two. At first glance it seemed to be closed tightly, but as I looked at it more closely, I noticed that it was open a fraction of an inch, as if the spring catch, which locked it automatically, had failed to snap when the door had last been shut. Vance pushed on the door gently with the tips of his fingers, and it swung inward slowly and ponderously.

"Deuced queer," he commented. "A vault for preserving valuable documents—and the door unlocked. I wonder. . ."

The light from the hall shone into the dark recess of the vault, and as Vance pushed the door further inward a white cord hanging from a ceiling light became visible. To the end of this cord was attached a miniature brass pestle which acted as a weight. Vance stepped immediately inside and jerked the cord, and the vault was flooded with light.

"Vault" hardly describes this small storeroom, except that the walls were unusually thick, and it had obviously been constructed to serve as a burglar-proof repository. The room was about five by seven feet, and the ceiling was as high as that of the hallway. The walls were lined with deep shelves from floor to ceiling, and these were piled with all manner of papers, documents, pamphlets, filing cases, and racks of test-tubes and vials labelled with mysterious symbols. Three of the shelves were devoted to a series of sturdy steel cash and security boxes. The floor was overlaid with small squares of black and white ceramic tile.

Although there was ample room for us both inside the vault, I remained in the hallway, watching Vance as he looked about him.

"Egoism, Van," he remarked, without turning toward me. "There probably isn't a thing here that any thief would deign to steal. Formulae, I imagine—the results of experimental researches—and such abstruse items, of no value or interest to any one but the professor himself. Yet he builds a special storeroom to keep them locked away from the world. . ."

Vance leaned over and picked up a batch of scattered typewritten papers which had evidently been brushed down from one of the shelves directly opposite the door. He glanced at them for a moment and carefully replaced them in the empty space on the shelf.

"Rather interestin', this disarray," he observed. "The professor was obviously not the last person in here, or he would certainly not have left his papers on the floor. . ." He wheeled about. "My word!"

he exclaimed in a low tone. "These fallen papers and that unlatched door. . .It could be, don't y' know." There was a suppressed excitement in his manner. "I say, Van, don't come in here; and, above all, don't touch this door-knob."

He took out his monocle and adjusted it carefully. Then he knelt down on the tiled floor and began a close inspection of the small squares, as if he were counting them. His action reminded me of the way he had inspected the tiling on the roof near the chair in which we had found young Swift. It occurred to me that he was seeking here what he had failed to find in the garden. His next words confirmed my surmise.

"It should be here," he murmured, as if to himself. "It would explain many things—it would form the first vague outline of a workable pattern. . ."

After searching about for a minute or two, he stopped abruptly and leaned forward eagerly. Then he took a small piece of paper from his pocket and adroitly flicked something onto it from the floor. Folding the paper carefully, he tucked it away in his waistcoat pocket. Although I was only a few feet from him and was looking directly at him, I could not see what it was that he had found.

"I think that will be all for the moment," he said, rising and pulling the cord to extinguish the light. Coming out into the hallway, he closed the vault door by carefully grasping the shank of the knob. Then he moved swiftly down the passageway, stepped through the door to the garden, and went directly to the dead man. Though his back was turned to me as he bent over the figure, I could see that he took the folded paper from his waistcoat pocket and opened it. He glanced repeatedly from the paper in his hand to the limp figure in the chair. At length he nodded his head emphatically, and rejoined me in the hallway. We descended the stairs to the apartment below.

Just as we reached the lower hall, the front door opened and Cecil Kroon entered. He seemed surprised to find us in the hall, and asked somewhat vaguely, as he threw his hat on a bench:

"Anything the matter?"

Vance studied him sharply and made no answer; and Kroon went on:

"I suppose the big race is over, damn it! Who won it—Equanimity?"

Vance shook his head slowly, his eyes fixed on the other.

"Azure Star won the race. I believe Equanimity came in fifth or sixth."

"And did Woody go in on him up to the hilt, as he threatened?"

Vance nodded. "I'm afraid he did."

"Good Gad!" Kroon caught his breath. "That's a blow for the chap. How's he taking it?" He looked away from Vance as if he would rather not hear the answer.

"He's not taking it," Vance returned quietly. "He's dead."

"No!" Kroon sucked in his breath with a whistling sound, and his eyes slowly contracted. When he had apparently recovered from the shock he spoke in a hushed voice: "So he shot himself, did he?"

Vance's eyebrows went up slightly.

"That's the general impression," he returned blandly. "You're not psychic—are you? I didn't mention how Swift died, but the fact is, he did die by a revolver shot. Superficially, I admit, it looks like suicide." Vance smiled coldly. "Your reaction is most interestin'. Why, for instance, did you assume that he shot himself, instead of—let us say— jumping off the roof?"

Kroon set his mouth in a straight line, and a look of anger came into his narrowed eyes. He fumbled in his pocket for a cigarette, and finally stammered:

"I don't know—exactly. . .except that—most people shoot themselves nowadays."

"Oh, quite." Vance's lips were still set in a stern smile. "Not an uncommon way of assisting oneself out of this troublous world. But, really y' know, I didn't mention suicide at all. Why do you take it for granted that his death was self-inflicted?"

Kroon became aggressive. "He was healthy enough when I left here. No one's going to blow a man's brains out in public like this."

"Blow his brains out?" Vance repeated. "How do you know he wasn't shot through the heart?" Kroon was now obviously flustered.

"I—I merely assumed—"

Vance interrupted the man's embarrassment.

"However," he said, without relaxing his calculating scrutiny, "your academic conclusions regarding a more or less public murder are not without some logic. But the fact remains, some one did actually shoot Swift through the head—and practically in public. Things like that do happen, don't y' know. Logic has very little bearing on life and death—and horse-racing. Logic is the most perfect artificial means of arriving at a false conclusion." He held a light to Kroon's cigarette. "However, I could bear to know just where you've been and just when you returned to the apartment house here."

Kroon's gaze wandered, and he took two deep puffs on his cigarette before he answered.

"I believe I remarked before I went out," he said, with an attempt at serenity, "that I was going to a relative's to sign some silly legal documents—"

"And may I have the name and address of your relative—an aunt, I believe you said?" Vance requested pleasantly. "I'm in charge of the situation here until the officials arrive."

Kroon took the cigarette from his mouth with a forced air of nonchalance and drew himself up haughtily.

"I cannot see," he replied stiffly, "that that information concerns any one but myself."

"Neither can I," admitted Vance cheerfully. "I was merely hopin' for frankness. But I can assure you, in view of what has happened here this afternoon, that the police will want to know exactly when you returned from your mysterious signing of documents."

Kroon smirked. "You surely don't think that I've been lingering outside in the hall, do you? I arrived a few minutes ago and came directly up here."

"Thanks awfully," Vance murmured. "And now I must ask you to join the others in the drawing-room, and to wait there until the police arrive. I trust you have no objections."

"None whatever, I assure you," Kroon returned with a display of cynical amusement. "The regular police will be a relief, after this amateur hocus-pocus." He swaggered up the hall toward the archway, with his hands thrust deep in his trousers pockets.

When Kroon had disappeared into the drawing-room, Vance went immediately to the front door, opened it quietly and, walking down the narrow public corridor, pressed the elevator button. A few moments later the sliding door opened and a dark, thin, intelligent-looking boy of perhaps twenty-two, in a light-blue uniform, looked out enquiringly.

"Going down?" he said respectfully.

"I'm not going down," Vance replied. "I merely wanted to ask you a question or two. I'm more or less connected with the District Attorney's office."

"I know you, Mr. Vance." The boy nodded alertly.

"A little matter has come up this afternoon," Vance said, "and I think you may be able to help me . . ."

"I'll tell you anything I know," agreed the boy.

"Excellent! Do you know a Mr. Kroon who visits the Garden apartment?—The gentleman is blond and has a waxed moustache."

"Sure, I know him," the boy returned promptly. "He comes up here nearly every afternoon. I brought him up today."

"About what time was that?"

"Two or three o'clock, I guess." The boy frowned. "Isn't he in there?"

Vance answered the question by asking another. "Have you been on the car all afternoon?"

"Sure I have—since noon. I don't get relieved till seven o'clock."

"And you haven't seen Mr. Kroon since you brought him up here early this afternoon?"

The boy shook his head. "No, sir; I haven't."

"I was under the impression," said Vance, "that Mr. Kroon went out about an hour ago and just returned."

Again the boy shook his head, and gave Vance a puzzled look.

"No. I only brought him up once today; and that was at least two hours ago. I haven't seen him since, going up or down."

The annunciator buzzed, and Vance quickly handed the boy a folded bill.

"Many thanks," he said. "That's all I wanted to know."

The boy pocketed the money and released the door as we turned back to the apartment.

When we re-entered the front hall, the nurse was standing in the doorway of the bedroom at the right of the entrance. There was a worried, inquisitive look in her eyes.

Vance closed the door softly and was about to start up the hall, but he hesitated and turned toward the girl.

"You look troubled, Miss Beeton," he said kindly. "But, after all, you should be accustomed to death."

"I am accustomed to it," she answered in a low voice. "But this is so different. It came so suddenly—without any warning. . .Although," she added, "Mr. Swift always impressed me as more or less the suicidal type."

Vance looked at the nurse appraisingly. "Your impression may have been correct," he said. "But it happens that Swift did not commit suicide."

The girl's eyes opened wide: she caught her breath and leaned against the casing of the door. Her face paled perceptibly.

"You mean someone shot him?" Her words were barely audible. "But who—who—?"

"We don't know." Vance's voice was matter-of-fact. "But we must find that out. . .Would you like to help me, Miss Beeton?"

She drew herself up; her features relaxed; and she was once more the unperturbed and efficient nurse.

"I'd be very glad to." There was more than a suggestion of eagerness in her words.

"Then I would like you to stand guard, as it were," he said, with a faint friendly smile. "I want to talk to Mr. Garden, and I don't want any one to go upstairs. Would you mind taking your post in this chair and notifying me immediately if any one should attempt to go up?"

"That's so little to ask," the girl replied, as she seated herself in a chair at the foot of the stairs.

Vance thanked her and proceeded to the den. Inside Garden and Zalia Graem were sitting close together on a tapestry davenport and talking in low, confidential tones. An indistinct murmur of voices from beyond the archway indicated that the other members of the group were in the drawing-room.

Garden and Miss Graem drew apart quickly as we stepped into the den. Vance ignored their apparent embarrassment and addressed Garden as if he were unaware that he had interrupted a *tête-à-tête*.

"I've called the District Attorney, and he has notified the police. They should be here any minute now. In the meantime, I'd like to see you alone." He turned his head to Miss Graem and added: "I hope you won't mind."

The girl stood up and arched her eyebrows. "Pray, don't consider me," she replied. "You may be as mysterious as you wish."

Garden rebuked her peevishly.

"Never mind the *hauteur*, Zalia." Then he turned to Vance. "Why didn't you ring the buzzer for me? I would have come up. I purposely stayed here in the den because I thought you might be wanting me."

"I did ring, don't y' know," Vance told him. "Twice, in fact. But as you didn't come up, I came down."

"There was no signal here," Garden assured him. "And I've been right here ever since I came downstairs."

"I can vouch for that," put in Miss Graem.

Vance's eyes rested on her for a moment, and there was the trace of a sardonic smile at the corners of his mouth.

"I'm dashed grateful for the corroboration," he murmured.

"Are you sure you pressed the button?" Garden asked Vance. "It's damned funny. That system hasn't failed in six years. Wait a minute. . ."

Going to the door he called loudly for Sneed, and the butler came into the room almost immediately.

"Go upstairs to the study, Sneed," Garden ordered, "and push the buzzer button."

"The buzzer is out of order, sir," the butler told him imperturbably. "I've already notified the telephone company and asked them to send a man to fix it."

"When did you know about it?" Garden demanded angrily.

The nurse, who had heard the conversation, left her chair and came to the doorway.

"I discovered this afternoon that the buzzer wasn't working," she explained; "so I told Sneed about it and suggested that he notify the telephone company."

"Oh, I see. Thank you, Miss Beeton." Garden turned back to Vance. "Shall we go upstairs now?"

Miss Graem, who had been looking on with a cynical and somewhat amused expression, started from the room.

"Why go upstairs?" she asked. "I'll fade into the drawing-room, and you can talk to your heart's content right here."

Vance studied the girl for a few seconds, and then bowed slightly.

"Thank you," he said. "That will be much better." He stood aside as she strolled leisurely into the hall and closed the door after her.

Vance dropped his cigarette into a small ash tray on the *tabouret* before the davenport and, moving swiftly to the door, reopened it. From where I stood in the den, I could see that Miss Graem, instead of going toward the drawing-room, was walking rapidly in the opposite direction.

"Just a moment, Miss Graem!" Vance's voice was peremptory. "Please wait in the drawing-room. No one is to go upstairs just now."

She swung about. "And why not?" Her face was flushed with anger, and her jaw protruded with defiance. "I have a right to go up," she proclaimed spiritedly.

Vance said nothing but shook his head in negation, his eyes holding hers.

She returned his look, but could not resist the power of his scrutiny. Slowly she came back toward him. A sudden change seemed to have come over her. Her eyes dimmed, and tears sprang into them.

"But you don't understand," she protested, in a broken voice. "I'm to blame for this tragedy—it wasn't the race. If it hadn't been for me Woody would be alive now. I—I feel terrible about it. And I wanted to go upstairs—to see him."

Vance put his hand on the girl's shoulder. "Really," he said softly, "there's nothing to indicate that you're to blame."

Zalia Graem looked up at Vance searchingly. "Then what Floyd has been trying to tell me is true—that Woody didn't shoot himself?"

"Quite true," said Vance.

The girl drew a deep breath, and her lips trembled. She took a quick impulsive step toward Vance, and resting her head against his arm, burst into tears.

Vance placed his hands on her arms and held her away from him.

"I say, stop this nonsense," he admonished her sternly. "And don't try to be so deuced clever. Run along to the drawing-room and have a highball. It'll buck you up no end."

The girl's face, suddenly became cynical, and she drew up her shoulders in an exaggerated shrug.

"*Bien, Monsieur* Lecoq," she retorted with a toss of the head. And brushing past him, she swaggered up the hall toward the drawing-room.

CHAPTER 6

An Interrupted Interview
Saturday, April 14; 4:50 p.m.

Vance watched her disappear. Then he turned and met the half wistful, half indignant gaze of Miss Beeton. He smiled at her a bit grimly and started back into the den. At this moment Mrs. Garden came through the archway with a look of resentful determination, and strode aggressively down the hall.

"Zalia has just told me," she said angrily, "that you forbade her to go upstairs. It's an outrage! But surely I may go up. This is my house, remember. You have no right whatever to prevent me from spending these last minutes with my nephew."

Vance turned to confront her. There was a pained look on his face, but his eyes were cold and stern.

"I have every right, madam," he said. "The situation is a most serious one, and if you will not accept that fact, it will be necess'ry for me to assume sufficient authority to compel you to do so."

"This is unbelievable!" the woman remonstrated indignantly.

Garden stepped to the den door.

"For Heaven's sake, mater," he pleaded, "be reasonable. Mr. Vance is quite right. And, anyway, what possible reason could you have for wanting to be with Woody now? We're in for enough scandal as it is. Why involve yourself further?"

The woman looked squarely at her son, and I had a feeling that some telepathic communication passed between them.

"It really doesn't make any particular difference," she conceded with calm resignation. But as she turned her eyes to Vance the look of cynical resentment returned. "Where, sir," she asked, "do you prefer that I remain until your policemen arrive?"

"I don't wish to seem too exacting, madam," Vance returned

quietly; "but I would deeply appreciate it if you remained in the drawing-room."

The woman raised her eyebrows, shrugged her shoulders, and, turning indifferently, went back up the hall.

"Frightfully sorry, Vance," apologized Garden. "The mater is a dowager. Not accustomed to taking orders. And she resents it. I doubt if she really has the slightest desire to sit by Woody's stiffening body. But she hates to be told what to do and what not to do. She'd probably have spent the day in bed, if Doc Siefert hadn't firmly told her not to get up."

"That's quite all right." Vance spoke indifferently, gazing with perplexed meditation at the tip of his cigarette. Then he came quickly to the den door. "Let's have our little chat—eh, what?" He stood aside for Garden to enter the room; then he followed and closed the door.

Garden sat down wearily at one end of the davenport and took a pipe from a small drawer in the *tabouret*. He got out his tobacco and slowly packed the pipe, while Vance walked to the window and stood looking out over the city.

"Garden," he began, "there are a few things that I'd like to have cleared up before the District Attorney and the police arrive." He turned about leisurely and sat down at the desk, facing Garden. The latter was having some difficulty getting his pipe lighted. When he had finally succeeded he looked up dejectedly and met Vance's gaze.

"Anything I can do to help," he mumbled, sucking on his pipe.

"A few necess'ry questions, don't y' know," Vance went on. "Hope they won't upset you, and all that. But the fact is, Mr. Markham will probably want me to take a hand in the investigation, since I was a witness to the preamble of this distressin' tragedy."

"I hope he does," Garden returned. "It's a damnable affair, and I'd like to see the axe fall, no matter whom it might behead." His pipe was still giving him trouble. "By the way, Vance," he went on quietly, "how did you happen to come here today? I've asked you so often to join our racing séance—and you pick the one day when the roof blows off the place."

Vance kept his eyes on Garden for a moment.

"The fact is," he said at length, "I got an anonymous telephone message last night, vaguely outlining the situation here and mentioning Equanimity."

Garden jerked himself up to keener attention. His eyes opened wide, and he took the pipe from his mouth.

"The devil you say!" he exclaimed. "That's a queer one. Man or woman?"

"Oh, it was a man," Vance replied casually. Garden pursed his lips and, after a moment's meditation, said quietly:

"Well, anyway, I'm damned glad you did come. . .What can I tell you that might be of help? Anything you want, old man."

"First of all, then," asked Vance, "did you recognize the revolver? I saw you looking at it rather apprehensively when we came out on the roof."

Garden frowned, busied himself for a moment with his pipe, and finally answered, as if with sudden resolution:

"Yes! I did recognize it, Vance. It belongs to the old gentleman—"

"Your father?"

Garden nodded grimly. "He's had it for years. Why he ever got it in the first place, I don't know—he probably hasn't the slightest idea how to use it. . ."

"By the by," Vance put in, "what time does your father generally return home from the University?"

"Why—why—" Garden hesitated and then continued: "On Saturdays he's always here early in the afternoon—rarely after three. Gives himself and his staff a half-holiday. . .But," he added, "father's very erratic. . ." His voice trailed off nervously.

Vance took two deep inhalations on his cigarette: he was watching Garden attentively. Then he asked in a soft tone:

"What's on your mind?—Unless, of course, you have good reason for not wanting to tell me."

Garden took a long breath and stood up. He seemed to be deeply troubled as he walked across the room and back.

"The truth is, Vance," he said, as he resumed his place on the davenport, "I don't even know where the *pater* is this afternoon. As soon as I came downstairs after Woody's death, I called him to give him the news. I thought he'd want to get here as soon as possible, in the circumstances. But I was told that he'd locked up the laboratory and left the University about two o'clock." Garden looked up quickly. "He's probably gone to the library for some research work. Or he may have swung round to Columbia. He spends a good bit of his time there."

I could not understand the man's perturbation; and I could see that it puzzled Vance as well. Vance endeavoured to put him at his ease.

"It really doesn't matter," he said, as if dismissing the subject. "It may be just as well that your father doesn't learn of the tragedy till later." He smoked for a moment. "But to get back to the revolver: where was it usually kept?"

"In the centre drawer of the desk upstairs," Garden told him promptly.

"And was the fact generally known to the other members of the household, or to Swift himself?"

Garden nodded. "Oh, yes. There was no secret about it. We often joked with the old gentleman about his 'arsenal.' Only last week, at dinner, he thought he heard some one in the garden and ran upstairs to see who it was. The mater called after him spoofingly: 'At last you may have a chance to use your precious revolver.' The old gentleman returned in a few minutes rather sheepishly. One of the flower-pots had been blown over and had rolled across the tiles. We all rode him good-naturedly for the rest of the meal."

"And the revolver was always loaded?"

"So far as I know, yes."

"And was there an extra supply of cartridges?"

"As to that, I cannot say," Garden answered; "but I don't think so."

"And here's a very important question, Garden," Vance went on. "How many of the people that are here today could possibly have known that your father kept this loaded revolver in his desk? Now, think carefully before answering."

Garden meditated for several moments. He looked off into space and puffed steadily on his pipe.

"I am trying to remember," he said reminiscently, "just who was here the day Zalia came upon the gun—"

"What day was that?" Vance cut in sharply.

"It was about three months ago," Garden explained. "You see, we used to have the telephone set-up connected upstairs in the study. But some of the western races came in so late that it began to interfere with the old gentleman's routine when he came home from the University. So we moved the paraphernalia down into the drawing-room. As a matter of fact, it was more convenient; and the mater didn't object—in fact, she rather enjoyed it—"

"But what happened on this particular day?" insisted Vance.

"Well, we were all upstairs in the study, going through the whole silly racing rigmarole that you witnessed this afternoon, when Zalia Graem, who always sat at the old gentleman's desk, began opening the drawers, looking for a piece of scratch paper on which to figure the *mutuels*. She finally opened the centre drawer and saw the revolver. She brought it out with a flourish and, laughing like a silly schoolgirl, pointed it around the room. Then she made some comments about the perfect gambling accommodations, drawing a parallel between the presence of the gun and the suicide room at Monte Carlo. 'All the conveniences of the Riviera,' she babbled. Or something to that effect. 'When you've lost your chemise, you can blow out your brains.' I reprimanded her—rather rudely, I'm afraid—and ordered her to put the revolver back in its place, as it was loaded—and just then a race came over the amplifier, and the episode was ended."

"Most interestin'," murmured Vance. "And can you recall how many of those present today were likewise present at Miss Graem's little *entr'acte*?"

"I rather think they were all there, if my memory is correct."

Vance sighed.

"A bit futile—eh, what? No possible elimination along that line."

Garden looked up, startled.

"Elimination? I don't understand. We were all downstairs here this afternoon except Kroon—and he was out—when the shot was fired."

"Quite—oh, quite," agreed Vance, leaning back in his chair. "That's the puzzlin' and distressin' part of this affair. No one could have done it, and yet someone did. But let's not tarry over the point. There are still one or two matters I want to ask you about."

"Go right ahead." Garden seemed completely perplexed. . .

At this moment there was a slight commotion in the hallway. It sounded as if a scuffle of some kind was in process, and a shrill, protesting voice mingled with the calm but determined tones of the nurse. Vance went immediately to the door and threw it open. There, just outside the den door, only a short distance from the stairway, were Miss Weatherby and Miss Beeton. The nurse had a firm hold on the other woman and was calmly arguing with her. As Vance stepped toward them, Miss Weatherby turned to face him and drew herself up arrogantly.

"What's the meaning of this?" she demanded. "Must I be mauled by a menial because I wish to go upstairs?"

"Miss Beeton has orders that no one is to go upstairs," Vance said sternly. "And I was unaware that she is a menial."

"But why can't I go upstairs?" the woman asked with dramatic emphasis. "I want to see poor Woody. Death is so beautiful; and I was very fond of Woody. By whose orders, pray, am I being denied this last communion with the departed?"

"By my orders," Vance told her coldly. "Furthermore, this particular death is far from beautiful, I assure you. Unfortunately, we are not living in a Maeterlinckian era. Swift's death is rather a sordid one, don't y' know. And the police will be here any minute. Until then no one will be permitted to disturb anything upstairs."

Miss Weatherby's eyes flashed.

"Then why," she demanded with histrionic indignation, "was this—this woman"—she glanced with exaggerated contempt at the nurse—"coming down the stairs herself when I came into the hall?"

Vance made no attempt to hide a smile of amusement.

"I'm sure I don't know. I may ask her later. But she happens to be under instructions from me to let no one go upstairs. Will you be so good, Miss Weatherby," he added, almost harshly, "as to return to the drawing-room and remain there until the officials arrive?"

The woman glared superciliously at the nurse, and then, with a toss of the head, strode toward the archway. There she turned and, with a cynical smirk, called back in an artificial tone:

"Blessings upon you, my children." Whereupon she disappeared into the drawing-room.

The nurse, obviously embarrassed, turned to resume her post, but Vance stopped her.

"Were you upstairs, Miss Beeton?" he asked in a kindly tone.

She was standing very erect, her face slightly flushed. But, for all her apparent mental disturbance, she was like a symbol of poise. She looked Vance frankly and firmly in the eye and slowly shook her head.

"I haven't left my post, Mr. Vance," she said quietly. "I understand my duty."

Vance returned her gaze for a moment, and then bowed his head slightly.

"Thank you, Miss Beeton," he said.

He came back into the den, and closing the door, addressed Garden again.

"Now that we have disposed temporarily of the theatrical queen,"— he smiled sombrely—"suppose we continue with our little chat."

Garden chuckled mildly and began repacking his pipe.

"Queer girl, Madge; always acting like a tragedienne—but I don't think she's ever really been on the stage. Suppressed theatrical ambition and that sort of thing. Dreams of herself as another Nazimova. And morbid as they come. Outside of that, she's a pretty regular sort. Takes her losses like an old general—and she's lost plenty the last few months. . ."

"You heard her tell me she was particularly fond of Swift," remarked Vance. "Just what did she mean by that?"

Garden shrugged. "Nothing at all, if you ask me. She didn't know that Woody was on earth, so to speak. But dead, Woody becomes a dramatic possibility."

"Yes, yes—quite," murmured Vance. "Which reminds me: what was the tiff between Swift and Miss Graem about? I noticed your little peace-maker advances this afternoon."

Garden became serious.

"I haven't been able to figure that situation out myself. I know they were pretty soft on each other some time ago—that is, Woody was pretty deep in the new-mown hay as far as Zalia went. Hovered round her all the time, and took all her good-natured bantering without a murmur. Then, suddenly, the embryonic love affair—or whatever it was—went sour. I'll-never-speak-to-you-again stuff. Like two kids. Both of them carrying around at least a cord of wood on each shoulder whenever the other was present. Obviously something had happened, but I never got the straight of it. It may have been a new flame on Woody's part—I rather imagine it was something of the kind. As for Zalia, she was never serious about it anyway. And I have an idea that Woody wanted that extra twenty thousand today for some reason connected with Zalia. . ." Garden stopped speaking abruptly and slapped his thigh. "By George! I wouldn't be surprised if that hard-bitten little gambler had turned Woody down because he was comparatively hard up. You can't tell about these girls today. They're as practical as the devil himself."

Vance nodded thoughtfully.

"Your observations rather fit with the remarks she made to me a little while ago. She, too, wanted to go upstairs to see Swift. Gave as her excuse the fact that she felt she was to blame for the whole sordid business."

Garden grinned.

"Well, there you are." Then he remarked judicially: "But you can never tell about women. One minute Zalia gives the impression of being superficial; and the next minute she'll make some comment that would almost lead you to believe she were an octogenarian philosopher. Unusual girl. Infinite possibilities there."

"I wonder." Vance smoked in silence for a moment. Then he went on: "There's another matter in connection with Swift which you might be able to clear up for me. Could you suggest any reason why, when I placed the bet on Azure Star for Miss Beeton this afternoon, Swift should have looked at me as if he would enjoy murdering me?"

"I saw that too," Garden nodded. "I can't say it meant anything much. Woody was always a weak sister where any woman was concerned. It took damned little to make him think he'd fallen in love. He may have become infatuated with the nurse—he'd been seeing her around here for the past few months. And now that you mention it, he's been somewhat poisonous toward me on several occasions because she was more or less friendly with me and ignored him entirely. But I'll say this for Woody: if he did have ideas about Miss Beeton, his taste is improving. She's an unusual girl—different. . ."

Vance nodded his head slowly and gazed with peculiar concentration out the window.

"Yes," he murmured. "Quite different." Then, as if bringing himself back from some alien train of thought, he crushed out his cigarette and leaned forward. "However, we'll drop speculation for the moment. . . Suppose you tell me something about the vault upstairs."

Garden glanced up in evident surprise.

"There's nothing to tell about that old catch-all. It's neither mysterious nor formidable. And it's really not a vault at all. Several years ago the *pater* found that he had accumulated a lot of private papers and experimental data that he didn't want casual callers messing in. So he had this fire-proof storeroom built to house these scientific treasures of his. The vault, as you call it, was built as much for mere privacy as for actual safe-keeping. It's just a very small room with shelves around the walls."

"Has everyone in the house access to it?" asked Vance.

"Anyone so inclined," replied Garden. "But who, in the name of Heaven, would want to go in there?"

"Really, y' know, I haven't the groggiest notion," Vance returned, "except that I found the door to it unlatched when I was coming downstairs a little while ago."

Garden shrugged carelessly, as if the matter was neither important nor unusual.

"Probably," he suggested, "the *pater* didn't shut the door tightly when he went out this morning. It has a spring lock."

"And the key?"

"The key is a mere matter of form. It hangs conveniently on a small nail at the side of the door."

"Accordingly," mused Vance, "the vault is readily accessible to any one in the household who cares to enter it."

"That's right," nodded the other. "But what are you trying to get at, Vance? What's the vault to do with poor Woody's death?"

"I'm not sure," returned Vance slowly, rising and going again to the window. "I wish I knew. I'm merely tryin' not to overlook any possibility."

"Your line of inquiry sounds pretty far-fetched to me," Garden commented indifferently.

"One never knows, does one?" Vance murmured, going to the door. "Miss Beeton," he called, "will you be good enough to run upstairs and see if the key to the vault door is in its place?"

A few moments later the nurse returned and informed Vance that the key was where it was always kept.

Vance thanked her and, closing the den door, turned again to Garden.

"There's one more rather important matter that you can clear up for me—it may have a definite bearing on the situation." He sat down in a low green leather chair and took out his cigarette case. "Can the garden be entered from the fire exit opening on the roof?"

"Yes, by George!" The other sat up with alacrity. "There's a gate in the east fence of the garden, just beside the privet hedge, which leads upon the terrace on which the fire exit of the building opens. When we had the fence built we were required to put this gate in because of the fire laws. But it's rarely used, except on hot summer nights. Still, if any one came up the main stairs to the roof and went out the emergency fire door, he could easily enter our garden by coming through that gate in the fence."

"Don't you keep the gate locked?" Vance was studying the tip of his cigarette with close attention.

"The fire regulations don't permit that. We merely have an old-fashioned barn-door lift-latch on it."

"That's most interestin'," Vance commented in a low voice. "Then, as I understand it, any one coming up the main stairway could walk out through the fire exit to the terrace, and enter your garden. And, of course, return the same way."

"That's true." Garden narrowed his eyes questioningly. "Do you really think that some one may have entered the garden that way and popped poor Woody off while we were all down here?"

"I'm doing dashed little thinking at the present moment," Vance answered evasively. "I'm trying to gather some material to think about, don't y' know. . ."

We could hear the sharp ringing of the entrance bell, and a door opening somewhere. Vance stepped out into the hall. A moment later the butler admitted District Attorney Markham and Sergeant Heath, accompanied by Snitkin and Hennessey.[1]

---

1. Snitkin and Hennessey were two detectives of the Homicide Bureau, who had worked as associates of Sergeant Heath on the various criminal cases with which Vance had previously been connected.

CHAPTER 7

Evidence of Murder
Saturday, April 14; 5:10 p.m.

"Well, what's the trouble, Vance?" Markham demanded brusquely. "I phoned Heath, as you requested, and brought him up with me."

"It's a bad business," Vance returned. "Same like I told you. I'm afraid you're in for some difficulties. It's no ordin'ry crime. Everything I've been able to learn so far contradicts everything else." He looked past Markham and nodded pleasantly to Heath. "Sorry to make you all this trouble, Sergeant."

"That's all right, Mr. Vance." Heath held out his hand in solemn good-nature. "Glad I was in when the Chief called. What's it all about, and where do we go from here?. . ."

Mrs. Garden came bustling energetically down the hallway.

"Are you the District Attorney?" she asked, eyeing Markham ferociously. Without waiting for an answer, she went on: "This whole thing is an outrage. My poor nephew shot himself and this gentleman here"—she looked at Vance with supreme contempt—"is trying to make a scandal out of it." Her eyes swept over Heath and the two detectives. "And I suppose you're the police. There's no reason whatever for your being here."

Markham looked steadfastly at the woman and seemed to take in the situation immediately.

"Madam, if things are as you say," he promised in a pacifying, yet grave, tone, "you need have no fear of any scandal."

"I'll leave the matter entirely in your hands, sir," the woman returned with calm dignity. "I shall be in the drawing-room, and I trust you will notify me the moment you have done what is necessary." She turned and walked back up the hall.

"A most tryin' and complicated state of affairs, Markham." Vance took the matter up again. "I admit the chap upstairs appears to have killed himself. But that, I think, is what every one is *supposed to believe.* Tableau superficially correct. Stage direction and décor fairly good. But the whole far from perfect. I observed several discrepancies. As a matter of fact, the chap did not kill himself. And there are several people here who should be questioned later. They're all in the drawing-room now—except Floyd Garden."

Garden, who had been standing in the doorway to the den, came forward, and Vance introduced him to Markham and Heath. Then Vance turned to the Sergeant.

"I think you'd better have either Snitkin or Hennessey remain down here and see that no one leaves the apartment for a little while." He addressed Garden. "I hope you won't mind."

"Not at all," Garden replied complacently. "I'll join the others in the drawing-room. I feel the need of a highball, anyway." He included us all in a curt bow and moved up the hall.

"We'd better go up to the roof now, Markham," said Vance. "I'll run over the whole matter with you. There are some strange angles to the case. I don't at all like it. Rather sorry I came today. It might have passed for a nice refined suicide, with no bother or suspicion—every one smugly relieved. But here I am. However. . ."

He moved down the hall, and Markham and Heath and I followed him. But before he mounted the stairs he stopped and turned to the nurse.

"You needn't keep watch here any longer, Miss Beeton," he said. "And thanks for your help. But one more favour: when the Medical Examiner comes, please bring him directly upstairs."

The girl inclined her head in acquiescence and stepped into the bedroom.

We went immediately up to the garden. As we stepped out on the roof, Vance indicated the body of Swift slumped in the chair.

"There's the johnnie," he said. "Just as he was found."

Markham and Heath moved closer to the huddled figure and studied it for a few moments. At length Heath looked up with a perplexed frown.

"Well, Mr. Vance," he announced querulously, "it looks like suicide, all right." He shifted his cigar from one corner of his mouth to the other.

Markham too turned to Vance. He nodded his agreement with the Sergeant's observation.

"It certainly has the appearance of suicide, Vance," he remarked.

"No—oh, no," Vance sighed. "Not suicide. A deuced brutal crime—and clever no end."

Markham smoked a while, still staring at the dead man sceptically; then he sat down facing Vance.

"Let's have the whole story before Doremus[1] gets here," he requested, with marked irritation.

Vance remained standing, his eyes moving aimlessly about the garden. After a moment he recounted succinctly, but carefully, the entire sequence of events of the afternoon, describing the group of people present, with their relationships and temperamental clashes; the various races and wagers; Swift's retirement to the garden for the results of the big Handicap; and, finally, the shot which had aroused us all and brought us upstairs. When he had finished, Markham worried his chin for a moment.

"I still can't see a single fact," he objected, "that does not point logically to suicide."

Vance leaned against the wall beside the study window and lighted a *Régie*.

"Of course," he said, "there's nothing in the outline I've given you to indicate murder. Nevertheless, it was murder; and that outline is exactly the concatenation of events which the murderer wants us to accept. We are supposed to arrive at the obvious conclusion of suicide. Suicide as the result of losing money on horses is by no means a rare occurrence, and only recently there has been an account of such a suicide in the papers.[2] It is not impossible that the murderer's scheme was influenced by this account. But there are other factors, psychological and actual, which belie this whole superficial and deceptive structure." He drew on his cigarette and watched the thin blue ribbon of smoke disperse in the light breeze from the river. "To begin with," he went on, "Swift was not the suicidal type. A trite observation—and one that is often untrue. But there can be little doubt of its truth in the present instance, despite the fact that young Garden has taken pains to convince me to the contr'ry. In the first place, Swift was a weakling and a highly imaginative one. Moreover, he was too hopeful and ambitious—too sure of his own judgment and good luck—to put himself out of the world simply because he had lost all his money. The fact that Equanimity might not win the race was an eventuality which, as

1. Doctor Emanuel Doremus, the Chief Medical Examiner of New York.
2. Vance was referring to the suicide of a man in Houston, Texas, who left the following note: "To the public—Race horses caused this. The greatest thing the Texas Legislature can do is to repeal and enforce the gambling law."

a confirmed gambler, he would have taken into consideration beforehand. In addition, his nature was such that, if he were greatly disappointed, the result would be self-pity and hatred of others. He might, in an emergency, have committed a crime—but it would not have been against himself. Like all gamblers, he was trusting and gullible; and I think it was these temperamental qualities which probably made him an easy victim for the murderer. . ."

"But see here, Vance." Markham leaned forward protestingly. "No amount of mere psychological analysis can make a crime out of a situation as seemingly obvious as this one. After all, this is a practical world; and I happen to be a member of a practical profession. I must have more definite reasons than you have given me before I would be justified in discarding the theory of suicide."

"Oh, I dare say," nodded Vance. "But I have more tangible evidence that the johnnie did not eliminate himself from this life. However, the psychological implications of the man's nature—the contradictions, so to speak, between his character and the present situation—were what led me in the first place to look for more specific and demonstrable evidence that he was not unassisted in his demise."

"Well, let's have it." Markham fidgeted impatiently in his chair.

"*Imprimis*, my dear Justinian, a bullet wound in the temple would undoubtedly cause more blood than you see on the brow of the deceased. There are, as you notice, only a few partly coagulated drops, whereas the vessels of the brain cannot be punctured without a considerable flow of blood. And there is no blood either on his clothes or on the tiles beneath his chair. Meanin' that the blood had been, perhaps, spilled elsewhere before I arrived on the scene—which was, let us say, within thirty seconds after we heard the shot—"

"But good Heavens, man!—"

"Yes, yes; I know what you're going to say. And my answer is that the gentleman did not receive the bullet in his temple as he sat in yonder chair with the head-phone on. He was shot elsewhere and brought here."

"A far-fetched theory," muttered Markham. "All wounds don't bleed the same."

Vance ignored the District Attorney's objection.

"And please take a good look at the poor fellow as he sits there, freed from all the horrors of the struggle for existence. His legs are stretched forward at an awkward angle. The trousers are twisted out of place and look most uncomfortable. His coat, though buttoned, is riding his shoulders, so that his collar is at least three inches above his exquisite mauve shirt. No man could endure to have his clothes so outrageously askew, even on the point of suicide—he would have straightened them out almost unconsciously. The *corpus delicti* shows every indication of having been dragged to the chair and placed in it."

Markham's eyes were surveying the limp figure of Swift as Vance talked.

"Even that argument is not entirely convincing," he said dogmatically, though his tone was a bit modified; "especially in view of the fact that he still wears the ear-phone. . ."

"Ah, exactly!" Vance took him up quickly. "That's another item to which I would call your attention. The murderer went a bit too far—there was a trifle too much thoroughness in the setting of the stage. Had Swift shot himself in that chair, I believe his first impulsive movement would have been to remove the head-phone, as it very easily could have interfered with his purpose. And it certainly would have been of no use to him after he had heard the report of the race. Furthermore, I seriously doubt if he would have come upstairs to listen to the race with his mind made up in advance that he was going to commit suicide in case his horse didn't come in. And, as I have explained to you, the revolver is one belonging to Professor Garden and was always kept in the desk in the study. Consequently, if Swift had decided, after the race had been run, to shoot himself, he would hardly have gone into the study, procured the gun, then come back to his chair on the roof and put the head-phone on again before ending his life. Undoubtedly he would have shot himself right there in the study—at the desk from which he had obtained the revolver."

Vance moved forward a little as if for emphasis.

"Another point about that head-phone—the point that gave me the first hint of murder—is the fact that the receiver at present is over Swift's right ear. Earlier today I saw Swift put the head-phone on for a minute, and he was careful to place the receiver over his left ear— the custom'ry way. The telephone receiver, d' ye see, Markham, has always been placed on the left side of the phone box, in order to leave the right hand free to make notations or for other emergencies. The result is, the left ear has adapted itself to hearing more distinctly over the wire than the right ear. And humanity, as a result, has accustomed itself to holding a telephone receiver to the left ear. Swift was merely conforming to custom and instinct when he placed the receiving end of the headphone on the left side of his head. But now the head-phone is on in reversed position, and therefore unnatural. I'm certain, Markham, that head-phone was placed on Swift after he was dead."

Markham meditated on this for several moments.

"Still, Vance," he said at length, "reasonable objections could be raised to all the points you have brought up. They are based almost entirely on theory and not on demonstrable facts."

"From a legal point of view, you're right," Vance conceded. "And if these had been my only reasons for believing that a crime had been committed, I wouldn't have summoned you and the doughty Sergeant. But, even so, Markham, I can assure you the few drops of blood you see on the chappie's temple could not have thickened to the extent they had when I first saw the body—they must have been exposed to the air for several minutes. And, as I say, I was up here approximately thirty seconds after we heard the shot."

"But that being the case," returned Markham in astonishment, "how can you possibly explain the fact?"

Vance straightened a little and looked at the District Attorney with unwonted gravity.

"Swift," he said, *"was not killed by the shot we heard."*

"That don't make sense to me, Mr. Vance," Heath interposed, scowling.

"Just a moment, Sergeant." Vance nodded to him in friendly fashion. "When I realized that the shot that wiped out this johnnie's existence was not the shot that we had heard, I tried to figure out where the fatal shot could have been fired without our hearing it below. And I've found the place. It was in a vault-like storeroom—practically sound-proof, I should say—on the other side of the passageway that leads to the study. I found the door unlocked and looked for evidence of some activity there. . ."

Markham had risen and taken a few nervous steps around the pool in the centre of the roof.

"Did you find any evidence," he asked, "to corroborate your theory?"

"Yes—unmistakable evidence." Vance walked over to the still figure in the chair and pointed to the thick-lensed glasses tipped forward on the nose. "To begin with, Markham, you will notice that Swift's glasses are in a position far from normal, indicatin' that they were put on hurriedly and inaccurately by some one else—just as was the head-phone."

Markham and Heath leaned over and peered at the glasses.

"Well, Mr. Vance," agreed the Sergeant, "they certainly don't look as if he had put 'em on himself."

Markham straightened up, compressed his lips, and nodded slowly.

"All right," he said; "what else?"

"Perpend, Markham." Vance pointed with his cigarette. "The left lens of the glasses—the one furthest from the punctured temple—is cracked at the corner, and there's a very small V-shaped piece missing where the crack begins—an indication that the glasses have been dropped and nicked. I can assure you that the lens was neither cracked nor nicked when I last saw Swift alive."

"Couldn't he have dropped his glasses on the roof here?" asked Heath.

"Possible, of course, Sergeant," Vance returned. "But he didn't. I carefully looked over the tiles round the chair, and the missin' bit of glass was not there."

Markham looked at Vance shrewdly.

"And perhaps you know where it is."

"Yes oh, yes." Vance nodded. "That's why I urged you to come here. That piece of glass is at present in my waistcoat pocket."

Markham showed a new interest.

"Where did you find it?" he demanded brusquely.

"I found it," Vance told him, "on the tiled floor in the vault across the hall. And it was near some scattered papers which could easily have been knocked to the floor by some one falling against them."

Markham's eyes opened incredulously, and he turned and studied the dead man again meditatively. At length he took a deep breath and pursed his lips.

"I'm beginning to see why you wanted me and the Sergeant here," he said slowly. "But what I don't understand, Vance, is that second shot that you heard. How do you account for it?"

Vance drew deeply on his cigarette.

"Markham," he answered, with quiet seriousness; "when we know how and by whom that second shot—which was obviously intended for us to hear—was fired, we will know who murdered Swift. . ."

At this moment the nurse appeared in the doorway leading to the roof. With her was Doctor Doremus, and behind the Medical Examiner were Captain Dubois and Detective Bellamy, the finger-print men, and Peter Quackenbush, the official police photographer.

CHAPTER 8

Disconnected Wires

Saturday, April 14; 5:30 p.m.

Miss Beeton indicated our presence on the roof with a professional nod as she stepped to one side, and the Medical Examiner strolled briskly toward us, with a "Thank you, my dear," thrown over his shoulder to the nurse.

"If I can be of any help—" the young woman offered.

"Not at the moment, thank you," replied Vance with a friendly smile; "though we may call on you later."

With an inclination of her head she indicated that she understood, and made her way back downstairs.

Doremus acknowledged our joint greetings with a breezy wave of the hand, and halted jauntily in front of Heath.

"Congratulations, Sergeant," he said in a bantering falsetto. "By Gad, congratulations!"

The Sergeant was immediately on his guard—he knew the peppery little Medical Examiner of old. "Well, what's it all about, doc?" Heath grinned.

"For once in your life," Doremus went on jocularly, "you picked the right time to summon me. Positively amazin', as Mr. Vance here would say. I wasn't eating or sleeping when your call came in. Nothing to do—bored with life, in fact. For the first time in history, you haven't dragged me away from my victuals or out from under my downy quilt. Why this sudden burst of charitable consideration?...Not a minim of vinegar in my system today. Bring on your corpses and I'll look 'em over without rancour."

Heath was amused in spite of his annoyance.

"I ain't arranging murders for your convenience. But if I caught you in an idle moment this time, it's fine with me...There's the fellow in the chair over there. It's Mr. Vance's find—and Mr. Vance has got ideas about it."

Doremus pushed his hat further back on his head, thrust his hands deep in his trousers pockets and stepped leisurely to the rattan chair with its lifeless occupant. He made a cursory examination of the limp figure, scrutinized the bullet hole, tested the arms and legs for *rigor mortis*, and then swung about to face the rest of us.

"Well, what about it?" he asked, in his easy cynical manner. "He's dead; shot in the head with a small-calibre bullet; and the lead's probably lodged in the brain. No exit hole. Looks as if he'd decided to shoot himself. There's nothing here to contradict the assumption. The bullet went into the temple, and is at the correct angle. Furthermore, there are powder marks, showing that the gun was held at very close range—almost a contact wound, I should say. There's an indication of singeing around the orifice."

He teetered on his toes and leered at the Sergeant.

"You needn't ask me how long he's been dead, for I can't tell you. The best I can do is to say that he's been dead somewhere between thirty minutes and a couple of hours. He isn't cold yet, and rigor mortis hasn't set in. The blood from the wound is only slightly coagulated, but the variations of this process—especially in the open air—do not permit an accurate estimate of the time involved:. . . What else do you want me to tell you?"

Vance took the cigarette from his mouth and addressed Doremus.

"I say, doctor; speakin' of the blood on the johnnie's temple, what would you say about the amount?"

"Too damned little, I'd say," Doremus returned promptly. "But bullet wounds have a queer way of acting sometimes. Anyway, there ought to be a lot more gore."

"Precisely," Vance nodded. "My theory is that he was shot elsewhere and brought to this chair."

Doremus made a wry face and cocked his head to one side.

"*Was* shot? Then you don't think it was suicide?" He pondered a moment. "It could be, of course," he decided finally. "There's no reason why a corpse can't be carried from one place to another. Find the rest of the blood and you'll probably know where his death occurred."

"Thanks awfully, doctor." Vance smiled faintly. "That did flash through my mind, don't y' know; but I believe the blood was wiped up. I was merely hopin' that your findings would substantiate my theory that he did not shoot himself while sitting in that chair, without any one else around."

Doremus shrugged indifferently.

"That's a reasonable enough assumption," he said. "There really ought to be more blood. And I can tell you that he didn't mop it up himself after the bullet was fired. He died instantly."

"Have you any other suggestions?" asked Vance.

"I may have when I've gone over the body more carefully after these babies"—he waved his hand toward the photographer and the finger-print men—"finish their hocus-pocus."

Captain Dubois and Detective Bellamy had already begun their routine, with the telephone table as the starting-point; and Quackenbush was adjusting his small metal tripod.

Vance turned to Dubois. "I say, Captain, give your special attention to the head-phone, the revolver, and the glasses. Also the door-knob of the vault across the hall inside."

Dubois nodded with a grunt, and continued his delicate labours.

Quackenbush, his camera having been set up, took his pictures and then waited by the passageway door for further instructions from the finger-print officers.

When the three men had gone inside, Doremus drew in an exaggerated sigh and spoke to Heath impatiently.

"How about getting your *corpus delicti* over on the settee? Easier to examine him there."

"O.K., doc."

The Sergeant beckoned to Snitkin with his head, and the two detectives lifted Swift's limp body and placed it on the same wicker divan where Zalia Graem had lain when she collapsed at the sight of the dead man.

Doremus went to work in his usual swift and efficient fashion. When he had finished the task, he threw a steamer rug over the dead man, and made a brief report to Vance and Markham.

"There's nothing to indicate a violent struggle, if that's what you're hoping for. But there's a slight abrasion on the bridge of the nose, as if his glasses had been jerked off; and there's a slight bump on the left side of his head, over the ear, which may have been caused by a blow of some kind, though the skin hasn't been broken."

"How, doctor," asked Vance, "would the following theory square with your findings:—that the man had been shot elsewhere, had fallen to a tiled floor, striking his head against it sharply, that his glasses had been torn off when the left lens came in contact with the floor, and that he was carried out here to the chair, and the glasses replaced on his nose?"

86

Doremus pursed his lips and inclined his head thoughtfully.

"That would be a very reasonable explanation of the lump on his head and the abrasion on the bridge of his nose." He jerked his head up, raised his eyebrows, and smirked. "So this is another of your cock-eyed murders, is it? Well, it's all right with me. But I'll tell you right now, you won't get an autopsy report tonight. I'm bored and need excitement; and I'm going to Madison Square Garden to see Strangler Lewis and Londos have it out on the mat." He thrust his chin out in good-natured belligerence at Heath. "And I'm not going to leave my seat number at the box-office either. That's fair warning to you, Sergeant. You can either postpone your future casualties until tomorrow, or worry one of my assistants."

He made out an order for the removal of the body, readjusted his hat, waved a friendly good-bye which included all of us, and disappeared swiftly through the door into the passageway.

Vance led the way into the study, and the rest of us followed him. We were barely seated when Captain Dubois came in and reported that there were no finger-prints on any of the objects Vance had enumerated.

"Handled with gloves," he finished laconically, "or wiped clean."

Vance thanked him. "I'm not in the least surprised," he added.

Dubois rejoined Bellamy and Quackenbush in the hall, and the three made their way down the stairs.

"Well, Vance, are you satisfied?" Markham asked.

Vance nodded. "I hadn't expected any fingerprints. Cleverly thought-out crime. And what Doremus found fills some vacant spots in my own theory. Stout fella, Doremus. For all of his idiosyncrasies, he understands his business. He knows what is wanted and looks for it. There can be no question that Swift was in the vault when he was shot; that he fell to the floor, brushing down some of the, papers; that he struck his head on the tiled floor, and broke the left lens of his glasses—you noted, of course, that the lump on his head is also on the left side—and that he was dragged into the garden and placed in the chair. Swift was a small, slender man; probably didn't weigh over a hundred and twenty pounds; and it would have been no great feat of strength for some one to have thus transported him after death. . ."

There were footsteps in the corridor and, as our eyes involuntarily turned toward the door, we saw the dignified elderly figure of Professor Ephraim Garden. I recognized him immediately from pictures I had seen.

He was a tall man, despite his stooped shoulders; and, though he was very thin, he possessed a firmness of bearing which made one feel that he had retained a great measure of the physical power that had obviously been his in youth. There was benevolence in the somewhat haggard face, but there was also shrewdness in his gaze; and the contour of his mouth indicated a latent hardness. His hair, brushed in a pompadour, was almost white and seemed to emphasize the sallowness of his complexion. His dark eyes and the expression of his face were like his son's; but he was a far more sensitive and studious type than young Garden.

He bowed to us with an old-fashioned graciousness and took a few steps into the study.

"My son has just informed me," he said in a slightly querulous voice, "of the tragedy that has occurred here this afternoon. I'm sorry that I did not return home earlier, as is my wont on Saturdays, for in that event the tragedy might have been averted. I myself would have been in the study here and would probably have kept an eye on my nephew. In any event, no one could then have got possession of my revolver."

"I am not at all sure, Doctor Garden," Vance returned grimly, "that your presence here this afternoon would have averted the tragedy. It is not nearly so simple a matter as it appears at first glance."

Professor Garden sat down in a chair of antique workmanship near the door and, clasping his hands tightly, leaned forward.

"Yes, yes. So I understand. And I want to hear more about this affair." The tension in his voice was patent. "Floyd told me that Woode's death had all the appearances of suicide, but that you do not accept that conclusion. Would it be asking too much if I requested further details with regard to your attitude in this respect?"

"There can be no doubt, sir," Vance returned quietly, "that your nephew was murdered. There are too many indications that contradict the theory of suicide. But it would be inadvisable, as well as unnecess'ry, to go into details at the moment. Our investigation has just begun."

"Must there be an investigation?" Professor Garden asked in tremulous protest.

"Do you not wish to see the murderer brought to justice?" Vance retorted coldly.

"Yes—yes; of course." The professor's answer was almost involuntary; but as he spoke his eyes drifted dreamily to the window overlooking the river, and he sank dejectedly a little lower into his chair. "It's most unfortunate, however," he murmured. Then he looked appealingly to Vance. "But are you sure you are right and that you are not creating unnecessary scandal?"

"Quite," Vance assured him. "Whoever committed the murder made several grave miscalculations. The subtlety of the crime was not extended through all phases of it. Indeed, I believe that some fortuitous incident or condition made certain revisions necess'ry at the last moment. . .By the by, doctor, may I ask what detained you this afternoon?—I gathered from your son that you usually return home long before this time on Saturdays."

"Of course, you may," the man replied with seeming frankness; but there was a startled look in his eyes as he gazed at Vance. "I had some obscure data to look up before I could continue with an experiment I'm making; and I thought today would be an excellent time to do it, since I close the laboratory and let my assistants go on Saturday afternoons."

"And where were you, doctor," Vance went on, "between the time you left the laborat'ry and the time of your arrival here?"

"To be quite specific," Professor Garden answered, "I left the University at about two and went to the public library where I remained until half an hour ago. Then I took a cab and came directly home."

"You went to the library alone?" asked Vance.

"Naturally I went alone," the professor answered tartly. "I don't take assistants with me when I have research work to do." He stood up suddenly. "But what is the meaning of all this questioning? Am I, by any chance, being called upon to furnish an alibi?"

"My dear doctor!" said Vance placatingly. "A serious crime has been committed in your home, and it is essential that we know—as a matter of routine—the whereabouts of the various persons in any way connected with the unfortunate situation."

"I see what you mean." Professor Garden inclined his head courteously and moved to the front window where he stood looking out to the low purple hills beyond the river, over which the first crepuscular shadows were creeping.

"I am glad you appreciate our difficulties," Vance said; "and I trust you will be equally considerate when I ask you just what was the relationship between you and your nephew?"

The man turned slowly and leaned against the broad sill.

"We were very close," he answered without hesitation or resentment. "Both my wife and I have regarded Woode almost as a son, since his parents died. He was not a strong person morally, and he needed both spiritual and material assistance. Perhaps because of this fundamental weakness in his nature, we have been more lenient with him than with our own son. In comparison with Woode, Floyd is a strong-minded and capable man, fully able to take care of himself."

Vance nodded with understanding.

"That being the case, I presume that you and Mrs. Garden have provided for young Swift in your wills."

"That is true," Professor Garden answered after a slight pause. "We have, as a matter of fact, made Woode and our son equal beneficiaries."

"Has your son," asked Vance, "any income of his own?"

"None whatever," the professor told him. "He has made a little money here and there, on various enterprises—largely connected with sports—but he is entirely dependent on the allowance my wife and I give him. It's a very liberal one—too liberal, perhaps, judged by conventional standards. But I see no reason not to indulge the boy. It isn't his fault that he hasn't the temperament for a professional career, and has no flair for business. And I see no point in his pursuing some uncongenial commercial routine, since there is no necessity for it. Both Mrs. Garden and I inherited our money; and while I have always regretted that Floyd had no interest in the more serious phases of life, I have never been inclined to deprive him of the things which apparently constitute his happiness."

"A very liberal attitude, doctor," Vance murmured; "especially for one who is himself so wholeheartedly devoted to the more serious things of life as you are...But what of Swift: did he have an independent income?"

"His father," the professor explained, "left him a very comfortable amount; but I imagine he squandered it or gambled most of it away."

"There's one more question," Vance continued, "that I'd like to ask you in connection with your will and Mrs. Garden's: were your son and nephew aware of the disposition of the estate?"

"I couldn't say. It's quite possible they were. Neither Mrs. Garden nor I have regarded the subject as a secret...But what, may I ask,"—Professor Garden gave Vance a puzzled look—"has this to do with the present terrible situation?"

"I'm sure I haven't the remotest idea," Vance admitted frankly. "I'm merely probin' round in the dark, in the hope of findin' some small ray of light."

Hennessey, the detective whom Heath had ordered to remain on guard below, came lumbering up the passageway to the study.

"There's a guy downstairs, Sergeant," he reported, "who says he's from the telephone company and has got to fix a bell or somethin'.

He's fussed around downstairs and couldn't find anything wrong there, so the butler told him the trouble might be up here. But I thought I'd better ask you before I let him come-up. How about it?"

Heath shrugged and looked inquiringly at Vance.

"It's quite all right, Hennessey," Vance told the detective. "Let him come up."

Hennessey saluted half-heartedly and went out.

"You know, Markham," Vance said, slowly and painstakingly lighting another cigarette, "I wish this infernal buzzer hadn't gone out of order at just this time. I abominate coincidences—"

"Do you mean," Professor Garden interrupted, "that inter-communicating buzzer between here and the den downstairs?. . .It was working all right this morning—Sneed summoned me to breakfast with it as usual."

"Yes, yes," nodded Vance. "That's just it. It evidently ceased functioning after you had gone out. The nurse discovered it and reported it to Sneed who called up the telephone company."

"It's not of any importance," the professor returned with a lackadaisical gesture of his hand. "It's a convenience, however, and saves many trips up and down the stairs."

"We may as well let the man attend to it, since he's here. It won't disturb us." Vance stood up. "And I say, doctor, would you mind joining the others downstairs? We'll be down presently, too."

The professor inclined his head in silent acquiescence and, without a word, went from the room.

Presently a tall, pale, youthful man appeared at the door to the study. He carried a small black tool-kit.

"I was sent here to look over a buzzer," he announced with surly indifference. "I didn't find the trouble downstairs."

"Maybe the difficulty is at this end," suggested Vance. "There's the buzzer behind the desk." And he pointed to the small black box with the push-button.

The man went over to it, opened his case of tools and, taking out a flashlight and a small screw-driver, removed the outer shell of the box. Fingering the connecting wires for a moment, he looked up at Vance with an expression of contempt.

"You can't expect the buzzer to work when the wires ain't connected," he commented.

Vance became suddenly interested. Adjusting his monocle, he knelt down and looked at the box.

"They're both disconnected—eh, what?" he remarked.

"Sure they are," the man grumbled. "And it don't look to me like they worked themselves loose, either."

"You think they were deliberately disconnected?" asked Vance.

"Well, it looks that way." The man was busy reconnecting the wires. "Both screws are loose, and the wires aren't bent—they look like they been pulled out."

"That's most interestin'." Vance stood up, and returned the monocle to his pocket meditatively. "It might be, of course. But I can't see why any one should have done it. . .Sorry for your trouble."

"Oh, that's all in the day's work," the man muttered, readjusting the cover of the box. "I wish all my jobs were as easy as this one." After a few moments he stood up. "Let's see if the buzzer will work now. Any one downstairs who'll answer if I press this?"

"I'll take care of that," Heath interposed, and turned to Snitkin. "Hop down to the den, and if you hear the buzzer down there, ring back."

Snitkin hurried out, and a few moments later, when the button was pressed, there came two short answering signals.

"It's all right now," the repair man said, packing up his tools and going toward the door. "So long." And he disappeared down the passageway.

Markham had been scrutinizing Vance closely for several minutes.

"There's something on your mind," he said seriously. "What's the point of this disconnected buzzer?"

Vance smoked for a moment in silence, looking down at the floor. Then he walked to the north window and looked out meditatively into the garden.

"I don't know, Markham. It's dashed mystifyin'. But I have a notion that the same person who fired the shot we heard disconnected those wires. . ."

Suddenly he stepped to one side behind the draperies and crouched down, his eyes still peering out cautiously into the garden. He raised a warning hand to us to keep back out of sight.

"Deuced queer," he said tensely. "That gate in the far end of the fence is slowly opening. . .Oh, my aunt!" And he swung swiftly into the passageway leading to the garden, beckoning to us to follow.

CHAPTER 9

Two Cigarette Stubs
Saturday, April 14; 6 p.m.

Vance ran past the covered body of Swift on the settee, and crossed to the garden gate. As he reached it he was confronted by the haughty and majestic figure of Madge Weatherby. Evidently her intention was to step into the garden, but she drew back abruptly when she saw us. Our presence, however, seemed neither to surprise nor to embarrass her.

"Charmin' of you to come up, Miss Weatherby," said Vance. "But I gave orders that every one was to remain downstairs."

"I had a right to come here!" she returned, drawing herself up with almost regal dignity.

"Ah!" murmured Vance. "Yes, of course. It might be, don't y' know. But would you mind explainin'?"

"Not at all." Her expression remained unchanged, and her voice was hollow and artificial. "I wished to ascertain if he could have done it."

"And who," asked Vance, "is this mysterious 'he'?"

"Who?" she repeated, throwing her head back sarcastically. "Why, Cecil Kroon!"

Vance's eyelids drooped, and he studied the woman narrowly for a brief moment. Then he said lightly:

"Most interestin'. But let that wait a moment. How did you get up here?"

"That was very simple." She tossed her head negligently. "I pretended to be faint and told your minion I was going into the butler's pantry to get a drink of water. I went out through the pantry door into the public hallway, came up the main stairs, and out on this terrace."

"But how did you know that you could reach the garden by this route?"

"I didn't know." She smiled enigmatically. "I was merely reconnoitring. I was anxious to prove to myself that Cecil Kroon could have shot poor Woody."

"And are you satisfied that he could have?" asked Vance quietly.

"Oh, yes," the woman replied with bitterness. "Beyond a doubt. I've known for a long time that Cecil would kill him sooner or later. And I was quite certain when you said that Woody had been murdered that Cecil had done it. But I did not understand how he could have gotten up here, after leaving us this afternoon. So I endeavoured to find out."

"And why, may I ask," said Vance, "would Mr. Kroon desire to dispose of Swift?"

The woman clasped her hands theatrically against her breast. Taking a step forward, she said in a histrionically sepulchral voice:

"Cecil was jealous—frightfully jealous. He's madly in love with me. He has tortured me with his attentions..." One of her hands went to her forehead in a gesture of desperation. "There has been nothing I could do. And when he learned that I cared for Woody, he became desperate. He threatened me. I was horribly frightened. I didn't dare break everything off with him—I didn't know what he might do. So I humoured him: I went about with him, hoping, hoping that this madness of his would subside. For a time I thought he was becoming more normal and rational. And then—today—this terrible crime!..." Her voice trailed off in an exaggerated sigh.

Vance's keen regard showed neither the sympathy her pompous recital called for, nor the cynicism which I knew he felt. There was only a studied interest in his gaze.

"Sad—very sad," he mumbled.

Miss Weatherby jerked her head up and her eyes flashed.

"I came up here to see if it were possible that Cecil could have done this thing. I came up in the cause of justice!"

"Very accommodatin'." Vance's manner had suddenly changed. "We're most appreciative, and all that sort of thing. But I must insist, don't y' know, that you return downstairs and wait there with the others. And you will be so good as to come through the garden and go down the apartment stairs."

He was brutally matter-of-fact as he drew the gate shut and directed the woman to the passageway door. She hesitated a moment and then followed his indicating finger. As she passed the wicker settee she stopped suddenly and sank to her knees.

"Oh, Woody, Woody!" she wailed dramatically. "It was all my fault!"

She covered her face with her hands and bent her head far forward in an attitude of abject misery.

Vance heaved a deep sigh, threw away his cigarette and, taking her firmly by one arm, lifted her to her feet.

"Really, y' know, Miss Weatherby," he said brusquely, leading her toward the door, "this is not a melodrama."

She straightened up with a stifled sob and went down the passageway toward the stairs.

Vance turned to the detective and nodded toward the entrance.

"Snitkin," he said wearily, "go downstairs and tell Hennessey to keep an eye on Sarah Bernhardt till we need her."

Snitkin grinned and followed Miss Weatherby below.

When we were back in the study Vance sank into a chair and yawned.

"My word!" he complained. "The case is difficult enough without these amateur theatricals."

Markham, I could see, had been both impressed and puzzled by the incident.

"Maybe it's not all dramatics," he suggested. "The woman made some very definite statements."

"Oh, yes. She would. She's the type." Vance took out his cigarette case. "Definite statements, yes. And misleadin'. Really, y' know, I don't for a moment believe she regards Kroon as the culprit."

"Well, what then?" snapped Markham.

"Nothing—really nothing." Vance sighed. "Vanity and futility. The lady is vanity—we're futility. Neither leads anywhere."

"But she certainly has something on her mind," protested Markham.

"So have we all. I wonder. . .But if we could read one person's mind completely, we'd probably understand the universe. Akin to omniscience, and that sort of thing."

"God Almighty!" Markham stood up and planted himself belligerently in front of Vance. "Can't you be rational?"

"Oh, Markham—my dear Markham!" Vance shook his head sadly. "What is rationality? However. . .As you say. There is something back of the lady's histrionics. She has ideas. But she's circuitous. And she wants us to be like those Chinese gods who can't proceed except in a straight line. Sad. But let's try makin' a turn. The situation is something like this: An unhappy lady slips out through the butler's pantry and presents herself on the roof-garden, hopin' to attract our attention. Having succeeded, she informs us that she has proved conclusively that a certain Mr. Kroon has done away with Swift because of amorous jealousy. That's the straight line—the longest distance between two points.—Now for the curve. The lady herself, let us assume, is the spurned and not the spurner. She resents it. She has a temper and is vengeful—and she comes to the roof here for the sole purpose of convincing us that Kroon is guilty. She's not beyond that sort of thing. She'd be jolly well glad to see Kroon suffer, guilty or not."

"But her story is plausible enough," said Markham aggressively. "Why try to find hidden meanings in obvious facts? Kroon could have done it. And your psychological theory regarding the woman's motives eliminates him entirely."

"My dear Markham—oh, my dear Markham! It doesn't eliminate him at all. It merely tends to involve the lady in a rather unpleasant bit of chicanery. The fact is, her little drama here on the roof may prove most illuminatin'."

Vance stretched his legs out before him and sank deeper into his chair.

"Curious situation. Y' know, Markham, Kroon deserted the party about fifteen or twenty minutes before the big race—legal matters to attend to for a maiden aunt, he explained—and he didn't appear again until after I had phoned you. Assumed immediately that Swift had shot himself. Also mentioned a couple of accurate details. All of which could have been either the result of actual knowledge or mere guess-work. Doubt inspired me to converse with the elevator boy. I learned that Kroon had not gone down or up in the elevator since his arrival here early in the afternoon. . ."

"What's that!" Markham exclaimed. "That's more than suspicious—taken with what we have just heard from this Miss Weatherby."

"I dare say." Vance was unimpressed. "The legal mind at work. But from my gropin' amateur point of view, I'd want more—oh, much more. However,"—Vance rose and meditated a moment—"I'll admit that a bit of lovin' communion with Mr. Kroon is definitely indicated." He turned to Heath. "Send the chappie up, will you, Sergeant? And be sweet to him. Don't annoy him. *La politesse.* No need to put him on his guard."

Heath nodded and started toward the door. "I get you, Mr. Vance."

"And Sergeant," Vance halted him; "you might question the elevator boy and find out if there is any one else in the building whom Kroon is in the habit of calling on. If so, follow it up with a few discreet inquiries."

Heath vanished down the stairs, and a minute or so later Kroon sauntered into the study with the air of a man who is bored and not a little annoyed.

"I suppose I'm in for some more tricky questions," he commented, giving Markham and Snitkin a fleeting contemptuous glance and letting his eyes come to rest on Vance with a look of resentment. "Do I take the third-degree standing or sitting?"

"Just as you wish," Vance returned mildly; and Kroon, after glancing about him, sat down leisurely at one end of the davenport. The man's manner, I could see, infuriated Markham, who leaned forward and asked in cold anger:

"Have you any urgent reasons for objecting to give us what assistance you can in our investigation of this murder?"

Kroon raised his eyebrows and smoothed the waxed ends of his moustache:

"None whatever," he said with calm superiority. "I might even be able to tell you who shot Woody."

"That's most interestin'," murmured Vance, studying the man indifferently. "But we'd much rather find out for ourselves, don't y' know. Much more sportin', what? And there's always the possibility that our own findin's might prove more accurate than the guesses of others."

Kroon shrugged maliciously and said nothing.

"When you deserted the party this afternoon, Mr. Kroon," Vance went on in an almost lackadaisical manner, "you gratuitously informed us that you were headed for a legal conference of some kind with a maiden aunt. I know we've been over this before, but I ask again: would you object to giving us, merely as a matter of record, the name and address of your aunt, and the nature of the legal documents which lured you so abruptly away from the Rivermont Handicap, after you had wagered five hundred dollars on the outcome?"

"I most certainly would object," returned Kroon coolly. "I thought you were investigating a murder; and I assure you my aunt had nothing to do with it. I fail to see why you should be interested in my family affairs."

"Life is full of surprises, don't y' know," murmured Vance. "One never knows where family affairs and murder overlap."

Kroon chuckled mirthlessly, but checked himself with a cough.

"In the present instance, I am happy to inform you that, so far as I am concerned, they do not overlap at all."

Markham swung round toward the man.

"That's for us to decide," he snapped. "Do you intend to answer Mr. Vance's question?"

Kroon shook his head.

"I do not! I regard that question as incompetent, irrelevant, and immaterial. Also frivolous."

"Yes, yes." Vance smiled at Markham. "It could be, don't y' know. However, let it pass, Markham. Present status: Name and address of maiden aunt, unknown; nature of legal documents, unknown; reason for the gentleman's reticence, also unknown."

Markham resentfully mumbled a few unintelligible words and resumed smoking his cigar while Vance continued the interrogation.

"I say, Mr. Kroon, would you also consider it irrelevant—and the rest of the legal verbiage—if I asked you by what means you departed and returned to the Garden apartment?"

Kroon appeared highly amused.

"I'd consider it irrelevant, yes; but since there is only one sane way I could have gone and come back, I'm perfectly willing to confess to you that I took a taxicab to and from my aunt's."

Vance gazed up at the ceiling as he smoked. "Suppose," he said, "that the elevator boy should deny that he took you either down or up in the car since your first arrival here this afternoon. What would you say?"

Kroon jerked himself up to attention.

"I'd say that he had lost his memory—or was lying."

"Yes, of course. The obvious retort. Quite." Vance's eyes moved slowly to the man on the davenport. "You will probably have the opportunity of saying just that on the witness stand."

Kroon's eyes narrowed and his face reddened. Before he could speak, Vance went on.

"And you may also have the opportunity of officially giving or withholding your aunt's name and address. The fact is, you may find yourself in the most distressin' need of an alibi."

Kroon sank back on the davenport with a supercilious smile.

"You're very amusing," he commented lightly. "What next? If you'll ask me a reasonable question, I'll be only too happy to answer. I'm a highly esteemed citizen of these States—always willing, not to say anxious, to assist the authorities—to aid in the cause of justice, and all that sort of rot." There was an undercurrent of venom in his contumelious tone.

"Well, let's see where we stand." Vance suppressed an amused smile. "You left the apartment at approximately a quarter to four, took the elevator downstairs and then a taxi, went to your aunt's to fuss a bit with legal documents, drove back in a taxi, and took the elevator upstairs. Bein' gone a little over half an hour. During your absence Swift was shot. Is that correct?"

"Yes." Kroon was curt.

"But how do you account for the fact that when I met you in the hall on your return, you seemed miraculously cognizant of the details of Swift's passing?"

"We've been over that, too. I knew nothing about it. You told me Swift was dead, and I merely surmised the rest."

"Yes—quite. No crime in accurate surmisals. Deuced queer coincidence, however. Taken with other facts. As likely as a five-horse win parlay. Extr'ordin'ry."

"I'm listening with great interest." Kroon had again assumed his air of superiority. "Why don't you stop beating about the bush?"

"Worth-while suggestion." Vance crushed out his cigarette and, drawing himself up in his chair, leaned forward and rested his elbows on his knees. "What I was leadin' up to was the fact that someone has definitely accused you of murdering Swift."

Kroon started, and his face went pale. After a few moments he forced a harsh guttural noise intended for a laugh. "And who, may I ask, has accused me?"

"Miss Madge Weatherby."

One corner of Kroon's mouth went up in a sneer of hatred.

"She would! And she probably told you that it was a crime of passion—caused by an uncontrollable jealousy."

"Just that," nodded Vance. "It seems you have been forcing your unwelcome attentions upon her, with dire threats; whereas, all the time, she was madly enamoured of Mr. Swift. And so, when the strain became too great, you eliminated your rival. Incidentally, she has a very pretty theory which fits the known facts, and which your own refusal to answer my questions bolsters up considerably."

"Well, I'll be damned!" Kroon got to his feet slowly and thrust his hands deep into his pockets. "I see what you're driving at. Why didn't you tell me this in the first place?"

"Waitin' for the final odds," Vance returned. "You hadn't laid your bet. But now that I've told you, do you care to give us the name and address of your maiden aunt and the nature of the legal documents you had to sign?"

"That's all damned nonsense," Kroon spluttered. "I don't need an alibi. When the time comes—" At this moment Heath appeared at the door, and walking directly to Vance, handed him a page torn from his note-book, on which were several lines of handwriting.

Vance read the note rapidly as Kroon looked on with malignant resentment. Then he folded the paper and slipped it into his pocket.

"When the time comes. . .," he murmured. "Yes—quite." He raised his eyes lazily to Kroon. "As you say. When the time comes. The time has now come, Mr. Kroon."

The man stiffened, but did not speak. I could see that he was aggressively on his guard.

"Do you, by any chance," Vance continued, "know a lady named Stella Fruemon? Has a snug little apartment on the seventeenth floor of this building—only two floors below. Says you were visitin' her around four o'clock today. Left her at exactly four-fifteen. Which might account for your not using the elevator. Also for your reluctance to give us your aunt's name and address. Might account for other things as well. . .Do you care to revise your story?"

Kroon appeared to be thinking fast. He walked nervously up and down the study floor.

"Puzzlin' and interestin' situation," Vance went on. "Gentleman leaves this apartment at—let's say—ten minutes to four. Family documents to sign. Doesn't enter the elevator. Appears in apartment two floors below within a few minutes—been a regular visitor there. Remains till four-fifteen. Then departs. Shows up again in this apartment at half-past four. In the meantime, Swift is shot through the head—exact time unknown. Gentleman is apparently familiar with various details of the shooting. Refuses to give information regarding his whereabouts during his absence. A lady accuses him of the murder, and demonstrates how he could have accomplished it. Also kindly supplies the motive. Fifteen minutes of gentleman's absence—namely, from four-fifteen to four-thirty—unaccounted for."

Vance drew on his cigarette.

"Fascinatin' assortment of facts. Add them up. Mathematically speakin', they make a total. . .I say, Mr. Kroon, any suggestions?"

Kroon came to a sudden halt and swung about.

"No!" he blurted. "Damn your mathematics! And you people hang men on such evidence!" He sucked in a deep noisy breath and made a despairing gesture. "All right, here's the story. Take it or leave it. I've been mixed up with Stella Fruemon for the past year. She's nothing but a gold-digger and blackmailer. Madge Weatherby got on to it. She's the jealous member of this combination—not me. And she cared about as much for Woode Swift as I did. Anyway, I got involved with Stella Fruemon. It came to a show-down, and I had to pay through the nose. To avoid scandal for my family, of course. Otherwise, I'd have thrown her through the window and called it my boy scout's good deed for the day. At any rate, we each got our lawyers, and a settlement was reached. She finally named a stiff figure and agreed to sign a general release from all claims. In the circumstances, I had no alternative. Four o'clock today was the time set for the completion of the transaction. My lawyer and hers were to be at her apartment. The certified check and the papers were ready. So I went down there a little before four to clean up the whole dirty business. And I cleaned it up and got out. I had walked down the two flights of stairs to her apartment, and at four-fifteen, when the hold-up was over, I told the lady she could go to hell, and I walked back up the stairs."

Kroon took a deep breath and frowned.

"I was so furious—and relieved—that I kept on walking without realizing where I was going. When I opened the door which I thought led into the public hallway outside the Garden apartment, I found I was out on the terrace of the roof." He cocked an angry eye at Vance. "I suppose that fact is suspicious too—walking up three flights of stairs instead of two—after what I'd been through?"

"No. Oh, no." Vance shook his head. "Quite natural. Exuberant spirits. Weight off the shoulders, and all that. Three flights of stairs seemin' like two. Light impost, so to speak. Horses run better that way. Don't feel the extra furlong, as it were. Quite comprehensible. . .But please proceed."

"Maybe you mean that—and maybe you don't." Kroon spoke truculently. "Anyway; it's the truth. . .When I saw where I was I thought I'd come through the garden and go down the stairway there. It was really the natural thing to do. . ."

"You knew about the gate leading into the garden, then?"

"I've known about it for years. Everybody who's been up here knows about it. On summer nights Floyd used to leave the gate open and we'd walk up and down the terrace. Anything wrong with my knowing about the gate?"

"No. Quite natural. And so, you opened the gate and entered the garden?"

"Yes."

"And that would be between a quarter after four and twenty minutes after four?"

"I wasn't holding a stop-watch on myself, but I guess that's close enough. . .When I entered the garden I saw Swift slumped down in his chair. His position struck me as funny, but I paid no attention to it until I spoke to him and got no answer. Then I approached and saw the revolver lying on the tiles, and the hole in his head. It gave me a hell of a shock, I can tell you, and I started to run downstairs to give the alarm. But I realized it would look bad for me. There I was, alone on the roof with a dead man. . ."

"Ah, yes. Discretion. So you played safe. Can't say that I blame you entirely—if your chronology is accurate. So, I take it, you re-entered the public stairway and came down to the front door of the Garden apartment."

"That's just what I did." Kroon's tone was as vigorous as it was resentful.

"By the by, during the brief time you were on the roof, or even after you returned to the stairway, did you hear a shot?"

Kroon looked at Vance in obvious surprise.

"A shot? I've told you the fellow was already dead when I first saw him."

"Nevertheless," said Vance, "there was a shot. Not the one that killed him, but the one that summoned us to the roof. There were two shots, don't y' know—although no one seems to have heard the first."

Kroon thought a moment.

"By George! I did hear something, now that you put it that way. I thought nothing of it at the time, since Woody was already dead. But just as I re-entered the stairway there was an explosion of some kind outside. I thought it was a car back-firing down in the street, and paid no attention to it."

Vance nodded with a puzzled frown.

"That's very interestin'. . ." His eyes drifted off into space. "I wonder. . ." After a moment he returned his gaze to Kroon. "But to continue your tale. You say you left the roof immediately and came downstairs. But there were at least ten minutes from the time you left the garden to the time I encountered you entering the apartment at the front door. How and where did you spend these ten intervening minutes?"

"I stayed on the landing of the stairs and smoked a couple of cigarettes. I was trying to pull myself together. After what I had been through, and then finding Woody shot, I was in a hell of a mental state."

Heath stood up quickly, one hand in his outside coat pocket, and thrust out his jaw belligerently toward the agitated Kroon.

"What kind of cigarettes do you smoke?" he barked.

The man looked at the Sergeant in bewilderment, and then said: "I smoke gold-tipped Turkish cigarettes. What about it?"

Heath drew his hand from his pocket and looked at something which he held on his palm.

"All right," he muttered. Then he addressed Vance. "I got the stubs here. Picked 'em up on the landing when I came up from the dame's apartment. Thought maybe they might have some connection."

"Well, well," sneered Kroon. "So the police actually found something!...What more do you want?" he demanded of Vance.

"Nothing for the moment, thank you," Vance, returned with exaggerated courtesy. "You have done very well by yourself this afternoon, Mr. Kroon. We won't need you any more...Sergeant, give instructions to Hennessey that Mr. Kroon may leave the apartment."

Kroon went to the door without a word.

"Oh, I say." Vance delayed him at the threshold. "Do you, by any chance, possess a maiden aunt?"

Kroon looked back over his shoulder with a vicious grin.

"No, thank God!" And he slammed the door noisily behind him.

CHAPTER 10

The $10,000 Bet
Saturday, April 14; 6:15 p.m.

"A good story," Markham commented dryly when Kroon had gone.

"Yes, yes. Good. But reluctant."Vance appeared disturbed.

"Do you believe it?"

"My dear Markham, I keep an open mind, neither believin' nor disbelievin'. Prayin' for facts. But no facts yet. Drama everywhere, but no substance. Kroon's story is at least consistent. One of the reasons why I'm sceptical. Always distrust consistency. Too easy to manufacture. And Kroon's shrewd no end."

"Still," put in Markham, "those cigarette butts which Heath found check with his story."

"Yes. Oh, yes."Vance nodded and sighed. "I don't doubt he smoked two cigarettes on the stair landing. But he could have smoked them just as well if he'd done the johnnie in. At the moment I'm suspectin' every one here. Lot of angles protrudin' from this case."

"On the other hand," objected Markham, "with that entrance from the main stairway to the door open to anybody, why couldn't an outsider have killed Swift?"

Vance looked up at him with a melancholy air.

"Oh, Markham—my dear Markham! The legalistic intelligence at work. Ever lookin' for loopholes. The prosecutin' attorney hopin' for the best. No. Oh, no. No outsider. Too many sound objections. The murder was too perfectly timed. Only some one present could have executed it so fittingly. Moreover, it was committed in yon vault. Only some one thoroughly familiar with the Garden household and the exact situation here this afternoon could have done it. . ."

There was a rustle in the passageway, and Madge Weatherby came rushing into the study, with Heath following and protesting vigorously. It was obvious that Miss Weatherby had dashed up the stairs before any one could interfere with her.

"What's the meaning of this?" she demanded imperiously. "You're letting Cecil Kroon go, after what I've told you? And I"—she indicated herself with a dramatic gesture—"*I* am being held here, a prisoner."

Vance rose wearily and offered her a cigarette. She brushed the proffered case aside and sat down rigidly.

"The fact is, Miss Weatherby," said Vance, returning to his chair, "Mr. Kroon explained his brief absence this afternoon lucidly and with im-pellin' logic. It seems that he was doing nothing more reprehensible than conferring with Miss Stella Fruemon and a brace of attorneys."

"Ah!" The woman's eyes glared with venom.

"Quite so. He was breaking off with the lady for ever and ever. Also getting a release from her and from her heirs, executors, adminis-trators, and assigns, from the beginning of the world to the day of the date of these presents—I believe that is the correct legal phraseology. Really, y' know, he never cared for her. He assured us she was quite a nuisance. Was rather vehement about it. No woman would ever domi-nate and blackmail him—or brave words to that effect. The Cezanne slogan modified: *Pas une gonzesse ne me mettra le grappin dessus.»*

"Is that the truth?" Miss Weatherby straightened in her chair.

"Yes, yes. No subterfuge. Kroon said you were jealous of Stella. Thought I'd relieve your mind."

"Why didn't he tell me, then?"

"There's always the possibility you didn't give him a chance."

The woman nodded vigorously.

"Yes, that's right. I wouldn't speak to him when he returned here this afternoon."

"Care to revamp your original theory?" asked Vance. "Or do you still think that Kroon is the culprit?"

"I—I really don't know now," the woman answered hesitantly. "When I last spoke to you I was terribly upset. . .Maybe it was all my imagination."

"Imagination—yes. Terrible and dangerous thing. Causes more mis-ery than actuality. Especially imagination stimulated by jealousy. 'Not poppy, nor mandragora, nor all the drowsy syrups of the world'. . ." He looked at the woman quizzically. "Since you're not so sure that Kroon did the deed, have you any other suggestions?"

There was a tense silence. Miss Weatherby's face seemed to con-tract: she drew in her lips. Her eyes almost closed.

"Yes!" she exploded, leaning toward Vance with a new enthusiasm.

"It was Zalia Graem who killed Woody! She had the motive, as you call it. She's capable of such things, too. She's breezy and casual enough on the outside. But inside she's a demon. She'd stop at nothing. There was something between her and Woody. Then she chucked him over. But he wouldn't let her alone. He kept on annoying her, and she ignored him. He didn't have enough money to suit her. You saw the way they acted toward each other today."

"Have you any idea as to how she managed the crime?" Vance asked quietly.

"She was out of the drawing-room long enough, wasn't she? Supposed to be telephoning. But does any one really know where she was, or what she was doing?"

"Poignant question. Situation very mysterious." Vance rose slowly and bowed to the woman. "Thanks awfully—we're most grateful. And we shall not hold you prisoner any longer. If we should need you later, we'll communicate with you."

When she had gone Markham grinned sourly. "The lady is well equipped with suspects. What do you make of this new accusation?"

Vance was frowning.

"Animosity shunted from Monsieur Kroon to La Graem. Yes. Queer situation. Logically speakin', this new accusation is more reasonable than her first. It has its points. . .If only I could get that disconnected buzzer out of my mind. It must fit somewhere. . .And that second shot—the one we all heard."

"Couldn't it have been a mechanism of some kind?" suggested Markham. "It's not difficult to effect a detonation by electric wires."

Vance nodded apathetically.

"I'd thought of that. But there's nothing about the buzzer to indicate that a gadget might have been attached to it. I looked carefully while the telephone man was working on it."

Vance again moved to the buzzer and inspected it with care. Then he gave his attention to the bookshelves surrounding it. He took down a dozen or so volumes and scrutinized the empty shelves and the uprights. Finally he shook his head and returned to his chair.

"No. Nothing there. The dust behind the books is thick and shows no signs of recent disturbance. No powder marks anywhere. And no indications of a mechanism."

"It could have been removed before the repair man arrived," theorized Markham without enthusiasm.

"Yes, another possibility. I had thought of that too. But the opportunity was lacking. I came in here immediately after I had found the johnnie shot. . ." He took the cigarette from his lips and straightened up. "By Jove! Some one might have slipped in here when we all dashed upstairs after the shot. Remote chance, though. And yet. . .Another curious thing, Markham: three or four different people tried to storm this aerie while I was in the den with Garden. All of them wished to be with the corpse for *post-mortem* communion—that sort of morbid rigmarole. I wonder. . .However, it's too late to work from that point now. Nothing to do but to jot down those facts for future reference."

"Does the buzzer connect with any other room besides the den?"

Vance shook his head.

"No. That's the only connection."

"Didn't you say there was some one in the den at the time you heard this shot?"

Vance's gaze swept past Markham, and it was several moments before he answered.

"Yes. Zalia Graem was there. Ostensibly telephonin'." His voice, I thought, was a little bitter; and I could see that his mind had gone off on a new line of thought.

Heath squinted and moved his head up and down. "Well, Mr. Vance, that gets us places."

Vance stared at him.

"Does it really, Sergeant? Where? It merely fuddles up the case—until we get some more information along the same line."

"We might get more information from the young woman herself," Markham put in sarcastically.

"Oh, yes. Quite. Obvious procedure. But I have a few queries to put to Garden first. Pavin' the way, as it were. I say, Sergeant, collect Floyd Garden and bring him here."

Garden came into the room uneasily and looking slightly haggard.

"What a mess!" he sighed, sinking dismally into a chair. He packed his pipe shakily. "Any light on the case?"

"A few fitful illuminations," Vance told him. "By the by, it seems that your guests walk in and out the front door without the formality of ringing or being announced. Is this practice custom'ry?"

"Oh, yes. But only when we're playing the races. Much more convenient. Saves annoyance and interruptions."

"And another thing: when Miss Graem was phoning in the den and you suggested that she tell the gentleman to call back later, did you actually know that it was a man she was talking to?"

Garden opened his eyes in mild surprise.

"Why, no. I was merely ragging her. Hadn't the faintest idea. But, if it makes any difference, I'm sure Sneed could give you the information, if Miss Graem won't. Sneed answered the phone, you know."

"It's of no importance." Vance brushed the matter aside. "It might interest you to know, however, that the buzzer in this room failed to function because someone had carefully disconnected the wires."

"The devil you say!"

"Oh, yes. Quite." Vance fixed Garden with a significant look. "This buzzer, if I understand it correctly, is operated only from the den, and when we heard the shot, Miss Graem was in the den. Incidentally, the shot we all heard was not the shot that killed Swift. The fatal shot had been fired at least five minutes before that. Swift never even knew whether he had won or lost his bet."

Garden's gaze was focused on Vance with wide-eyed awe. A smothered exclamation escaped his half-parted lips. Quickly he drew himself together and, standing up, let his eyes roam vaguely about the room.

"Good God, man!" He shook his head despondently. "This thing is getting hellish. I see your implication about the buzzer and the shot we heard. But I can't see just how the trick was done." He turned to Vance with an appealing look. "Are you sure about those disconnected wires and what you say was a second shot?"

"Quite sure." Vance's tone was casual. "Sad, what? By the by, Miss Weatherby tried to convince us that Miss Graem shot Swift."

"Has she any grounds for such an accusation?"

"Only that Miss Graem had a grudge of some kind against Swift and detested him thoroughly, and that, at the supposed time of his demise, Miss Graem was absent from the drawing-room. Doubts that she was in the den phoning all the time. Thinks she was up here, busily engaged in murder."

Garden drew rapidly on his pipe and seemed to be thinking.

"Of course, Madge knows Zalia pretty well," he admitted with reluctance. "They go about a great deal together. Madge may know the inside story of the clash between Zalia and Woody. I don't. Zalia might have thought she had sufficient cause to end Woody's career. She's an amazing girl. One never quite knows what she will do next."

"Do you yourself regard Miss Graem as capable of a cold-blooded, skilfully planned murder?"

Garden pursed his lips and frowned. He coughed once or twice, as if to gain time; then he spoke.

"Damn it, Vance! I can't answer that question. Frankly, I don't know who is and who isn't capable of murder. The younger set today are all bored to death, intolerant of every restraint, living beyond their means, digging up scandal, seeking sensations of every type. Zalia is little different from the rest, as far as I can see. She always seems to be stepping on the gas and exceeding the speed limits. How far she would actually go, I'm not prepared to say. Who is, for that matter? It may be merely a big circus parade with her, or it may be fundamental—a violent reaction from respectability. Her people are eminently respectable. She was brought up strictly—even forced into a convent for a couple of years, I believe. Then broke loose and is now having her fling. . ."

"A vivid, though not a sweet, character sketch," murmured Vance. "One might say offhand that you are rather fond of her but don't approve."

Garden laughed awkwardly.

"I can't say that I dislike Zalia. Most men do like her—though I don't think any of them understand her. I know I don't. There's some impenetrable wall around her. And the curious thing is, men like her although she doesn't make the slightest effort to gain their esteem or affection. She treats them shabbily—actually seems to be annoyed by their attentions."

"A poisonous, passive Dolores, so to speak."

"Yes, something like that, I should say. She's either damned superficial or deep as hell—I can't make up my mind which. As to her status in this present situation. . .well, I don't know. It wouldn't surprise me in the least if Madge was right about her. Zalia has staggered me a couple of times—can't exactly explain it. You remember, when you asked me about father's revolver, I told you Zalia had discovered it in that desk and staged a scene with it in this very room. Well, Vance, my blood went cold at the time. There was something in the way she did it, and in the tone of her voice, that made me actually fear that she was fully capable of shooting up the party and then walking about the room to chuckle at the corpses. No reason for my feelings, perhaps; but, believe me, I was damned relieved when she put the gun back and shut the drawer. . .All I can say," he added, "is that I don't wholly understand her."

"No. Of course not. No one can wholly understand another person. If any one could he'd understand everything. Not a comfortin' thought. . .Thanks awfully for the recital of your fears and impressions. You'll look after matters downstairs for a while, won't you?"

Garden seemed to breathe more freely on being dismissed, and, with a mumbled acquiescence, moved toward the door.

"Oh, by the by," Vance called after him. "One other little point I wish to ask you about."

Garden waited politely.

"Why," asked Vance, blowing a ribbon of smoke toward the ceiling, "didn't you place Swift's bet on Equanimity?"

The man gave a start, and his jaw dropped. He barely rescued his pipe from falling to the floor.

"You didn't place it, don't y' know," Vance went on dulcetly, gazing at Garden with dreamy, half-closed eyes. "Rather interestin' point, in view of the fact that your cousin was not destined to live long enough to collect the wager, even if Equanimity had won. And, in the circumstances, had you placed it, you would now be saddled with a ten-thousand-dollar debt—since Swift is no longer able to settle."

"God Almighty, stop it, Vance!" Garden exploded. He sank limply into a chair. "How the hell do you know I didn't place Woode's bet?"

Vance regarded the man with searching eyes.

"No bookie would take a bet of that size five minutes before post time. He couldn't absorb it. He would have to lay a lot of it off—he might even have to place some of it out of town—Chicago or Detroit. He'd need time, don't y' know. A ten-thousand-dollar bet would usually have to be placed at least an hour before the race was run. I've done a bit of hobnobbin' with bookies and race-track men."

"But Hannix—"

"Don't make a Wall-Street financier of Hannix for my benefit," Vance admonished quietly. "I know these gentlemen of the chalk and eraser as well as you do. And another thing: I happened to be sitting in a strategic position near your table when you pretended to place Swift's bet. You very deftly pulled the cord taut over the plunger of the telephone when you picked up the receiver. You were talking into a dead phone."

Garden drew himself together and capitulated with a weary shrug.

"All right, Vance," he said. "I didn't place the bet. But if you think, for one moment, that I had any suspicion that Woody was going to be shot this afternoon, you're wrong."

"My dear fellow!" Vance sighed with annoyance. "I'm not thinkin'. Higher intelligence not at work at the moment. Mind a blank. Only tryin' to add up a few figures. Ten thousand dollars is a big item. It changes our total—eh, what?. . .But you haven't told me why you didn't place the bet. You could have placed it. You had sufficient indication that Swift was going to wager a large sum on Equanimity, and it would only have been necess'ry to inform him that the bet had to be placed early."

Garden rose angrily, but beneath his anger was a great perturbation.

"I didn't want him to lose the money," he asserted aggressively. "I knew what it would mean to him."

"Yes, yes. The Good Samaritan. Very touchin'. But suppose Equanimity had won, and your cousin had survived—what about the pay-off?"

"I was fully prepared to run that risk. It wasn't a hell of a lot. What did the old oat-muncher pay, anyway?—less than two to one. A dollar and eighty cents to the dollar, to be exact. I would have been out eighteen thousand dollars. But there wasn't a chance of Equanimity's coming in—I was quite certain of that. I took the chance for Woody's sake. I was being decent—or weak—I don't know which. If the horse had won, I'd have paid Woody myself—and he would never have known that it wasn't Hannix's money."

Vance looked at the man thoughtfully.

"Thanks for the affectin' confession," he murmured at length. "I think that will be all for the moment."

As he spoke, two men with a long coffin-like wicker basket bustled into the passageway. Heath was at the door in two strides.

"The Public Welfare boys after the body," he announced over his shoulder.

Vance stood up.

"I say, Sergeant, have them go down the outside stairway. No use returning through the apartment." He addressed Garden again. "Would you mind showing them the way?"

Garden nodded morosely and went out on the roof. A few moments later the two carriers, with Garden leading the way, disappeared through the garden gate with their grim burden.

CHAPTER 11

The Second Revolver
Saturday, April 14; 6:25 p.m.

Markham regarded Vance with dismal concern. "What's the meaning of Garden's not placing that bet?"

Vance sighed.

"What's the meaning of anything? Yet, it's from just such curious facts as this that some provisional hypothesis may evolve."

"I certainly can't figure out what bearing Garden's conduct has on the case, unless—"

Vance interrupted him quickly.

"No. Puzzlin' situation. But everything we have learned so far might mean something. Provided, of course, we could read the meanin'. Emotion may be the key."

"Don't be so damned occult," snapped Markham. "What's on your mind?"

"My dear Markham! You're too flatterin'. Nothing whatever. I'm seekin' for something tangible. The other gun, for instance. The one that went off somewhere when the chappie was already dead. It should be here or hereabouts. . ." He turned to Heath. "I say, Sergeant, could you and Snitkin take a look for it? Suggested itiner'ry: the roof-garden and the flowerbeds, the terrace, the public stairs, the lower hallway. Then the apartment proper. Assumption: any one present may have had it. Follow up all the known local migrations of every one downstairs. If it's here it'll probably be in some tempor'ry hidin'-place, awaitin' further disposal. Don't ransack the place. And don't be too dashed official. Sweetness and light does it."

Heath grinned. "I know what you mean, Mr. Vance."

"And, Sergeant, before you start reconnoitrin', will you fetch

Hammle. You'll probably find him at the bar downstairs, ingesting a Scotch-and-soda."

When Heath had gone, Vance turned to Markham.

"Hammle may have some good counsel to offer, and he may not. I don't like the man—sticky sort. We might as well get rid of him—at least tempor'rily. The place is frightfully cluttered. . ."

Hammle strutted pompously into the study and was cursorily presented to Markham. Through the window, in the gathering dusk, I could catch glimpses of Heath and Snitkin moving along the flower boxes.

Vance waved Hammle to a chair and studied him a moment with a melancholy air, as if endeavouring to find an excuse for the man's existence.

The interview was brief and, as it turned out, of peculiar significance. The significance lay, not so much in what Hammle said, as in the result of the curiosity which Vance's questions aroused in the man. It was this curiosity which enabled him later to supply Vance with important information.

"It is not our desire to keep you here any longer than necess'ry, Mr. Hammle,"—Vance began the interview with marked distaste—"but it occurred to me to ask you if you have any ideas that might be helpful to us in solving Swift's murder."

Hammle coughed impressively and appeared to give the matter considerable thought.

"No, I have none," he at length admitted. "None whatever. But of course one can never tell about these things. The most insignificant facts can really be interpreted seriously, provided one has given them sufficient thought. As for myself, now, I haven't duly considered the various approaches to the subject."

"Of course," Vance agreed, "there hasn't been a great deal of time for serious thought concerning the situation. But I thought there might be something in the relationships of the various people here this afternoon—and I am assuming that you are fairly familiar with them all—that might inspire you to make a suggestion."

"All I can say," returned Hammle, carefully weighing his words, "is that there were many warring elements in the gathering—that is to say, many peculiar combinations. Oh, nothing criminal." He waved his hand quickly in deprecation. "I would have you understand that absolutely. But there was a combination of this and that, which might lead to—well, to anything."

"To murder, for instance?"

Hammle frowned. "Now, murder is a very, very serious business." His tone bordered on the sententious. "But, Mr. Vance, you can take it from me, in all solemnity, I wouldn't put even murder past any of those present today. No, by Gad!"

"That's an amazin' indictment," muttered Vance; "but I'm glad to have your opinion and we'll consider it...By the by, didn't you notice anything irregular in Garden's placing Swift's large bet on Equanimity at the last minute?"

Hammle's countenance went quickly blank. He presented Vance momentarily with a perfect "poker face." Then, unable to withstand the direct scrutiny of Vance's cold gaze, he puckered up his mouth into a shrewd smile.

"Why deny it?" he chuckled. "The laying of that bet was not only irregular—it was damned near impossible. I don't know a book-maker in New York who would take such an amount when there was not even enough time to throw some 'come-back money' into the totalizator. A swell time this Hannix would have had trying to balance his book with a cloudburst like that at the last minute! The whole transaction struck me as damned peculiar. Couldn't imagine what Garden was up to."

Vance leaned forward, and his eyelids drooped as he focused his gaze on Hammle.

"That might easily have had some bearing on the situation here this afternoon, and I'd like very much to know why you didn't mention it."

For a brief moment the man seemed flustered; but almost immediately he settled back in his chair with a complacent look, and extended his hands, palms up.

"Why should I become involved?" he asked with cynical suavity. "I have never believed in bothering too much with other people's concerns. I've too many problems of my own to worry about."

"That's one way of looking at life," Vance drawled. "And it has its points. However..." He contemplated the tip of his cigarette, then asked: "Would your discretion permit you to comment on Zalia Graem?"

Hammle sat up with alacrity.

"Ah!" He nodded his head significantly. "That's something to think about. There are varied possibilities in that girl. You may be on the right track. A most likely suspect for the murder. You never can tell about women, anyway. And, come to think of it, the shooting must have taken place during the time she was out of the room. She's a good pistol shot, too. I recall once when she came out to my estate on

Long Island—she did a bit of target practice that afternoon. Oh, she knows weapons as most women know bonnets, and she's as wild as a two-year-old filly at her first barrier."

Vance nodded and waited.

"But don't think, for a minute," Hammle hurried on, "that I am intimating that she had anything to do with Swift's death. Absolutely not! But the mention of her name gave me pause." As he finished speaking he nodded his head sagely.

Vance stood up with a stifled yawn.

"It's quite evident," he said, "you're not in the mood to be specific. I wasn't looking for generalities, don't y' know. Consequently I may want to have another chat with you. Where can you be reached later, should we need you?"

"If I am permitted to go now, I shall return to Long Island immediately," Hammle answered readily, glancing speculatively at his watch. "Is that all you wish at the moment?"

"That is all, thank you."

Hammle again referred to his watch, hesitated a moment, and then left us.

"Not a nice person, Markham,"Vance commented dolefully when Hammle had gone. "Not at all a nice person. As you noticed, every one, according to him, is fitted for the role of killer—every one except himself, of course. A smug creature. And that unspeakable waistcoat! And the thick soles of his shoes! And the unpressed clothes! Oh, very careless and sportin'—and very British. The uniform of the horse-and-dog gentry. Animals really deserve better associates."

He shrugged sadly and, going to the buzzer, pressed the button.

"Queer reports on that Graem girl." He walked back to his chair musingly. "The time has come to commune with the lady herself. . ."

Garden appeared at the door.

"Did you ring for me, Vance?"

"Yes."Vance nodded. "The buzzer is working now. Sorry to trouble you, but we would like to see Miss Graem. Would you do the honours?"

Garden hesitated, his eyes fixed sharply on Vance. He started to say something, changed his mind and, with a muttered "Right-o," swung about and returned downstairs.

Zalia Graem swaggered into the room, her hands in her jacket pockets, and surveyed us with breezy cynicism.

"My nose is all powdered for the inquisition," she announced with a twisted smile. "Is it going to take long?"

"You might better sit down."Vance spoke with stern politeness.

"Is it compulsory?" she asked.

Vance ignored the question, and she leaned back against the door.

"We're investigating a murder, Miss Graem,"—Vance's voice was courteous but firm—"and it will be necess'ry to ask you questions that you may deem objectionable. But please believe that it will be for your own good to answer them frankly."

"Am I a suspect? How thrilling!"

"Every one I've talked to thus far thinks so." He looked at the girl significantly.

"Oh, so that's how the going is! I'm in for a sloppy track, and I can't mud. How perfectly beastly!" She frowned. "I thought I detected a vague look of fear in people's eyes. I think I will sit down, after all." She threw herself into a chair and gazed up with simulated dejection. "Am I to be arrested?"

"Not just at the minute. But certain matters must be straightened out. It may be worth your while to help us."

"It sounds ghastly. But go ahead."

"First," said Vance, "we'd like to know about the feud between you and Swift."

"Oh, the devil!" the girl exclaimed disgustedly. "Must that be raked up? There was really nothing to it. Woody bothered the life out of me. I felt sorry for him and went around with him a bit when he implored me to and threatened to resort to all the known forms of suicide if I didn't. Then it became too much for me, and I decided to draw a line across the page. But I'm afraid I didn't go about it in a nice way. I told him I was extravagant and cared only for luxuries, and that I could never marry a poor man. I had a silly notion it might snap him out of his wistful adoration. It worked, after a fashion. He got furious and said nasty things—which, frankly, I couldn't forgive. So he took the high road, and I took the low—or the other way round."

"And so, the conclusion we may draw is that he played the horses heavily in the forlorn hope of amassing a sufficient fortune to overcome your aversion to his poverty—and that his bet on Equanimity today was a last fling—"

"Don't say that!" the girl cried, her hands tightening over the arms of the chair. "It's a horrible idea, but—it might be true. And I don't want to hear it."

Vance continued to study her critically.

"Yes, as you say. It might be true. On the other hand. . .however, we'll let it pass." Then he asked quickly: "Who telephoned you today, just before the Rivermont Handicap?"

"Tartarin de Tarascon," the girl replied sarcastically.

"And had you instructed this eminent adventurer to call you at just that time?"

"What has that to do with anything?"

"And why were you so eager to take the call on the den phone and shut the door?"

The girl leaned forward and looked at Vance defiantly.

"What are you trying to get at?" she demanded furiously.

"Are you aware," Vance went on, "that the den downstairs is the only room directly connected by wires with this room up here?"

The girl seemed unable to speak. She sat pale and rigid, her eyes fixed steadily on Vance.

"And do you know," he continued, without change of intonation, "that the wires at this end of the line had been disconnected? And are you aware that the shot which we heard downstairs was not the one that ended Swift's life—that he was shot in the vault off the hall, several minutes before we heard the shot?"

"You're being ghastly," the girl cried. "You're making up nightmares—nightmares to frighten me. You're implying terrible things. You're trying to torture me into admitting things that aren't true, just because I was out of the room when Woody was shot. . ."

Vance held up his hand to stop her reproaches. "You misinterpret my attitude, Miss Graem," he said softly. "I asked you, a moment ago, for your own sake, to answer my questions frankly. You refuse. In those circumstances, you should know the facts as they appear to others." He paused. "You and Swift were not on good terms. You knew, as did the others, that he usually went up to the roof before races. You knew where Professor Garden kept his revolver. You're familiar with guns and a good pistol shot. A telephone call for you is perfectly timed. You disappear. Within the next five minutes Swift is shot behind that steel door. Another five minutes pass; the race is over; and a shot is heard. That shot could conceivably have been fired by a mechanism. The buzzer wires up here had been disconnected, obviously for some specific purpose. At the time of the second shot you were at the other end of those wires. You almost fainted at the sight of Swift. Later you tried to go upstairs. . .Adding all this up: you had a motive, a sufficient knowledge of the situation, access to the criminal agent, the ability to act, and the opportunity." Vance paused again. "Now are you ready to be frank, or have you really something to hide?"

A change came over the girl. She relaxed, as if from a sudden attack of weakness. She did not take her eyes from Vance, and appeared to be appraising him and deciding what course to follow.

Before she managed to speak Heath stamped up the passageway and opened the study door. He carried a woman's black-and-white tweed top-coat over his arm. He cocked an eyebrow at Vance and nodded triumphantly.

"I take it, Sergeant," Vance drawled, "your quest has been successful. You may speak out." He turned to Zalia Graem and explained: "Sergeant Heath has been searching for the gun that fired the second shot."

The girl became suddenly animated and leaned forward attentively.

"I followed the route you suggested, Mr. Vance," Heath reported. "After going over the roof and the stairs and the hall of the apartment, I thought I'd look through the wraps hanging in the hall closet. The gun was in the pocket of this." He threw the coat on the davenport and took a .38 gun-metal revolver from his pocket. He broke it and showed it to Vance and Markham. "Full of blanks and one of 'em has been discharged."

"Very good, Sergeant," Vance complimented him. "Whose coat is this, by the by?"

"I don't know yet, Mr. Vance; but I'm going to find out pronto."

Zalia Graem had risen and come forward.

"I can tell you whose coat that is," she said. "It belongs to Miss Beeton, the nurse. I saw her wearing it yesterday."

"Thanks awfully for the identification," returned Vance, his eyes resting dreamily on her.

She gave him a wry smile and returned to her chair.

"But there's a question still pending," Vance said; "—to wit: are you ready to be frank now?"

"All right." She focused her gaze on Vance again. "Lemmy Merrit, one of the various scions of the horsy aristocracy that infests our eastern seaboard, asked me to drive out to Sands Point with him for the polo game tomorrow. I thought I might dig up some more exciting engagement and told him to call me here this afternoon at half-past three for a final yes or no. I purposely stipulated that time, so I wouldn't miss the running of the Handicap. As you know, he didn't call till after four, with excuses about not having been able to get to a telephone. I tried to get rid of him in a hurry, but he was persistent—the only virtue he possesses, so far as I know. I left him dangling on the wire when I came out to listen to the race, and then went back for a farewell and have-a-nice-time-without-me. Just as I hung up I heard what sounded like a shot and came to the door, to find every one hurrying along the hall. An idea went through my head that maybe Woody had shot himself—that's why I went mid-Victorian and almost passed out when I saw him. That's everything. I know nothing about wires, buzzers, or mechanical devices; and I haven't been in this room for a week. However, I'll incriminate myself to the extent of admitting that I didn't like Woody, and that on many occasions I had the desire to blow his brains out. And, as you say, I am a pretty good shot."

Vance rose and bowed.

"Thanks for your ultimate candour, Miss Graem. I'm deuced sorry I had to torture you to obtain it. And please ignore the nightmares you accused me of manufacturing. I'm really grateful to you for helping me fill in the pattern."

The girl frowned as her intense gaze rested on Vance.

"I wonder if you don't really know more about this affair than you pretend."

"My dear Miss Graem! I do not pretend to know anything about it." Vance went to the door and held it open for her. "You may go now, but we shall probably want to see you again tomorrow, and I must ask for your promise that you will stay at home where you will be available."

"Don't worry, I'll be at home." She shrugged and then added: "I'm beginning to think that maybe Ogden Nash had the right idea."

As she went out, Miss Beeton was coming up the passageway toward the study. The two women passed each other without speaking.

"I'm sorry to trouble you, Mr. Vance," the nurse apologized, "but Doctor Siefert has just arrived and asked me to inform you that he wished very much to see you as soon as possible. Mr. Garden," she added, "has told him about Mr. Swift's death."

At that moment her gaze fell on the tweed coat, and a slight puzzled frown lined her forehead. Before she could speak Vance said:

"The Sergeant brought your coat up here. He didn't know whose it was. We were looking for something." Then he added quickly: "Please tell Doctor Siefert that I will be very glad to see him at once. And ask him if he will be good enough to come here to the study."

Miss Beeton nodded and went out, closing the door softly behind her.

CHAPTER 12

Poison Gas
Saturday, April 14; 6:40 p.m.

Vance went to the window and looked out for some time in silence. It was obvious he was deeply troubled. Markham respected his perturbation and did not speak. It was Vance himself who at length broke the silence.

"Markham," he said, his eyes scanning the brilliant sunset colours across the river, "the more I see of this case the less I like it. Every one seems to be trying to pin the posy of guilt on the other chap. And there's fear wherever I turn. Guilty consciences at work."

"But every one," returned Markham, "seems pretty well agreed that this Zalia Graem had a hand in it."

Vance inclined his head.

"Oh, yes," he murmured. "I had observed that fact. I wonder. . ."

Markham studied Vance's back for several moments.

"Do you think Doctor Siefert will be of any help?" he asked.

"He might be, of course," Vance replied. "Evidently he wants to see me. But I imagine it's curiosity as much as anything else. However, there's little that anyone who was not actually here can tell us. The difficulty in this case, Markham, lies in trying to weed out a multiplicity of misleading items. . ."

There was a soft knock, and Vance turned from the window. He was confronted by Garden, who had opened the study door without waiting for a summons.

"Sorry, Vance," Garden apologized, "but Doc Siefert is downstairs and says he'd like to see you, if convenient, before he goes."

Vance looked at the man a moment and frowned.

"Miss Beeton informed me of the fact a few minutes ago. I asked her to tell the doctor I would be glad to see him at once. I can't understand his sending you also. Didn't the nurse give him the message?"

"I'm afraid not. I know Siefert sent Miss Beeton up here, and I assumed, as I imagine Siefert did, that you had detained her." He looked round the room with a puzzled expression. "The fact is, I thought she was still up here."

"You mean she hasn't returned downstairs?" Vance asked.

"No, she hasn't come down yet."

Vance took a step forward.

"Are you sure of that, Garden?"

"Yes, very sure." Garden nodded vigorously. "I've been in the front hall, near the foot of the stairs, ever since Doc Siefert arrived."

Vance walked thoughtfully to a small table and broke the ashes from his cigarette.

"Did you see any of the others come down?" he asked Garden.

"Why, yes," Garden told him. "Kroon came down and went out. And then Madge Weatherby also came down and went out. And shortly after the nurse had gone up with Siefert's message to you, Zalia came down and hurried away. But that's all. And, as I say, I've been down there in the front hall all the time."

"What about Hammle?"

"Hammle? No, I haven't seen anything of him. I thought he was still here with you."

"That's deuced queer." Vance moved slowly to a chair and sat down with a perplexed frown. "It's possible you missed him. However, it doesn't matter." He had lifted his head a little and was watching Garden speculatively. "Ask the doctor to come up, will you?"

When Garden had left us Vance sat smoking and staring at the ceiling. I knew from the droop of his eyelids that he was disturbed. He moved restlessly in his chair and finally leaned forward, resting his elbows on his knees.

"Deuced queer," he muttered again.

"For Heaven's sake, Vance," Markham commented irritably. "It's entirely possible Garden wasn't watching the stairs as closely as he imagines."

"Yes. Oh, yes." Vance nodded vaguely. "Everyone worried. No one on the alert. Normal mechanisms not functioning. Still, the stairs are visible half way up the hall, and the hall itself isn't very spacious. . ."

"It's quite possible Hammle went down the main stairs from the terrace, wishing, perhaps, to avoid the others."

"He hadn't his hat up here with him," Vance returned without looking up. "He would have had to enter the front hall and pass Garden to get it. No point in such silly manoeuvres. . .But it isn't Hammle

I'm thinking of. It's Miss Beeton. I don't like it. . ." He got up slowly and took out another cigarette. "She's not the kind of girl that would neglect taking my message to Siefert immediately, unless for a very good reason."

"A number of things might have happened—" Markham began, but Vance cut in.

"Yes, of course. That's just it. Too many things have happened here today already." He went to the north window and looked out into the garden. Then he returned to the centre of the room and stood for a moment in tense meditation. "As you say, Markham." His voice was barely audible. "Something may have happened. . ." Suddenly he threw his cigarette into an ash tray and turned on his heel. "Oh, my word! I wonder. . .Come, Sergeant. We'll have to make a search—immediately."

He opened the door quickly and started down the hall. We followed him with vague apprehension, not knowing what was in his mind and with no anticipation of what was to follow. Vance peered out through the garden door. Then he turned back, shaking his head.

"No, it couldn't have been there. We would have been able to see." His eyes moved inquiringly up and down the hall, and after a moment a strange, startled look came into them. "It could be!" he exclaimed. "Oh, my aunt! Damnable things are happening here. Wait a second."

He rapidly retraced his steps to the vault door. Grasping the knob, he rattled it violently; but the door was now locked. Taking the key from its nail, he inserted it hurriedly into the lock. As he opened the heavy door a crack, a pungent, penetrating odour assailed my nostrils. Vance quickly drew back.

"Out into the air!" he called over his shoulder, in our direction. "All of you!"

Instinctively we made for the door to the garden.

Vance held one hand over his nose and mouth and pushed the vault door further inward. Heavy amber-coloured fumes drifted out into the hall, and I felt a stifling, choking sensation. Vance staggered back a short step, but kept his hand on the door-knob.

"Miss Beeton! Miss Beeton!" he called. There was no response; and I saw Vance put his head down and move forward into the dense fumes that were emanating from the open door. He sank to his knees on the threshold and leaned forward into the vault. The next moment he had straightened up and was dragging the limp body of the nurse out into the passageway.

The whole episode took much less time than is required to relate it. Actually no more than ten seconds had elapsed from the time he had inserted the key into the lock. I knew what an effort he was making, for even as I stood outside the garden door, where the fumes were comparatively thin, I felt half suffocated, and Markham and Heath were choking and coughing.

As soon as the girl was out of the vault, Vance took her up in his arms and carried her unsteadily out into the garden, where he placed her gently on the wicker settee. His face was deathly pale; his eyes were watering; and he had difficulty with his breathing. When he had released the girl, he leaned heavily against one of the iron posts which supported the awning. He opened his mouth wide and sucked the fresh air into his lungs.

The nurse was gasping stertorously and clutching her throat. Although her breast was rising and falling convulsively, her whole body was limp and lifeless.

At that moment Doctor Siefert stepped through the garden door, a look of amazement on his face. He had all the outward appearance of the type of medical man Vance had described to us the night before. He was about sixty, conservatively but modishly attired, and with a bearing studiously dignified and self-sufficient.

With a great effort Vance drew himself erect.

"Hurry, doctor," he called. "It's bromin gas." He made a shaky gesture with one hand toward the prostrate figure of the nurse.

Siefert came rapidly forward, moved the girl's body into a more comfortable position and opened the collar of her uniform.

"Nothing but the air can help her," he said, as he moved one end of the settee around so that it faced the cool breeze from the river. "How are you feeling, Vance?"

Vance was dabbing his eyes with a handkerchief. He blinked once or twice and smiled faintly.

"I'm quite all right." He went to the settee and looked down at the girl for a moment. "A close call," he murmured.

Siefert inclined his head gravely.

At this moment Hammle came strutting up briskly from a remote corner of the garden.

"Good Gad!" he exclaimed. "What's the matter?"

Vance turned to the man in angry surprise.

"Well, well," he greeted him. "The roll call is complete. I'll tell you later what's the matter. Or perhaps you will be able to tell me. Wait over there." And he jerked his head in the direction of a chair nearby.

Hammle glared in resentment and began spluttering; but Heath, who had come quickly to his side, took him firmly by the arm and led him diplomatically to the chair Vance had indicated. Hammle sat down meekly and took out a cigarette.

"I wish I'd taken the earlier train to Long Island," he muttered.

"It might have been better, don't y' know," murmured Vance, turning away from him.

The nurse's strangled coughing had abated somewhat. Her breathing was deeper and more regular, and the gasping had partly subsided. Before long she struggled to sit up.

Siefert helped her.

"Breathe as deeply and rapidly as you can," he said. "It's air you need."

The girl made an effort to follow instructions, one hand braced against the back of the settee, and the other resting on Vance's arm.

A few minutes later she was able to speak, but with considerable difficulty.

"I feel—better now. Except for the burning—in my nose and throat."

Siefert sent Heath for some water and when the Sergeant had fetched it Miss Beeton drank a glassful in choking gulps. In another two or three minutes she seemed to have recovered to a great extent. She looked up at Vance with frightened eyes.

"What happened?" she asked.

"We don't know yet." Vance returned her gaze with obvious distress. "We only know that you were poisoned with bromin gas in the vault where Swift was shot. We were hoping that you could tell us about it yourself."

She shook her head vaguely, and there was a dazed look in her eyes.

"I'm afraid I can't tell you very much. It all happened so unexpectedly—so suddenly. All I know is that when I went to tell Doctor Siefert he might come upstairs, I was struck on the head from behind, just as I passed the garden door. The blow didn't render me entirely unconscious, but it stunned me so that I was unaware of anything or anybody around me. Then I felt myself being caught from behind, turned about, and forced back up the passageway and into the vault. I have a faint recollection of the door being shut upon me, although I wasn't sufficiently rational to protest or even to realize what had happened. But I was conscious of the fact that inside the vault there was a frightful suffocating smell. I was leaning up against the wall and it was very painful to breathe. . .I felt myself sinking—and that's the last I remember. . ." She shuddered. "That's all I knew—until just now."

"Yes. Not a pleasant experience. But it could have been much worse." Vance spoke in a low voice and smiled gravely down at the girl. "There's a bad bruise on the back of your head. That too might have been worse, but the starched band of your cap probably saved you from more serious injury."

The girl had got to her feet and stood swaying a little as she steadied herself against Vance.

"I really feel all right now." She looked at Vance wistfully. "And I have you to thank—haven't I?"

Siefert spoke gruffly. "A few more minutes of that bromin gas would have proved fatal. Whoever found you and got you out here did so just in time."

The girl had not taken her eyes from Vance.

"How did you happen to find me so soon?" she asked him.

"Belated reasoning," he answered. "I should have found you several minutes before—the moment I learned that you had not returned downstairs. But at first it was difficult to realize that anything serious could have happened to you."

"I can't understand it even now," the girl said with a bewildered air.

"Neither can I—entirely," returned Vance. "But perhaps I can learn something more."

Going quickly to the pitcher of water Heath had brought, he dipped his handkerchief into it. Pressing the handkerchief against his face, he disappeared into the passageway. A minute or so later he returned. In his hand he held a jagged piece of thin curved glass, about three inches long.

It was part of a broken vial, and still clinging to it was a small paper label on which was printed the symbol "Br."

"I found this on the tiled floor, in the far corner of the vault. It was just beneath one of the racks which holds Professor Garden's assortment of chemicals. There's an empty space in the rack, but this vial of bromin couldn't have fallen to the floor accidentally. It could only have been taken out deliberately and broken at the right moment." He handed the fragment of glass to Heath. "Take this, Sergeant, and have it gone over carefully for fingerprints. But if, as I suspect, the same person that killed Swift handled it, I doubt if there will be any telltale marks on it. However. . ."

Heath accepted the bit of glass gingerly, rolled it in his handkerchief and thrust it into his pocket.

"If it does show any finger-prints," he grumbled, "it'll be the first we found around here."

Vance turned to Markham, who had been standing near the rock pool during the entire scene, looking on with aggressive bewilderment.

"Bromin," he explained, "is a common reagent. It's to be found in almost every chemist's laborat'ry. It's one of the halogens, and, though it's never found free in nature, it occurs in various compounds. Incidentally, it got its name from the Greek *bromos*, which means stench. It hasn't figured very often as a criminal agent, although accidental cases of bromin poisoning are numerous. But it was used extensively during the war in the manufacture of gas bombs, for it volatilizes on coming in contact with the air. And bromin gas is suffocating and deadly. Whoever planned this lethal chamber for Miss Beeton wasn't without cruelty."

"It was a dastardly thing, Vance," Siefert burst out, his eyes flashing.

Vance nodded and his eyes moved to the nurse. "Yes. All of that, doctor. So was Swift's murder. . .How are you feeling now, Miss Beeton?"

"A little shaky," she answered with a weak smile. "But nothing more." She was leaning against one end of the settee.

"Then we'll carry on, what?"

"Of course," she returned in a low voice.

Floyd Garden stepped out from the hallway at this moment. He coughed and looked at us with blinking, inquisitive eyes.

"What's this beastly odour in the hall?" he asked. "It's gotten downstairs, and Sneed is already crying like a lost baby. Is anything wrong?"

"Not now. No," Vance returned. "A little bromin gas a few minutes ago; but the air will be clear in a little while. No casualties. Every one doing well. . .Did you want to see me?"

Garden looked round at the group on the roof with a puzzled air.

"Awfully sorry to interrupt you, Vance; but the fact is, I came for the doctor." His eyes rested on Siefert, and he smiled dryly. "It's the usual thing, doc," he said. "The mater seems almost in a state of collapse—she assured me vigorously that she hadn't an ounce of strength left. I got her to go to bed—which she seemed perfectly willing to do. But she insists on seeing you immediately. I never know when she means it and when she doesn't. But that's the message."

A worried look came into Siefert's eyes, and he took a slow deep breath before answering.

"I'll come at once, of course," he said. He looked at the nurse and then lifted his gaze to Vance. "Will you excuse me?"

Vance bowed. "Certainly, doctor. But I think Miss Beeton had better remain here in the air for a while longer."

"Oh, by all means. By all means. If I need her I'll send word. But I trust that won't be necessary." And Siefert left the roof reluctantly, with Garden following him.

Vance watched them until they turned through the door of the passageway; then he spoke to the nurse.

"Please sit here a few minutes, Miss Beeton. I want to have a talk with you. But first I'd like a minute or two with Mr. Hammle."

The nurse nodded her assent and sat down a little wearily on the settee.

Vance beckoned curtly to Hammle. "Suppose we go inside for a moment."

Hammle rose with alacrity. "I was wondering how much longer you gentlemen were going to keep me here."

Vance led the way into the study, and Markham and I followed behind Hammle.

"What were you doing on the roof, Mr. Hammle?" asked Vance. "I told you some time ago, after our brief interview, that you might go."

Hammle fidgeted. He was patently apprehensive and wary.

"There's no crime in going out into the garden for a while—is there?" he asked with unimpressive truculence.

"None whatever," Vance returned casually. "I was wonderin' why you preferred the garden to going home. Devilish things have been happening in the garden this afternoon."

"As I told you, I wish I had gone. How did I know—?"

"That's hardly the point, Mr. Hammle." Vance cut him short. "It doesn't answer my question."

"Well now, look here," Hammle explained fulsomely; "I had just missed a train to Long Island, and it was more than an hour until the next one. When I went out of here and started to go downstairs, I suddenly said to myself, 'It'll be pleasanter waiting in the garden than in the Pennsylvania Station.' So I went out on the roof and hung around. And here I am."

Vance regarded the man shrewdly and nodded his head. "Yes, as you say. Here you are. More or less in evidence. By the by, Mr. Hammle, what did you see while you were waiting in the garden for the next train?"

"Not a thing—absolutely!" Hammle's tone was aggressive. "I walked along the boxwood hedges, smoking, and was leaning over the parapet by the gate, looking out at the city, when I heard you come out carrying the nurse."

Vance narrowed his eyes: it was obvious he was not satisfied with Hammle's explanation.

"And you saw no one else either in the garden or on the terrace?"

"Not a soul," the man assured him.

"And you heard nothing?"

"Not until you gentlemen came out."

Vance stood regarding Hammle for several moments. Then he turned and walked toward the garden window.

"That will be all for the moment," he said brusquely. "But we shall probably want to see you tomorrow."

"I'll be at home all day. Glad to be of any service." Hammle shot a covert look at Vance, made his *adieux* quickly, and went out down the passageway.

CHAPTER 13

The Azure Star

Saturday, April 14; 7 p.m.

Vance returned at once to the garden. Miss Beeton drew herself up a little as he approached her.

"Do you feel equal to a few questions?" he asked her.

"Oh, yes." She smiled with more assurance now, and rose.

Dusk was settling rapidly over the city. A dull slate colour was replacing the blue mist over the river. The skies beyond the Jersey hills were luminous with the vivid colours of the sunset, and in the distance tiny specks of yellow light were beginning to appear in the windows of the serried buildings. A light breeze was blowing from the north, and the air was cool.

As we crossed the garden to the balustrade, Miss Beeton took a deep breath and shuddered slightly.

"You'd better have your coat," Vance suggested. He returned to the study and brought it out to her. When he had helped her into it she turned suddenly and looked at him inquiringly.

"Why was my coat brought to the study?" she asked. "It's been worrying me frightfully. . .with all the terrible things that have been going on today."

"Why should it worry you?" Vance smiled at the girl. "A misplaced coat is surely not a serious matter." His tone was reassuring. "But we really owe you an explanation. You see, two revolvers figured in Swift's death. One of them we all saw on the roof here—that was the one with which the chap was killed. But no one downstairs heard the shot because the poor fellow met his end in Professor Garden's storeroom vault—"

"Ah! That was why you wanted to know if the key was in its place." The girl nodded.

"The shot we all heard," Vance went on, "was fired from another revolver after Swift's body had been carried from the vault and placed in the chair out here. We were naturally anxious to find that other weapon, and Sergeant Heath made a search for it. . ."

"But—but—my coat?" Her hand went out and she clutched at Vance's sleeve as a look of understanding came into her frightened eyes.

"Yes," Vance said, "the Sergeant found the revolver in the pocket of your top-coat. Some one had put it there as a tempor'ry hiding-place."

She recoiled with a sudden intake of breath. "How dreadful!" Her words were barely audible.

Vance put his hand on her shoulder.

"If you had not come to the study when you did and seen the coat, we would have returned it to the closet downstairs and saved you all this worry."

"But it's too terrible!. . .And then this—this attempt on my life. I can't understand. I'm frightened."

"Come, come," Vance exhorted the girl. "It's over now, and we need your help."

She gazed directly into his eyes for several minutes. Then she gave him a faint smile of confidence.

"I'm very sorry," she said simply. "But this house—this family—they've been doing queer things to my nerves for the past month. I can't explain it, but there's something frightfully wrong here. . .I was in charge of an operating room in a Montreal hospital for six months, attending as many as six and eight operations a day; but that never affected me the way this household does. There, at least, I could see what was going on—I could help and know that I was helping. But here everything goes on in dark corners, and nothing I do seems to be of any use. Can you imagine a surgeon suddenly going blind in the middle of a *laparotomy* and trying to continue without his sight? That's how I feel in this strange place. . .But please don't think I am not ready to help—to do anything I can for you. You, too, always have to work in the dark, don't you?"

"Don't we all have to work in the dark?" Vance murmured, without taking his eyes from her. "Tell me who you think could have been guilty of the terrible things that have happened here."

All fear and doubt seemed to have left the girl. She moved toward the balustrade and stood looking over the river with an impressive calm and self-control.

"Really, I don't know," she answered with quiet restraint. "There are several possibilities, humanly speaking. But I haven't had time to think about it clearly. It all happened so suddenly. . ."

"Yes, quite," put in Vance. "Things like that usually do come suddenly and without previous warning."

"Woode Swift's death wasn't at all the sort of thing I would expect to happen here," the girl went on. "I wouldn't have been surprised at some act of impulsive violence, but this premeditated murder, so subtle and so carefully planned, seems alien to the atmosphere here. Besides, it isn't a loving family, except on the surface. Psychologically, every one seems at cross purposes—full of hidden hatreds. No contacts anywhere—I mean, no understanding contacts. Floyd Garden is saner than the others. His interests are narrow, to be sure, but, on his own mental level, he has always impressed me as being straightforward and eminently human. He's dependable, too, I think. He's intolerant of subtleties and profundities, and has always taken the course of ignoring the existence of those qualities which have caused friction between the other members of the household. Maybe I'm wrong about it, but that has been my impression."

She paused and frowned.

"As for Mrs. Garden, I feel that by nature she is shallow and is deliberately creating for herself a deeper and more complex mode of life, which she doesn't in the least understand. That, of course, makes her unreasonable and dangerous. I have never had a more unreasonable patient. She has no consideration whatever for others. Her affection for her nephew has never seemed genuine to me. He was like a little clay model that she had made and prized highly. If she had an idea

for another figurine, I feel that she would have wet the clay and remodelled it into a new object of adoration."

"And Professor Garden?"

"He's a researcher and scientist, of course, and, therefore, not altogether human, in the conventional sense. I have thought sometimes that he isn't wholly rational. To him people and things are merely elements to be converted into some new chemical combination. Do you understand what I am trying to say?"

"Yes, quite well," Vance assured her. "Every scientist imagines himself an *Übermensch*. Power is his god. Many of the world's greatest scientists have been regarded as madmen. Perhaps they were. Yes. A queer problem. The possession of power induces weakness. Silly notion, what? The most dangerous agency in the world is science. Especially dangerous to the scientist himself. Every great scientific discoverer is a Frankenstein. However. . .What is your impression of the guests who were present today?"

"I don't feel competent to pass judgment on them," the girl replied seriously. "I can't entirely understand them. But each one strikes me as dangerous in his own way. They are all playing a game—and it seems to be a game without rules. To them the outcome justifies the methods they use. They seem to be mere seekers after sensation, trying to draw the veil of illusion over life's realities because they are not strong enough to face the facts."

"Yes, quite. You have clear vision." Vance scrutinized the girl beside him. "And you took up nursing because you are able to face the realities. You are not afraid of life—or of death."

The girl looked embarrassed.

"You're making too much of my profession. After all, I had to earn my living, and nursing appealed to me."

"Yes, of course. It would." Vance nodded. "But tell me, wouldn't you rather not have to work for your living?"

She looked up.

"Perhaps. But isn't it natural for every woman to prefer luxury and security to drudgery and uncertainty?"

"No doubt," said Vance. "And speakin' of nursing, just what do you think of Mrs. Garden's condition?"

Miss Beeton hesitated before she answered:

"Really, I don't know what to say. I can't understand it. And I rather suspect that Doctor Siefert himself is puzzled by it. Mrs. Garden is obviously a sick woman. She shows many of the symptoms of that nervous, erratic temperament exhibited by people suffering from cancer. Though she's much better some days than others, I know that she suffers a great deal. Doctor Siefert tells me she is really a neurological case; but I get the feeling, at times, that it goes much deeper—that an obscure physiological condition is producing the neurological symptoms she shows."

"That's most interestin'. Doctor Siefert mentioned something of the kind to me only a few days ago." Vance moved nearer to the girl. "Would you mind telling me something of your contacts with the members of the household?"

"There's very little to tell. Professor Garden practically ignores me—half the time I doubt if he even knows I am here. Mrs. Garden alternates between periods of irritable admonition and intimate confidence. Floyd Garden has always been pleasant and considerate. He has wanted me to be happy here, and has often apologized for his mother's abominable treatment of me at times. I've rather liked him for his attitude."

"And what of Swift—did you see much of him?" The girl seemed reluctant to answer and looked away; but she finally turned back to Vance.

"The truth is, Mr. Swift asked me several times to go to dinner and the theatre with him. He was never objectionable in his advances; but he did rather annoy me occasionally. I got the impression, though, that he was one of those unhappy men who feel their inferiority and seek to bolster themselves up with the affections of women. I think that he was really concerned with Miss Graem, and merely turned to me through pique."

Vance smoked for a few moments in silence. Then he said:

"What of the big race today? Had there been much discussion about it?"

"Oh, yes. For over a week I've heard little else here. A curious tension has been growing in the house. I heard Mr. Swift remark to Floyd Garden one evening that the Rivermont Handicap was his one remaining hope, and that he thought Equanimity would win. They immediately went into a furious argument regarding Equanimity's chances."

"Was it generally known to the other members of the afternoon gatherings how Swift felt about this race and Equanimity?"

"Yes, the matter was freely discussed for days.—You see," the girl added in explanation, "it's impossible for me not to overhear some of these afternoon discussions; and Mrs. Garden herself often takes part in them and then discusses them with me later."

"By the by," asked Vance, "how did you come to bet on Azure Star?"

"Frankly," the girl confessed shyly, "I've been mildly interested in the horse-betting parties here, though I've never had any desire to make a wager myself. But I overheard you tell Mr. Garden that you had picked Azure Star, and the name was so appealing that I asked Mr. Garden to place that bet for me. It was the first time I ever bet on a horse."

"And Azure Star came in." Vance sighed. "Too bad. Actually you bet against Equanimity, you know—he was the favourite. A big gamble. Most unfortunate that you won. Beginner's luck, d' ye see, is always fatal."

The girl's face became suddenly sombre, and she looked steadily at Vance for several moments before she spoke again.

"Do you really think it will prove fatal?"

"Yes. Oh, yes. Inevitable. You won't be able to resist making other wagers. One doesn't stop with the first bet if one wins. And, invariably, one loses in the end."

Again the girl gave Vance a long and troubled look; then her gaze drifted to the darkening sky overhead.

"But Azure Star is a beautiful name, isn't it?" She pointed upward. "There's one now."

We all looked up. High above we saw a single bright star shining with blue luminosity in the cloudless sky. After a moment Vance moved toward the parapet and looked out over the waters of the river to the purpling hills and the still glowing sunset colours in the west. The sharp forms of the great gaunt buildings of the city to the south cut the empyrean like the unreal silhouettes on a theatrical drop.

"No city in the world," Vance said, "is as beautiful as New York seen from a vantage point like this in the early twilight." (I wondered at his sudden change of mood.)

He stepped up on the parapet and looked down into the great abyss of deep shadows and flickering lights far below. A curious chill of fear ran over me—the sort of fear I have always felt when I have seen acrobatic performers perilously balanced high above a circus arena. I knew Vance had no fear of heights and that he possessed an abnormal sense of equilibrium. But I nevertheless drew in an involuntary breath; my feet and lower limbs began to tingle; and for a moment I actually felt faint.

Miss Beeton was standing close to Markham, and she, too, must have experienced something of the sensation I felt, for I saw her face go suddenly pale. Her eyes were fixed on Vance with a look of apprehensive horror, and she caught at Markham's arm as if for support.

"Vance!" It was Markham's stern voice that broke the silence. "Come down from there!"

Vance jumped down and turned to us.

"Frightfully sorry," he said. "Height does affect most people. I didn't realize." He looked at the girl. "Will you forgive me?..."

As he spoke Floyd Garden stepped out on the roof through the passageway door.

"Sorry, Vance," he apologized, "but Doc Siefert wants. Miss Beeton downstairs—if she feels equal to it. The mater is putting on one of her acts."

The nurse hurried away immediately, and Garden strolled up to Vance. He was again fussing with his pipe.

"A beastly mess," he mumbled. "And you've certainly put the fear of God and destruction into the hearts of the pious boys and girls here this afternoon. They all got the jitters after you talked with them." He looked up. "The fact is, Vance, if you should want to see Kroon or Zalia Graem or Madge Weatherby for any reason this evening, they'll be here. They've all asked to come. Must return to the scene of the crime, or something of that kind. Need mutual support. And, to tell you the truth, I'm damned glad they're coming. At least we can talk the thing over and drink highballs; and that's better than fussing and worrying about it all alone."

"Perfectly natural. Quite." Vance nodded. "I understand their feelings—and yours—perfectly. . .Beastly mess, as you say. . .And now suppose we go down."

Doctor Siefert met us at the foot of the stairs.

"I was just coming up for you, Mr. Vance. Mrs. Garden insists on seeing you gentlemen." Then he added in a low tone: "She's in a tantrum. A bit hysterical. Don't take anything she may say too seriously."

We entered the bedroom. Mrs. Garden, in a salmon-pink silk dressing-gown, was in bed, bolstered up by a collection of pillows. Her face was drawn and, in the slanting rays of the night-light, seemed flabby and unhealthy. Her eyes glared demoniacally as she looked at us, and her fingers clutched nervously at the quilt. Miss Beeton stood at the far side of the bed, looking down at her patient with calm concern; and Professor Garden leaned heavily against the window-sill opposite, his face a mask of troubled solicitude.

"I have something to say, and I want you all to hear it." Mrs. Garden's voice was shrill and strident. "My nephew has been killed to-day—and I know who did it!" She glared venomously at Floyd Garden who stood near the foot of the bed, his pipe hanging limply from the corner of his mouth. "*You* did it!" She pointed an accusing finger at her son. "You've always hated Woody. You've been jealous of him. No one else had any reason to do this despicable thing. I suppose I should lie for you and shield you. But to what end? So you could kill somebody else? Perhaps—perhaps even me, or your father. No! The time has come for the truth. You killed Woody, and I know you killed him. And I know why you did it. . ."

Floyd Garden stood through this tirade without moving and without perceptible emotion. He kept his eyes on his mother with cynical indifference. When she paused he took the pipe from his mouth and with a sad smile said:

"And why did I do it, mater?"

"Because you were jealous of him. Because you knew that I had divided my estate equally between you two—and you want it all for yourself. You always resented the fact that I loved Woody as well as you. And now you think that by having got Woody out of the way, you'll get everything when I die. But you're mistaken. You'll get nothing! Do you hear me? Nothing! Tomorrow I'm going to change my will." Her eyes were full of frantic gloating: she was like a woman who has suddenly gone out of her mind. "I'm going to change my will, do you understand? Woody's share will go to your father, with the stipulation that you will never get or inherit a dollar of it. And

135

your share will go to charity." She laughed hysterically and beat the bed with her clenched fists.

Doctor Siefert had been watching the woman closely. He now moved a little nearer the bed.

"An ice-pack, immediately," he said to the nurse; and she went quickly from the room. Then he busied himself with his medicine case and deftly prepared a hypodermic injection.

"I won't let you give me that," the woman on the bed screamed. "There's nothing the matter with me. I'm tired of taking your drugs."

"Yes, I know. But you'll take this, Mrs. Garden." Doctor Siefert spoke with calm assurance.

The woman relaxed under his patient dictatorial scrutiny and permitted him to give her the injection. She lay back on the pillows, staring blankly at her son. The nurse returned to the room and arranged the ice-bag for her patient.

Doctor Siefert then quickly made out a prescription and turned to Miss Beeton.

"Have this filled at once. A teaspoonful every two hours until Mrs. Garden falls asleep."

Floyd Garden stepped forward and took the prescription.

"I'll phone the pharmacy," he said. "It'll take them only a few minutes to send it over." And he went out of the room.

After a few final instructions to Miss Beeton, the doctor led the way to the drawing-room, and the rest of us followed, leaving the nurse rearranging Mrs. Garden's pillows. Professor Garden, who during the painful scene had stood with his back to us, gazing out of the window into the night, still remained there, looking like a hunched gargoyle framed by the open casement. As we passed the den door, we could hear Floyd Garden telephoning.

"I think Mrs. Garden will quiet down now," Doctor Siefert remarked to Vance when we reached the drawing-room. "As I told you, you mustn't take her remarks seriously when she's in this condition. She will probably have forgotten about it by tomorrow."

"Her bitterness, however, did not seem entirely devoid of rationality," Vance returned.

Siefert frowned but made no comment on Vance's statement. Instead he said in his quiet, well-modulated voice, as he sat down leisurely in the nearest chair: "This whole affair is very shocking. Floyd Garden gave me but few details when I arrived. Would you care to enlighten me further?"

Vance readily complied. He briefly went over the entire case, beginning with the anonymous telephone message he had received the night before. (Not by the slightest sign did the doctor indicate any previous knowledge of that telephone call. He sat looking at Vance with serene attentiveness, like a specialist listening to the case history of a patient.) Vance withheld no important detail from him. He explained about the races and the wagers, Swift's withdrawal to the roof, the actions of the other members of the party, the shot, the finding of Swift's body, the discoveries in the vault, the matter of the disconnected buzzer wires, the substance of his various interviews with the members of the Garden family and their guests, and, finally, the finding of the second revolver in the nurse's coat.

"And the rest," Vance concluded, "you yourself have witnessed."

Siefert nodded very slowly two or three times, as if to infer that he had received a clear and satisfactory picture of the events of the afternoon.

"A very serious situation," he commented gravely, as if making a diagnosis. "Some of the things you have told me seem highly significant. A shrewdly conceived murder—and a vicious one. Especially the hiding of the revolver in Miss Beeton's coat and the attempt on her life with the bromin gas in the vault. I don't understand that phase of the situation."

Vance looked up quickly.

"Do you understand any other phase of the situation?"

"No, no. I did not mean to imply that," Siefert hastened to answer. "I was merely thinking that while Swift's death could conceivably be explained on rational grounds, I fail to see any possible reason for this dastardly attempt to involve Miss Beeton and then to end her life."

"But I seriously doubt," said Vance, "that the revolver was put in Miss Beeton's coat pocket with any intention of incriminating her. I imagine it was to have been taken out of the house at the first opportunity. But I agree with you that the bromin episode is highly mystifyin'." Vance, without appearing to do so, was watching the doctor closely. "When you asked to see me on your arrival here this afternoon," he went on, "I was hoping that you might have some suggestion which, coming from one who is familiar with the domestic situation here, might put us on the track to a solution."

Siefert solemnly shook his head several times. "No, no. I am sorry, but I am completely at a loss myself. When I asked to speak to you and Mr. Markham it was because I was naturally deeply interested in the situation here and anxious to hear what you might have to say about it." He paused, shifted slightly in his chair, and then asked: "Have you formed any opinion from what you have been able to learn?"

"Yes. Oh, yes." Vance's gaze drifted from the doctor to the beautiful T'ang horse which stood on a nearby cabinet. "Frankly, however, I detest my opinion. I'd hate to be right about it. A sinister, unnatural conclusion is forcing itself upon me. It's sheer horror." He spoke with unwonted intensity.

Siefert was silent, and Vance turned to him again.

"I say, doctor, are you particularly worried about Mrs. Garden's condition?"

A cloud overspread Siefert's countenance, and he did not answer at once.

"It's a queer case," he said at length, with an obvious attempt at evasion. "As I recently told you, it has me deeply puzzled. I'm bringing Kattelbaum up tomorrow."[1]

"Yes. As you say. Kattelbaum." Vance looked at the doctor dreamily. "My anonymous telephone message last night mentioned radioactive sodium. But equanimity is essential. Yes. By all means. Not a nice case, doctor—not at all a nice case. . .And now I think we'll be toddlin'." Vance rose and bowed with formal brusqueness. Siefert also got up.

"If there is anything whatever that I can do for you. . .," he began.

"We may call on you later," Vance returned, and walked toward the archway.

Siefert did not follow us, but turned and moved slowly toward one of the front windows, where he stood looking out, with his hands clasped behind him. We re-entered the hallway and found Sneed waiting to help us with our coats.

We had just reached the door leading out of the apartment when the strident tones of Mrs. Garden's voice assailed us again. Floyd Garden was standing just inside the bedroom door, looking over at his mother.

"Your solicitude won't do you any good, Floyd," Mrs. Garden cried. "Being kind to me now, are you? Telephoning for the prescription—all attention and loving kindness. But don't think you're pulling the wool over my eyes. It won't make any difference. Tomorrow I change my will! Tomorrow. . ."

We continued on our way out, and heard no more.

But Mrs. Garden did not change her will. The following morning she was found dead in bed.

---

1. Hugo Kattelbaum, though a comparatively young man, was one of the country's leading authorities on cancer, and his researches on the effect of radium on the human viscera had, for the past year, been receiving considerable attention in the leading medical journals.

CHAPTER 14

Radioactive Sodium

Sunday, April 15; 9 a.m.

Shortly after nine o'clock the next morning there was a telephone call from Doctor Siefert. Vance was still abed when the telephone rang, and I answered it. (I had been up for several hours: the events of the preceding day had stirred me deeply, and I had been unable to sleep.) The doctor's voice was urgent and troubled when he asked that I summon Vance immediately. I had a premonition of further disaster as I roused Vance. He seemed loath to get up and complained cynically about people who rise early in the morning. But he finally slipped into his Chinese robe and sandals and, lighting a *Régie*, went protestingly into the anteroom.

It was nearly ten minutes before he came out again. His resentment had given way, and as he stepped across to the table and rang for Currie, there was a look of keen interest in his eyes.

"Breakfast at once," he ordered when his old butler appeared. "And put out a sombre suit and my black Homburg. And, by the by, Currie, a little extra coffee. Mr. Markham will be here soon and may want a cup."

Currie went out, and Vance turned back to his bedroom. At the door he stopped and turned to me with a curious look.

"Mrs. Garden was found dead in her bed this morning," he drawled. "Poison of some kind. I've phoned Markham, and we'll be going to the Garden apartment as soon as he comes. A bad business, Van,—very bad. There's too much betting going on in that house." And he went on into the bedroom.

Markham arrived within half an hour. In the meantime Vance had dressed and was finishing his second cup of coffee.

"What's the trouble now?" Markham demanded irritably, as he came into the library. "Perhaps now that I'm here, you'll be good enough to forgo your cryptic air."

139

"My dear Markham—oh, my dear Markham!" Vance looked up and sighed. "Do sit down and have a cup of coffee while I enjoy this cigarette. Really, y' know, it's deuced hard to be lucid on the telephone." He poured a cup of coffee, and Markham reluctantly sat down. "And please don't sweeten the coffee," Vance went on. "It has a delightfully subtle bouquet, and it would be a pity to spoil it with saccharine."

Markham, frowning defiantly, put three lumps of sugar in the cup.

"Why am I here?" he growled.

"A profoundly philosophical question," smiled Vance. "Unanswerable, however. Why are any of us here? Why anything? But, since we are all here without knowing the reason therefore, I'll pander to your pragmatism." He drew deeply on his cigarette and settled back lazily in his chair. "Siefert phoned me this morning, just before I called you. Explained he didn't know your private number at home and asked me to apologize to you for not notifying you direct."

"Notifying me?" Markham set down his cup.

"About Mrs. Garden. She's dead. Found so this morning in bed. Probably murdered."

"Good God!"

"Yes, quite. Not a nice situation. No. The lady died some time during the night—exact hour unknown as yet. Siefert says it might have been caused by an overdose of the sleeping medicine he prescribed for her. It's all gone. And he says there was enough of it to do the trick. On the other hand, he admits it might have been something else. He's very noncommittal. No external signs he can diagnose. Craves our advice and succour. Hence his summons."

Markham pushed his cup aside with a clatter and lighted a cigar.

"Where's Siefert now?" he asked.

"At the Gardens'. Very correct. Standing by, and all that. The nurse phoned him shortly after eight this morning—it was she who made the discovery when she took Mrs. Garden's breakfast in. Siefert hastened over and after viewing the remains and probing round a bit called me. Said that, in view of yesterday's events, he didn't wish to go ahead until we got there."

"Well, why don't we get along?" snapped Markham, standing up.

Vance sighed and rose slowly from his chair.

"There's really no rush. The lady can't elude us. And Siefert won't desert the ship. Moreover, it's a beastly hour to drag one out of bed. Y' know, Markham, an entertainin' monograph could be written about the total lack of consideration on the part of murderers. They think only of themselves. No fellow feelin'. Always upsettin' the normal routine. And they never declare a holiday—not even on a Sunday morning. . .However, as you say. Let's toddle."

"Hadn't we better notify Heath?" suggested Markham.

"Yes—quite," returned Vance, as we went out. "I called the Sergeant just after I phoned you. He's been up half the night working on the usual police routine. Stout fella, Heath. Amazin' industry. But quite futile. If only such energy led anywhere beyond steel filing cabinets. I always think tenderly of Heath as a perpetuator of archives. . ."

Miss Beeton admitted us to the Garden apartment. She looked drawn and worried, but she gave Vance a faint smile of greeting which he returned.

"I'm beginning to think this nightmare will never end, Mr. Vance," she said.

Vance nodded sombrely, and we went on into the drawing-room where Doctor Siefert, Professor Garden, and his son were awaiting us.

"I'm glad you've come, gentlemen," Siefert greeted us, coming forward.

Professor Garden sat at one end of the long davenport, his elbows resting on his knees, his face in his hands. He barely acknowledged our presence. Floyd Garden got to his feet and nodded abstractedly in our direction. A terrible change seemed to have come over him. He looked years older than when we had left him the night before, and his face, despite its tan, showed a greenish pallor. His eyes moved vaguely about the room; he was visibly shaken.

"What a hell of a situation!" he mumbled, focusing watery eyes on Vance. "The mater accuses me last night of putting Woody out of the way, and then threatens to cut me off in her will. And now she's dead! And it was I who took charge of the prescription. The doc says it could have been the medicine that killed her."

Vance looked at the man sharply.

"Yes, yes," he said in a low, sympathetic tone. "I thought of all that, too, don't y' know. But it certainly won't help you to be morbid about it. How about a Tom Collins?"

"I've had four already," Garden returned dispiritedly, sinking back into his chair. But almost immediately he sprang to his feet again. He pointed a finger at Vance, and his eyes filled with apprehension and entreaty.

"For God's sake," he burst out, "it's up to you to find out the truth. I'm on the spot—what with my going out of the room with Woody yesterday, my failure to place his bet, then the mater's accusation, and that damned will of hers, and the medicine. You've got to find out who's guilty. . ."

As he was talking the door bell had rung, and Heath came up the hallway.

"Sure, we're gonna find out," came the pugnacious voice of the Sergeant from the archway. "And it ain't gonna be so well with you when we do."

Vance turned quickly round. "Oh, I say, Sergeant. Less animation, please. This is hardly the time. Too early in the morning." He went to Garden and, putting a hand on the man's shoulder, urged him back into his chair. "Come, buck up," he said; "we'll need your help, and if you work up a case of jitters you'll be useless."

"But don't you see how deeply involved I am?" Garden protested weakly.

"You're not the only one involved," Vance returned calmly. He turned to Siefert. "I think, doctor, we should have a little chat. Possibly we can get the matter of your patient's death straightened out a bit. Suppose we go upstairs to the study, what?"

As we stepped through the archway into the hall, I glanced back. Young Garden was staring after us with a hard, determined look. The professor had not moved, and took no more notice of our going than he had of our coming.

In the study Vance went directly to the point.

"Doctor, the time has come when we must be perfectly frank with each other. The usual conventional considerations of your profession must be temporarily put aside. A matter far more urgent is involved now, and it requires more serious consideration than the accepted relationship between doctor and patient. Therefore, I shall be altogether candid with you and trust that you can see your way to being equally candid with me."

Siefert, who had taken a chair near the door, looked at Vance a trifle uneasily.

"I regret that I do not understand what you mean," he said in his suavest manner.

"I merely mean," replied Vance coolly, "that I am fully aware that it was you who sent me the anonymous telephone message Friday night."

Siefert raised his eyebrows slightly.

"Indeed! That's very interesting."

"Not only interestin'," drawled Vance, "but true. How I know it was you need not concern us at the moment. I only beg of you to admit that it is so, and to act accordingly. The fact has a direct bearing on this tragic case, and unless you will assist us with a frank statement, a grave injustice may be done—an injustice that could not be squared with any existing code of medical ethics."

Siefert hesitated for several moments. He withdrew his eyes hastily from Vance and looked thoughtfully out of the window toward the west.

"Assuming, for the sake of argument," he said with deliberation, like a man carefully choosing his words, "that it was I who phoned you Friday night, what then?"

Vance watched the man with a faint smile.

"It might be, don't y' know," he said, "that you were cognizant of the situation here, and that you had a suspicion—or let us say, a fear—that something tragic was impending." Vance took out his cigarette case and lighted a cigarette. "I fully understood the import of that message, doctor—as you intended. That is why I happened to be here yesterday afternoon. The significance of your reference to the *Aeneid* and the inclusion of the word 'equanimity' did not escape me. I must say, however, that your advice to investigate radioactive sodium was not entirely clear—although I think I now have a fairly lucid idea as to the implication. However, there were some deeper implications in your message, and this is the time, d' ye see, when we should face this thing together with complete honesty."

Siefert brought his eyes back to Vance in a long appraising glance, and then shifted them to the window again. After a minute or two he stood up, clasped his hands behind him, and strode across the room. He looked out over the Hudson with troubled concern. Then he turned and, nodding as if in answer to some question he had put to himself, said:

"Yes, I did send you that message. Perhaps I was not entirely loyal to my principles when I did so, for I had little doubt that you would guess who sent it and would understand what I was trying to convey to you. But I realize that nothing can be gained now by not being frank with you. . .The situation in this household has bothered me for a long time, and lately I've had a sense of imminent disaster, All of the factors of late have been ripening for this final outburst. And I felt so strongly about them that I could not resist sending an anonymous message to you, in the hope that the vague eventualities I anticipated might be averted."

"How long have you felt this vague premonition?" asked Vance.

"For the past three months, I should say. Although I have acted as the Gardens' physician for many years, it was not until last fall that Mrs. Garden's changing condition came to my notice. I thought little of it at first, but, as it grew worse and I found myself unable to diagnose it satisfactorily, a curious suspicion forced itself on me that the change was not entirely natural. I began coming here much more frequently than had been my custom, and during the last couple of months I had felt many subtle undercurrents in the various relationships of the household, which I had never sensed before. Of course, I knew that Floyd and Swift never got along particularly well—that there was some deep animosity and jealousy between them. I also knew the conditions of Mrs. Garden's will. Furthermore, I knew of the gambling on the horses that had become part of the daily routine here. Neither Floyd nor Woode kept anything from me—you see, I have always been their confidant as well as their physician—and their reactions toward their personal affairs—which, unfortunately, included horse-racing—were well known to me."

Siefert paused with a frown.

"As I say, it has been only recently that I have felt something deeper and more significant in all this interplay of temperaments; and this feeling grew to such proportions that I actually feared a violent climax of some kind—especially as Floyd told me only a few days ago that his cousin intended to stake his entire remaining funds on Equanimity in the big race yesterday. So overpowering was my feeling in regard to the whole situation here that I decided to do something about it, if I could manage it without divulging any professional confidences. But you saw through my subterfuge, and, to be wholly candid with you, I'm rather glad you did."

Vance nodded. "I appreciate your scruples in the matter, doctor. I only regret that I was unable to forestall these tragedies. That, as it happened, was beyond human power." Vance looked up quickly. "By the by, doctor, did you have any definite suspicions when you phoned me Friday night?"

Siefert shook his head with emphasis. "No. Frankly, I was baffled. I merely felt that some sort of explosion was imminent. But I hadn't the slightest idea in what quarter that explosion would occur."

"Can you say from what quarter the causes for your apprehension arose?"

"No. Nor can I say whether my feeling had to do with Mrs. Garden's state of health alone, or whether I was influenced also by the subtle antagonism between Floyd and Woode Swift. I asked myself the question many times, without finding a satisfactory answer. At times, however, I could not resist the impression that the two factors were in some way closely related. Hence my phone message, in which, by inference, I called your attention to both Mrs. Garden's peculiar illness and the tense atmosphere that had developed round the daily betting on the races."

Vance smoked a while in silence. "And now, doctor, will you be so good as to give us the full details about this morning?"

Siefert drew himself up in his chair.

"There's practically nothing to add to the information I gave you over the phone. Miss Beeton called me a little after eight o'clock and informed me that Mrs. Garden had died some time during the night. She asked for instructions, and I told her that I would come at once. I was here half an hour or so later. I could find no determinable cause for Mrs. Garden's death, and assumed it might have been her heart until Miss Beeton called my attention to the fact that the bottle of medicine sent by the druggist was empty..."

"By the by, doctor, what was the prescription you made out for your patient last night?"

"A simple barbital solution."

"Why did you not prescribe one of the ordin'ry barbiturate compounds?"

"Why should I?" Siefert asked with obvious annoyance. "I always prefer to know exactly what my patient is getting. I'm old-fashioned enough to take little stock in proprietary mixtures."

"And I believe you told me on the telephone that there was sufficient barbital in the prescription to have caused death."

"Yes." The doctor nodded. "If taken at one time."

"And Mrs. Garden's death was consistent with barbital poisoning?"

"There was nothing to contradict such a conclusion," Siefert answered. "And there was nothing to indicate any other cause."

"When did the nurse discover the empty bottle?"

"Not until after she had phoned me, I believe."

"Could the taste of the solution be detected if it were given to a person without his knowledge?"

"Yes—and no," the doctor replied judicially. "The taste is a bit acrid; but it is a colourless solution, like water, and if it were drunk fast the taste might go unnoticed."

Vance nodded. "Therefore, if the solution had been poured into a glass and water had been added, Mrs. Garden might conceivably have drunk it all without complaining about the bitter taste?"

"That's wholly possible," the doctor told him. "And I cannot help feeling that something of that kind took place last night. It was because of this conclusion that I called you immediately."

Vance, smoking lazily, was watching Siefert from under speculative eyelids. Moving slightly in his chair and crushing out his cigarette in a small jade ash tray at his side, he said:

"Tell me something of Mrs. Garden's illness, doctor, and why radioactive sodium should have suggested itself to you."

Siefert brought his eyes sharply back to Vance.

"I was afraid you would ask me that. But this is no time for squeamishness. I must trust wholly to your discretion." He paused, as if determining how he might best approach a matter which was obviously distasteful to him. "As I've already said, I don't know the exact nature of Mrs. Garden's ailment. The symptoms have been very much like those accompanying radium poisoning. But I have never prescribed any of the radium preparations for her—I am, in fact, profoundly sceptical of their efficacy. As you may know, we have had many untoward results from the haphazard, unscientific administration of these radium preparations."[2]

He cleared his throat before continuing.

"One evening while reading the reports of the researches made in California on radioactive sodium, or what might be called artificial radium, which has been heralded as a possible medium of cure for cancer, I suddenly realized that Professor Garden himself was actively interested in this particular line of research and had done some very creditable work in the field. The realization was purely a matter of association, and I gave it little thought at first. But the idea persisted, and before long some very unpleasant possibilities began to force themselves upon me."

Again the doctor paused, a troubled look on his face.

"About two months ago I suggested to Doctor Garden that, if it were at all feasible, he put Miss Beeton on his wife's case. I had already come to the conclusion that Mrs. Garden required more constant attention and supervision than I could afford her, and Miss Beeton, who is a registered nurse, had, for the past year or so, been working with Doctor Garden in his laboratory—in fact, it was I who had sent her to him when he mentioned his need of a laboratory assistant. I was particularly anxious to have her take Mrs. Garden's case, rather than some other nurse, for I felt that from her observations some helpful suggestions might result. The girl had been on several difficult cases of mine, and I was wholly familiar with her competency and discretion."

"And have Miss Beeton's subsequent observations been helpful to you, doctor?" asked Vance.

2. Doctor Siefert was undoubtedly alluding to recent distressing stories in the press of radium poisoning—one of the death of a prominent steel manufacturer and sportsman, presumably resulting from the continued use of a radioactive water extensively advertised as a cure for various ailments; and another of the painful and fatal poisoning of several women and girls whose occupation was painting so-called *radiolite* watch-dials.

"No, I can't say that they have," Siefert admitted, "despite the fact that Doctor Garden still availed himself of her services occasionally in the laboratory, thereby giving her an added opportunity of keeping an eye on the entire situation. But, on the other hand, neither have they tended to dissipate my suspicions."

"I say, doctor,"Vance asked after a moment, "could this new radio-active sodium be administered to a person without his knowing it?"

"Oh, quite easily," Siefert assured him. "It could, for instance, be substituted in a shaker for ordinary salt and there would be nothing to arouse the slightest suspicion."

"And in quantities sufficient to produce the effects of radium poisoning?"

"Undoubtedly."

"And how long would it be before the effects of such administrations proved fatal?"

"That's impossible to say."

Vance was studying the tip of his cigarette. Presently he asked: "Has the nurse's presence in the house resulted in any information regarding the general situation here?"

"Nothing that I had not already known. In fact, her observations have merely substantiated my own conclusions. It's quite possible, too, that she herself may unwittingly have augmented the animosity between young Garden and Swift, for she has intimated to me once or twice that Swift had annoyed her occasionally with his attentions; and I have a very strong suspicion that she is personally interested in Floyd Garden."

Vance looked up with augmented interest.

"What, specifically, has given you that impression, doctor?"

"Nothing specific," Siefert told him. "I have, however, observed them together on several occasions, and my impression was that some sentiment existed there. Nothing that I can put my finger on, though. But one night when I was walking up Riverside Drive I happened to see them together in the park—undoubtedly a stroll together."

"By the by, doctor, have young Garden and the nurse been acquainted only since she came here to take care of his mother?"

"Oh, no," said Siefert. "But their previous acquaintance was, I imagine, more or less casual. You see, during the time Miss Beeton was Doctor Garden's laboratory assistant she had frequent occasion to come to the apartment here, to work with the professor in his study—stenographic notes and transcription, records, and the like. And she naturally became acquainted with Floyd and Woode Swift and Mrs. Garden herself. . ."

The nurse appeared at the door at that moment to announce the arrival of the Medical Examiner, and Vance asked her to bring Doctor Doremus up to the study.

"I might suggest," said Siefert quickly, "that, with your consent, it would be possible to have the Medical Examiner accept my verdict of death due to an accidental overdose of barbital and avoid the additional unpleasantness of an autopsy."

"Oh, quite." Vance nodded. "That was my intention." He turned to the District Attorney. "All things considered, Markham," he said, "I think that might be best. There's nothing to be gained from an autopsy. We have enough facts, I think, to proceed without it. Undoubtedly Mrs. Garden's death was caused by the barbital solution. The radioactive sodium is a separate and distinct issue."

Markham nodded in reluctant acquiescence as Doremus was led into the room by Miss Beeton. The Medical Examiner was in vile humour and complained bitterly about having been summoned personally on a Sunday morning. Vance placated him somewhat and introduced him to Doctor Siefert. After a brief interchange of explanations and comments Doremus readily agreed to Markham's suggestion that the case be regarded as resulting from an overdose of barbital solution.

Doctor Siefert rose and looked hesitantly at Vance. "You will not need me further, I trust."

"Not at the moment, doctor." Vance rose also and bowed formally. "We may, however, communicate with you later. Again our thanks for your help and your candour. . .Sergeant, will you accompany Doctor Siefert and Doctor Doremus below and take care of any necess'ry details. . .And, Miss Beeton, please sit down for a moment. There are a few questions I want to ask you."

The girl came forward and seated herself in the nearest chair, as the three men went down the passageway.

CHAPTER 15

Three Visitors

Sunday, April 15; 10:45 a.m.

"I don't mean to trouble you unduly, Miss Beeton," said Vance; "but we should like to have a firsthand account of the circumstances surrounding the death of Mrs. Garden."

"I wish there was something definite I could tell you," the nurse replied readily in a business-like manner, "but all I know is that when I arose this morning, a little after seven, Mrs. Garden seemed to be sleeping quietly. After dressing I went to the dining-room and had my breakfast; and then I took a tray in to Mrs. Garden. She always had tea and toast at eight o'clock, no matter how late she may have retired the night before. It wasn't until I had drawn up the shades and closed the windows, that I realized something was wrong. I spoke to her and she didn't answer me; and when I tried to rouse her I got no response. I saw then that she was dead. I called Doctor Siefert at once, and he came over as quickly as he could."

"You sleep, I believe, in Mrs. Garden's room?"

The nurse inclined her head. "Yes. You see, Mrs. Garden frequently needed some small service in the night."

"Had she required your attention at any time during the night?"

"No. The injection Doctor Siefert gave her before he left her seemed to have quieted her and she was sleeping peacefully when I went out—"

"You went out last night?. . .What time did you leave the house?" asked Vance.

"About nine o'clock. Mr. Floyd Garden suggested it, assuring me that he would be here and that he thought I needed a little rest. I was very glad of the opportunity, for I was really fatigued and unnerved."

"Had you no professional qualms about leaving a sick patient at such a time?"

149

"Ordinarily I might have had," the girl returned resentfully; "but Mrs. Garden had never shown me any consideration. She was the most selfish person I ever knew. Anyway, I explained to Mr. Floyd Garden about giving his mother a teaspoonful of the medicine if she should wake up and show any signs of restlessness. And then I went out into the park."

"At what time did you return, Miss Beeton?"

"It must have been about eleven," she told him. "I hadn't intended to stay out so long, but the air was invigorating, and I walked along the river almost to Grant's tomb. When I got back I went immediately to bed."

"Mrs. Garden was asleep when you came in?" The girl turned her eyes to Vance before answering.

"I—I thought—she was asleep," she said hesitantly. "Her colour was all right. But perhaps—even then—"

"Yes, yes. I know," Vance put in quickly. "However. . ." He inspected his cigarette for a moment. "By the by, did you notice anything changed—anything, let us say, out of place—in the room, on your return?"

The nurse shook her head slowly.

"No. Everything seemed the same to me. The windows and shades were just as I had left them, and—Wait, there was something. The glass I had left on the night-table with drinking water was empty. I refilled it before going to bed."

Vance looked up quickly. "And the bottle of medicine?"

"I didn't particularly notice that; but it must have been just as I had left it, for I remember a fleeting sense of relief because Mrs. Garden hadn't needed a dose of the medicine."

Vance seemed profoundly puzzled and said nothing for some time. Then he glanced up suddenly.

"How much light was there in the room?"

"Only a dim shaded night-light by my bed."

"In that case, you might conceivably have mistaken an empty bottle for one filled with a colourless fluid."

"Yes, of course," the nurse returned reluctantly. "That must have been the case. Unless. . ." Her voice trailed off.

Vance nodded and finished the sentence for her. "Unless Mrs. Garden drank that medicine deliberately some time later." He studied the girl a moment. "But that isn't altogether reasonable. I don't care for the theory. Do you?"

She returned his gaze with complete frankness, and made a slight negative gesture of the head.

"No," she said. Then she added quickly: "But I wish it were true."

"Quite," agreed Vance. "It would be somewhat less terrible."

"I know what you mean." She took a deep tremulous breath and shuddered slightly.

"Tell me, when did you discover that all the medicine was gone?" Vance asked.

"Shortly before Doctor Siefert arrived this morning. I moved the bottle when I was arranging the table, and realized it was empty."

"I think that will be all just now, Miss Beeton." Vance glanced at the girl sombrely and then turned away. "Really, y' know, I'm deuced sorry. But you'd better not plan on leaving here just yet. We will undoubtedly want to see you again today."

As she got up her eyes rested on Vance with an enigmatic look. She seemed about to say something further, but instead she turned quickly and went from the room.

Heath must have been waiting in the passageway for the girl's dismissal, for just as she was going out, he came in to report that Siefert and Doremus had departed, and that Floyd Garden had made the arrangements for the removal of his mother's body.

"And what do we do now, Mr. Vance?" Heath asked.

"Oh, we carry on, Sergeant." Vance was unusually serious. "I want to talk to Floyd Garden first. Send him up. And call one of your men; but stay on the job downstairs yourself till he arrives. We may get this affair cleared up today."

"That wouldn't make me sore, Mr. Vance," returned Heath fervently, as he went toward the door.

Markham had risen and was pacing the floor, drawing furiously on his cigar.

"Evidently you see some light in this damnable situation," he grumbled to Vance. "I wish I could." He stopped and turned. "Are you serious about the possibility of getting this thing cleared up today?"

"Oh, quite. It could be, don't y' know." Vance cocked an eye whimsically at Markham. "Not legally, of course. Not a case for the law. No. Legal technicalities quite useless in such an emergency. Deeper issues involved. Human issues, d' ye see?"

"You're talking nonsense," Markham muttered. "You and your damned pseudo-subtle moods!"

"I can change the mood," Vance offered cheerfully. "I'm frank to confess that I like the situation even less than you do. But there's no other procedure indicated. The law is helpless against it at present. And, frankly, I'm not interested in your law. I want justice."

Markham snorted. "And just what do you intend to do?"

Vance looked past Markham into some remote world of his own imagining. "I shall try to stage a tragic drama," he said evenly. "It may be effective. If it fails, I'm afraid there's no help for us."

Markham snorted again. "Philo Vance—impresario!"

"Quite," Vance nodded. "Impresario. As you say. Aren't we all?"

Markham looked at him steadily for a while. "When does the curtain go up?"

"Anon."

Footsteps sounded in the passageway, and Floyd Garden entered the study. He appeared deeply shaken. "I can't stand much today. What do you want?" His tone was unduly resentful. He sat down and seemed to ignore us entirely as he fussed nervously with his pipe.

"We understand just how you feel," Vance said. "It was not my intention to bother you unnecess'rily. But if we are to get at the truth, we must have your cooperation."

"Go ahead, then," Garden mumbled, his attention still on his pipe.

Vance waited until the man got his pipe going. "We must have as many details as possible about last night. Did your expected guests come?"

Garden nodded cheerlessly. "Oh, yes. Zalia Graem, Madge Weatherby, and Kroon."

"And Hammle?"

"No, thank Heaven!"

"Didn't that strike you as a bit odd?"

"It didn't strike me as odd at all," Garden grumbled. "It struck me only as a relief. Hammle's all right, but he's a frightful bore—cold-blooded, self-sufficient. I never feel that the man has any real blood in him. Horses, dogs, foxes, game—anything but human beings. If one of his damned hounds had died he'd have taken it more to heart than Woody's death. I was glad he didn't show up."

Vance nodded with understanding. "Was there any one else here?"

"No, that was all."

"Which of your visitors arrived first?"

Garden took the pipe from his mouth and looked up swiftly. "Zalia Graem. She came at half-past eight, I should say. Why?"

"Merely garnerin' facts," Vance replied indifferently. "And how long after Miss Graem came in did Miss Weatherby and Kroon arrive?"

"About half an hour. They came a few minutes after Miss Beeton had gone out."

Vance returned the man's steady scrutiny.

"By the by, why did you send the nurse out last night?"

"She looked as if she needed some fresh air," Garden answered with a show of complete frankness. "She'd had a tough day. Moreover, I didn't think there was anything seriously wrong with the mater. And I was going to be here myself and could have got her anything she might have needed." His eyes narrowed slightly. "Shouldn't I have let the nurse go out?"

"Yes. Oh, yes. Quite humane, don't y' know. A tryin' day for her."

Garden shifted his gaze heavily to the window, but Vance continued to study the man closely.

"What time did your guests depart?" he asked.

"A little after midnight. Sneed brought in sandwiches about half-past eleven. Then we had another round of highballs. . ." The man turned his eyes sharply back to Vance. "Does it matter?"

"I don't know. Perhaps not. However, it could. . .Did they all depart at the same time?"

"Yes. Kroon had his car below, and offered to drop Zalia at her apartment."

"Miss Beeton had returned by then, of course?"

"Yes, long before that. I heard her come in about eleven."

"And after your guests had gone, what did you do?"

"I sat up for half an hour or so, had another drink and a pipe; then I shut up the front of the house and turned in."

"Your bedroom is next to your mother's, I believe."

Garden nodded. "Father's been sharing it with me since the nurse has been here."

"Had your father retired when you went to your bedroom?"

"No. He rarely turns in before two or three in the morning. He works up here in the study till all hours."

"Was he up here last night?"

Garden looked a little disturbed.

"I imagine so. He couldn't very well have been anywhere else. He certainly didn't go out."

"Did you hear him when he came to bed?"

"No."

Vance lighted another cigarette, took several deep inhalations on it, and settled himself deeper in his chair.

"To go back a bit," he said casually. "The sleeping medicine Doctor Siefert prescribed for your mother seems to constitute a somewhat crucial point in the situation. Did you have occasion to give her a dose of it while the nurse was out?"

153

Garden drew himself up sharply and set his jaw. "No, I did not," he said through his teeth.

Vance took no notice of the change in the man's manner.

"The nurse, I understand, gave you explicit instructions about the medicine before she went out. Will you tell me exactly where this was?"

"In the hall," Garden answered with a puzzled frown. "Just outside the den door. I had left Zalia in the drawing-room and had gone to tell Miss Beeton she might go out for a while. I waited to help her on with her coat. It was then she told me what to do in case the mater woke up and was restless."

"And when she had gone you returned to the drawing-room?"

"Yes, immediately." Garden still looked puzzled. "That's exactly what I did. And a few minutes later Madge and Kroon arrived."

There was a short silence during which Vance smoked thoughtfully.

"Tell me, Garden," he said at length, "did any of your guests enter your mother's room last night?"

Garden's eyes opened wide: colour came back into his face, and he sprang to his feet.

"Good God, Vance! Zalia was in mother's room!"

Vance nodded slowly. "Very interestin'. Yes, quite. . .I say, do sit down. Light your beastly pipe, and tell us about it."

Garden hesitated a moment. He laughed harshly and resumed his seat.

"Damn it! You take it lightly enough," he complained. "That may be the whole explanation."

"One never knows, does one?" Vance returned indifferently. "Carry on."

Garden had some difficulty getting his pipe going again. For a moment or two he sat with clouded, reminiscent eyes gazing out of the east window.

"It must have been about ten o'clock," he said at length. "The mater rang the little bell she keeps on the table beside her bed, and I was about to answer it when Zalia jumped up and said she would see what the mater wanted. Frankly, I was glad to let her go, after the scene you witnessed here yesterday—I had a feeling I might still be *persona non grata* there. Zalia came back in a few minutes and casually reported that the mater only wanted to have her water glass refilled."

"And did you yourself go into your mother's room at any time during Miss Beeton's absence?"

"No, I did not!" Garden looked defiantly at Vance.

"And you're sure that no one else entered your mother's room during the nurse's absence?"

"Absolutely."

I could tell by Vance's expression that he was not satisfied with Garden's answers. He broke the ashes from his cigarette with slow deliberation. His eyelids drooped a little with puzzled speculation. Without looking up, he asked:

"Were Miss Weatherby and Kroon in the drawing-room with you during their entire visit?"

"Yes—with the exception of ten minutes or so, when they walked out on the balcony."

"And you and Miss Graem remained in the drawing-room?"

"Yes. I was in no particular mood to view the nocturnal landscape—nor, apparently, was Zalia."

"About what time did Miss Weatherby and Kroon go out on the balcony?"

Garden thought a moment. "I'd say it was shortly before the nurse returned."

"And who was it," Vance went on, "that first suggested going home?"

Garden pondered the question.

"I believe it was Zalia."

Vance got up.

"Awfully good of you, Garden, to let us bother you with these queries at such a time," he said kindly. "We're deuced grateful. . .You won't be leaving the house today?"

Garden shook his head as he too stood up. "Hardly," he said. "I'll stay in with father. He's pretty well broken up. By the way, would you care to see him?"

Vance waved his hand negatively.

"No. That won't be necess'ry just now."

Garden went morosely from the room, his head down, like a man weighted with a great mental burden.

When he had gone Vance stood for a moment in front of Markham, eyeing him with cynical good-nature.

"Not a nice case, Markham. As I said. Frankly speakin', do you see any titbit for the law to get its teeth into?"

"No, damn it!" Markham blurted angrily. "No two things hang together. There's no straight line in any direction. Every thread in the case is tangled with every other thread. Heaven knows, there are enough motives and opportunities. But which are we to choose as a starting-point?. . .And yet," he added grimly, "a case could be made out—"

"Oh, quite," Vance interrupted. "A case against any one of various persons. And one case as good—or as bad—as another. Every one has acted in a perfect manner to bring suspicion upon himself." He sighed. "A sweet situation."

"And fiendish," supplemented Markham. "If it weren't for that fact, I'd be almost inclined to call it two suicides and let it go at that."

"Oh, no, you wouldn't," countered Vance with an affectionate shake of the head. "Neither would I. Really, y' know, that's not the way to be humane." He moved toward the window and looked out. "But I have things pretty well in hand. The pattern is shaping itself perfectly. I've fitted together all the pieces, Markham,—all but one. And I hold that piece too, but I don't know where it goes, or how it fits into the ensemble."

Markham looked up. "What's the piece that's bothering you, Vance?"

"Those disconnected wires on the buzzer. They bother me frightfully. I know they have a bearing on the terrible things that have been going on here. . ." He turned from the window and walked up and down the room several times, his head down, his hands thrust deep into his pockets. "Why should those wires have been disconnected?" he murmured, as if talking to himself. "How could they have been related to Swift's death or to the shot we heard? There was no mechanism. No, I'm convinced of that. After all, the wires merely connect two buzzers. . .a signal. . .a signal between upstairs and downstairs. . .a signal—a call—a line of communication. . ."

Suddenly he stopped his meditative pacing. He was now facing the door into the passageway and he stared at it as if it were something strange—as if he had never seen it before.

"Oh, my aunt!" he exclaimed. "My precious aunt! It was too obvious." He wheeled about to Markham, a look of self-reproach on his face. "The answer was here all the time," he said. "It was simple—and I was looking for complexities. . .The picture is complete now, Markham. Everything fits. Those disconnected wires mean that there's another murder contemplated—a murder that was intended from the first, but that did not come off." He took a deep breath. "This business must be cleared up today. Yes. . ."

He led the way downstairs. Heath was smoking gloomily in the lower hall.

"Sergeant," Vance said to him, "phone Miss Graem, Miss Weatherby, Kroon—and Hammle. Have them all here late this afternoon—say six o'clock. Floyd Garden can help you in getting in touch with them."

"They'll be here, all right, Mr. Vance," Heath assured him.

"And Sergeant, as soon as you have taken care of this, telephone me. I want to see you this afternoon. I'll be at home. But wait here for Snitkin and leave him in charge. No one is to come here but those I've asked you to get, and no one is to leave the apartment. And, above all, no one is to be permitted to go upstairs either to the study or the garden. . .I'm staggerin' along now."

"I'll be phoning you by the time you get home, Mr. Vance."

Vance went to the front door but paused with his hand on the knob.

"I think I'd better speak to Garden about the gathering before I go. Where is he, Sergeant?"

"He went into the den when he came downstairs," Heath told him with a jerk of the head.

Vance walked up the hall and opened the den door. I was just behind him. As the door swung inward and Vance stepped over the threshold, we were confronted by an unexpected *tableau*. Miss Beeton and Garden were standing just in front of the desk, outlined against the background of the window. The nurse's hands were pressed to her face, and she was leaning against Garden, sobbing. His arms were about her.

At the sound of Vance's entry they drew away from each other quickly. The girl turned her head to us with a sudden motion, and I could see that her eyes were red and filled with tears. She caught her breath and, turning with a start, half ran through the connecting door into the adjoining bedroom.

"I'm frightfully sorry," Vance murmured. "Thought you were alone."

"Oh, that's all right," Garden returned, although it was painfully evident the man was embarrassed. "But I do hope, Vance," he added with a forced smile, "that you won't misunderstand. Everything, you know, is in an emotional upheaval here. I imagine Miss Beeton had all she could stand yesterday and today, and when I found her in here she seemed to break down, and—put her head on my shoulder. I was merely trying to comfort her. I can't help feeling sorry for the girl."

Vance raised his hand in good-natured indifference.

"Oh, quite, Garden. A harassed lady always welcomes a strong masculine shoulder to weep on. Most of them leave powder on one's lapel, don't y' know; but I'm sure Miss Beeton wouldn't be guilty of that. . .Dashed sorry to interrupt you, but I wanted to tell you before I went that I have instructed Sergeant Heath to have all your guests of yesterday here by six o'clock this afternoon. Of course, we'll want you and your father here, too. If you don't mind, you might help the Sergeant with the phone numbers."

"I'll be glad to, Vance," Garden returned, taking out his pipe and beginning to fill it. "Anything special in mind?"

Vance turned toward the door.

"Yes. Oh, yes. Quite. I'm hopin' to clear this matter up later on. Meanwhile I'm running along. Cheerio." And he went out, closing the door.

As we walked down the outer hall to the elevator, Vance said to Markham somewhat sadly: "I hope my plan works out. I don't particularly like it. But I don't like injustice, either. . ."

CHAPTER 16

Through the Garden Door

Sunday, April 15; afternoon

We had been home but a very short time when Sergeant Heath telephoned as he had promised. Vance went into the anteroom to answer the call and closed the door after him. A few minutes later he rejoined us and, ringing for Currie, ordered his hat and stick.

"I'm running away for a while, old dear," he said to Markham. "In fact, I'm joining the doughty Sergeant at the Homicide Bureau. But I sha'n't be very long. In the meantime, I've ordered lunch for us here."

"Damn the lunch!" grumbled Markham. "What are you meeting Heath for?"

"I'm in need of a new waistcoat," Vance told him lightly.

"That explanation's a great help," Markham snorted.

"Sorry. It's the only one I can offer at present," Vance returned.

Markham stared at him, disgruntled, for several minutes.

"Why all this mystery?" he demanded.

"Really, y' know, Markham, it's necess'ry." Vance spoke seriously. "I'm hoping to work out this beastly affair tonight."

"For Heaven's sake, Vance, what are you planning?" Markham stood up in futile desperation.

Vance took a pony of brandy and lighted a *Régie*. Then he looked at Markham affectionately.

"I'm plannin' to entice the murderer into making one more bet—a losing bet. . .Cheerio." And he was gone.

Markham fumed and fretted during Vance's absence. He showed no inclination to talk, and I left him to himself. He tried to interest himself in Vance's library, but evidently found nothing to hold his attention. Finally he lit a cigar and settled himself in an easy chair before the window, while I busied myself with some notes I was preparing for Vance.

It was a little after half-past two when Vance returned to the apartment.

"Everything is in order," he announced as he came in. "There are no horses running today, of course, but nevertheless I'm looking forward to a big wager being laid this evening. If the bet isn't placed, we're in for it, Markham. Every one will be present, however. The Sergeant, with Garden's help, has got in touch with all those who were present yesterday, and they will foregather again in the Gardens' drawing-room at six o'clock. I myself have left a message for Doctor Siefert, and I hope he gets it in time to join us. I think he should be there. . ." He glanced at his watch and, ringing for Currie, ordered a bottle of 1919 Montrachet chilled for our lunch.

"If we don't tarry too long at table," he said, "we'll be able to hear the second half of the Philharmonic programme. Melinoff is doing Grieg's piano concerto, and I think it might do us all a bit of spiritual good. A beautiful climax, Markham—one of the most stirring in all music—simple, melodious, magistral. Curious thing about Grieg: it's taken the world a long time to realize the magnitude of the man's genius. One of the truly great composers. . ."

But Markham did not go with us to the concert. He pleaded an urgent political appointment at the Stuyvesant Club, but promised to meet us at the Garden apartment at six o'clock. As if by tacit agreement, no word regarding the case was spoken during lunch. When we had finished Markham excused himself and departed for the club, while Vance and I drove to Carnegie Hall. Melinoff gave a competent, if not an inspired, performance, and Vance seemed in a more relaxed frame of mind as we started for home.

Sergeant Heath was waiting for us when we reached the apartment.

"Everything's set, sir," he said to Vance; "I got it here."

Vance smiled a little sadly. "Excellent, Sergeant. Come into the other room with me while I get out of these Sunday togs."

Heath picked up a small package wrapped in brown paper, which he had evidently brought with him, and followed Vance into the bedroom. Ten minutes later they both came back into the library. Vance was now wearing a heavy dark tweed sack suit; and on Heath's face was a look of smug satisfaction.

"So long, Mr. Vance," he said, shaking hands. "Good luck to you." And he lumbered out.

We arrived at the Garden apartment a few minutes before six o'clock. Detectives Hennessey and Burke were in the front hall. As soon as we were inside Burke came up and, putting his hand to his mouth, said to Vance *sotto voce*:

"Sergeant Heath told me to tell you everything's all right. He and Snitkin are on the job."

Vance nodded and started up the stairs.

"Wait down here for me, Van," he said over his shoulder. "I'll be back immediately."

I wandered into the den, the door of which was ajar, and walked aimlessly about the room, looking at the various pictures and etchings. One behind the door attracted my attention—I think it was a Blampied—and I lingered before it for several moments. Just then Vance entered the room. As he came in he threw the door open wider, half pocketing me in the corner behind it, where I was not immediately noticeable. I was about to speak to him, when Zalia Graem came in.

"Philo Vance." She called his name in a low, tremulous voice.

He turned and looked at the girl with a quizzical frown.

"I've been waiting in the dining-room," she said. "I wanted to see you before you spoke to the others."

I realized immediately, from the tone of her voice, that my presence had not been noticed, and my first impulse was to step out from the corner. But, in the circumstances, I felt there could be nothing in her remarks which would be beyond the province of my privilege of hearing, and I decided not to interrupt them.

Vance continued to look squarely at the girl, but did not speak. She came very close to him now.

"Tell me why you have made me suffer so much," she said.

"I know I have hurt you," Vance returned. "But the circumstances made it imperative. Please believe that I understand more of this case than you imagine I do."

"I am not sure that I understand." The girl spoke hesitantly. "But I want you to know that I trust you." She looked up at him, and I could see that her eyes were glistening. Slowly she bowed her head. "I have never been interested in any man," she went on—and there was a quaver in her voice. "The men I have known have all made me unhappy and seemed always to lead me away from the things I longed for. . ." She caught her breath. "You are the one man I have ever known whom I could—care for."

So suddenly had this startling confession come, that I did not have time to make my presence known, and after Miss Graem finished speaking I remained where I was, lest I cause her embarrassment.

161

Vance placed his hands on the girl's shoulders and held her away from him.

"My dear," he said, with a curiously suppressed quality in his voice, "I am the one man for whom you should not care." There was no mistaking the finality of his words.

Behind Vance the door to the adjoining bedroom opened suddenly, and Miss Beeton halted abruptly on the threshold. She was no longer wearing the nurse's uniform, but a plain tailored tweed suit, severe in cut.

"I'm sorry," she apologized. "I thought Floyd—Mr. Garden—was in here."

Vance looked at her sharply.

"You were obviously mistaken, Miss Beeton."

Zalia Graem was staring at the nurse with angry resentment.

"How much did you hear," she asked, "before you decided to open the door?"

Miss Beeton's eyes narrowed and there was a look of scorn in her steady gaze.

"You perhaps have something to hide," she answered coldly, as she walked across the room to the hall door and went toward the drawing-room.

Zalia Graem's eyes followed her as if fascinated, and then she turned back to Vance.

"That woman frightens me," she said. "I don't trust her. There's something dark—and cruel—back of that calm self-sufficiency of hers. . .And you've been so kind to her—but you have made *me* suffer."

Vance smiled wistfully at the girl.

"Would you mind waiting in the drawing-room a little while?. . ."

She gave him a searching look and, without speaking, turned and went from the den.

Vance stood for some time gazing at the floor with a frown of in-decision, as if loath to proceed with whatever plans he had formulated. Then he turned to the window.

I took this opportunity to come out from my corner, and just as I did so Floyd Garden appeared at the hall door.

"Oh, hello, Vance," he said. "I didn't know you had returned until Zalia just told me you were in here. Anything I can do for you?"

Vance swung around quickly.

"I was just going to send for you. Every one here?"

Garden nodded gravely. "Yes, and they're all frightened to death—all except Hammle. He takes the whole thing as a lark. I wish some-body had shot him instead of Woody."

162

"Will you send him in here," Vance asked. "I want to talk to him. I'll see the others presently."

Garden walked up the hall, and at that moment I heard Burke speaking to Markham at the front door. Markham immediately joined us in the den.

"Hope I haven't kept you waiting," he greeted Vance.

"No. Oh, no." Vance leaned against the desk. "Just in time. Every one's here except Siefert, and I'm about to have Hammle in here for a chat. I think he'll be able to corroborate a few points I have in mind. He hasn't told us anything yet. And I may need your moral support."

Markham had barely seated himself when Hammle strutted into the den with a jovial air. Vance nodded to him brusquely and omitted all conventional preliminaries.

"Mr. Hammle," he said, "we're wholly familiar with your philosophy of minding your own business and keeping silent in order to avoid all involvements. A defensible attitude—but not in the present circumstances. This is a criminal case, and in the interest of justice to every one concerned, we must have the whole truth. Yesterday afternoon you were the only one in the drawing-room who had even a partial view down the hallway. And we must know everything you saw, no matter how trivial it may seem to you."

Hammle, assuming his poker expression, remained silent; and Markham leaned forward glowering at him.

"Mr. Hammle"—he spoke with cold, deadly calm—"if you don't wish to give us here what information you can, you will be taken before the Grand Jury and put under oath."

Hammle gave in. He spluttered and waved his arms.

"I'm perfectly willing to tell you everything I know. You don't have to threaten me. But to tell you the truth," he added suavely, "I didn't realize how serious the matter was." He sat down with pompous dignity and assumed an air which was obviously meant to indicate that for the time being he was the personification of law, order and truth.

"First of all, then," said Vance, without relaxing his stern gaze, "when Miss Graem left the room, ostensibly to answer a telephone call, did you notice exactly where she went?"

"Not exactly," Hammle returned; "but she turned to the left, toward the den. You understand, of course, that it was impossible for me to see very far down the hall, even from where I sat."

"Quite." Vance nodded. "And when she came back to the drawing-room?"

"I saw her first opposite the den door. She went to the hall closet where the hats and wraps are kept, and then came back to stand in the archway until the race was over. After that I didn't notice her either coming or going, as I had turned to shut off the radio."

"And what about Floyd Garden?" asked Vance. "You remember he followed Swift out of the room. Did you notice which way they went, or what they did?"

"As I remember, Floyd put his arm around Swift and led him into the dining-room. After a few moments they came out. Swift seemed to be pushing Floyd away from him, and then he disappeared down the hall toward the stairs. Floyd stood outside the dining-room door for several minutes, looking after his cousin, and then went down the hall after him; but he must have changed his mind, for he came back into the drawing-room in short order."

"And you saw no one else in the hall?"

Hammle shook his head ponderously. "No. No one else."

"Very good." Vance took a deep inhalation on his cigarette. "And now let's go to the roof-garden, figuratively speaking. You were in the garden, waiting for a train, when the nurse was almost suffocated with bromin gas in the vault. The door into the passageway was open, and if you had been looking in that direction you could easily have seen who passed up and down the corridor." Vance looked at the man significantly. "And I have a feelin' you were looking through that door, Mr. Hammle. Your reaction of astonishment when we came out on the roof was a bit overdone. And you couldn't have seen much of the city from where you had been standing, don't y' know."

Hammle cleared his throat and grinned.

"You have me there, Vance," he admitted with familiar good-humour. "Since I couldn't make my train, I thought I'd satisfy my curiosity and stick around for a while to see what happened. I went out on the roof and stood where I could look through the door into the passageway—I wanted to see who was going to get hell next, and what would come of it all."

"Thanks for your honesty." Vance's face was coldly formal. "Please tell us now exactly what you saw through that doorway while you were waiting, as you've confessed, for something to happen."

Again Hammle cleared his throat.

"Well, Vance, to tell you the truth, it wasn't very much. Just people coming and going. First I saw Garden go up the passageway toward the study; and almost immediately he went back downstairs. Then Zalia Graem passed the door on her way to the study. Five or ten

164

minutes later the detective—Heath, I think his name is—went by the door, carrying a coat over his arm. A little later—two or three minutes, I should say—Zalia Graem and the nurse passed each other in the passageway, Zalia going toward the stairs, and the nurse toward the study. A couple of minutes after that Floyd Garden passed the door on his way to the study again—"

"Just a minute," Vance interrupted. "You didn't see the nurse return downstairs after she passed Miss Graem in the passageway?"

Hammle shook his head emphatically. "No. Absolutely not. The first person I saw after the two girls was Floyd Garden going toward the study. And he came back past the door in a minute or so. . ."

"You're quite sure your chronology is accurate?"

"Absolutely."

Vance seemed satisfied and nodded.

"That much checks accurately with the facts as I know them," he said. "But are you sure no one else passed the door, either coming or going, during that time?"

"I would swear to that."

Vance took another deep puff on his cigarette.

"One more thing, Mr. Hammle: while you were out there in the garden, did any one come out on the roof from the terrace gate?"

"Absolutely not. I didn't see anybody at all on the roof."

"And when Garden had returned downstairs, what then?"

"I saw you come to the window and look out into the garden. I was afraid I might be seen, and the minute you turned away I went over to the far corner of the garden, by the gate. The next thing I knew, you gentlemen were coming out on the roof with the nurse."

Vance moved forward from the desk against which he had been resting.

"Thank you, Mr. Hammle. You've told me exactly what I wanted to know. It may interest you to learn that the nurse informed us she was struck over the head in the passageway, on leaving the study, and forced into the vault which was full of bromin fumes."

Hammle's jaw dropped and his eyes opened. He grasped the arms of his chair and got slowly to his feet.

"Good Gad!" he exclaimed. "So that's what it was! Who could have done it?"

"A pertinent question," returned Vance casually. "Who could have done it, indeed? However, the details of your secret observations from the garden have corroborated my private suspicions, and it's possible I may be able to answer your question before long. Please sit down again."

Hammle shot Vance an apprehensive look and resumed his seat. Vance turned from the man and looked out of the window at the darkening sky. Then he swung about to Markham. A sudden change had come over his expression, and I knew, by his look, that some deep conflict was going on within him.

"The time has come to proceed, Markham," he said reluctantly. Then he went to the door and called Garden.

The man came from the drawing-room immediately. He seemed nervous, and eyed Vance with inquisitive anxiety.

"Will you be so good as to tell every one to come into the den," Vance requested.

With a barely perceptible nod Garden turned back up the hall; and Vance crossed the room and seated himself at the desk.

CHAPTER 17

An Unexpected Shot

Sunday, April 15; 6:20 p.m.

Zalia Graem was the first to enter the den. There was a strained, almost tragic look on her drawn face. She glanced at Vance appealingly and seated herself without a word. She was followed by Miss Weatherby and Kroon, who sat down uneasily beside her on the davenport. Floyd Garden and his father came in together. The professor appeared dazed, and the lines on his face seemed to have deepened during the past twenty-four hours. Miss Beeton was just behind them and stopped hesitantly in the doorway, looking uncertainly at Vance.

"Did you want me too?" she asked diffidently.

"I think it might be best, Miss Beeton," said Vance. "We may need your help."

She gave him a nod of acquiescence and, stepping into the room, sat down near the door.

At that moment the front door bell rang, and Burke ushered Doctor Siefert into the den.

"I just got your message, Mr. Vance, and came right over." He looked about the room questioningly and then brought his eyes back to Vance.

"I thought you might care to be present," Vance said, "in case we can reach some conclusion about the situation here. I know you are personally interested. Otherwise I wouldn't have telephoned you."

"I'm glad you did," said Siefert blandly, and walked across to a chair before the desk.

Vance lighted a cigarette with slow deliberation, his eyes moving aimlessly about the room. There was a tension over the assembled group. But as future events indicated, no one could have known what was in Vance's mind or his reason for bringing them all together.

The taut silence was broken by Vance's voice. He spoke casually, but with a curious emphasis.

"I have asked you all to come here this afternoon in the hope that we could clear up the very tragic situation that exists. Yesterday Woode Swift was murdered in the vault upstairs. A few hours later I found Miss Beeton locked in the same vault, half suffocated. Last night, as you all know by now, Mrs. Garden died from what we have every reason to believe was an overdose of barbital prescribed by Doctor Siefert. There can be no question that these three occurrences are closely related—that the same hand participated in them all. The pattern and the logic of the situation point indisputably to that assumption. There was, no doubt, a diabolical reason for each act of the murderer—and the reason was fundamentally the same in each instance. Unfortunately, the stage setting for this multiple crime was so confused that it facilitated every step of the murderer's plan, and at the same time tended to disperse suspicion among many people who were entirely innocent."

Vance paused for a moment.

"Luckily, I was present when the first murder was committed, and I have since been able to segregate the various facts connected with the crime. In that process of segregation I may have seemed unreasonable and, perhaps, harsh to several persons present. And during the process of my brief investigation, it has been necess'ry for me to withhold any expression of my personal opinions for fear of providing the perpetrator with an untimely warning. This, of course, would have proved fatal, for so cleverly was the whole plot conceived, so fortuitous were many of the circumstances connected with it, that we would never have succeeded in bringing the crime home to the true culprit. Consequently, an interplay of suspicion between the innocent members and guests of this household was essential. If I have offended any one or seemed unjust, I trust that, in view of the abnormal and terrible circumstances, I may be forgiven—"

He was interrupted by the startling sound of a shot ominously like that of the day before. Everyone in the room stood up quickly, aghast at the sudden detonation. Every one except Vance. And before any one could speak, his calm authoritative voice was saying:

"There is no need for alarm. Please sit down. I expressly arranged that shot for all of you to hear—it will have an important bearing on the case. . ."

Burke appeared suddenly at the door.

"Was that all right, Mr. Vance?"

"Quite all right," Vance told him. "The same revolver and blanks?"

"Sure. Just like you told me. And from where you said. Wasn't it like you wanted it?"

"Yes, precisely," nodded Vance. "Thanks, Burke." The detective grinned broadly and moved away down the hall.

"That shot, I believe," resumed Vance, sweeping his eyes lazily over those present, "was similar to the one we heard yesterday afternoon—the one that summoned us to Swift's dead body. It may interest you to know that the shot just fired by Detective Burke was fired from the same revolver, with the same cartridges, that the murderer used yesterday—*and from about the same spot.*"

"But this shot sounded as if it were fired down here somewhere," cut in Siefert.

"Exactly," said Vance with satisfaction. "It was fired from one of the windows on this floor."

"But I understood that the shot yesterday came from upstairs." Siefert looked perplexed.

"That was the general, but erroneous, assumption," explained Vance. "Actually it did not. Yesterday, because of the open roof door and the stairway, and the closed door of the room from which the shot was fired, and mainly because we were psychologically keyed to the idea of a shot from the roof, it gave us all the impression of coming from the garden. We were misled by our manifest, but unformulated, fears."

"By George, you're right, Vance!" It was Floyd Garden who spoke almost excitedly. "I remember wondering at the time of the shot where it could have come from, but naturally my mind went immediately to Woody, and I assumed it came from the garden."

Zalia Graem turned quickly to Vance.

"The shot yesterday didn't sound to me as if it came from the garden. When I came out of the den I wondered why you were all hurrying upstairs."

Vance returned her gaze squarely.

"No, it must have sounded much closer to you," he said. "But why didn't you mention that important fact yesterday when I talked with you about the crime?"

"I—don't know," the girl stammered. "When I saw Woody dead up there, I naturally thought I'd been mistaken."

"But you couldn't have been mistaken," returned Vance, half under his breath. His eyes drifted off into space again. "And after the revolver had been fired yesterday from a downstairs window, it was surreptitiously placed in the pocket of Miss Beeton's top-coat in the

169

hall closet. Had it been fired from upstairs it could have been hidden to far better advantage somewhere on the roof or in the study. Sergeant Heath, having searched both upstairs and down, later found it in the hall closet." He turned again to the girl. "By the by, Miss Graem, didn't you go to that closet after answering your telephone call here in the den?"

The girl gasped.

"How—how did you know?"

"You were seen there," explained Vance. "You must remember that the hall closet is visible from one end of the drawing-room."

"Oh!" Zalia Graem swung around angrily to Hammle. "So it was you who told him!"

"It was my duty," returned Hammle, drawing himself up righteously.

The girl turned back to Vance with flashing eyes.

"I'll tell you why I went to the hall closet. I went to get a handkerchief I had left in my handbag. Does that make me a murderer?"

"No. Oh, no." Vance shook his head and sighed. "Thank you for the explanation. . .And will you be so good as to tell me exactly what you did last night when you answered Mrs. Garden's summons?"

Professor Garden who had been sitting with bowed head, apparently paying no attention to any one, suddenly looked up and let his hollow eyes rest on the girl with a slight show of animation.

Zalia Graem glared defiantly at Vance.

"I asked Mrs. Garden what I could do for her, and she requested me to fill the water glass on the little table beside her bed. I went into the bathroom and filled it; then I arranged her pillows and asked her if there was anything else she wanted. She thanked me and shook her head; and I returned to the drawing-room."

Professor Garden's eyes clouded again, and he sank back in his chair, once more oblivious to his surroundings.

"Thank you," murmured Vance, nodding to Miss Graem and turning to the nurse. "Miss Beeton," he asked, "when you returned last night, was the bedroom window which opens on the balcony bolted?"

The nurse seemed surprised at the question. But when she answered, it was in a calm, professional tone.

"I didn't notice. But I know it was bolted when I went out—Mrs. Garden always insisted on it. I'm sorry I didn't look at the window when I returned. Does it really matter?"

"No, not particularly." Vance then addressed Kroon. "I understand you took Miss Weatherby out on the balcony last night. What were you doing there during the ten minutes you remained outside?"

Kroon bristled. "If you must know, we were fighting about Miss Fruemon—"

"We were not!" Miss Weatherby's shrill voice put in. "I was merely asking Cecil—"

"That's quite all right." Vance interrupted the woman sharply and waved his hand deprecatingly. "Questions or recriminations—it really doesn't matter, don't y' know." He turned leisurely to Floyd Garden. "I say, Garden, when you left the drawing-room yesterday afternoon, to follow Swift on your errand of mercy, as it were, after he had given you his bet on Equanimity, where did you go with him?"

"I led him into the dining-room." The man was at once troubled and aggressive. "I argued with him for a while, and then he came out and went down the hall to the stairs. I watched him for a couple of minutes, wondering what else I might do about it, for, to tell you the truth, I didn't want him to listen in on the race upstairs. I was pretty damned sure Equanimity wouldn't win, and he didn't know I hadn't placed his bet. I was rather worried about what he might do. For a minute I thought of following him upstairs, but changed my mind. I decided there was nothing more to be done about it except to hope for the best. So I returned to the drawing-room."

Vance lowered his eyes to the desk and was silent for several moments, smoking meditatively.

"I'm frightfully sorry, and all that," he murmured at length, without looking up; "but the fact is, we don't seem to be getting any forrader. There are plausible explanations for everything and everybody. For instance, during the commission of the first crime, Doctor Garden was supposedly at the library or in a taxicab. Floyd Garden, according to his own statement, and with the partial corroboration of Mr. Hammle here, was in the dining-room and the lower hallway. Mr. Hammle himself, as well as Miss Weatherby, was in the drawing-room. Mr. Kroon explains that he was smoking somewhere on the public stairway, and left two cigarette butts there as evidence. Miss Graem, so far as we can ascertain, was in the den here, telephoning. Therefore, assuming—merely as a hypothesis—that any one here could be guilty of the murder of Swift, of the apparent attempt to murder Miss Beeton, and of the possible murder of Mrs. Garden, there is nothing tangible to substantiate an individual accusation. The performance was too clever, too well conceived, and the innocent persons seem unconsciously and involuntarily to have formed a conspiracy to aid and abet the murderer."

Vance looked up and went on.

"Moreover, nearly every one has acted in a manner which conceivably would make him appear guilty. There have been an amazing number of accusations. Mr. Kroon was the first victim of one of these unsubstantiated accusations. Miss Graem has been pointed out to me as the culprit by several persons. Mrs. Garden last night directly accused her son. In fact, there has been a general tendency to involve various people in the criminal activities here. From the human and psychological point of view the issue has been both deliberately and unconsciously clouded, until the confusion was such that no clear-cut outline remained. And this created an atmosphere which perfectly suited the murderer's machinations, for it made detection extremely difficult and positive proof almost impossible. . .And yet," Vance added, "some one in this room is guilty."

He rose dejectedly. I could not understand his manner: it was so unlike the man as I had always known him. All of his assurance seemed gone, and I felt that he was reluctantly admitting defeat. He turned and looked out of the window into the gathering dusk. Then he swung round quickly, and his eyes swept angrily about the room, resting for a brief moment on each one present.

"Furthermore," he said with a *staccato* stress on his words, *"I know who the guilty person is!"*

There was an uneasy stir in the room and a short tense silence which was broken by Doctor Siefert's cultured voice.

"If that is the case, Mr. Vance—and I do not doubt the sincerity of your statement—I think it your duty to name that person."

Vance regarded the doctor thoughtfully for several moments before answering. Then he said in a low voice: "I think you are right, sir." Again he paused and, lighting a fresh cigarette, moved restlessly up and down in front of the window. "First, however," he said, stopping suddenly, "there's something upstairs I wish to look at again—to make sure. . .You will all please remain here for a few minutes." And he moved swiftly toward the door. At the threshold he hesitated and turned to the nurse. "Please come with me, Miss Beeton. I think you can help me."

The nurse rose and followed Vance into the hall. A moment later we could hear them mounting the stairs.

A restlessness swept over those who remained below. Professor Garden got slowly to his feet and went to the window, where he stood looking out. Kroon threw a half-smoked cigarette away and, taking out his case offered it to Miss Weatherby. As they lighted their cigarettes they murmured something to each other which I could not distinguish.

Floyd Garden shifted uncomfortably in his chair and resumed his nervous habit of packing his pipe. Siefert moved around the room, pretending to inspect the etchings, and Markham's eyes followed his every move. Hammle cleared his throat loudly several times, lighted a cigarette, and busied himself with various papers which he took from his pocket folder. Only Zalia Graem remained unruffled. She leaned her head against the back of the davenport and, closing her eyes, smoked languidly. I could have sworn there was the trace of a smile at the corners of her mouth. . .

Fully five minutes passed, and then the tense silence of the room was split by a woman's frenzied and terrifying cry for help, from somewhere upstairs. As we reached the hallway the nurse came stumbling down the stairs, holding with both hands to the, bronze railing. Her face was ghastly pale, and there was a wild, frightened look in her eyes.

"Mr. Markham! Mr. Markham!" she called hysterically. "Oh, my God! The most terrible thing has happened!"

She had just reached the foot of the stairs when Markham came up to her. She stood clutching the railing for support.

"It's Mr. Vance!" she panted excitedly. "He's—gone!"

A chill of horror passed over me, and every one in the hall seemed stunned. I noticed—as something entirely apart from my immediate perceptions—Heath and Snitkin and Peter Quackenbush, the official police photographer, step into the hall through the main entrance. Quackenbush had his camera and tripod with him; and the three men stood calmly just inside the door, detached from the amazed group around the foot of the stairs. I vaguely wondered why they were accepting the situation with such smug indifference. . .

In broken phrases, interspersed with gasping sobs, the nurse was explaining to Markham.

"He went over.—Oh, God, it was horrible! He said he wanted to ask me something, and led me out into the garden. He began questioning me about Doctor Siefert, and Professor Garden, and Miss Graem. And while he talked he moved over to the parapet—you remember where he stood last night. He got up there again, and looked down. I was frightened—the way I was yesterday. And then—and then—while I was talking to him—he bent over, and I could see—oh, God!—he had lost his balance." She stared at Markham wild-eyed. "I reached toward him. . .and suddenly he wasn't there any more. . .He had gone over!. . ."

Her eyes lifted suddenly over our heads and peered past us transfixed. A sudden change came over her. Her face seemed contorted into a hideous mask. Following her horrified gaze, we instinctively turned and glanced up the hallway toward the drawing-room. . .

There, near the archway, looking calmly toward us, was Vance.

I have had many harrowing experiences, but the sight of Vance at that moment, after the horror I had been through, affected me more deeply than any shock I can recall. A numbness overcame me, and I could feel cold perspiration breaking out all over my body. The sound of Vance's voice merely tended to upset me further.

"I told you last night, Miss Beeton," he was saying, his eyes resting sternly on the nurse, "that no gambler ever quits with his first winning bet, and that in the end he always loses." He came forward a few steps. "You won your first gamble, at long odds, when you murdered Swift. And your poisoning of Mrs. Garden with the barbital also proved a winning bet. But when you attempted to add me to your list of victims, because you suspected I knew too much—you lost. That race was fixed—you hadn't a chance."

Markham was glaring at Vance in angry amazement.

"What is the meaning of all this?" he fairly shouted, despite his obvious effort to suppress his excitement.

"It merely means, Markham," explained Vance, "that I gave Miss Beeton an opportunity to push me over the parapet to what ordinarily would have been certain death. And she took that opportunity. This afternoon I arranged for Heath and Snitkin to witness the episode; and I also arranged to have it permanently recorded."

"Recorded? Good God! What do you mean?" Markham seemed half dazed.

"Just that," returned Vance calmly. "An official photograph taken with a special lens adapted to the semi-light—for the Sergeant's archives." He looked past Markham to Quackenbush. "You got the picture, I hope," he said.

"I sure did," the man returned with a satisfied grin. "At just the right angle too. A pippin."

The nurse, who had been staring at Vance as if petrified, suddenly relaxed her hold on the stair railing, and her hands went to her face in a gesture of hopelessness and despair. Then her hands dropped to her sides to reveal a face of haggard defeat.

"Yes!" she cried at Vance; "I tried to kill you. Why shouldn't I? You were about to take everything—everything—away from me."

She turned quickly and ran up the stairs. Almost simultaneously Vance dashed forward.

"Quick, quick!" he called out. "Stop her before she gets to the garden."

But before any of us realized the significance of his words, Vance was himself on the stairs. Heath and Snitkin were just behind him, and the rest of us, stupefied, followed. As I came out on the roof, I could see Miss Beeton running toward the far end of the garden, with Vance immediately behind her. Twilight had nearly passed, and a deep dusk had settled over the city. As the girl leaped up on the parapet at the same point where Vance had stood the night before, she was like a spectral silhouette against the faintly glowing sky. And then she disappeared down into the deep shadowy abyss, just before Vance could reach her. . .

CHAPTER 18

The Scratch Sheet

Sunday, April 15; 7:15 p.m.

A half hour later we were all seated in the den again. Heath and the detectives had gone out immediately after the final catastrophe to attend to the unpleasant details occasioned by Miss Beeton's suicide.

Vance was once more in the chair at the desk. The tragic termination of the case seemed to have saddened him. He smoked gloomily for a few minutes. Then he spoke.

"I asked all of you to stay because I felt you were entitled to an explanation of the terrible events that have taken place here, and to hear why it was necess'ry for me to conduct the investigation in the manner I did. To begin with, I knew from the first that I was dealing with a very shrewd and unscrupulous person, and I knew it was some one who was in the house yesterday afternoon. Therefore, until I had some convincing proof of that person's guilt, it was imperative for me to appear to doubt every one present. Only in an atmosphere of mutual suspicion and recrimination—in which I myself appeared to be as much at sea as any one else—was it possible to create in the murderer that feeling of security which I felt would lead to his final undoing.

"I was inclined to suspect Miss Beeton almost from the first, for, although every one here had, through some act, drawn suspicion upon himself, only the nurse had the time and the unhampered opportunity to commit the initial crime. She was entirely unobserved when she put her plan into execution; and so thoroughly familiar was she with every arrangement of the household, that she had no difficulty in timing her every step so as to insure this essential privacy. Subsequent events and circumstances added irresistibly to my suspicion of her. For instance, when Mr. Floyd Garden informed me where the key to the vault was kept, I sent her to see if it was in place, without indicating to her where its place was, in order to ascertain if she knew where the key hung. Only some one who knew exactly how to get into the vault at a moment's notice could have been guilty of killing Swift. Of course, the fact that she did know was not definite proof of her guilt, as there were others who knew; but at least it was a minor factor in the case against her. If she had not known where the key was kept, she would have been automatically eliminated. My request that she look for the key was made with such casualness and seeming indifference that it apparently gave her no inkling of my ulterior motive.

"Incidentally, one of my great difficulties in the case has been to act in such a way, at all times, that her suspicions would not be aroused at any point. This was essential because, as I have said, I could hope to substantiate my theory of her guilt only by making her feel sufficiently secure to do or say something which would give her away.

"Her motive was not clear at first, and, unfortunately, I thought that by Swift's death alone she had accomplished her purpose. But after my talk with Doctor Siefert this morning, I was able to understand fully her whole hideous plot. Doctor Siefert pointed out definitely her interest in Floyd Garden, although I had had hints of it before. For instance, Floyd Garden was the only person here about whom she spoke to me with admiration. Her motive was based on a colossal ambition—the desire for financial security, ease and luxury; and mixed with this over-weaning desire was a strange twisted love. These facts became clear to me only today."

Vance glanced at young Garden.

"It was you she wanted," he continued. "And I believe her self-assurance was such that she did not doubt for a minute that she would be successful in attaining her goal."

Garden sprang to his feet.

"Good God, Vance!" he exclaimed. "You're right. I see the thing now. She has been making up to me for a long time; and, to be honest with you, I may have said and done things which she could have construed as encouragement—God help me!" He sat down again in dejected embarrassment.

"No one can blame you," Vance said kindly. "She was one of the shrewdest women I have ever encountered. But the point of it all is, she did not want only you—she wanted the Garden fortune as well. That's why, having learned that Swift would share in the inheritance, she decided to eliminate him and leave you sole beneficiary. But this murder did not, by any means, constitute the whole of her scheme."

Vance again addressed us in general.

"Her whole terrible plot was clarified by some other facts that Doctor Siefert brought out this morning during my talk with him. The death, either now or later, of Mrs. Garden was also an important integer of that plot; and Mrs. Garden's physical condition had, for some time, shown certain symptoms of poisoning. Of late these symptoms have increased in intensity. Doctor Siefert informed me that Miss Beeton had been a laborat'ry assistant to Professor Garden during his experiments with radioactive sodium, and had often come to the apartment here for the purpose of typing notes and attending to other duties which could not conveniently be performed at the University. Doctor Siefert also informed me that she had actually entered the household here about two months ago, to take personal charge of Mrs. Garden's case. She had, however, continued to assist Professor Garden occasionally in his work and naturally had access to the radioactive sodium he had begun to produce; and it was since she had come here to live that Mrs. Garden's condition had grown worse—the result undoubtedly of the fact that Miss Beeton had greater and more frequent opportunities for administering the radioactive sodium to Mrs. Garden. Her decision to eliminate Mrs. Garden, so that Floyd Garden would inherit her money, undoubtedly came shortly after she had become the professor's assistant and had, through her visits to the apartment, become acquainted with Floyd Garden and familiar with the various domestic arrangements here."

Vance turned his eyes to Professor Garden.

"And you too, sir," he said, "were, as I see it, one of her intended victims. When she planned to shoot Swift I believe she planned a double murder—that is, you and Swift were to be shot at the same time. But, luckily, you had not returned to your study yesterday afternoon at the time fixed for the double shooting, and her original plan had to be revised."

"But—but," stammered the professor, "how could she have killed me and Woody too?"

"The disconnected buzzer wires gave me the answer this morning," explained Vance. "Her scheme was both simple and bold. She knew that, if she followed Swift upstairs before the big race, she would have no difficulty in enticing him into the vault on some pretext or other—especially in view of the fact that he had shown a marked interest in her. Her intention was to shoot him in the vault, just as she did, and then go into the study and shoot you. Swift's body would then have been placed in the study, with the revolver in his hand. It would appear like murder and suicide. As for the possibility of the shot in the study being heard downstairs, I imagine she had tested that out beforehand under the very conditions obtaining yesterday afternoon. Personally, I am of the opinion that a shot in the study could not be heard down here during the noise and excitement of a race broadcast, with the study door and windows shut. For the rest, her original plan would have proceeded just as her revised one did. She would merely have fired two blanks out of the bedroom window instead of one. In the event that you should have guessed her intent when she entered the study, and tried to summon help, she had previously disconnected the wires of the buzzer just behind your chair at the desk."

"But, good Lord!" exclaimed Floyd Garden in an awed tone. "It was she herself who told Sneed about the buzzer being out of order."

"Precisely. She made it a point to be the one to discover that fact, in order to draw suspicion entirely away from herself; for the natural assumption, she must have reasoned, would be that the person who had disconnected the wires for some criminal purpose would be the last one to call attention to them. It was a bold move, but it was quite in keeping with her technique throughout."

Vance paused. After a moment he went on.

"As I say, her plan had to be revised somewhat because Doctor Garden had not returned. She had chosen the Rivermont Handicap as the background for her manoeuvres, for she knew Swift was placing a large bet on the race—and if he lost, it would give credence to the theory of suicide. As for the shooting of Doctor Garden, that would, of course, be attributed to his attempt to thwart his nephew's suicide. And, in a way, Doctor Garden's absence helped her, though it required quick thinking on her part to cover up this unexpected gap in her well-laid plans. Instead of placing Swift in the study, as she originally intended, she placed him in his chair on the roof. She carefully wiped up the blood in the vault so that no trace of it remained on the floor. A nurse with operating-room experience in removing blood from sponges, instruments, operating table and floor, would have known how. Then she came down and fired a blank shell out of the bedroom window just as soon as the outcome of the race had been declared official. Substantiatin' suicide.

"Of course, one of her chief difficulties was the disposal of the second revolver—the one she fired down here. She was confronted with the necessity either of getting rid of the revolver—which was quite impossible in the circumstances—or of hiding it safely till she could remove it from the apartment; for there was always the danger that it might be discovered and the whole technique of the plot be revealed. Since she was the person apparently least under suspicion, she probably considered that placing it temporarily in the pocket of her own top-coat, would be sufficiently safe. It was not an ideal hiding-place; but I have little doubt that she was frustrated in an attempt to hide it somewhere on the roof or on the terrace upstairs, until she could take it away at her convenience without being observed. She had no opportunity to hide the revolver upstairs after we had first gone to the roof and discovered Swift's body. However, I think it was her intention to do just this when Miss Weatherby saw her on the stairs and resentfully called my attention to the fact. Naturally, Miss Beeton denied having been on the stairs at all. And the significance of the situation did not occur to me at the moment; but I believe that she had the revolver on her person at the time Miss Weatherby saw her. She evidently thought she would have sufficient time while I was in the den, to run to the roof and hide the revolver; but when she had barely started upstairs, Miss Weatherby came unexpectedly out of the drawing-room with the intention of going to the garden herself. It was immediately after that, no doubt, that she dropped the revolver into her coat pocket in the hall closet. . ."

"But why," asked Professor Garden, "didn't she fire the revolver upstairs in the first place—it would certainly have made the shot sound more realistic—and then hide it in the garden before coming down?"

"My dear sir! That would have been impossible, as you can readily see. How would she have got back downstairs? We were ascending the stairs a few seconds after we heard the shot, and would have met her coming down. She could, of course, have come down by the public stairs and re-entered the apartment at the front door without being seen; but in that event she could not have established her presence down here at the time the shot was fired—and this was of utmost importance to her. When we reached the foot of the stairs, she was standing in the doorway of Mrs. Garden's bedroom, and she made it clear that she had heard the shot. It was, of course, a perfect alibi, provided the technique of the crime had not been revealed by the evidence she left in the vault. . .No. The shot could not have been fired upstairs. The only place she could have fired it and still have established her alibi, was out of the bedroom window."

He turned to Zalia Graem.

"Now do you see why you felt so definitely that the shot did not sound as if it came from the garden? It was because, being in the den, you were the person nearest to the shot when it was fired and could more or less accurately gauge the direction from which it came. I'm sorry I could not explain that fact to you when you mentioned it, but Miss Beeton was in the room, and it was not then the time to reveal my knowledge to her."

"Well, anyway, you were horrid about it," the girl complained. "You acted as if you believed the reason I heard the shot so distinctly was that I had fired it."

"Couldn't you read between the lines of my remarks? I was hoping you would."

She shook her head. "No, I was too worried at the time; but I'll confess that when you asked Miss Beeton to go to the roof with you, the truth dawned on me."

(The moment she made this remark I recalled that she was the only person in the room who was entirely at ease when Vance had gone upstairs.)

There was another brief silence in the room, which was broken by Floyd Garden.

"There's one point that bothers me, Vance," he said. "If Miss Beeton counted on our accepting the suicide theory, what if Equanimity had won the race?"

"That would have upset her entire calculations," answered Vance. "But she was a great gambler. And, remember, she was playing for the highest stakes. She was practically betting her life. I'll warrant it was the biggest wager ever made on Equanimity."

"Good God!" Floyd Garden murmured. "And I thought Woody's bet was a big one!"

"But, Mr. Vance," put in Doctor Siefert, frowning, "your theory of the case does not account for the attempt made on her own life."

Vance smiled faintly.

"There was no attempt on her life, doctor. When Miss Beeton left the study, a minute or so after Miss Graem, to take my message to you, she went instead into the vault, shut the door, making sure this time that the lock snapped, and gave herself a superficial blow on the back of the head. She had reason to believe, of course, that it would be but a short time before we looked for her; and she waited till she heard the key in the lock before she broke the vial of bromin. It is possible that when she went out of the study she had begun to fear that I might have some idea of the truth, and she enacted this little melodrama to throw me off the track. Her object undoubtedly was to throw suspicion on Miss Graem."

Vance looked at the girl sympathetically.

"I think when you were called from the drawing-room to the

phone, Miss Graem—at just the time Miss Beeton was on her way upstairs to shoot Swift—she decided to use you, should it be necess'ry to save herself. Undoubtedly she knew of your feud with Swift, and capitalized it; and she also undoubtedly realized that you would be a suspect in the eyes of the others who were here yesterday. That is why, my dear, I sought to lead her on by seeming to regard you as the culprit. And it had its effect. . .I hope you can find it in your heart to forgive me for having made you suffer."

The girl did not speak—she seemed to be struggling with her emotions.

Siefert had leaned forward and was studying Vance closely.

"As a theory, that may be logical," he said with sceptical gravity. "But, after all, it is only a theory."

Vance shook his head slowly.

"Oh, no, doctor. It's more than a theory. And you should be the last person to put that name on it. Miss Beeton herself—and in your presence—gave the whole thing away. Not only did she lie to us, but she contradicted herself when you and I were on the roof and she was recovering from the effects of the bromin gas—effects, incidentally, which she was able to exaggerate correctly as the result of her knowledge of medicine."

"But I don't recall—"

Vance checked him. "Surely, doctor, you remember the story she told us. According to her voluntary account of the episode, she was struck on the head and forced into the vault; and she fainted immediately as the result of the bromin gas; then the next thing she knew was that she was lying on the settee in the garden, and you and I were standing over her."

Siefert inclined his head.

"That is quite correct," he said, frowning at Vance.

"And I am sure you also remember, doctor, that she looked up at me and thanked me for having brought her out into the garden and saved her, and also asked me how I came to find her so soon."

Siefert was still frowning intently at Vance.

"That also is correct," he admitted. "But I still don't understand wherein she gave herself away."

"Doctor," asked Vance, "if she had been unconscious, as she said, from the time she was forced into the vault to the time she spoke to us in the garden, how could she possibly have known who it was that had found her and rescued her from the vault? And how could she have known that I found her soon after she had entered the vault?. . .You see, doctor, she was never unconscious at all: she was taking no chances whatever of dying of bromin gas. As I have said, it was not until I had started to unlock the door that she broke the vial of bromin; and she was perfectly aware who entered the vault and carried her out to the garden. Those remarks of hers to me were a fatal error on her part."

Siefert relaxed and leaned back in his chair with a faint wry smile. "You are perfectly right, Mr. Vance. That point escaped me entirely."

"But," Vance continued, "even had Miss Beeton not made the mistake of lying to us so obviously, there was other proof that she alone was concerned in that episode. Mr. Hammle here conclusively bore out my opinion. When she told us her story of being struck on the head and forced into the vault, she did not know that Mr. Hammle had been in the garden observing every one who came and went in the passageway. And she was alone in the corridor at the time of the supposed attack. Miss Graem, to be sure, had just passed her and gone downstairs; and the nurse counted on that fact to make her story sound plausible, hoping, of course, that it would produce the effect she was striving for—that is, to make it appear that Miss Graem had attacked her."

Vance smoked in silence for a moment.

"As for the radioactive sodium, doctor, Miss Beeton had been administering it to Mrs. Garden, content with having her die slowly of its cumulative effects. But Mrs. Garden's threat to erase her son's name from her will necessitated immediate action, and the resourceful girl decided on an overdose of the barbital last night. She foresaw, of course, that this death could easily be construed as an accident or as another suicide. As it happened, however, things were even more propitious for her, for the events of last night merely cast further suspicion on Miss Graem.

"From the first I realized how difficult, if not impossible, it would be to prove the case against Miss Beeton; and during the entire investigation I was seeking some means of trapping her. With that end in view, I mounted the parapet last night in her presence, hoping that it might suggest to her shrewd and cruel mind a possible means of removing me from her path, if she became convinced that I had guessed too much. My plan to trap her was, after all, a simple one. I asked you all to come here this evening, not as suspects, but to fill the necess'ry roles in my grim drama."

Vance sighed deeply before continuing.

"I arranged with Sergeant Heath to equip the post at the far end of the garden with a strong steel wire such as is used in theatres for flying and levitation acts. This wire was to be just long enough to reach as far as the height of the balcony on this floor. And to it was attached the usual spring catch which fastens to the leather equipment worn by the performer. This equipment consists of a heavy cowhide vest resembling in shape and cut the old Ferris waist worn by young girls in post-Victorian days, and even later. This afternoon Sergeant Heath brought such a leather vest—or what is technically known in theatrical circles as a 'flying corset'—to my apartment, and I put it on before I came here...You might be interested in seeing it. I took it off a little while ago, for it's frightfully uncomfortable..."

He rose and went through the door into the adjoining bedroom. A few moments later he returned with the leather "corset." It was made of very heavy brown leather, with a soft velour finish, and was lined with canvas. The sides, instead of being seamed, were held together by strong leather thongs laced through brass eyelets. The closing down the middle was effected by a row of inch-wide leather straps and steel buckles by which the vest was tightened to conform to the contour of the person who wore it. There were adjustable shoulder straps of leather, and thigh straps strongly made and cushioned with thick rolls of rubber.

Vance held up this strange garment.

"Here it is," he said. "Ordinarily, the buckles and straps are in front and the attachment for the spring catch is in back. But for my purpose this had to be reversed. I needed the rings in front because the wire had to be attached at this point when my back was turned to Miss Beeton." He pointed to two heavy overlapping iron rings, about two inches in diameter, held in place by nuts and bolts in a strip of canvas, several layers in thickness, in the front of the corset.

Vance threw the garment on the desk.

"This waistcoat, or corset," he said, "is worn under the actor's costume; and in my case I put on a loose tweed suit today so that the slightly protruding rings in front would not be noticeable.

"When I took Miss Beeton upstairs with me, I led her out into the garden and confronted her with her guilt. While she was protesting, I mounted the parapet, standing there with my back to her, ostensibly looking out over the city, as I had done last evening. In the semi-darkness I snapped the wire to the rings on the front of my leather vest without her seeing me do so. She came very close to me as she talked, but for a minute or so I was afraid she would not take advantage of the situation. Then, in the middle of one of her sentences, she lurched toward me with both hands outstretched, and the impact sent me over the parapet. It was a simple matter to swing myself over the balcony railing. I had arranged for the drawing-room door to be unlatched, and I merely disconnected the suspension wire, walked in, and appeared in the hallway. When Miss Beeton learned that I had witnesses to her act, as well as a photograph of it, she realized that the game was up.

"I admit, however, that I had not foreseen that she would resort to suicide. But perhaps it is just as well. She was one of those women who through some twist of nature—some deep-rooted wickedness—personify evil. It was probably this perverted tendency which drew her into the profession of nursing, where she could see, and even take part in, human suffering."

Vance leaned back in his chair and smoked abstractedly. He seemed to be deeply affected, as were all of us. Little more was said—each, of us, I think, was too much occupied with his own thoughts for any further discussion of the case. There were a few desultory questions, a few comments, and then a long silence.

Doctor Siefert was the first to take his departure. Shortly afterward the others rose restlessly.

I felt shaken from the sudden let-down of the tension through which I had been going, and walked into the drawing-room for a drink of brandy. The only light in the room came through the archway from the chandelier in the hall and from the after-glow of the sky which faintly illumined the windows, but it was sufficient to enable me to make my way to the little cabinet bar in the corner. I poured myself a pony of brandy and, drinking it quickly, stood for a moment looking out of the window over the slatey waters of the Hudson.

I heard some one enter the room and cross toward the balcony, but I did not look round immediately. When I did turn back to the room I saw the dim form of Vance standing before the open door to the balcony, a solitary, meditative figure. I was about to speak to him when Zalia Graem came softly through the archway and approached him.

"Good-by, Philo Vance," she said.

"I'm frightfully sorry," Vance murmured, taking her extended hand. "I was hoping you would forgive me when you understood everything."

"I do forgive you," she said. "That's what I came to tell you."

Vance bowed his head and raised her fingers to his lips.

The girl then withdrew her hand slowly and, turning, went from the room.

Vance watched her till she had passed through the archway. Then he moved to the open door and stepped out on the balcony.

When Zalia Graem had gone, I went into the den where Markham sat talking with Professor Garden and his son. He looked up at me as I entered, and glanced at his watch.

"I think we'd better be going, Van," he said. "Where's Vance?"

I went reluctantly back into the drawing-room to fetch him. He was still standing on the balcony, gazing out over the city with its gaunt spectral structures and its glittering lights.

* * * * * * * *

To this day Vance has not lost his deep affection for Zalia Graem. He has rarely mentioned her name, but I have noted a subtle change in his nature, which I attribute to the influence of that sentiment. Within a fortnight after the Garden murder case, Vance went to Egypt for several months; and I have a feeling that this solitary trip was motivated by his interest in Miss Graem. One evening after his return from Cairo he remarked to me: "A man's affections involve a great responsibility. The things a man wants most must often be sacrificed because of this exacting responsibility." I think I understood what was in his mind. With the multiplicity of intellectual interests that occupied him, he doubted (and I think rightly so) his capacity to make any woman happy in the conventional sense.

As for Zalia Graem, she married Floyd Garden the following year, and they are now living on Long Island, only a few miles distant from Hammle's estate. Miss Weatherby and Kroon are still seen together; and there have been rumours from time to time that she is about to sign a contract with a Hollywood motion-picture producer. Professor Garden is still living in his penthouse apartment, a lonely and somewhat pathetic figure, completely absorbed in his researches.

A year or so after the tragedies at the Garden apartment, Vance met Hannix, the book-maker, at Bowie. It was a casual meeting, and I doubt if Vance remembered it afterward. But Hannix remembered. One day, several months later, when Vance and I were sitting in the downstairs dining-hall of the club-house at Empire, Hannix came over and drew up a chair.

"What's happened to Floyd Garden, Mr. Vance?" he asked. "I haven't heard from him for over a year. Given up the horses?"

"It's possible, don't y' know," Vance returned with a faint smile.

"But why?" demanded Hannix. "He was a good sport, and I miss him."

"I dare say." Vance nodded indifferently. "Perhaps he grew a bit weary of contributing to your support."

"Now, now, Mr. Vance." Hannix assumed an injured air and extended his hands appealingly. "That was a cruel remark. I never held out with Mr. Garden for the usual bookie maximum. Believe, me, I paid him *mutuel* prices on any bet up to half a hundred. . .By the way, Mr. Vance,"—Hannix leaned forward confidentially—"the Butler Handicap is coming up in a few minutes, and the slates are all quoting Only One at eight. If you like the colt, I'll give you ten on him. He's got a swell chance to win."

Vance looked at the man coldly and shook his head. "No, thanks, Hannix. I'm already on Discovery."

Discovery won that race by a length and a half. Only One, incidentally, finished a well-beaten second.

The Kidnap
Murder Case

Non semper ea sunt, quae videntur; decipit
Frons prima multos.

—Phaedrus.

Characters of the Book

Philo Vance

John F.-X. Markham—*District Attorney of New York County.*

Ernest Heath—*Sergeant of the Homicide Bureau.*

Kaspar Kenting—*A play-boy and gambler, who mysteriously disappears from his home.*

Kenton Kenting—*A broker; brother of Kaspar and technical head of the Kenting family.*

Madelaine Kenting—*Kaspar Kenting's wife.*

Eldridge Fleel—*A lawyer; a friend of the Kenting family and their attorney.*

Mrs. Andrews Falloway—*Madelaine Kenting's mother.*

Fraim Falloway—*Madelaine Kenting's brother.*

Porter Quaggy—*Another friend of the Kentings.*

Weem—*The Kenting butler and houseman.*

Gertrude—*The Kenting cook and maid; wife of Weem.*

Snitkin—*Detective of the Homicide Bureau.*

Hennessey—*Detective of the Homicide Bureau.*

Burke—*Detective of the Homicide Bureau.*

Guilfoyle—*Detective of the Homicide Bureau.*

Sullivan—*Detective of the Homicide Bureau.*

Captain Dubois—*Finger-print expert.*

Detective Bellamy—*Finger-print expert.*

William McLaughlin—*Patrolman on night duty on West 86th Street.*

Currie—*Vance's valet.*

CHAPTER 1

Kidnapped!
Wednesday, July 20; 9:30 a.m.

Philo Vance, as you may remember, took a solitary trip to Egypt immediately after the termination of the Garden murder case.[1] He did not return to New York until the middle of July. He was considerably tanned, and there was a tired look in his wide-set grey eyes. I suspected, the moment I greeted him on the dock, that during his absence he had thrown himself into Egyptological research, which was an old passion of his.

"I'm fagged out, Van," he complained good-naturedly, as we settled ourselves in a taxicab and started uptown to his apartment. "I need a rest. We're not leavin' New York this summer—you won't mind, I hope. I've brought back a couple of boxes of archaeological specimens. See about them tomorrow, will you?—there's a good fellow."

Even his voice sounded weary. His words carried a curious undertone of distraction; and the idea flashed through my mind that he had not altogether succeeded in eliminating from his thoughts the romantic memory of a certain young woman he had met during the strange and fateful occurrences in the penthouse of Professor Ephraim Garden.[2] My surmise must have been correct, for it was that very evening, when he was relaxing in his roof-garden, that Vance remarked to me, apropos of nothing that had gone before: "A man's affections involve a great responsibility. The things a man wants most must often be sacrificed because of this exacting responsibility." I felt quite certain then that his sudden and prolonged trip to Egypt had not been an unqualified success as far as his personal objective was concerned.

For the next few days Vance busied himself in arranging, classifying

1. *The Garden Murder Case*, 1935).
2. This famous case had taken place just three months earlier.

and cataloguing the rare pieces he had brought back with him. He threw himself into the work with more than his wonted interest and enthusiasm. His mental and physical condition showed improvement immediately, and it was but a short time before I recognized the old vital Vance that I had always known, keen for sports, for various impersonal activities, and for the constant milling of the undercurrents of human psychology.

It was just a week after his return from Cairo that the famous Kidnap murder case broke. It was an atrocious and clever crime, and more than the usual publicity was given to it in the newspapers because of the wave of kidnapping cases that had been sweeping over the country at that time. But this particular crime of which I am writing from my voluminous notes was very different in many respects from the familiar "snatch"; and it was illumined by many sinister high lights. To be sure, the motive for the crime, or, I should say, crimes, was the sordid one of monetary gain; and superficially the technique was similar to that of the numerous cases in the same category. But through Vance's determination and fearlessness, through his keen insight into human nature, and his amazing flair for the ramifications of human psychology, he was able to penetrate beyond the seemingly conclusive manifestations of the case.

In the course of this investigation Vance took no thought of any personal risk. At one time he was in the gravest danger, and it was only through his boldness, his lack of physical fear, and his deadly aim and quick action when it was a matter of his life or another's—partly the result, perhaps, of his World-War experience which won him the *Croix de Guerre*—that he saved the lives of several innocent persons as well as his own, and eventually put his finger on the criminal in a scene of startling tragedy.

There was a certain righteous indignation in his attitude during this terrible episode—an attitude quite alien to his customarily aloof and cynical and purely academic point of view—for the crime itself was one of the type he particularly abhorred.

As I have said, it was just a week after his return to New York that Vance was unexpectedly, and somewhat against his wishes, drawn into the investigation. He had resumed his habit of working late at night and rising late; but, to my surprise, when I entered the library at nine o'clock on that morning of July 20, he was already up and dressed and had just finished the Turkish coffee and the *Régie* cigarette that constituted his daily breakfast. He had on his patch-pocket grey tweed suit and a pair of heavy walking boots, which almost invariably indicated a contemplated trip into the country.

Before I could express my astonishment (I believe it was the first time in the course of our relationship that he had risen and started the day before I had) he smilingly explained to me with his antemeridian drawl:

"Don't be shocked by my burst of energy, Van. It really can't be helped, don't y' know. I'm driving out to Dumont, to the dog show. I've a little chap entered in the puppy and American-bred classes, and I want to take him into the ring myself. He's a grand little fellow, and this is his debut.[3] I'll return for dinner."

I was rather pleased at the prospect of being left alone for the day, for there was much work for me to do. I admit that, as Vance's legal advisor, monetary steward and general overseer of his affairs, I had allowed a great deal of routine work to accumulate during his absence, and the assurance of an entire day, without any immediate or current chores, was most welcome to me.

As Vance spoke he rang for Currie, his old English butler and major-domo, and asked for his hat and chamois gloves. Filling his cigarette case, he waved a friendly good-bye to me and started toward the door. But just before he reached it, the front doorbell sounded, and a moment later Currie ushered in John F.-X. Markham, District Attorney of New York County.[4]

"Good heavens, Vance!" exclaimed Markham. "Going out at such an early hour? Or have you just come in?" Despite the jocularity of his words, there was an unwonted sombreness in his face and a worried look in his eyes, which belied the manner of his greeting.

Vance smiled with a puzzled frown.

"I don't like the expression on your Hellenic features this morning, old dear. It bodes ill for one who craves freedom and surcease from earthly miseries. I was just about to escape by hieing me to a dog show in the country. My little Sandy—"

"Damn your dogs and your dog shows, Vance!" Markham growled. "I've serious news for you."

Vance shrugged his shoulders with resignation and heaved an exaggerated sigh.

"Markham—my very dear Markham! How did you time your

---

3. As I learned later, he was referring to his Scottish terrier, Pibroch Sandyman. Incidentally, this dog won the puppy class that day and received Reserve Winners as well. Later he became a Champion.

4. Markham and Vance had been close friends for over fifteen years, and, although Vance's unofficial connection with the District Attorney's office had begun somewhat in the spirit of an experimental adventure, Markham had now come to depend implicitly upon his friend as a vital associate in his criminal investigations.

visit so accurately? Thirty seconds later and I would have been on my way and free from your clutches."Vance threw his hat and gloves aside. "But since you have captured me so neatly, I suppose I must listen, although I am sure I shall not like the tidin's. I know I'm going to hate you and wish you had never been born. I can tell from the doleful look on your face that you're in for something messy and desire spiritual support." He stepped a little to one side. "Enter, and pour forth your woes."

"I haven't time—"

"Tut, tut." Vance moved nonchalantly to the centre-table and pointed to a large comfortable upholstered chair. "There's always time. There always has been time—there always will be time. Represented by n, don't y' know. Quite meaningless—without beginning and without end, and utterly indivisible. In fact, there's no such thing as time—unless you're dabblin' in the fourth dimension. . . ."

He walked back to Markham, took him gently by the arm and, ignoring his protests, led him to the chair by the table.

"Really, y' know, Markham, you need a cigar and a drink. Let calm be your watchword, my dear fellow,—always calm. Serenity. Consider the ancient oaks. Or, better yet, the eternal hills—or is it the everlasting hills? It's been so long since I penned poesy. Anyway, Swinburne did it much better. . . . *Eheu, eheu! . . .*"

As he babbled along, with seeming aimlessness, he went to a small side-table and, taking up a crystal decanter, poured some of its contents into a tulip-shaped glass, and set it down before the District Attorney. "Try that old Amontillado." He then moved the humidor forward. "And these panatelas are infinitely better than the cigars you carry around to dole out to your constituents."

Markham made a restless, annoyed gesture, lighted one of the cigars, and sipped the old syrupy sherry.

Vance seated himself in a near-by chair and carefully lighted a *Régie.*

"Now try me," he said. "But don't make the tale too sad. My heart is already at the breaking-point."

"What I have to tell you is damned serious." Markham frowned and looked sharply at Vance. "Do you like kidnappings?"

"Not passionately," Vance answered, his face darkening. "Beastly crimes, kidnappings. Worse than poisonings. About as low as a criminal can sink." His eyebrows went up. "Why?"

"There's been a kidnapping during the night. I learned about it half an hour ago. I'm on my way—"

"Who and where?"Vance's face had now become sombre too.

"Kaspar Kenting. Heath and a couple of his men are at the Kenting house in 86th Street now. They're waiting for me."

"Kaspar Kenting ..."Vance repeated the name several times, as if trying to recall some former association with it. "In 86th Street, you say?"

He rose suddenly and went to the telephone stand in the anteroom where he opened the directory and ran his eye down the page.

"Is it number 86 West 86th Street, perhaps?"

Markham nodded. "That's right. Easy to remember."

"Yes—quite." Vance came strolling back into the library, but instead of resuming his chair he stood leaning against the end of the table. "Quite," he repeated. "I seemed to remember it when you mentioned Kenting's name. . . . The domicile's an interestin' old landmark. I've never seen it, however. Had a fascinatin' reputation once. Still called the Purple House."

"Purple house?" Markham looked up. "What do you mean?"

"My dear fellow! Are you entirely ignorant of the history of the city which you adorn as District Attorney? The Purple House was built by Karl K. Kenting back in 1880, and he had the bricks and slabs of stone painted purple, in order to distinguish his abode from all others in the neighbourhood, and to flaunt it as a challenge to his numerous enemies. 'With a house that colour,' he used to say, 'they won't have any trouble finding me, if they want me.' The place became known as the Purple House. And every time the house was repainted, the original colour was retained. Sort of family tradition, don't y' know. . . . But what about your Kaspar Kenting?"

"He disappeared some time last night," Markham explained impatiently. "From his bedroom. Open window, ladder, ransom note thumb-tacked to the window-sill. No doubt about it."

"Details familiar—eh, what?" mused Vance. "And I presume the ransom note was concocted with words cut from a newspaper and pasted on a sheet of paper?"

Markham looked astonished.

"Exactly! How did you guess it?"

"Nothing new or original about it—what? Highly conventional. Bookish, in fact. But not being done this season in the best kidnapping circles. . . . Curious case. . . . How did you learn about it?"

"Eldridge Fleel was waiting at my office when I arrived this morning. He's the lawyer for the Kenting family. One of the executors for the old man's estate. Kaspar Kenting's wife naturally notified him at once at his home—called him before he was up. He went to the house, looked over the situation, and then came directly to me."

"Level-headed chap, this Fleel?"

"Oh, yes. I've known the man for years. Good lawyer. He was wealthy and influential once, but was badly hit by the depression. We were both members of the Lawyers' Club, and we had offices in the same building on lower Broadway before I was cursed with the District Attorneyship. . . . I got in touch with Sergeant Heath immediately, and he went up to the house with Fleel. I told them I'd be there as soon as I could. I dropped off here, thinking—"

"Sad . . . very sad," interrupted Vance with a sigh, drawing deeply on his cigarette. "I still wish you had made it a few minutes later. I'd have been safely away. You're positively ineluctable."

"Come, come, Vance. You know damned well I may need your help." Markham sat up with a show of anger. "A kidnapping isn't a pleasant thing, and the city's not going to like it. I'm having enough trouble as it is.[5] I can't very well pass the buck to the federal boys. I'd rather clean up the mess from local headquarters. . . . By the way, do you know this young Kaspar Kenting?"

"Slightly," Vance answered abstractedly. "I've run into the johnnie here and there, especially at old Kinkaid's Casino[6] and at the race-tracks. Kaspar's a gambler and pretty much a ne'er-do-well. Full of the spirit of frivolity and not much else. Ardent play-boy, as it were. Always hard up. And trusted by no one. Can't imagine why any one would want to pay a ransom for him."

Vance slowly exhaled his cigarette smoke, watching the long blue ribbons rise and disperse against the ceiling.

"Queer background," he murmured, almost as if to himself. "Can't really blame the chappie for being such a blighter. Old Karl K., the author of his being, was a bit queer himself. Had more than enough money, and left it all to the older son, Kenyon K., to dole out to Kaspar as he saw fit. I imagine he hasn't seen fit very often or very much. Kenyon is the solid-citizen type, in the worst possible meaning of the phrase. Came to the Belmont track in the highest of dudgeons one afternoon and led Kaspar righteously home. Probably goes to church regularly. Marches in parades. Applauds the high notes of sopranos. Feels positively nude without a badge of some kind. That sort of johnnie. Enough to drive any younger brother to

---

5. There had been several recent kidnappings at this time, two of a particularly atrocious nature, and the District Attorney's office and the Commissioner of Police were being constantly and severely criticized by the press for their apparent helplessness in the situation.
6. Vance was referring to the gambling establishment which figured so prominently in the *Casino Murder Case*.

hell. . . . The old man, as you must know, wasn't a block from which you could expect anything in the way of fancy chips. A rabid and fanatical Ku-Klux-Klanner. . . ."

"You mean his initials?" asked Markham.

"No. Oh, no. His convictions." Vance looked at Markham inquiringly. "Don't you know the story?"

Markham shook his head despondently.

"Old K. K. Kenting originally came from Virginia and was a King Kleagle in that sheeted Order.[7] So rabid was he that he changed the C in his name, Carl, to a K, and gave himself a middle initial, another K, so that his monogram would be the symbol of his fanatical passion. And he went even further. He had two sons and a daughter, and he gave them all names beginning with K, and added for each one a middle initial K—Kenyon K. Kenting, Kaspar K. Kenting, and Karen K. Kenting. The girl died shortly after Karl himself was gathered to Abraham's bosom. The two sons remaining, being of a new generation and less violent, dropped the middle K—which never stood for anything, by the by."

"But why a purple house?"

"No symbolism there," returned Vance. "When Karl Kenting came to NewYork and went into politics he became boss of his district. And he had an idea his sub-Potomac enemies were going to persecute him; so, as I say, he wanted to make it easy for 'em to find him. He was an aggressive and fearless old codger."

"I seem to remember they eventually found him, and with a vengeance," Markham mumbled impatiently.

"Quite." Vance nodded indifferently. "But it took two machine-guns to translate him to the Elysian Fields. Quite a scandal at the time. Anyway, the two sons, while wholly different from each other, are both unlike their father."

Markham stood up with deliberation.

"That may all be very interesting," he grumbled; "but I've got to get to 86th Street. This may prove a crucial case, and I can't afford to ignore it." He looked somewhat appealingly at Vance.

Vance rose likewise and crushed out his cigarette.

"Oh, by all means," he drawled. "I'll be delighted to toddle along. Though I can't even vaguely imagine why kidnappers should select

---

7. Vance was mistaken about this, as Kenting belonged to the old, or original, Klan, in which there was no such title as King Keagle. This title did not come into existence until 1915, with the modern Klan. Kenting probably had been a Grand Dragon (or State head) in the original Klan.

Kaspar Kenting. The Kentings are no longer a reputedly wealthy family. True, they might be able to produce a fairly substantial sum on short notice, but they're not, d' ye see, in the class which professional kidnappers enter up on their list of possible victims. . . . By the by, do you know how much ransom was demanded?"

"Fifty thousand. But you'll see the note when we get there. Nothing's been touched. Heath knows I'm coming."

"Fifty thousand . . ." Vance poured himself a pony of his Napoléon cognac. "That's most interestin'. Not an untidy sum—eh, what?"

When he had finished his brandy he rang again for Currie.

"Really, y' know," he said to Markham—his tone had suddenly changed to one of levity—, "I can't wear chamois gloves in a purple house. Most inappropriate."

He asked Currie for a pair of doeskin gloves, his *wanghee* cane, and a town hat. When they were brought in he turned to me.

"Do you mind calling MacDermott[8] and explainin'?" he asked. "The old boy himself will have to show Sandy. . . . And do you care to come along, Van? It may prove more fascinatin' than it sounds."

Despite my accumulated work, I was glad of the invitation. I caught MacDermott on the telephone just as he was packing his crated entries into the station-wagon. I wasted few words on him, in true Scotch fashion, and immediately joined Vance and Markham in the lower hallway where they were waiting for me.

We entered the District Attorney's car, and in fifteen minutes we were at the scene of what proved to be one of the most unusual criminal cases in Vance's career.

---

8. Robert A. MacDermott was Vance's kennel manager.

CHAPTER 2

The Purple House
Wednesday, July 20; 10:30 a.m.

The Kenting residence in 86th Street was not as bizarre a place as I had expected to see after Vance's description of it. In fact, it differed very little from the other old brownstone residences in the street, except that it was somewhat larger. I might even have passed it or driven by it any number of times without noticing it at all. This fact was, no doubt, owing to the dullness of its faded colour, since the house had apparently not been repainted for several years, and sun and rain had not spared it. Its tone was so dingy and superficially nondescript that it blended unobtrusively with the other houses of the neighbourhood. As we approached it that fateful morning it appeared almost a neutral grey in the brilliant summer sunshine.

On closer inspection I could see that the house had been built of bricks put together in English cross bond with weathered mortar joints, trimmed at the cornices, about the windows and door, and below the eaves, with great rectangular slabs of brownstone. Only in the shadow along the eaves and beneath the projections of the sills was there any distinguishable tint of purple remaining. The architecture of the house was conventional enough—a somewhat free adaptation of combined Georgian and Colonial, such as was popular during the middle of the last century.

The entrance, which was several feet above the street level and reached by five or six broad sandstone steps, was a spacious one; and there was the customary glass-enclosed vestibule. The windows were high, and old-fashioned shutters folded back against the walls of the house. Instead of the regulation four stories, the house consisted of only three stories, not counting the sunken basement; and I was somewhat astonished at this fact when it came to my attention, for the structure was even higher than its neighbours. The windows, however, were not on a line with those in the other houses, and I realized that the ceilings of the "Purple House" must be unusually high.

Another thing which distinguished the Kenting residence from the neighbouring buildings was the existence of a fifty-foot court to the east. This court was covered with a neatly kept lawn, with hedges on all four sides. There were two flower-beds—one star-shaped and the other in the form of a crescent; and an old gnarled maple tree stood at the rear, with its branches extending almost the entire width of the yard. Only a low iron picket fence, with a swinging gate, divided the yard from the street.

This refreshing quadrangle was bathed with sunshine, and it seemed a very pleasant spot, with its blooming hedges and its scattered painted metal chairs. But there was one sinister note—one item which in itself was not sinister at all, but which had acquired a malevolent aspect from the facts Markham had related to us in Vance's apartment that morning. It was a long, heavy ladder, such as outdoor painters use, leaning against the house, with its upper end just below a second-story window—the window nearest the street.

The "Purple House" itself was set about ten feet in from the sidewalk, and we immediately crossed the irregular flagstones and proceeded up the steps to the front door. But there was no need to ring the bell. Sergeant Ernest Heath, of the Homicide Bureau, greeted us in the vestibule. After saluting Markham, whom he addressed as Chief, he turned to Vance with a grin and shook his head ponderously.

"I didn't think you'd be here, Mr. Vance," he said good-naturedly. "Ain't this a little out of your line? But howdy, anyway." And he held out his hand.

"I myself didn't think I'd be here, Sergeant. And everything is out of my line today except dog shows. Fact is, I almost missed the present pleasure of seeing you." Vance shook hands with him cordially, and cocked one eye inquiringly. "What's the exhibit I'm supposed to view?"

"You might as well have stayed home, Mr. Vance," Heath told him. "Hell, there's nothing to this case. It ain't even a fancy one. A little routine police work is all that's needed to clear it up. There ain't a chance for what you call psychological deduction."

"My word!" sighed Vance. "Most encouragin', Sergeant. I hope you're right. Still, since I'm here, don't y' know, I might as well look around in my amateurish way and try to learn what it's all about. I promise not to complicate matters for you."

"That's a little more than O.K. with me, Mr. Vance," the Sergeant grinned, and, opening the heavy glass-panelled oak door, he led us into the dingy but spacious hallway, and then through partly-opened sliding doors at the right, into a stuffy drawing-room.

"Cap Dubois and Bellamy[1] are upstairs, getting the finger-prints; and Quackenbush[2] took a few shots and went away." Heath seated himself at a small Jacobean desk and drew out his little black leather-bound note-book. "Chief," he said to Markham, "I think maybe you'd better get the whole story direct from Mrs. Kenting, the wife of the gentleman who was kidnapped."

I now noticed three other persons in the room. At the front window stood a solid, slightly corpulent man of successful, professional mien. He turned and came forward as we entered, and Markham bowed to him cordially and greeted him by the name Fleel. He was the lawyer of the Kenting family.

At his side was a somewhat aggressive middle-aged man, rather thin, with a serious and pinched expression. Fleel introduced him to us cursorily, with a careless wave of the hand, as Kenyon Kenting, the brother of the missing man. Then the lawyer turned stiffly to the other side of the room, and said in a suave, businesslike voice:

"But I particularly wish to present you gentlemen to Mrs. Kaspar Kenting."

We all turned to the pale, terrified woman seated at one end of a small davenport, in the shadows of the west wall. She appeared at first glance to be in her early thirties; but I soon realized that my guess might be ten years out, one way or the other. She seemed exceedingly thin, even beneath the full folds of the satin dressing-gown she wore; and although her eyes were large and frankly appealing, there was in her features evidence of a shrewd competency amounting almost to hardness. It struck me that a painter could have used her for the perfect model of the clinging, nervous, whiny woman. But, on the other hand, she impressed me as being capable of assuming the role of a strong-minded and efficient person when the occasion demanded. Her hair was thin and stringy and of the lustreless ashen-blond variety; and her eyelashes and eyebrows were so sparse and pale, that she gave the impression, sitting there in the dim light, of having none at all.

When Fleel presented us to her she nodded curtly with a frightened air, and kept her eyes focused sharply on Markham. Kenyon

---

1. Captain Dubois and Detective Bellamy were finger-print experts attached to the New York Police Department.

2. Peter Quackenbush was the official police photographer.

Kenting went directly to her and, sitting down on the edge of the sofa, put his arm half around her and patted her gently on the back.

"You must be brave, my dear," he said in a tone that was almost endearing. "These gentlemen have come to help us, and I'm sure they'll be wanting to know all you can tell them about the events of last night."

The woman drew her eyes slowly away from Markham and looked up wistfully and trustingly at her brother-in-law. Then she nodded her head slowly, in complete and confiding acquiescence and again turned her eyes to Markham.

Sergeant Heath broke gruffly into the scene.

"Don't you want to go upstairs, Chief, and see the room from where the snatch was made? Snitkin's on duty up there, to see that nothing is moved around or changed."

"I say, just a moment, Sergeant." Vance sat down on the sofa beside Mrs. Kenting. "I'd like to ask Mrs. Kenting a few questions first." He turned to the woman. "Do you mind?" he asked in a mild, almost deferential tone. As she silently shook her head in reply he continued: "Tell me, when did you first learn of your husband's absence?"

The woman took a deep breath, and after a barely perceptible hesitation answered in a slightly rasping, low-pitched voice which contrasted strangely with her colourless, semi-anaemic appearance.

"Early this morning—about six o'clock, I should say. The sun had just risen."[3]

"And how did you happen to become aware of his absence?"

"I wasn't sleeping well last night," the woman responded. "I was restless for some unknown reason, and the early morning sun coming through the shutters into my room not only awakened me, but prevented me from going back to sleep. Then I thought I heard a faint unfamiliar sound in my husband's room—you see, we occupy adjoining rooms on the next floor—and it seemed to me I heard some one moving stealthily about. There was the unmistakable sound of footsteps across the floor—that is, like some one walking around in soft slippers."

She took another deep breath, and shuddered slightly.

"I was already terribly nervous, anyway, and these strange noises frightened me, for Kaspar—Mr. Kenting—is usually sound asleep at that hour of the morning. I got up, put on my slippers, threw a dressing-gown around me, and went to the door which connects our two rooms. I called to my husband, but got no answer. Then I called again,

---

3. The official time of sunrise on that day was 4:45, local mean time, or 4:41, Eastern standard time; but daylight saving time was then in effect, and Mrs. Kenting's reference to sunrise in New York at approximately six o'clock was correct.

and still again, in louder tones, at the same time knocking at the door. But there was no response of any kind—and I realized that everything had suddenly become quiet in the room. By this time I was panicky; so I pulled open the door quickly and entered the room. . . ."

"Just a moment, Mrs. Kenting," Vance interrupted. "You speak of having been startled by an unfamiliar sound in your husband's room this morning, and you say you heard some one walking about in the room. Just what kind of sound was it that first caught your attention?"

"I don't know exactly. It might have been some one moving a chair, or dropping something, or maybe it was just a door surreptitiously opened and shut. I can't describe it any better than that."

"Could it have been a scuffle of some kind—I mean, did it sound as if more than one person might have been making the noise?"

The woman shook her head vaguely.

"I don't think so. It was over too quickly for that. I should say it was a sound that was not intended—something accidental—do you see what I mean? I can't imagine what it could have been—so many things might have happened. . . ."

"When you entered the room, were the lights on?" Vance asked, with what appeared to be almost utter indifference.

"Yes," the woman hastened to answer animatedly. "That was the curious thing about it. Not only was the chandelier burning brightly, but the light beside the bed also. They were a ghastly yellow in the day-light."

"Are the two fixtures controlled with the same switch?" Vance asked, frowning down at his unlighted *Régie*.

"No," the woman told him. "The switch for the chandelier is near the hall door, while the night-lamp is connected to an outlet in the baseboard and is worked by a switch on the lamp itself. And another strange thing was that the bed had not been slept in."

Vance's eyebrows rose slightly, but he did not look up from his fixed contemplation of the cigarette between his fingers.

"Do you know what time Mr. Kenting came to his bedroom last night?"

The woman hesitated a moment and flashed a glance at Kenyon Kenting.

"Oh, yes," she said hurriedly. "I heard him come in. It must have been soon after three this morning. He had been out for the evening, and I happened to be awake when he got back—or else the unlocking and closing of the front door awakened me—I really don't know. I heard him enter his bedroom and turn on the lights. Then I heard him telephoning to some one in an angry voice. Right after that I fell asleep again."

"You say he was out last night. Do you know where or with whom?"

Mrs. Kenting nodded, but again she hesitated. Finally she answered in the same brittle, rasping voice:

"A new gambling casino was opened in Jersey yesterday, and my husband was invited to be a guest at the opening ceremonies. His friend Mr. Quaggy called for him about nine o'clock—"

"Please repeat the name of your husband's friend."

"Quaggy—Porter Quaggy. He's a very trustworthy and loyal man, and I've never objected to my husband's going out with him. He has been more or less a friend of the family for several years, and he always seems to know just how to handle my husband when he shows an inclination to go a little too far in his—his, well, his drinking. Mr. Quaggy was here at the house yesterday afternoon, and it was then that he and Kaspar made arrangements to go together to the new casino."

Vance nodded slightly, and directed his gaze to the floor as if trying to connect something the woman had told him with something already in his mind.

"Where does Mr. Quaggy live?" he asked.

"Just up the street, near Central Park West, at the Nottingham. . . ." She paused, and drew a deep breath. "Mr. Quaggy's a frequent and welcome visitor here."

Vance threw Heath a significant *coup d'oeil*, and the Sergeant made a note in the small leather-bound black book which lay before him on the desk.

"Do you happen to know," Vance continued, still addressing the woman, "whether Mr. Quaggy returned to the house last night with Mr. Kenting?"

"Oh, no; I'm quite sure he did not," was the prompt reply. "I heard my husband come in alone and mount the stairs; and I heard him alone in his bedroom. As I said, I dozed off shortly afterwards, and didn't wake up again until after the sun rose."

"May I offer you a cigarette?" said Vance, holding out his case.

The woman shook her head slightly and glanced questioningly at Kenyon Kenting.

"No, thank you," she returned. "I rarely smoke. But I don't in the least mind others smoking, so please light your own cigarette."

With a courteous bow in acknowledgment, Vance proceeded to do so, and then asked:

"When you found that your husband was not in his room at six this morning, and that the lights were on and the bed had not been slept in, what did you think?—and what did you do?"

"I was naturally upset and troubled and very much puzzled," Mrs. Kenting explained; "and just then I noticed that the big side window overlooking the lawn was open and that the Venetian blind had not been lowered. This was queer, because Kaspar was always fussy about this particular blind in the summer-time because of the early morning sun. I immediately ran to the window and looked down into the yard, for a sudden fear had flashed through my mind that perhaps Kaspar had fallen out. . . . You see," she added reluctantly, "my husband often has had too much to drink when he comes home late at night. . . . It was then I saw the ladder against the house; and I was wondering about that vaguely, when suddenly I noticed that horrible slip of paper pinned to the window-sill. Immediately I realized what had happened, and why I had heard those peculiar noises in his room. The realization made me feel faint."

She paused and dabbed gently at her eyes with a lace-trimmed handkerchief.

"When I recovered a little from the shock of this frightful thing," she continued, "I went to the telephone and called up Mr. Fleel. I also called Mr. Kenyon Kenting here—he lives on Fifth Avenue, just across the park. After that I simply ordered some black coffee, and waited, frantic, until their arrival. I said nothing about the matter to the servants, and I didn't dare inform the police until I had consulted with my brother-in-law and especially with Mr. Fleel, who is not only the family's legal advisor, but also a very close friend. I felt that he would know the wisest course to follow."

"How many servants are there here?" Vance asked.

"Only two—Weem, our butler and houseman, and his wife, Gertrude, who cooks and does maid service."

"They sleep where?"

"On the third floor, at the rear."

Vance had listened to the woman's account of the tragic episode with unusual attentiveness, and while to the others he must have seemed casual and indifferent, I had noticed that he shot the narrator several appraising glances from under his lazily drooping eyelids.

At last he rose and, walking to the desk, placed his half-burnt cigarette in a large onyx ash receiver. Turning to Mrs. Kenting again, he asked quietly:

"Had you, or your husband, any previous warning of this event?"

Before answering, the woman looked with troubled concern at Kenyon Kenting.

"I think, my dear," he encouraged her, in a ponderous, declamatory tone, "that you should be perfectly frank with these gentlemen."

The woman shifted her eyes back to Vance slowly, and after a moment of indecision said:

"Only this: several nights, recently, after I had retired, I have heard Kaspar dialling a number and talking angrily to some one over the telephone. I could never distinguish any of the conversation—it was simply a sort of muffled muttering. And I always noticed that the next day Kaspar was in a terrible humour and seemed worried and agitated about something. Twice I tried to find out what the trouble was, and asked him to explain the phone calls; but each time he assured me nothing whatever was wrong, and refused to tell me anything except that he had been speaking to his brother regarding business affairs. . . ."

"That was wholly a misleading statement on Kaspar's part," put in Kenyon Kenting with matter-of-fact suavity. "As I've already said to Mrs. Kenting, I can't remember ever having had any telephone conversation with Kaspar at night. Whenever we had business matters to discuss he either came to my office, or we talked them over here at the house. . . . I can't understand these phone conversations—but, of course, they may have no relation whatsoever to this present enigma."

"As you say, sir." Vance nodded. "No plausible connection with this crime apparent. But one never knows, does one? . . ." His eyes moved slowly back to Mrs. Kenting. "Was there nothing else recently which you can recall, and which might be helpful now?"

"Yes, there was." The woman nodded with a show of vigour. "About a week ago a strange, rough-looking man came here to see Kaspar—he looked to me like an underworld character. Kaspar took him immediately into the drawing-room here and closed the doors. They remained in the room a long time. I had gone up to my *boudoir*, but when the man left the house I heard him say to Kaspar in a loud tone, 'There are ways of getting things.' It wasn't just a statement—the words sounded terribly unfriendly. Almost like a threat."

"Has there been anything further?" Vance asked.

"Yes. Several days later, the same man came again, and an even more sinister-looking individual was with him. I got only the merest glimpse of them as Kaspar led them into this room and closed the doors. I can't even remember what either of them looked like—except that I'm sure they were dangerous men and I know they frightened me. I asked Kaspar about them the next morning, but he evaded the question and said merely that it was a matter of business and I wouldn't understand. That was all I could get out of him."

Kenyon Kenting had turned his back to the room and was looking out of the window, his hands clasped behind him.

"I hardly think these two mysterious callers," he commented with pompous finality, without turning, "have any connection with Kaspar's kidnapping."

Vance frowned slightly and cast an inquisitive glance at the man's back.

"Can you be sure of that, Mr. Kenting?" he asked coldly.

"Oh, no—oh, no," the other replied apologetically, swinging about suddenly and extending one hand in an oratorical gesture. "I can't be sure. I merely meant it isn't logical to suppose that two men would expose themselves so openly if they contemplated a step attended by such serious consequences as a proven kidnapping. Besides, Kaspar had many strange acquaintances, and these men were probably in no way connected with the present situation."

Vance kept his eyes fixed on the man, and his expression did not change.

"It might be, of course, as you say," he remarked lightly. "Also it might not be—what? Interestin' speculation. But quite futile. I wonder. . . ." He drew himself up and, meditatively taking out his cigarette case, lighted another *Régie*. "And now I think we might go above, to Mr. Kaspar Kenting's bedroom."

We all rose and went toward the sliding doors.

As we came out into the main hall, the door to a small room just opposite was standing ajar, and through it I saw what appeared to be a miniature museum of some kind. There were the slanting cases set against the walls, and a double row of larger cases down the centre of the room. It looked like a private exhibition, arranged on the lines of the more extensive ones seen in any public museum.

"Ah! a collection of semiprecious stones," commented Vance. "Do you mind if I take a brief look?" he asked, addressing Mrs. Kenting. "Tremendously interested in the subject, don't y' know."[4]

The woman looked a little astonished, but answered at once.

"By all means. Go right in."

"Your own collection?" Vance inquired casually.

"Oh, no," the woman told him—somewhat bitterly, it seemed to me. "It belonged to Mr. Kenting senior. It was here in the house when I first came, long after his death. It was part of the estate he left—residuary property, I believe they call it."

---

4. Although Vance never collected semiprecious stones himself, he had become deeply interested in the subject as early as his college days.

Fleel nodded, as if he considered Mrs. Kenting's explanation correct and adequate.

Much to Markham's impatience and annoyance, Vance immediately entered the small room and moved slowly along the cases. He beckoned to me to join him.

Neatly arranged in the cases were specimens, in various shapes and sizes, of aquamarine, topaz, spinel, tourmaline, and zircon; rubelite, amethyst, alexandrite, peridot, hessonite, pyrope, demantoid, almandine, kinzite, andalusite, turquoise, and jadeite. Many of these gemstones were beautifully cut and lavishly faceted, and I was admiring their lustrous beauty, impressed by what I assumed to be their great value, when Vance murmured softly:

"A most amazin' and disquietin' collection. Only one gem of real value here, and not a rare specimen among the rest. A schoolgirl's assortment, really. Very queer. And there seem to be many blank spaces. Judgin' by the vacancies and general distribution, old Kenting must have been a mere amateur. . . ."

I looked at him in amazement. Then his voice trailed off, and he suddenly wheeled about and returned to the hall.

"A most curious collection," he murmured again.

"Semiprecious stones were one of my father's hobbies," Kenting returned.

"Yes, yes. Of course." Vance nodded abstractedly. "Most unusual collection. Hardly representative, though. . . . Was your father an expert, Mr. Kenting?"

"Oh, yes. He studied the subject for many years. He was very proud of this gem-room, as he called it."

"Ah!"

Kenting shot the other a peculiar, shrewd look but said nothing; and Vance at once followed Heath toward the wide stairway.

212

CHAPTER 3

The Ransom Note
Wednesday, July 20; 11 a.m.

As we entered Kaspar Kenting's bedroom, Captain Dubois and Detective Bellamy were just preparing to leave it.

"I don't think there's anything for you, Sergeant," Dubois reported to Heath after his respectful greetings to Markham. "Just the usual kind of marks and smudges you'd find in any bedroom—and they all check up with the finger-prints on the silver toilet set and the glass in the bathroom. Can't be any one else's finger-prints except the guy what lives here. Nothing new anywhere."

"And the window-sill?" asked Heath with desperate hopefulness.

"Not a thing, Sarge,—absolutely not a thing," Dubois replied. "And I sure went over it carefully. If any one went out that window during the night, they certainly wiped it clean, or else wore gloves and was mighty careful. And there's just the kind of finish on that window-sill—that old polished ivory finish—that'll take finger-prints like smoke-paper. . . . Anyhow, I may have picked up a stray print here and there that'll check with something we've got in the files. I'll let you know more about it, of course, when we've developed and enlarged what we got."

The Sergeant seemed greatly disappointed.

"I'll be wanting you later for the ladder," he told Dubois, shifting the long black cigar from one corner of his mouth to the other. "I'll get in touch with you when we're ready."

"All right, Sergeant." Dubois picked up his small black case. "That'll be a tough job though. Don't make it too late in the afternoon—I'll want all the light I can get." And he waved a friendly farewell to Heath and departed, followed by Bellamy.

Kaspar Kenting's bedroom was distinctly old-fashioned, and conventional in the extreme. The furniture was shabby and worn. A wide Colonial bed of mahogany stood against the south wall, and there was a mahogany chest of drawers, with a hanging mirror over it, near the entrance to the room. Several easy chairs stood here and there about the room, and a faded flower-patterned carpet covered the floor. In one corner at the front of the room was a small writing-table on which stood a French telephone.

There were two windows in the room, one at the front of the house, overlooking the street; the other was in the east wall, and I recognized it at once as the window to which Mrs. Kenting said she had run in her fright. It was thrown wide open, with the Venetian blind drawn up to the top, and the outside shutters were invisible from where we stood; whereas the front window was half closed, with its blind drawn half-way down. At the rear of the room, to the right of the bed, was a door, now wide open. Beyond it another bedroom, similar to the one in which we stood, was identifiable: it was obviously Mrs. Kenting's boudoir. Between Kaspar Kenting's bed and the east wall two narrower doors led into the bathroom and a closet respectively.

The electric lights were still burning with a sickly illumination in the old-fashioned crystal chandelier hanging from the centre of the ceiling, and in the standard modern fixture near the head of the bed.

Vance looked about him with seeming indifference; but I knew that not a single detail of the setting escaped him. His first words were directed to the missing man's wife.

"When you came in here this morning, Mrs. Kenting, was this hall door locked or bolted?"

The woman looked uncertain and faltered in her answer.

"I—I—really, I can't remember. It must have been unlocked, or else I would probably have noticed it. I went out through the door when the coffee was ready, and I don't recall unlocking it."

Vance nodded understandingly.

"Yes, yes; of course," he murmured. "A deliberate act like unlocking a door would have made a definite mental impression on you. Simple psychology. . . ."

"But I really don't know, Mr. Vance. . . . You see," she added hurriedly, "I was so upset. . . . I wanted to get out of this room."

"Oh, quite. Wholly natural. But it really doesn't matter." Vance dismissed the subject. Then he went to the open window and looked down at the ladder.

As he did so Heath took from his pocket a knife such as boy scouts use, and pried loose the thumbtack which held a soiled and wrin-

214

kled sheet of paper to the broad window-sill. He picked up the paper gingerly and handed it to Markham. The District Attorney took it and looked at it, his face grim and troubled. I glanced over his shoulder as he read it. The paper was of the ordinary typewriter quality and had been trimmed irregularly at the edges to disguise its original size. On it were pasted words and separate characters in different sizes and styles of type, apparently cut from a newspaper. The uneven lines, crudely put together, read:

> If you want him back safe price will be 50 thousands $ otherwise killed will let you no ware & when to leave money later.

This ominous communication was signed with a cabalistic signature consisting of two interlocking uneven squares which were outlined with black ink. (I am herewith including a copy of the ransom note which was found that morning at the Kenting home.)

Vance had turned back to the room, and Markham handed him the note. Vance glanced at it, as if it were of little interest to him, and read it through quickly, with the faint suggestion of a cynical smile.

"Really, y' know, Markham old dear, it isn't what you could possibly term original. It's been done so many times before."

He was about to return the paper to Markham when he suddenly drew his hand back and made a new examination of the note. His eyes grew serious and clouded, and the smile faded from his lips. "Interestin' signature," he murmured. He took out his monocle and, carefully adjusting it, scrutinized the paper closely. "Made with a Chinese pencil," he announced, "—a Chinese brush—held vertically—and with China ink. . . . And those small squares . . ." His voice trailed off.

"Sure!" Sergeant Heath slapped his thigh and puffed vigorously at his cigar. "Same as the holes like I've seen in Chinese money."

"Quite so, Sergeant." Vance was still studying the cryptic signature. "Not illuminatin', however. But worth remembering." He returned his monocle to his waistcoat pocket and gave the paper back to Markham. "Not an upliftin' case, old dear. . . . Let's stagger about a bit. . . ."

He moved to the chest of drawers and adjusted his cravat before the mirror: then he smoothed back his hair and flicked an imaginary speck of dust from the left lapel of his coat. Markham glowered, and Heath made an expressive grimace of disgust.

"By the by, Mrs. Kenting," Vance asked casually, "is your husband, by any chance, bald?"

"Of course not," she answered indignantly. "What makes you ask that?"

"Queer—very queer," murmured Vance. "All the necess'ry toilet articles are in place on the top of this low-boy except a comb."

"I—don't understand," the woman returned in amazement. She moved swiftly across the room and stood beside Vance. "Why, the comb is gone!" she exclaimed in a tone of bewilderment. "Kaspar always kept it right here." And she pointed to a vacant place on the faded silk covering of what had obviously served Kaspar Kenting as a dresser.

"Most extr'ordin'ry. Let's see whether your husband's toothbrush is also missing. Do you know where he kept it?"

"In the bathroom, of course,"—Mrs. Kenting seemed frightened and breathless—"in a little rack beside the medicine cabinet. I'll see." As she spoke she turned and went quickly toward the door nearest the east wall. She pushed it open and stepped into the bathroom. After a moment she rejoined us.

"It's not there," she remarked dejectedly. "It isn't where it should be—and I've looked in the cabinet for it too."

"That's quite all right," Vance returned. "Do you remember what clothes your husband was wearing last night when he went to the opening of the casino in New Jersey with Mr. Quaggy?"

"Why, he wore evening dress, of course," the woman answered without hesitation. "I mean, he wore a tuxedo."

Vance walked quickly across the room and, opening the door beside the bathroom, looked into the narrow clothes closet. After a brief inspection of its contents he turned and again addressed Mrs. Kenting who now stood near the open east window, her hands clasped on her breast, and her eyes wide with apprehension.

"But his dinner jacket is hanging here in the closet, Mrs. Kenting. Has he more than one? . . ."

The woman shook her head vaguely.

"And I say, I suppose that Mr. Kenting wore the appropriate evening oxfords with his dinner coat."

"Naturally," the woman said.

"Amazin'," murmured Vance. "There are a pair of evening oxfords standin' neatly on the floor of the closet, and the soles are dampish—it was rather wet out last night, don't y' know, after the rain."

Mrs. Kenting moved slowly across the room to where Kenyon Kenting was standing and put her arm through his, seeming to lean against him. Then she said in a low voice, "I really don't understand, Mr. Vance."

Vance gave the woman and her brother-in-law a thoughtful glance and stepped inside the closet. But he turned back to the room in a moment and once more addressed Mrs. Kenting.

"Are you familiar with your husband's wardrobe?" he asked.

"Of course, I am," she returned with an undertone of resentment. "I help him select the materials for all his clothes."

"In that case," Vance said politely, "you can be of great assistance to me if you will glance through this closet and tell me whether anything is missing."

Mrs. Kenting withdrew her arm from that of her brother-in-law and, with a dazed and slightly startled expression, joined Vance at the clothes closet. As he took a step to one side, she turned her back to him and gave her attention to the row of hangers. Then she faced him with a puzzled frown.

"His Glen Urquhart suit is missing," she said. "It's the one he generally wears when he goes away for a week-end or a short trip."

"Very interestin'," Vance murmured. "And is it possible for you to tell me what shoes he may have substituted for his evening oxfords?"

The woman's eyes narrowed, and she looked at Vance with dawning comprehension.

"Yes!" she said, and immediately swung about to inspect the shoe rack in the closet. After a moment she again turned to Vance with a look of bewilderment in her eyes. "One pair of his heavy tan bluchers are not here," she announced in a hollow, monotonous tone. "That's what Kaspar generally wears with his Glen Urquhart."

Vance bowed graciously and muttered a conventional "thank-you," as Mrs. Kenting returned slowly to Kenyon Kenting and stood rigid and wide-eyed beside him.

Vance turned back into the closet and it was but a minute before he came out and walked to the window. Between his thumb and forefinger he held a small cut gem—a ruby, I thought—which he examined against the light.

"Not a genuine ruby," he murmured. "Merely a balas-ruby—the two are often confused. A necess'ry item, to be sure, for a representative collection of gem-stones, but of little worth in itself. . . . By the by, Mrs. Kenting, I found this in the outer side-pocket of your husband's dinner jacket. I took the liberty of ascertaining whether he had transferred the contents of his pockets when he changed his clothes after returning home last night. This bit of balas-ruby was all I found. . . ."

He looked at the stone again and placed it carefully in his waistcoat pocket. Then he took out another cigarette and lighted it slowly and thoughtfully.

"Another thing that would interest me mildly," he remarked, looking vaguely before him, "is what kind of pyjamas Mr. Kenting wears."

"Shantung silk," Mrs. Kenting asserted, stepping suddenly forward. "I just gave him a new supply on his birthday." She was looking directly at Vance, but now her eyes shifted quickly to the bed.

"There's a pair on—" She left the sentence unfinished, and her pale eyes opened still wider. "They're not there!" she exclaimed excitedly.

"No. As you say. Bed neatly turned down. Slippers in place. Glass of orange juice on the night-stand. But no pyjamas laid out. I did notice the omission. A bit curious. But it may have been an oversight . . ."

"No," the woman interrupted emphatically. "It was not an oversight. I placed his pyjamas at the foot of the bed myself, as I always do."

"Thin Shantung?" Vance asked, without looking at her.

"Yes—the sheerest summer-weight."

"Might easily be rolled up and placed in a pocket?"

The woman nodded vaguely. She was now staring at Vance.

"What do you mean?" she asked. "Tell me, what is it?"

218

"I really don't know." Vance spoke with kindliness. "I'm merely observing things. There is no answer as yet. It's most puzzlin'."

Markham had been standing in silence near the door, watching Vance with grim curiosity. Now he spoke.

"I see what you're getting at, Vance," he said. "The situation is damnably peculiar. I don't know just how to take it. But, at any rate, if the indications are correct, I think we can safely assume that we are not dealing with inhuman criminals. When they came here and took Mr. Kenting to be held for ransom, they at least permitted him to get dressed, and to take with him two or three of the things a man misses most when he's away from home."

"Yes, yes. Of course." Vance spoke without enthusiasm. "Most kind of them—eh, what? If true."

"If true?" repeated Markham aggressively. "What else have you in mind?"

"My dear Markham!" protested Vance mildly. "Nothing whatever. Mind an utter blank. Evidence points in various directions. Whither go we?"

"Well, anyway," put in Sergeant Heath, "I don't see that there's any reason to worry about any harm coming to the fella. It looks to me like the guys who did the job were only after the money."

"It could be, of course, Sergeant." Vance nodded. "But I think it is a bit early to jump to conclusions." He gave Heath a significant look under drooped eyelids, and the Sergeant merely shrugged his shoulders and said no more.

Fleel had been watching and listening attentively, with a shrewd, judicial air.

"I think, Mr. Vance," he said, "I know what is in your mind. Knowing the Kentings as well as I do, and knowing the circumstances in this household for a great number of years, I can assure you that it would be no shock to either of them if you were to state exactly what you think regarding this situation."

Vance looked at the man for several seconds with the suggestion of an amused smile. At length he said: "Really, y' know, Mr. Fleel, I don't know exactly what I do think."

"I beg to differ with you, sir," the lawyer returned in a court-room manner. "And from my personal knowledge—the result of my many years of association with the Kenting family—I know that it would be heartening—I might even say, an act of mercy—if you stated frankly that you believe, as I am convinced you do, that Kaspar planned this *coup* himself for reasons that are only too obvious."

Vance looked at the man with a slightly puzzled expression and then said noncommittally: "If you believe that to be the case, Mr. Fleel, what procedure would you suggest be followed? You have known the young man for a long time and are possibly in a position to know how best to handle him."

"Personally," answered Fleel, "I think it is about time Kaspar should be taught a rigorous lesson. And I think we shall never have a better opportunity. If Kenyon agrees, and is able to provide this preposterous sum, I would be heartily in favour of following whatever further instructions are received, and then letting the law take its course on the ground's of extortion. Kaspar must be taught his lesson." He turned to Kenting. "Don't you agree with me, Kenyon?"

"I don't know just what to say," Kenting returned in an obvious quandary. "But somehow I feel that you are right. However, remember that we have Madelaine to consider."

Mrs. Kenting began crying softly and dabbing her eyes.

"Still," she demurred, "Kaspar may not have done this terrible thing at all. But if he did . . ."

Fleel swung round again to Vance. "Don't you see what I meant when I asked you to state frankly your belief? It would, I am sure, greatly relieve Mrs. Kenting's anxiety, even though she thought her husband was guilty of having planned this whole frightful affair."

"My dear sir!" returned Vance. "I would be glad to say anything which might relieve Mrs. Kenting's anxiety regarding the fate of her husband. But I assure you that at the present moment the evidence does not warrant extending the comfort of any such belief, either to you or to any member of the Kenting family. . . ."

At this moment there was an interruption. At the hall door appeared a short, middle-aged man with a sallow moon-like face, sullen in expression. Scant, colourless blond hair lay in straight long strands across his bulging pate, in an unsuccessful effort to cover up his partial baldness. He wore thick-lensed rimless glasses through which one of his watery blue eyes looked somehow different from the other, and he stared at us as if he resented our presence. He had on a shabby butler's livery which was too big for him and emphasized his awkward posture. A cringing and subservient self-effacement marked his general attitude despite his air of insolence.

"What is it, Weem?" Mrs. Kenting asked, with no more than a glance in the man's direction.

"There is a gentleman—an officer—at the front door," the butler answered in a surly tone, "who says he wants to see Sergeant Heath."

"What's his name?" snapped Heath, eyeing the butler with belligerent suspicion.

The man looked at Heath morosely and answered, "He says his name is McLaughlin."

Heath nodded curtly and looked up at Markham.

"That's all right, Chief," he said. "McLaughlin was the man on this beat last night, and I left word at the Bureau to send him up here as soon as they could locate him. I thought he might know something, or maybe he saw something, that would give us a line on what happened here last night." Then he turned back to the butler. "Tell the officer to wait for me. I'll be down in a few minutes."

"Just a moment, Weem,—have I the name right?" Vance put in. "You're the butler here, I understand."

The man inclined his head.

"Yes, sir," he said, in a low rumbling voice.

"And your wife is the cook, I believe?"

"Yes, sir."

"What time did you and your wife go to bed last night?"

The butler hesitated a moment, and then looked shiftily at Mrs. Kenting, but her back was to him.

He transferred his weight from one foot to the other before he answered Vance.

"About eleven o'clock. Mr. Kenting had gone out, and Mrs. Kenting said she would not need me any more after ten o'clock."

"Your quarters are at the rear of the third floor, I believe?"

"Yes," the man returned with an abrupt, stiff nod.

"I say, Weem," Vance went on, "did either you or your wife hear anything unusual in the house, after you had gone to your quarters?"

The man again shifted his weight.

"No," he answered. "Everything was quiet until I went to sleep—and I didn't wake up till Mrs. Kenting rang for coffee around six."

"Then you didn't hear Mr. Kenting return to the house—or any one else moving about the house between eleven o'clock last night and six this morning?"

"No, nobody—I was asleep."

"That's all, Weem." Vance nodded curtly and turned away. "You'd better take the Sergeant's message to Officer McLaughlin."

The butler shuffled away lackadaisically.

"I think," Vance said to Heath, "it was a good idea to get McLaughlin. . . . There's really nothing more to be done up here just now. Suppose we go down and find out what he can tell us."

"Right!" And the Sergeant started toward the door, followed by Vance, Markham, and myself.

Vance paused leisurely just before reaching the door and turned to the small writing-table at the front of the room, on which the telephone stood. He regarded it contemplatively as he approached it. Opening the two shallow drawers, he peered into them. He took up the bottle of ink which stood at the rear of the table, just under the low stationery rack, and read the label. Setting the ink-bottle back in its place, he turned to the small wastepaper basket beside the table and bent over it.

When he rose he asked Mrs. Kenting:

"Does your husband do his writing at this table?"

"Yes, always," the woman answered, staring at Vance with a puzzled frown.

"And never anywhere else?"

The woman shook her head slowly.

"Never," she told him. "You see, he has very little correspondence, and that writing-table was always more than adequate for his needs."

"But did he never need any paste or mucilage?" Vance asked. "I don't see any here."

"Paste?" Mrs. Kenting appeared still more puzzled. "Why, no. As a matter of fact, I don't believe there's any in the house. . . . But why—why do you ask?"

Vance looked up at the woman and smiled at her somewhat sympathetically.

"I'm merely trying to learn the truth about everything, and I beg that you forgive any questions which seem irrelevant."

The woman made no reply, and Vance again went toward the door where Markham and Heath and I were waiting, and we all went out into the hall.

As we reached the narrow landing half-way down the stairs, Markham suddenly stopped, letting Heath proceed on his way. He took Vance by the arm, detaining him.

"See here, Vance," he said aggressively, but in a subdued tone, so that no one in the room from which we had just come should overhear him. "This kidnapping doesn't strike me as being entirely on the level. And I don't believe you yourself think that it is."

"Oh, my Markham!" deplored Vance. "Art thou a mind-reader?"

"Drop that," continued Markham angrily. "Either the kidnappers have no intention of harming young Kenting, or else—as Fleel suggests—Kenting staged the whole affair and kidnapped himself."

"I am waiting patiently for the question I fear is *en route*," sighed Vance with resignation.

"What I want to know," Markham went on doggedly, "is why you refused to offer any hope, or to admit the possibility of either of these hypotheses, when you know damn well that the mere expression of such an opinion by you would have mitigated the apprehensions of both Mrs. Kenting and the young fellow's brother."

Vance heaved a deep sigh and gazed at Markham a moment with a look of mock commiseration.

"Really, y' know, Markham," he said lightly, but with a certain seriousness, "you're a most admirable character, but you're far too naive for this unscrupulous world. Both you and your legal friend, Fleel, are quite wrong in your suppositions. I assure you, don't y' know, that I am not sufficiently cruel to extend false hopes to any one."

"What do you mean by that, Vance?" Markham demanded.

"My word, Markham! I can mean only one thing."

Vance continued to gaze at the District Attorney with sympathetic affection and lowered his voice.

"The chappie, I fear, is already dead."

CHAPTER 4

A Startling Declaration
Wednesday, July 20; 11:45 a.m.

There was something as startling as it was ominous about Vance's astonishing words. However, even in the dim light of the stairway I could see the serious expression on his face, and the finality of his tone convinced me that there was little or no doubt in his mind as to the truth of his words regarding Kaspar Kenting's fate.

Markham was stunned for a moment, but he was, I could see, frankly sceptical. The various bits of evidence uncovered in Kaspar Kenting's room seemed to point indisputably toward a very definite conclusion, which was quite the reverse of the conclusion which Vance had evidently reached. And I was sure that Markham felt as I did about it, and that he was as much surprised and confused as I at Vance's amazing statement. Markham did not relinquish his hold on Vance's arm. He apparently recovered his poise almost immediately and spoke in a hoarse undertone.

"You have a reason for saying that, Vance?"

"Tut, tut, my dear fellow," Vance returned lightly "This is neither the place nor the time to discuss the matter. I'll be quite willin' to point out all the obvious evidence to you later on. We are not dealing here with surface indications—those are quite consistent with the pattern which has been so neatly cut out for us. We are dealing with falsifications and subtleties; and I abhor them. . . . We'd better wait a while, don't y' know. At the moment I am most anxious to hear what McLaughlin has to say to the Sergeant. Let's descend and listen, what?"

Markham shrugged, gave Vance a nettled look, and relaxed his grip on the other's arm.

"Have it your own way," he grumbled. "Anyway," he added stubbornly, "I think you're wrong."

"It could be, of course," returned Vance with a nod. "Really, I'd like to believe it."

Slowly he went down the remaining steps to the lower hallway. Markham and I followed in silence.

McLaughlin, a heavy-footed Irishman, was just entering the drawing-room in answer to a peremptory beckoning finger from the Sergeant, who had preceded him. The officer looked overgrown and abnormally muscular in his tight civilian suit of blue serge. I caught a whimsical look in Vance's eyes as his glance followed the man through the open sliding doors.

Weem was just closing the street door, with his sullen, indifferent manner. A moment after we had reached the lower hallway, he turned and, without a glance in our direction as he passed us, went swiftly but awkwardly toward the rear of the house. Vance watched him pass from our line of vision, shook his head musingly, and then went toward the drawing-room.

McLaughlin (whom I remembered from the famous case of Alvin Benson,[1] when he came to that fateful house on West 48th Street, to report the presence of a mysterious grey Cadillac) was just about to speak to the Sergeant when he heard us enter the drawing-room. Recognizing Markham, he saluted respectfully and stepped to one side, facing us and waiting for orders.

"McLaughlin," Heath began—his tone carried that official gruffness he always displayed to his inferior officers, much to Vance's amusement—"something damn wrong happened in this house last night—or maybe it was early this morning, to be more exact. What time are you relieved from your beat here?"

"Regular time—eight o'clock," answered the man. "I was just fixing to go to bed an hour ago when the Inspector—"

"All right, all right," snapped Heath. "I ordered the Department to send you up. We need a report.—Listen: where were you around six o'clock this morning?"

"Doing my duty, sir," the officer assured Heath earnestly; "walking down the other side of the street opposite here, makin' my regular rounds."

"Did you see anybody, or anything, that looked suspicious?" demanded the Sergeant, thrusting his jaw forward belligerently.

The man started slightly and squinted as if trying to recall something.

"I did, at that, Sergeant!" he said. "Only I wouldn't say as how it

---

1. *The Benson Murder Case*, 1926.

was suspicious at the time, although the idea passed through my mind. But there wasn't any cause to take action."

"What was it, McLaughlin? Shoot everything, whether you think it's important or not."

"Well, Sergeant, a coupé—it was a dirty green colour—pulled up on this side of the street along about that time. There were two men in it, and one of the guys got out and opened the hood and took a look at the engine. I came across the street and gave the car the once-over. But everything seemed on the up-and-up, and I didn't bother 'em. Anyhow, I stood there and watched, and pretty soon the driver got in and the coupé drove away. When it went down the block toward Columbus Avenue, the exhaust was open.... Well, Sergeant, there was nothing I could do about it then, so I went back across the street and walked on up to Broadway."

"That all you noticed?"

"No, it ain't, Sergeant." McLaughlin was looking a little uncomfortable. "I was just coming round the corner from Central Park West, back into 86th Street again, about twenty minutes later, when the same coupé went by me like hell—only, this time it was headed east instead of west—and it turned into the park—"

"How do you know it was the same coupé, McLaughlin?"

"Well, I ain't takin' no oath on it, Sergeant," the officer answered; "but it was the same kinda car, and the same dirty-green colour, and the exhaust was still open. And there was two guys in it, just like before, and the driver looked to me like the same big, smooth-faced guy who had his head stuck in the hood when I first crossed the street to look the situation over." McLaughlin took a deep breath and gave the Sergeant an apprehensive look, as if he expected a reprimand.

"You didn't see or hear anything else?" growled Heath. "It musta been pretty light at that time of the morning, with the sun up."

"Not another thing, Sergeant," the officer asserted, with obvious relief. "When I first seen the car I was headed toward Columbus; and I went on down to Broadway, and then swung round through 87th Street to Central Park West and over again on 86th. As I says, it took me about twenty minutes."

"Exactly where was that coupé when you first got a squint at it?"

"Right along the curb, about a hundred feet up the street from here, toward the park."

"Why didn't you ask some questions of them guys in the car?"

"I told you before, there was nothing suspicious about 'em—not until they went by me, going in the other direction. When I first seen 'em I thought they was just a couple of bums goin' home from a joy-ride. They was quiet and polite enough, and didn't act like trouble. These guys was plenty sober, and they was total strangers to me. There wasn't no reason to interfere with 'em—honest to God!"

Heath thought for a moment and puffed on his cigar.

"Which way did the car go when it entered the park?"

"Well, Sergeant, it went into the transverse, as if it was headed for the east side. Even if I'd wanted to grab the gorillas I wouldn'ta had time. Before I coulda got the call-box on the Avenue and talked to the fella over there, the car woulda been to hell and gone. And there was no car or taxi anywhere round that I coulda chased 'em in. Anyway, I figured they was on the level."

Heath turned with annoyance and paced impatiently up and down the room.

"I say, officer," put in Vance, "were both occupants of the coupé white men?"

"Sure they was, sir." The officer answered emphatically, but with an air of deference which he had not shown to the Sergeant. Vance was standing beside Markham, and McLaughlin must have assumed that Vance was speaking for the District Attorney, as it were.

"And couldn't there have been a third man in the coupé?" Vance proceeded. "A smaller man, let us say, whom you didn't see—on his knees, and hidden from view, perhaps?"

"Well, there mighta been, sir,—I ain't swearin' there wasn't. I didn't open either one of the doors and look in. But there was plenty of room in the car for him to be sittin' up. Why should he be lying on the floor?"

"I haven't the remotest idea—except that he might have been hiding because he didn't wish to be seen," Vance returned apathetically.

"Gosh!" muttered McLaughlin. "You think there was three men in that car?"

"Really, McLaughlin, I don't know," Vance drawled. "It would simplify matters if we knew there had been three men in the car. I crave a small pussy-footed fellow."

The Sergeant had stopped his pacing across the room and now stood near the desk, listening to Vance with an amused interest.

"I don't getcha at all, Mr. Vance," he muttered respectfully. "Two tough guys is enough for any snatch."

"Oh, quite, Sergeant. As you say. Two are quite sufficient," Vance returned somewhat cryptically. Again he addressed himself to McLaughlin. "By the by, officer, did you, by any chance, stumble upon a ladder during your nocturnal circuit in these parts last night?"

"I seen a ladder, if that's what you mean," the man admitted. "It was leanin' up against that maple tree in the garden out here. I noticed it when it began to get light. But I figured it was only being used to prune the tree, or something. There certainly wasn't any use in reportin' a ladder in a gent's yard, was there?"

"Oh, no," Vance assured him indifferently. "Silly idea, going about reportin' ladders—eh, what? . . . That ladder's still in the yard, officer; only, this morning it was restin' up against the house, under an open window."

"Honest to God?" McLaughlin's eyes grew bigger. "I hope it was O.K. not to report it."

"Oh, quite," Vance encouraged him. "It wouldn't have done a particle of good, anyway. Some one, don't y' know, moved it from the tree and placed it against the house while you were strollin' up Broadway and round 87th Street. Probably doesn't mean anything of any particular importance, however. . . . I say, did you ever notice a ladder in this yard before?"

The man shook his head ponderously.

"No, sir," he said, with a certain vague emphasis. "Can't say that I ever have. They generally keep that yard looking pretty neat and nice."

"Thanks awfully." Vance sauntered to the sofa and sat down lazily, stretching his legs out before him. It was obvious he had no other questions to put to the officer.

Heath straightened up and took the cigar from his mouth.

"That's all, McLaughlin. Much obliged for coming down. Go on home and hit the hay. I may, and may not, want to see you again later."

The officer saluted half-heartedly and went toward the door.

"Look here, Sergeant," he said, halting and turning around. "Do you mind telling me what happened here last night? You got me worryin' about that coupé."

"Oh, nothing much happened, I guess. A phoney snatch of some kind. It don't look serious, but we have to check up. Young fella named Kaspar Kenting ain't anywhere abouts. And there was a cockeyed ransom note."

The officer seemed speechless for a moment. Then he half gasped.

"Honest? Jeez!"

"Do you know him, McLaughlin?"

"Sure I know him. I see him lots of times coming home at all hours of the mornin'. Half the time he's pie-eyed."

228

Heath showed no further inclination to talk, and McLaughlin went lumbering from the room. A moment later the front door shut noisily after him.

"What now, Mr. Vance?" Heath was again resting his weight against the desk, puffing vigorously on his cigar.

Vance drew in his legs, as if with great effort, and sighed.

"Oh, much more, Sergeant," he yawned in answer. "You haven't the faintest idea of how much I'd really like to learn about a number of things. . . ."

"But see here, Vance," interrupted Markham, "I first want to know what you meant by that statement you made as we were coming down the stairs. I can't see it at all, and I'd bet money that fellow Kaspar is as safe as you or I."

"I'm afraid you'd lose your wager, old dear."

"But all the evidence points—" began Markham.

"Please, oh, please, Markham," implored Vance. "Must we necessarily lean wherever a finger points? I say, let's get the completed picture first. Then we can speak with more or less certainty about the indications. Can't a johnnie hazard a guess without being quizzed by the great Prosecutor for the Common People?"

"Damn it, Vance!" Markham returned angrily; "drop the persiflage and get down to business. I want to know why you said what you did on the stairs, in the face of all the evidence to the contrary. Are you in possession of any facts to which I have not had access?"

"Oh, no—no," replied Vance mildly, stretching out still further in the chair. "You've seen and heard everything I have. Only, we interpret the findin's in different ways."

"All right." Markham made an effort to curb his impatience. "Let's hear how you interpret these facts."

"Pardon me, Chief," put in Heath; "I didn't hear what Mr. Vance said to you on the stairs. I don't know what his ideas on the case are."

Markham took the cigar from his mouth and looked at the Sergeant.

"Mr. Vance doesn't believe that Kaspar Kenting was kidnapped merely for money or that he may have walked out and staged the kidnapping himself. He said he thinks that the fellow is already dead."

Heath spun round abruptly to Vance.

"The hell you say!" he exclaimed. "How in the name of God did you get such an idea, Mr. Vance?"

Vance smoked a moment before replying. Then he spoke as if the explanation were of no importance:

"My word, Sergeant! It seems sufficiently indicated."

He paused again and looked back meditatively to the District Attorney, who was standing before him, teetering impatiently on his toes.

"Do you really think, Markham, that your plotting Kaspar would have gone to the Jersey casino to indulge in a bit of gamblin' on his big night—that is to say, on the night he intended to carry out his grand *coup* involvin' fifty thousand dollars?"

"And why not?" Markham wanted to know.

"It's quite obvious this criminal undertaking was carefully prepared in advance. The note itself is sufficient evidence of this, with its letters and words painstakingly cut out and all neatly pasted on a piece of disguised paper."

"The criminal undertaking, as you call it, need not necessarily have been prepared very far in advance," objected Markham. "Kaspar would have had time to do his cutting and pasting when he returned from the casino."

"Oh, no, I don't think so," Vance returned at once. "I took a good look at the desk and the wastepaper basket. No evidence whatever of such activity. Moreover, the johnnie's phone call in the wee hours of the morning shows a certain amount of expectation on his part of getting the matter of his financial difficulties settled."

"Go on," said Markham, as Vance paused once more.

"Very good," continued Vance. "Why should Kaspar Kenting have taken three hours to change to street clothes after he had returned from his pleasant evening of desult'ry gambling? A few minutes would have sufficed. And another question: Why should he wait until bright daylight before going forth? The darkness would have been infinitely safer and better suited to his purpose."

"How do you know he didn't go much earlier—before it was daylight?" demanded Markham.

"But, my dear fellow," explained Vance, "the ladder was still leanin' against the tree around dawn, when McLaughlin saw it, and therefore was not placed against the window until after sun-up. I'm quite sure that, had Kaspar planned a disappearance, he would have placed the ladder at the window ere he departed—eh, what?"

"I see what you mean, Mr. Vance," Heath threw in eagerly. "And Mrs. Kenting herself told us that she heard some one in the room at six o'clock this morning."

"True, Sergeant; but that's not the important thing," Vance answered casually. "As a matter of fact, I don't think it was Kaspar at all whom Mrs. Kenting says she heard in her husband's room at that hour this morning. . . . And, by the by, Markham, here's still another question

230

to be considered: Why was the communicatin' door between Kaspar's room and his wife's left unlocked, if the gentleman contemplated carrying out a desperate and important plot that night? He would certainly not have left that door unlocked if he planned any such action. He would have guarded against any unwelcome intrusion on the part of his wife, who had merely to turn the knob and walk in and spoil all the fun, as it were. . . . And, speakin' of the door, you remember the lady opened it at six, right after hearin' some one walkin' in the room in what she described as soft slippers. But when she went into the room there was no one there. Ergo: Whoever it was she heard must have left the room hurriedly when she first knocked and called to her husband. And don't forget that it is his heavy blucher shoes that are gone—not his slippers. If it had been Kaspar she heard, imitatin' a slipper-shod gentleman, and if Kaspar had quickly gone out the hall door and down the front stairs, she would certainly have heard him, as she was very much on the alert at that moment. And, also, if he'd scrambled through the window and down the ladder with his heavy shoes on, he could hardly have done so without a sound. But the tellin' question in this connection is: Why, if the soft-footed person in the master bedroom was Kaspar, did he wait till his wife knocked on the door and called to him before he made a precipitate getaway? He could have left at any time during the three hours after he had come home from his highballs and roulette-playin'. All of which, I rather think, substantiates the assumption that it was another person that the lady heard at six o'clock this morning."

Markham's head moved slowly up and down. His cigar had gone out, but he paid no attention to it.

"I'm beginning to see what you mean, Vance; and I can't say your conclusions leave me happy. But what I want to know is—"

"Just a moment, Markham old dear. Just a wee moment." Vance raised his hand to indicate that he had something further to say. "If it had been Kaspar that Mrs. Kenting heard at six o'clock, he would hardly have had time, before he scooted off at his wife's knock, to collect his comb and toothbrush and pyjamas. Why should the chappie have bothered to take them, in the first place? True, they are things he could well make use of on his hypothetical jaunt for the purpose of getting hold of brother Kenyon's lucre, but he would hardly go to that trouble on so vital and all-important a venture,—the toilet articles would be far too trivial and could easily be bought wherever he was going, if he was finicky about such details. Furthermore, if so silly a plot had been planned by him he would have equipped himself sur-

231

reptitiously beforehand and would have had the beautifyin' accessories waitin' for him wherever he had decided to go, rather than grabbin' them up at the last minute."

Markham made no comment, and after a moment or two Vance resumed.

"Carryin' the supposition a bit forrader, he would have realized that the absence of these necess'ry articles would be highly suspicious and would point too obviously to the impression he would have wished to avoid—namely, his own wilful participation in the attempt to extort the fifty thousand dollars. I'd say, y' know, that these items for the gentleman's toilet were collected and taken away—in order to give just this impression—by the soft-footed person heard by Mrs. Kenting. . . . No, no, Markham. The comb and the toothbrush and the pyjamas and the shoes are only textural details—like the cat, the shawl-fringe, the posies, the ribbon, and the bandanna in Manet's *Olympia*. . . ."

"Manufactured evidence—that's your theory, is it?" Markham spoke without any show of aggressiveness or antagonism.

"Exactly," nodded Vance. "Far too many leadin' clues. Really, the culprit overdid it. An *embarras de richesses*. Whole structure does a bit of topplin' of its own weight. Very thorough. Too dashed thorough. Nothing left to the imagination."

Markham took a few steps up the room, turned, and then walked back.

"You think it's a real kidnapping then?"

"It could be," murmured Vance. "But that doesn't strike me as wholly consistent either. Too many counter-indications. But I'm only advancin' a theory. For instance, if Kaspar was allowed time to change his suit and shoes—as we know he did—he had time to call out, or to make a disturbance of some kind which would have upset all the kind-hearted villain's plans. Hanging up his dinner jacket so carefully, transferring things from his pockets, and putting away his oxfords in the closet, all indicate leisure in the process—a leisure which the kidnappers would hardly have permitted. Kidnappers are not benevolent persons, Markham."

"Well, what *do* you think happened?" Markham asked in a subdued, worried tone.

"Really, I don't know." Vance studied the tip of his cigarette with concern. "We do know, however, that Kaspar had an engagement last night which kept him out until three this morning; and that upon his return here he telephoned to some one and then changed to street clothes. It might therefore be assumed that he made some appointment to be kept between three and six and saw no necessity of going to bed in the interval. This would also account for the leisurely changing of his attire; and it is highly possible he went quietly out through the front door when he fared forth to keep his early-morning rendezvous. Assumin' that this theory is correct, I'd say further that he expected to return anon, for he left all the lights on. And one more thing: I think it safe to assume that the door from his bedroom into the hall was unlocked this morning—otherwise, Mrs. Kenting would have remembered unlocking it when she ordered coffee and went downstairs."

"And even if everything you say is true," argued Markham, "what could have happened to him?"

Vance sighed deeply.

"All we actually know at the moment, my dear Markham," he answered, "is that the johnnie did not come back. He seems to have disappeared. At any rate, he isn't here."

"Even so,"—Markham drew himself up with a slight show of annoyance—"why do you take it for granted that Kaspar Kenting is already dead?"

"I don't take it for granted." Vance, too, drew himself up and spoke somewhat vigorously. "I said merely that I *feared* the johnnie is already dead. If he did not, as it were, kidnap himself, d' ye see, and if he wasn't actually kidnapped as the term is commonly understood, then the chances are he was murdered when he went forth to keep his appointment. His disappearance and the elaborate clues arranged hereabouts to make it appear like a deliberate self-abduction, imply a connection between his appointment and the evidence we observed in his room. Therefore, it's more than likely, don't y' know, that if he were held alive and later released, he could relate enough—whom he had the appointment with, for instance—to lead us to the guilty person or persons. His immediate death would have been the only safe course."

As Vance spoke Heath had come forward and stood close to Markham.

"Your theory, Mr. Vance, sounds reasonable enough the way you tell it," the Sergeant commented doggedly. "But still and all—"

Vance had risen and was breaking his cigarette in an ash tray.

"Why argue about the case, Sergeant," he interrupted, "when, as yet, there is so little evidence to go on? . . . Let's dawdle about a bit longer and learn more about things."

"Learn what, and about what things?" Markham almost barked.

Vance was in one of his most dulcet moods.

"Really, if we knew, Markham, we wouldn't have to learn, would we? But Kenyon Kenting, I ween, harbours a number of fruitful items:—I'm sure a bit of social intercourse with the gentleman would be most illuminatin'. And then there's your friend, Mr. Fleel, the trusted Justinian of the Kenting household: I've a feelin' he might be prevailed upon to suggest a few details here and there and elsewhere. And Mrs. Kenting herself might cast a few more rays of light into the darkness. And let's not overlook old Mrs. Falloway—Mrs. Kenting's mother, y' know—who I think lives here. Exceptional old dowager. I met her once or twice before she became an invalid. Fascinatin' creature, Markham; bulgin' with original ideas, and shrewd no end. And it could be that even the butler Weem would be willin' to spin a yarn or two—he appears displeased and restive enough to give vent to some unflatterin' family confidences. . . . Really, y' know, I think all these seemingly trivial matters should be attended to ere we depart."

"Don't worry about such things, Vance," Markham advised him gravely. "They are all routine matters, and they'll be taken care of at the proper time."

"Oh, Markham—my dear Markham!" Vance was lighting another cigarette. "The present time is always the proper time." He took a few inhalations and blew the smoke forth indolently. "Really, I'm rather interested in the case, don't y' know. It has most amazin' possibilities. And as long as you've deprived me of attendin' the dog show today, I think I'll do a bit of snoopin' here and about."

"All right," Markham acquiesced. "What is it you wish to focus your prodigious powers on first?"

"My word, such flattery!" exclaimed Vance. "I haven't a single pro-digious power—I'm a mere broken reed. But I simply can't bear not to inspect that ladder."

Heath chuckled.

"Well, that's easy, Mr. Vance. Come on round to the yard. No trouble getting in from the street."

And he started energetically toward the front door.

234

CHAPTER 5

On the Rungs of the Ladder
Wednesday, July 20; 12:30 p.m.

We followed the Sergeant through the ponderous front door, down the stone steps, and across the flagstones. The sun was still shining brightly, and there was hardly a cloud in the sky. The light was so brilliant that for a moment it almost blinded me after the dimness of the Kenting interior. The Sergeant led the way thirty or forty feet east, along the sidewalk, until he came to the small gate in the low iron fence which divided the attractively sodded court of the Kenting house from the street. The gate was not on the latch, but stood slightly ajar, and the Sergeant pushed it wide open with his foot.

Heath was first to enter the enclosure, and he walked ahead with arms outstretched, holding us back from a too precipitate intrusion, like a prudent brood-hen guiding her recalcitrant and over-ambitious chicks.

"Don't come too close," he admonished us with a solemn air. "There are footprints at the bottom of the ladder and we gotta save 'em for Cap Jerym's[1] plaster casts."

"Well, well," smiled Vance. "Maybe you'll permit me to come as near as Captain Jerym will have to go to perform his sculpture?"

"Sure." Heath grinned. "But I don't want them footprints interfered with. They may be the best clue we'll get."

"Dear me!" sighed Vance. "As important as all that, Sergeant?"

Heath leaned forward and scowled as Vance stood beside him.

"Look at this one, Mr. Vance,"—and the Sergeant pointed to an impression in the border of the hedge within a foot of where the ladder stood.

"My word!" exclaimed Vance. "I'm abominably flattered by even such consideration as letting me come within viewing distance of

---

1. Captain Anthony P. Jerym, Bertillon expert of the New York Police Department.

235

the bally footprints." Again taking out his monocle he adjusted it carefully and, kneeling down on the lawn, inspected the imprint. He took several moments doing so, and a puzzled frown slowly spread over his face as he carefully scrutinized the mark in the neatly raked soil of the hedge.

"You know, sir, we was lucky," Heath asserted. "It drizzled most of yesterday afternoon, and around about eight o'clock last night it got to raining pretty hard, though it did clear up before midnight."

"Really, Sergeant! I knew it only too well!" Vance did not look up. "I planned to go to the tennis matches at Forest Hills yesterday afternoon, to see young Henshaw[2] play, but I simply couldn't bear the inclement weather." He said nothing more for several moments—his entire interest seemed to be centred on the footprint he was inspecting. At length he murmured without turning: "Rather small footprint here—eh, what?"

"I'll say it is," agreed Heath. "Mighta been a dame. And it looks like it was made with flat slippers of some kind. There's no heel mark."

"No, no heel mark," agreed Vance abstractedly. "As you say, no heel mark. Quite right. Obvious, in fact. Curious. I wonder. . . ."

He leaned closer to the impression in the sod of the hedge, and went on:

"But really, y' know, I shouldn't say the print was made by a slipper—unless, of course, you wish to call a sandal a slipper."

"Is that it, Mr. Vance?" The Sergeant was half contemptuous and half interested.

"Yes, yes; rather plain," Vance returned in a low voice. "Not an ordin'ry sandal, either. A Chinese sandal I'd say. Slightly turned-up tip."

"A Chinese sandal?" Heath's tone was almost one of ridicule now.

"More than likely, don't y' know." Vance rose and brushed the soil from his trousers.

"I suppose you'll be telling us next that this whole case is just another Tong war." Heath evidently did not deem Vance's conclusion worthy of serious consideration.

Vance was still leaning forward, rubbing vigorously at a spot on one knee. He stopped suddenly and, ignoring the Sergeant's raillery, leaned still farther forward.

"And, by Jove! here's another imprint." He pointed with his cigarette to a slight depression in the lawn just at the foot of the ladder.

The Sergeant leaned over curiously.

---

2. The sensational Davis cup winner and America's first seeded player at the time.

"So it is, sir!" he exclaimed, and his tone had become respectful. "I didn't see that one before."

"It really doesn't matter, y' know. Similar to the other one." Vance stepped past Heath and grasped the ladder with both hands.

"Look out, sir!" cautioned Heath angrily. "You'll make finger-prints on that ladder."

Vance relaxed his hold on the ladder momentarily, and turned to Heath with an amused smile.

"I'll at least give Dubois and Bellamy something to work on," he said lightly. "I fear there won't be any other finger-prints on this irrelevant exhibit. And it will be rather difficult to pin the crime on me. I've an unimpeachable alibi. Sittin' at home with Van Dine here, and readin' a bedtime story from Boccaccio."

Heath was spluttering. Before he could answer, Vance turned, grasped the ladder again, and lifted it so that its base was clear of the ground. Then he set it down several inches to the right.

"Really, Sergeant, you have nothing whatever to be squeamish about. Cheer up, and be more trustin'. Consider the lilies, and don't forget that the snail's on the thorn."

"What's lilies and snails gotta do with it?" demanded Heath irritably. "I'm tryin' to tell you—"

Before the Sergeant could protest Vance had thrown his cigarette carelessly away and was moving quickly up the ladder, rung by rung. When he was about three-quarters of the way up he stopped and made his way down. When he had descended and stood again on the lawn, he carefully and deliberately lighted another cigarette.

"I'm rather afraid to look and see just what happened. It would be most humiliatin' if I were wrong. However. . . ."

Again he lifted the ladder and moved it still farther to the right. Then he went a second time on his knees and inspected the new imprints which the two uprights of the ladder had made in the ground. After a moment he looked studiously at the original imprints of the ladder; and I could see that he was comparing the two sets.

"Very interestin'," he murmured as he rose and turned to Heath.

"What's interesting?" demanded the Sergeant. He again seemed to be nettled by Vance's complete disregard of the risk of making finger-prints on the ladder.

"Sergeant," Vance told him seriously, "the imprints I just made when I mounted the ladder are of practically the same depth as the imprints made by the ladder last night." Vance took a deep puff on his cigarette. "Do you see the significance of the results of that little test of mine?"

Heath corrugated his forehead, pursed his lips, and looked at Vance questioningly.

"Well, Mr. Vance, to tell you the truth—" He hesitated. "I can't say as I do see what it means—except that you've maybe spoiled a lot of good finger-prints."

"It means several other things. And don't stew so horribly about your beloved hypothetical fingerprints." Vance broke the ashes from his cigarette against the ladder, and sat down lazily on the second rung. "*Imprimis*, it means that two men were not on the ladder at the same time last night—or, rather, this morning. Secondly, it means that whoever was on that ladder was a very slight person who could not have weighed over 120 or 130 pounds. Thirdly, it means that Mr. Kaspar Kenting was not kidnapped *via* yon open window at all. . . . Does any of that help?"

"I still can't see it." Heath was holding his cigar meditatively between thumb and forefinger.

"My dear Sergeant!" sighed Vance. "Let us reflect and analyze for a moment. When the ladder was placed against this window between dawn and six o'clock, before the sun had come up, the ground was much softer than it is now, and any weight or pressure on the ladder would have created imprints of a certain depth in the moist sod. At the present time the soil is obviously drier and harder, for the sun has been shining on it for several hours. However, you noted—did you not?—that the ladder sank into the ground—or, rather, made impressions in the ground—when I mounted it, of equal depth with that of the earlier imprints. I have a feelin' that if I had mounted the ladder when the ground was considerably damper the ladder would have gone in deeper—eh, what?"

"I getcha now," blurted Heath. "The guy who went up that ladder early this morning musta been a damn sight lighter than you, Mr. Vance."

"Right-o, Sergeant." Vance smiled musingly. "It was a very small person. And if two persons had been on that ladder—that is, Mr. Kaspar Kenting and his supposed abductor—I rather think the original impressions made by the ladder would have been far deeper."

"Sure they would." Heath was gazing down at the two sets of impressions as if hypnotized.

"Therefore," Vance went on casually, "aren't we justified in assuming that only one person stepped on this ladder early this morning, and that that person was a very slight and fragile human being?"

Heath looked up at Vance with puzzled admiration.

"Yes, sir. But where does that get us?"

"The findings, as it were," continued Vance, "taken in connection with the footprints, seem to tell us that a Chinese gentleman of small stature was the only person who used this ladder. Pure supposition, of course, Sergeant; but I rather opine that—"

"Yes, yes," Markham interrupted. He had been drawing vigorously on his cigar, giving his earnest attention to the demonstration and Vance's subsequent conversation with Heath. He now nodded comprehendingly. "Yes," he repeated. "You see some connection between these footprints and the more-or-less Chinese signature on that ransom note."

"Oh, quite—quite," agreed Vance. "You show amazin' perspicacity. That's precisely what I was thinkin'."

Markham was silent for a moment.

"Any other ideas, Vance?" he demanded somewhat peevishly.

"Oh, no—not a thing, old dear." Vance blew a ribbon of smoke into the air, and rose lackadaisically.

He cast a meditative glance back at the ladder and at the trimmed privet hedge behind it, which ran the full length of the house. He stood motionless for a moment and squinted.

"I say, Markham," he commented in a low voice; "there's something shining there in the hedge. I don't think it's a leaf that's reflecting the light at that one spot."

As he spoke he moved quickly to a point just at the left of where the ladder now stood. He looked down at the small green leaves of the privet for a moment, and then, reaching forward with both hands, he separated the dense foliage and leaned over, as if seeking something.

"Ah! . . . My word!"

As Vance separated the foliage still farther, I saw a silver-backed dressing comb wedged between two closely forked branches of the privet.

Markham, who was standing at an angle to Vance, started forward.

"What is it, Vance?" he demanded.

Vance, without answering him, reached down and retrieving the comb, turned and held it out in the palm of his hand.

"It's just a comb, as you see, old dear," he said. "An ordin'ry comb from a gentleman's dressing set. Ordin'ry, except for the somewhat elaborate scrollwork of the silver back." He glanced at the astonished Heath. "Oh, no need to be upset, Sergeant. The scrolled silver wouldn't take any clear finger-prints, anyway. And I'm quite certain you wouldn't find any, in any event."

"You think that's Kaspar Kenting's missing comb?" asked Markham quickly.

"It could be, of course," nodded Vance. "I rather surmise as much. It was just beneath the open window of the chappie's *boudoir.*"

Heath was shaking his head somewhat shamefacedly.

"How the hell did Snitkin and I miss that?" His tone carried a tinge of regret and self-criticism.

"Oh, cheer up, Sergeant," Vance encouraged him good-naturedly. "You see, it was caught in the hedge before reaching the ground, and was jolly well hidden by the density of the leaves. I happened to be standing at just the right angle to get a glimpse of it through the leaves with the sun on it. . . . I imagine that whoever dropped it couldn't find it either, and, as time was pressin', the curs'ry search was abandoned. Interestin' item—what?" He tucked the comb into his upper waist-coat pocket.

Markham was still scowling, his eyes fixed inquiringly on Vance.

"What do you think about it?" he asked.

"Oh, I'm not thinkin', Markham." Vance started toward the gate. "I'm utterly exhausted. Let's stagger back into the Kenting domicile."

As we entered the front door, Mrs. Kenting, Kenyon Kenting, and Fleel were just descending the stairs.

Vance approached them and asked, "Do any of you happen to know anything about that ladder in the yard?"

"I never saw it before this morning," Mrs. Kenting answered slowly, in a deadened voice.

"Nor I," added her brother-in-law. "I can't imagine where it came from, unless it was brought here last night by the kidnappers."

"And I, of course," said Fleel, "would have no way of knowing anything about any ladders here. I haven't been here for a long time, and I never remember seeing a ladder around the premises before."

"You're quite sure, Mrs. Kenting," pursued Vance, "the ladder doesn't belong here? Might it, perhaps, have been kept somewhere at the rear of the house without your having seen it?" He looked at the woman with a slight frown.

"I'm quite sure it doesn't belong here," she said in the same muf-fled tone of voice. "Had it ever been here, I should have known about it. And, anyway, we have no need of such a ladder."

"Most curious," murmured Vance. "The ladder was resting against the maple tree in your courtyard early this morning when Officer McLaughlin passed the house."

"The maple tree?" Kenyon Kenting spoke with noticeable aston-ishment. "Then it was moved from the maple tree to the side of the house later?"

"Exactly. Obviously the people concerned in this affair made two trips here last night. Very confusin'—what?"

Vance dismissed the subject, and, reaching in his pocket, brought out the comb he had found in the privet hedge, and held it out to the woman.

"By the by, Mrs. Kenting, is this, by any chance, your husband's comb?"

The woman stared at it with frightened eyes.

"Yes, yes!" she exclaimed almost inaudibly. "That's Kaspar's comb. Where did you find it, Mr. Vance,—and what does it mean?"

"I found it in the privet hedge just beneath his window," Vance told her. "But I don't know yet what it means, Mrs. Kenting."

Before the woman could ask further questions Vance turned quickly to Kenyon Kenting and said:

"We should like to have a little chat with you, Mr. Kenting. Where can we go?"

The man looked around as if slightly dazed and undecided.

"I think the den might be the best place," he said. He walked down the hall to a room just beyond the still open entrance to the gem-room, and, throwing the door wide, stepped to one side for us to enter. Mrs. Kenting and Fleel proceeded through the sliding doors into the drawing-room on the opposite side of the hall.

241

CHAPTER 6

$50,000

Wednesday, July 20; 12:45 p.m.

Kenyon Kenting followed us into the den and, closing the door, stepped to a large leather armchair, and sat down uneasily on the edge of it.

"I will be very glad to tell you anything I know," he assured us. Then he added, "But I'm afraid I can be of little help."

"That, of course, remains to be seen," murmured Vance. He had gone to the small bay window and stood looking out with his hands deep in his coat pockets. "First of all, we wish to know just what the financial arrangement is between you and your brother. I understand that when your father died the estate was all left at your disposal, and that whatever money Kaspar Kenting should receive would be subject to your discretion."

Kenting nodded his head repeatedly, as if agreeing; but it was evident that he was thinking the matter over. Finally he said:

"That is quite right. Fleel, however, was appointed the custodian, so to speak, of the estate. And I wish to assure you that not only have I maintained this house for Kaspar, but have given him even more money than I thought was good for him."

"Your brother is a bit of a spendthrift—eh, what?"

"He is very wasteful—and very fond of gambling." Kenting spoke in a guarded semi-resentful tone. "He is constantly making demands on me for his gambling debts. I've paid a great many of them, but I had to draw the line somewhere. He has a remarkable facility for getting into trouble. He drinks far too much. He has always been a very difficult problem—especially in view of the fact that Madelaine, his wife, has to be considered."

"Did you always decide these monet'ry matters entirely by yourself?" Vance asked the man casually. "Or did you confer with Mr. Fleel about them?"

Kenting shot Vance a quick look and then glanced down again.

"I naturally consulted Mr. Fleel on any matters of importance regarding the estate. He is co-executor, appointed by my father. In minor matters this is not necessary, of course; but I do not have a free hand, as the distribution of the money is a matter of joint responsibility; and, as I say, Mr. Fleel has, in a way, complete legal charge of it. But I can assure you that there were never any clashes of opinion on the subject,—Fleel is wholly reasonable and understands the situation thoroughly. I find it an ideal arrangement."

Vance smoked for several moments in silence, while the other man looked vaguely before him. Then Vance turned from the window and sat down in the swivel chair before the old-fashioned roll-top desk of oak at one side of the window.

"When was the last time you saw your brother?" he asked, busying himself with his cigarette.

"The day before yesterday," the man answered promptly. "I generally see him at least three times a week—either here or at my office downtown—there are always minor matters of one kind or another to decide on, and he naturally depends a great deal on my judgment. In fact, the situation is such that even the ordinary household expenses have always been referred to me."

Vance nodded without looking up.

"And did your brother bring up the subject of finances on Monday?"

Kenyon Kenting fidgeted a bit and shifted his position in the chair. He did not answer at once. But at length he said, in a half-hearted tone, "I would prefer not to go into that, inasmuch as I regard it as a personal matter, and I cannot see that it has any bearing on the present situation."

Vance studied the man for a moment.

"That is a point for us to decide, I believe," he said in a peculiarly hard voice. "We should like you to answer the question."

Kenting looked again at Vance and then fixed his eyes on the wall ahead of him.

"If you deem it necessary, of course—" he began. "But I would much prefer to say nothing about it."

"I'm afraid, sir," put in Markham, in his most aggressive official manner, "we must insist that you answer the question."

Kenting shrugged reluctantly and settled back in his chair, joining the tips of his fingers.

"Very well," he said resignedly. "If you insist. On Monday my brother asked me for a large sum of money—in fact, he was persistent about it, and became somewhat hysterical when I refused him."

"Did he state what he required this money for?" asked Vance.

"Oh, yes," the man said angrily. "The usual thing—gambling and unwarranted debts connected with some woman."

"Would you be more specific as to the gambling debts?" pursued Vance.

"Well, you know the sort of thing." Kenting again shifted in his chair. "Roulette, black-jack, the bird-cage, cards—but principally horses. He owed several book-makers some preposterous amount."

"Do you happen to know the names of any of these book-makers?"

"No, I don't." Once more the man glanced momentarily at Vance then lowered his eyes. "Wait—I think one of them had a name something like Hannix."[1]

"Ah! Hannix, eh?" Vance contemplated his cigarette for a few moments. "What was so urgent about this as to produce hysterics?"

"The fact is," the other went on, "Kaspar told me the men were unscrupulous and dangerous, and that he feared for himself if he did not pay them off immediately. He said he had already been threatened."

"That doesn't sound like Hannix," mused Vance. "Hannix looks pretty hard, I know, but he's really a babe at heart. He's a shrewd gentleman, but hardly a vicious one. . . . And I say, Mr. Kenting, what was the nature of your brother's debts in connection with the mysterious lady you mentioned? Jewellery, perhaps?"

The man nodded vigorously.

"Yes, that's just it," he said emphatically.

"Well, well. Everything seems to be running true to form. Your brother's position was not in the least original—what? Gamblin' debts, liquor, and ladies cravin' precious gems. Most conventional, don't y' know." A faint smile played over Vance's lips. "And you denied your brother the money?"

"I had to," asserted Kenting. "The amount would almost have beggared the estate, what with so much tied up in what we've come to call 'frozen assets.' It was far more than I could readily get together at the time, and anyway, I would have had to take the matter up with Fleel, even if I had been inclined to comply with Kaspar's demands. And I knew perfectly well that Fleel would not

---

1. This was the same Mr. Hannix whom Vance had already met both at Bowie and at Empire, and who had acted as Floyd Garden's book-maker before that young man lost his interest in racing as a result of the tragic events related in *The Garden Murder Case*.

approve my doing so. He has a moral as well as legal responsibility, you understand."

Vance took several deep inhalations on his *Régie* and sent a succession of ribbons of blue smoke toward the old discoloured Queen-Anne ceiling.

"Did your brother approach Mr. Fleel about the matter?"

"Yes, he did," the other returned. "Whenever I refuse him anything he goes immediately to Fleel. As a matter of fact, Fleel has always been more sympathetic with Kaspar than I have. But Kaspar's demand this time was too utterly outrageous, and Fleel turned him down as definitely as I did. And—although I don't like to say so—I really think Kaspar was grossly exaggerating his needs. Fleel got the same impression, and mentioned to me over the phone the next morning that he was very angry with Kaspar. He told me, too, that legally he was quite helpless in the matter and could not accommodate Kaspar, even if he had personally wanted to."

"Has Mrs. Kenting any money of her own?" Vance asked unexpectedly.

"Nothing—absolutely nothing!" the man assured him. "She is entirely dependent upon what Kaspar gives her—which, of course, means some part of what I allow him from the estate. Often I think that he does not do the right thing by her and deprives her of many of the things she should have, so that he himself can fritter the money away." A scowl came over the man's face. "But there's nothing I can do about it. I have tried to remonstrate with him, but it's worse than useless."

"In view of this morning's occurrence," suggested Vance, "it may be that your brother was not unduly exaggerating about the necessity for this money."

Kenting became suddenly serious, and his eyes wandered unhappily about the room.

"That is a horrible thought, sir," he said, half under his breath. "But it is one that occurred to me immediately when I arrived here early this morning. And you can be sure it left me uncomfortable."

Vance regarded the man dubiously as he addressed him again.

"When you receive further instructions regarding the ransom money, what do you intend to do about it—that is to say, just what is your feeling in the matter?"

Kenting rose from his chair and stood looking down at the floor. He appeared deeply troubled.

"As a brother," he said slowly, "what can I do? I suppose I must

245

manage somehow to get the money and pay it. I can't let Kaspar be murdered. . . . It's a frightful situation."

"Yes—quite," agreed Vance.

"And then there's Madelaine. I could never forgive myself. . . . I say again, it's a frightful situation."

"Nasty mess. Rather. Still, I have a groggy notion," Vance went on, "that you won't be called upon to pay the ransom money at all. . . . And, by the by, Mr. Kenting, you didn't mention the amount that your brother asked for when you last saw him. Tell me: how much did he want to get him out of his imagin'ry difficulties?"

Kenting raised his head sharply and looked at Vance with a shrewdness he had not hitherto displayed during the interview. Withal, he seemed ill at ease and took a few nervous steps back and forth before replying.

"I was hoping you wouldn't ask me that question," he said regret-fully. "I avoided it purposely, for I am afraid it might create an erroneous impression."

"How much was it?" snapped Markham. "We must get on with this."

"Well, the truth is," Kenting stammered with evident reluctance, "Kaspar wanted fifty thousand dollars. Sounds incredible, doesn't it?" he added apologetically.

Vance leaned back in the swivel chair and looked unseeingly at one of the old etchings over the desk.

"I imagined that was the figure," he murmured. "Thanks awfully, Mr. Kenting. We sha'n't bother you any more just now, except that I should like to know whether Mrs. Kenting's mother, Mrs. Falloway, still lives here in the Purple House."

Kenting seemed surprised at the question.

"Oh, yes," he said with disgruntled emphasis. "She still occupies the front suite on the third floor with her son, Mrs. Kenting's brother. But the woman is crippled now and can get about only with a cane. She rarely is able to come downstairs, and she almost never goes outdoors."

"What about the son?" asked Vance.

"He's the most incompetent young whippersnapper I've ever known. He always seems to be sickly and has never earned so much as a penny. He's perfectly content to live here with his mother at the expense of the Kenting estate." The man's manner now had something of resentment and venom in it.

"Most unpleasant and annoyin' situation—what?" Vance rose and put out his cigarette. "Does Mrs. Falloway or her son know about what happened here last night?"

"Oh, yes," the man told him. "Both Madelaine and I spoke to them about it this morning, as we saw no point in keeping the matter a secret."

"And we, too, should like to speak to them," said Vance. "Would you be so good as to take us upstairs?"

Kenting seemed greatly relieved.

"I'll be glad to," he said, and started for the door. We followed him upstairs.

Mrs. Falloway was a woman between sixty and sixty-five years old. She was of heavy build and seemed to possess a corresponding aggressiveness. Her skin was somewhat wrinkled, but her thick hair was almost black, despite her years. There was an unmistakable masculinity about her, and her hands were large and bony, like those of a man. She had an intelligent and canny expression, and her features were large and striking. Withal, there was a wistful feminine look in her eyes. She impressed me as a woman with an iron will, but also with an innate sense of loyalty and sympathy.

When we entered her room that morning Mrs. Falloway was sitting placidly in a wicker armchair in front of the large bay window. She wore an antiquated black alpaca dress which fell in voluminous folds about her and completely hid her feet. An old-fashioned hand-crocheted afghan was thrown over her shoulders. On the floor beside her chair lay a long heavy Malakka cane with a shepherd's-crook gold handle.

At an old and somewhat dilapidated walnut secretary sat a thin, sickly youth, with straight dark hair which fell forward over his forehead, and large, prominent features. There was no mistaking mother and son. The pale youth held a magnifying glass in one hand and was moving it back and forth over a page of exhibits in a stamp album which was propped up at an angle facing the light.

"These gentlemen wish to speak to you, Mrs. Falloway," Kenyon Kenting said in an unfriendly tone. (It was obvious that an antagonism of some kind existed between the woman and this man on whose bounty she depended.) "I won't remain," Kenting added. "I think I'd better join Madelaine." He went to the door and opened it. "I'll be downstairs if you should need me." This last remark was addressed to Vance.

When he had gone, Vance took a few steps toward the woman with an air of solicitation.

"Perhaps you remember me, Mrs. Falloway—" he began.

"Oh, very well, Mr. Vance. It is very pleasant to see you again. Do sit down in that armchair there, and try to imagine that this meagre room is a Louis-Seize salon." There was a note of apology in her voice, accompanied by an unmistakable undertone of rancour.

Vance bowed formally.

"Any room you grace, Mrs. Falloway," he said, "becomes the most charming of salons." He did not accept her invitation to sit down, however, but remained standing deferentially.

"What do you make of this situation?" she went on. "And do you really think anything has happened to my son-in-law?" Her voice was hard and low-pitched.

"I really cannot say just yet," Vance answered. "We were hopin' you might be able to help us." He casually presented the others of us, and the woman acknowledged the introductions with dignified graciousness.

"This is my son, Fraim," she said, waving with a bony hand toward the anaemic young man at the secretary.

Fraim Falloway rose awkwardly and inclined his head without a word; then he sank back listlessly into his chair.

"Philatelist?" asked Vance, studying the youth.

"I collect American stamps." There was no enthusiasm in the lethargic voice, and Vance did not pursue the subject.

"Did you hear anything in the house early this morning?" Vance went on. "That is, did you hear Mr. Kaspar Kenting come in—or any kind of a noise between three and six o'clock?"

Fraim Falloway shook his head without any show of interest.

"I didn't hear anything," he said. "I was asleep."

Vance turned to the mother.

"Did you hear anything, Mrs. Falloway?"

"I heard Kaspar come in—he woke me up banging the front door shut." She spoke with bitterness. "But that's nothing new. I went to sleep again, however, and didn't know anything had happened until Madelaine and Mr. Kenyon Kenting informed me of it this morning, after my breakfast."

"Could you suggest any reason," asked Vance, "why any one should wish to kidnap Kaspar Kenting?"

The woman uttered a harsh, mirthless chuckle.

"No. But I can give you many reasons why any one should *not* wish to kidnap him," she returned with a hard, intolerant look. "He is not an admirable character," she went on, "nor a pleasant person to have around. And I regret the day my daughter married him. However," she added—and it seemed to me grudgingly—"I wouldn't wish to see any harm come to the scamp."

"And why not, mater?" asked Fraim Falloway with a whine. "You know perfectly well he has made us all miserable, including Sis. Personally, I think it's good riddance." The last words were barely audible.

"Don't be vindictive, son," the woman reproved him with a sudden softening in her tone, as the youth turned back to his stamps.

Vance sighed as if this interchange between mother and son bored him.

"Then you are not able, Mrs. Falloway, to suggest any reason for Mr. Kenting's sudden disappearance, or tell us anything that might be at all helpful?"

"No. I know nothing, and have nothing to tell you." Mrs. Falloway closed her lips with an audible sound.

"In that case," Vance returned politely, "I think we had better be going downstairs."

The woman picked up her cane and struggled to her feet, despite Vance's protestations.

"I wish I could help you," she said with sudden kindness. "But I am so well isolated these days with my infirmity. Walking, you know, is quite a painful process for me. I'm afraid I'm growing old."

She limped beside us slowly to the door, her son, who had risen, holding her tightly by one arm and casting reproachful glances at us.

In the hall Vance waited till the door was shut.

"An amusing old girl," he remarked. "Her mind is as young and shrewd as it ever was.... Unpleasant young citizen, Fraim. He's as ill as the old lady, but he doesn't know it. Endocrine imbalance," Vance continued as we went downstairs. "Needs medical attention. I wonder when he had a basal metabolism taken last. I'd say his chart would read in the minus thirties. May be thyroid. But it's more than possible, y' know, he needs the suprarenal hormone."

Markham snorted.

"He simply looks like a weakling to me."

"Oh, yes. Doubtless. As you say, devoid of stamina. And full of resentment against his fellow-men and especially against his brother-in-law. At any rate, an unpleasant character, Markham."

"A queer and unwholesome case," Markham commented, half to himself, and then lapsed into thoughtful silence as he descended the stairs with Vance. When we had reached the lower hall Vance went immediately toward the drawing-room and stepped inside.

Mrs. Kenting, who seemed perturbed and ill at ease, sat rigidly upright on the small sofa where we had first seen her. Her brother-in-law sat beside her, looking at her with a solicitous, comforting air.

Fleel was leaning back in an easy chair near the desk, smoking a cigar and endeavouring to maintain a judicious and unconcerned mien.

Vance glanced about him casually and, drawing up a small, straight-backed chair beside the sofa, sat down and addressed himself to the obviously unhappy woman.

"I know you told us, Mrs. Kenting," he began, "that you could not describe the men who called on your husband several nights ago. I wish, however, you would make an effort to give us at least a general description of them."

"It's strange that you should ask me that," the woman said. "I was just speaking to Kenyon about them and trying to recall what they looked like. The fact is, Mr. Vance, I paid little attention to them, but I know that one of them was a large man and seemed to me to have a very thick neck. And, as I recall, there was a lot of grey in his hair; and he may have had a clipped moustache—I really don't remember: it's all very vague. That was the man who came twice. . . ."

"Your description, madam," remarked Vance, nodding his head, "corresponds to the appearance of a certain gentleman I have in mind; and if it is the same person, your impression regarding the clipped moustache is quite correct—"

"Oh, who was he, Mr. Vance?" The woman leaned forward eagerly with a show of nervous animation. "Do you think you know who is responsible for this terrible thing?"

Vance shook his head and smiled sadly.

"No," he said, "I'm deuced sorry I cannot offer any hope in that particular quarter. If this man who called on your husband is the one I think it is, he is merely a good-natured book-maker who is at times aroused to futile anger when his clients fail to pay their debts. I'm quite sure, don't y' know, that if he should pop in here again at the present moment, you would find him inclined to exert his efforts in your behalf. I fear that we must dismiss him as a possibility. . . . But, by the by, Mrs. Kenting," Vance continued quickly, "can you tell me anything definite about the second man that called on your husband?"

The woman shook her head vaguely.

"Almost nothing, Mr. Vance," she returned. "I'm very sorry, but I caught only a glimpse of him. However, I recall that he was much shorter than the first man, and very dark. And my impression is that he was very well dressed. I remember thinking at the time that he seemed far less dangerous than his companion. But I do know that, in the fleeting glimpses I had of both the men, they struck me as being undesirable and untrustworthy characters. And I admit I worried about them on Kaspar's account. . . . Oh, I do wish I could tell you more, but I can't."

Vance thanked her with a slight bow.

"I can understand just how you felt, and how you feel now," he said in a kindly tone. "But I hardly think that either of these two objectionable visitors are in any way connected with your husband's disappearance. If they had really contemplated anything, I seriously doubt that they would have come here to their proposed victim's home and run the risk of being identified later. The second man—whom you describe as short, dark, and dapper—was probably a gambling-house keeper who had an account against your husband for overenthusiastic wagering. I can easily understand how he might be acquainted with the book-making gentleman who makes his livelihood through the cupidity of persons who persist in the belief that past-performance figures are an indication of how any horse will run at a given time."

As Vance spoke he rose from his chair and turned to Fleel, who had been listening intently to Vance's brief interchange with Mrs. Kenting.

"Before we go, sir," Vance said, "we wish to speak with you for a moment in the den. There are one or two points with which I feel you may be able to help us. . . . Do you mind?"

The lawyer rose with alacrity.

"I'll be very glad to do whatever I can to be of assistance," he said. "But I'm of the opinion I can tell you nothing more than you already know."

251

CHAPTER 7

The Black Opals
Wednesday, July 20; 1:15 p.m.

In the den Fleel seated himself with an easy, confident air and waited for Vance or Markham to speak. His manner was businesslike and competent, despite a certain lack of energy. I had a feeling he could, if he wished, supply us with more accurate and reasoned information than any of the members of the family. But Vance did not question him to any great extent. He seemed uninterested in any phase of the case on which the lawyer might have had information or suggestions to offer.

"Mr. Kenting tells us," Vance began, "that his brother demanded a large sum of money recently, to meet his debts, and that, when the demand was refused, Kaspar went to you as one of the executors of the estate."

"That is quite correct," Fleel responded, taking the cigar from his mouth and smoothing the wrapper with a moistened forefinger. "I, too, refused the demand; for, to begin with, I did not entirely believe the story Mr. Kaspar Kenting told me. He has cried 'wolf' so often that I have become sceptical, and did nothing about it. Moreover, Mr. Kenyon Kenting and I had consented to give him a large sum of money—ten thousand dollars, to be exact—only a few weeks ago. There were similar difficulties in which he said he had become involved at the time. We did it then, of course, for his wife's sake more than for his own—as, indeed, we had often done it before; but, unfortunately, no benefit ever accrued to her from these advances on her husband's patrimony."

"Did Mr. Kaspar see you personally?" asked Vance.

"No, he did not. He called me on the telephone," Fleel replied. "Frankly, I didn't ask him for any details other than those he volunteered, and I was rather brusque with him. . . . I might say that Kaspar has been a trying problem to the executors of the estate."

"Despite which," continued Vance, "I imagine his brother, as well as you yourself, will do everything possible to get him back, even to meeting the terms of the ransom note. Am I right?"

"I see nothing else to be done," the lawyer said without enthusiasm. "Unless, of course, the situation can be satisfactorily adjusted without payment of the ransom money. Of course we don't know for certain whether or not this is a *bona fide* kidnapping. Kidnapping is a damnable crime. . . ."

"Quite," agreed Vance with a sigh. "It places every one in a most irksome predicament. But, of course, there is nothing to be done until we have some further word from the supposed abductors. . . ."

Vance looked up and added quickly:

"By the by, Mrs. Kenting has informed us that Kaspar spoke to some one on the telephone when he came home in the early hours of this morning, and that he became angry. I wonder if it could have been you he called again?"

"Yes, damn it!" the lawyer returned with stern bitterness. "It was I. He woke me up some time after three, and became very vituperative when I refused to alter my previous decision. In fact, he said that both Kenyon and I would regret our penuriousness in refusing to help him, as he was certain it would result in some mischief, but did not say just what guise it might take. As a matter of fact, he sounded very much upset, and flew off the handle. But, I frankly admit, I didn't take him too seriously, for I had been through the same sort of thing with him before. . . . It seems now," the lawyer added a little uncomfortably, "that he was telling the truth for once—that it wasn't just an idle conjecture; and I am wondering if Kenyon and I shouldn't have investigated the situation before taking a definite stand."

"No, no; I think not," murmured Vance. "I doubt that it would have done any good. I have an idea the situation was not a new development—although there are, to be sure, few enough facts in hand at present on which to base an opinion. I don't like the outlook at all. It has too many conflictin' elements. . . . By the by, Mr. Fleel,"—Vance looked frankly at the man—"just how large a sum did Kaspar Kenting ask you for?"

"Too large an amount even to have been considered," returned the lawyer. "He asked for thirty thousand dollars."

"Thirty thousand," Vance repeated. "That's very interestin'." He rose lazily to his feet and straightened his clothes. "That will be all, I think, for the moment, Mr. Fleel," he said. "And many thanks for the trouble you've taken. There's little left to be done at the moment, aside from the usual routine. We will, of course, guard the matter as best we can. And we will get in touch with you if there is any new development."

Fleel stood up and bowed stiffly.

"You can always reach me through my office during the day, or through my home in the evening." He took an engraved card from his pocket and handed it to Vance. "There are my phone numbers, sir. . . . I think I shall remain a while with Mrs. Kenting and Kenyon." And he went from the den.

Markham, looking serious and puzzled, held Vance back.

"What do you make of that discrepancy in the amount, Vance?" he asked in a gruff, lowered tone.

"My dear Markham!" Vance shook his head solemnly. "There are many things we cannot make anything of at the present moment. One never knows—does one?—at this stage of the game. Perhaps young Kaspar, having failed with his brother, reduced the ante, as it were, in approaching Fleel, thinking he might get better results at the lower figure. Curious though; the amount demanded in the ransom note corresponds to what he told Kenyon he needed. On the other hand—I wonder. . . . However, let's commune with the butler before we toddle on."

Vance went to the door and opened it. Just outside stood Weem, bending slightly forward, as if he had been eavesdropping. Instead of showing any signs of embarrassment, the man looked up truculently and turned away.

"See here, Weem," Vance halted him. "Step inside a moment," he said with an amused smile. "You can hear better; and, anyway, there are one or two questions we'd like to put to you."

The man turned back without a word and entered the den with an air of sulkiness. He looked past us all with his watery eyes and waited.

"Weem, how long have you been the Kenting butler?" asked Vance.

"Going on three years," was the surly response.

"Three years," repeated Vance thoughtfully. "Good. . . . Have you any ideas, Weem, as to what happened here last night?" Vance reached in his pocket for his cigarette case.

"No, sir; none whatever," the butler returned, without looking at any of us. "But nothing would surprise me in this house. There are too many people who'd like to get rid of Mr. Kaspar."

"Are you, by any chance, one of them?" asked Vance lightly, watching the other with faint amusement.

"I'd just as soon never see him again." The answer came readily, in a disgruntled, morose tone.

"And who else do you think feels the same way about Mr. Kaspar Kenting?" Vance went on.

"Mrs. Falloway and young Mr. Falloway have no love for him, sir." There was no change in the man's tone. "And even Mrs. Kenting herself has had more than enough of him, I think. She and Mr. Kenyon are very good friends—and there was never any great love between the two brothers. . . . Mr. Kaspar is a very difficult man to get along with—he is very unreasonable. Other people have some rights, sir; but he doesn't think so. He's the kind of man that strikes his wife when he has too much to drink—"

"I think that will be all," Vance broke in sharply. "You're an unspeakable gossip, Weem." He turned away with a look of keen distaste, and the butler shuffled from the room without any sign of displeasure or offence.

"Come, Markham," said Vance. "Let's get out into the air. I don't like it in this house—I don't at all like it."

"But it strikes me—" began Markham.

"Oh, don't let your conscience bother you," interrupted Vance. "The only course we can possibly take is to wait for the next step on the part of our dire plotters." Although Vance spoke in a bantering tone, it was obvious from the deliberate way he lighted a cigarette that he was deeply troubled. "Something will happen soon, Markham. The next move will be expertly engineered, I'll wager. The case is by no means ended with this concocted kidnappin'. Too many loose ends—oh, far too many." He moved across the room. "Patience, my dear chap." He threw the admonition lightly over his shoulder to Markham. "We're supposed to be bustlin' with various anticipated activities. Some one is hopin' we'll take just the route indicated for us and thus be led entirely off the track. But, I say, let's not be gullible. Patience is our watchword. Patience and placidity. Nonchalance. Let the other johnnies make the next move. Live patiently and learn. Imitate the mountain—Mohammed is trudgin' your way."

Markham stood still in the centre of the room, looking down at the worn early-American art square. He seemed to be pondering something that bothered him.

"See here, Vance," he said after a brief silence, lifting his head and looking squarely at the other. "You speak of 'plotters' and 'johnnies'—both plural. You really think, then, that this damnable situation is the doing of more than one person?"

"Oh, yes—undoubtedly," Vance returned readily. "Far too many diverse activities for just one. A certain co-ordination was needed—and one person cannot be in two different places at the same time, don't y' know. Oh, undoubtedly more than one person. One lured the gentleman away from the house; another—possibly two—took care of the chappie at the place appointed by the first; and I rather think it more than likely there was at least another who arranged the elaborate setting in Kaspar's room—but this is not necess'rily correct, as any one of the three might have returned for the stage setting and been the person that Mrs. Kenting heard in the bedroom."

"I see what you mean." Markham nodded laboriously. "You're thinking of the two men whom McLaughlin saw in the car in the street here this morning."

"Oh, yes. Quite." Vance's response was spoken casually. "They fit into the picture nicely. But neither of them was a small man, and I doubt if either of them was the ladder-climber in the smallish Chinese sandals. Considerable evidence against that conclusion. That is why I say I'm inclined to think that there may have been still another helper who attended to the details of the *boudoir* setting—makin' four in all."

"But, good heavens!" argued Markham; "if there were several persons involved in the affair, it may be just another gang kidnapping, after all."

"It's always possible, of course, despite the contr'ry indications," Vance returned. "However, Markham, although I have said that there were undoubtedly several persons taking part in the execution of the plot, I am thoroughly convinced there is only a single mind at work on the case—the main organizing culprit, so to speak—some one who merely secured the necess'ry help—what the newspapers amusingly designate as a master-mind. And the person who planned and manipulated this whole distressin' affair is some one who is quite intimately *au courant* with the conditions in the Kenting house here. The various episodes have dovetailed together far too neatly to have been managed by an outsider. And really, y' know, I hardly think that the Purple House harbours, or is in any way related to, a professional kidnapper."

Markham shook his head sceptically.

"Granting," he said, "for the sake of hypothesis, that you are correct so far, what could have been the motive for such a dastardly act by any one who was close to Kaspar?"

"Money—unquestionably money," Vance ventured. "The exact amount named in the pretty little kindergarten paste-and-paper note attached to the window-sill. . . . Oh, yes; that was a very significant item. Some one wishes the money immediately. It is urgently needed. I rather think a genuine kidnapper—and especially a gang of kidnappers operating for themselves—would not have been so hasty in stating the exact sum, but would have let that little detail wait until a satisfact'ry contact was established and negotiations were definitely under way. And of course, if it had really been Kaspar who had abducted himself for the sake of the gain, the note could be easily understood; but once we eliminate Kaspar as the author of this crime, then we are confronted with the necessity of evolving an entirely new interpretation of the facts. The crime then becomes one of desperation and immediacy, with the money as an imperative desideratum."

"I am not so sure you are right this time, Vance," said Markham seriously.

Vance sighed.

"Neither am I, Markham old dear." He went to the door and opened it. "Let's move along." And he walked up the hall.

Vance stopped at the drawing-room door, bade the occupants a brief farewell; and a minute later we were descending the outside steps of the house into the noonday sunshine of the street.

We entered the District Attorney's car and drove toward Central Park. When we had almost reached the corner of Central Park West, Vance leaned forward suddenly and, tapping the chauffeur on the shoulder, requested him to stop at the entrance to the Nottingham Hotel which we were just passing.

"Really, y' know, Markham," he said as he stepped out of the car, "I think it might be just as well if we paid a little visit to the as-yet-unknown Mr. Quaggy. Queer name—what? He was the last person known to have been with young Kaspar. He's a gentleman of means and a gentleman of leisure, as well as a gentleman of nocturnal habits. He may be at home, don't y' know. . . . But I think we'd better go directly to his apartment without apprising him of the visit by being announced." He turned to Heath. "I am sure you can manage that, Sergeant,—unless you forgot to bring your pretty gilt badge with you this morning."

Heath snorted.

"Sure, we'll go right to his rooms, if that's what you want, Mr. Vance. Don't you worry about that. This ain't the first time I've had to handle these babies in a hotel."

Heath was as good as his word. We had no difficulty in obtaining the number of Quaggy's apartment and being taken up in the elevator without an announcement.

In answer to our ringing, the door was opened by a generously proportioned coloured woman, in a Hoover apron and an old stocking tied round her head.

"We want to see Mr. Quaggy." Heath's manner was as intimidating as it was curt.

The negress looked frightened.

"I don't think Mr. Quaggy—" she began in a tremulous voice.

"Never mind what you think, Aunt Jemima." Heath cut her short. "Is your boss here, or isn't he?" He flashed his badge. "We're from the police."

"Yes, sir; yes, sir. He's here." The woman was completely cowed by this time. "He's in the sittin'-room, over yonder."

The Sergeant brushed past her to the archway at the end of the foyer, toward which she waved her arm. Markham, Vance and I followed him.

The room into which we stepped was comfortably and expensively furnished, differing little from the conventional exclusive hotel-apartment living-room. There was a mahogany cellarette near a built-in modern fireplace, comfortable overstuffed chairs covered with brocaded satin that was almost colourless, a baby grand piano in one corner, two parchment-shaded table-lamps with green pottery bases, and a small glass-doored Tudor bookcase filled with colourful assorted volumes. At the front end of the room were two windows facing on the street, hung with heavy velour drapes and topped with scrolled-metal cornices.

As we entered, a haggard, dissipated-looking man of about forty rose from a low lounging chair in one corner of the room. He seemed both surprised and resentful at our intrusion. He was an attractive man, with finely chiselled features, but not a man whom one could call handsome. He was unmistakably the gambler type—that is, the type one sees habitually at gaming houses and the race-track. There was weariness and pallor in his face that morning, and his eyelids were oedematous and drawn down at the corners, like those of a man suffering with Bright's disease. He was still in evening clothes, and his linen was the worse for wear. He wore patent leather pumps which showed distinct traces of dried mud. Before he could speak Vance addressed him courteously.

"Forgive our unceremonious entry. You're Mr. Porter Quaggy, I believe?" The man's eyes became cold.

"What if I am?" he demanded. "I don't understand why you—"

"You will in a moment, sir," Vance broke in ingratiatingly. And he introduced himself, as well as Markham and Heath and me. "We have

258

just come from the Kentings' down the street," he went on. "A calamity took place there early this morning, and we understand from Mrs. Kaspar Kenting that Mr. Kenting was with you last night."

Quaggy's eyes narrowed to mere slits. "Has anything happened to Kaspar?" he asked. He turned to the cellarette and poured himself a generous drink of whiskey. He gulped it down and repeated his question.

"We'll get to that later," Vance replied. "Tell me, what time did you and Mr. Kenting get home last night?"

"Who said I was with him when he came home?" The man was obviously on his guard.

"Mrs. Kenting informed us that you and her husband went together to the opening of a casino in Jersey last night, and that Mr. Kenting returned somewhere around three o'clock in the morning. Is that correct?"

The man hesitated.

"Even if it is true, what of it?" he asked after a moment.

"Nothing—really nothing of any importance," murmured Vance. "Just lookin' for information. I note you're still bedecked in your evenin' togs. And your pumps are a bit muddy. It hasn't rained since yesterday, don't y' know. Offhand, I'd say you'd been sittin' up all night."

"Isn't that my privilege?" grumbled the other.

"I think you'd better do some straight talking, Mr. Quaggy," put in Markham angrily. "We're investigating a crime, and we haven't time to waste. You'll save yourself a lot of trouble, too. Unless, of course, you're afraid of implicating yourself. In that event, I'll allow you time to communicate with your attorney."

"Attorney hell!" snapped Quaggy. "I don't need any lawyers. I've nothing to be afraid of, and I'll speak for myself. . . . Yes, I went with Kaspar last night to the new casino in Paterson, and we got back, as Mrs. Kenting says, around three o'clock—"

"Did you go to the Kenting house with Mr. Kenting?" asked Vance.

"No; our cab came down Central Park West, and I got out here. I wish now I had gone with him. He asked me to—said he was worried as the devil about something, and wanted to put me up for the night. I thought he was stewed, and didn't pay any attention to him. But after he had gone on, I got to thinking about what he'd said—he's always getting into trouble of one kind or another—and I walked down there about an hour later. But everything seemed all right. There was a light in Kaspar's room, and I merely figured he hadn't gone to bed yet. So I decided not to disturb him."

Vance nodded understandingly.

"Did you, by any chance, step into the side yard?"

"Just inside the gate," the other admitted.

"Was the side window of his room open? And was the blind up?"

"The window might have been open or shut, but the blind was down. I'm sure of that because the light was coming from around the edges."

"Did you see a ladder anywhere in the court?"

"A ladder? No, there was no ladder. What would a ladder be doing there?"

"Did you remain there long, Mr. Quaggy?"

"No. I came back here and had a drink."

"But you didn't go to bed, I notice."

"It's every man's privilege to sit up if he wants to, isn't it?" Quaggy asked coldly. "The truth is, I began to worry about Kaspar. He was in a hell of a mood last night—all steamed up. I never saw him just that way before. To tell you the truth, I half expected something to happen to him. That's why I went down to the house."

"Was it only Mr. Kaspar Kenting that you were thinking about?" Vance inquired with a shrewd, fixed look. "I understand you're a close friend of the family and are very highly regarded by Mrs. Kenting."

"Glad to know it," muttered the man, meeting Vance's gaze squarely. "Madelaine is a very fine woman, and I should hate to see anything happen to her."

"Thanks awfully for the information," murmured Vance. "I think I see your point of view perfectly. Well, your premonitions were quite accurate. Something did happen to the young gentleman, and Mrs. Kenting is frightfully distressed."

"Is he all right?" asked Quaggy quickly.

"We're not sure yet. The fact is, Mr. Quaggy, your companion of yestereve has disappeared—superficial indications pointin' to abduction."

"The hell you say!" The man showed remarkable control and spoke without change of expression.

"Oh, yes—quite," Vance said disinterestedly.

Quaggy went to the cellarette again and poured himself another drink of whiskey. He offered the bottle to us all in general, and getting no response from us, replaced it on the stand.

"When did this happen?" he asked between swallows of the whiskey.

"Oh, early this morning some time," Vance informed him. "That's why we're here. Thought maybe you could give us an idea or two."

Quaggy finished the remainder of his glass of whiskey.

"Sorry, I can't help you," he said as he put down the glass. "I've told you everything I know."

"That's frightfully good of you," said Vance indifferently. "We may want to talk to you later, however."

"That's all right with me." The man turned, without looking up from the liquor stand. "Ask me whatever you want whenever you damn please. But it won't get you anywhere, for I've already told you all I know."

"Perhaps you'll recall an additional item or two when you are rested."

"If you mean when I'm sober, why don't you say so?" Quaggy asked with annoyance.

"No, no, Mr. Quaggy. Oh, no. I think you're far too shrewd and cautious a man to permit yourself the questionable luxury of inebriety. Clear head always essential, don't y' know. Helps no end in figuring percentages quickly."

Vance was at the archway now, and I was just behind him. Markham and Heath had already preceded us. Vance paused for a moment and looked down at a small conventional desk which stood near the entrance. Quickly he adjusted his monocle and scrutinized the desk. On it lay a crumpled piece of tissue paper in the centre of which reposed two perfectly matched dark stones, with a remarkable play of colour in them—a pair of black opals!

When we were back in the car and headed downtown, Markham, after a minute or two spent in getting his cigar going, said:

"Too many factors seem to counteract your original theory, Vance. If this affair was plotted so carefully to be carried out at a certain time, how do you account for the fact that Kaspar seemed to have a definite premonition of something dire and unforeseen happening to him?"

"Premonition?" Vance smiled slightly. "I'm afraid you're waxing esoteric, old dear. After Hannix's threat and after, perhaps, a bit of pressure thrown in by the other gentleman to whom he owed money, Kaspar was naturally in a sensitive and worried state of mind. He took their blustering, but harmless, talk too seriously. Suffered from fright and craved the comfort of company. Probably why he went to the casino—trying to put his despondency out of mind. With the threats of the two creditors uppermost in his consciousness, he used them as an argument with both his brother and Fleel. And his invitin' Quaggy home with him was merely part of this perturbation. Simple. Very simple."

"You're still stubborn enough to believe it had nothing to do with the facts of the case?" asked Markham irritably.

"Oh, yes, yes—quite," Vance replied cheerfully. "I can't see that his psychic warnings had anything whatsoever to do with what actually befell him later. . . . By the by, Markham,"—Vance changed the subject—"there were two rather amazin' black opals on the desk in Quaggy's apartment. Noticed them as I was going out."

"What's that!" Markham turned in surprise. Then a look of understanding came into his eyes. "You think they came from the Kenting collection?"

"It's possible." Vance nodded slowly. "The collection was quite deficient in black opals when I gazed upon it. The few remainin' specimens were quite inferior. No self-respectin' connoisseur would have admitted them to his collection unless he already had more valuable ones to offset them. Those that Quaggy had were undoubtedly a pair of the finest specimens from New South Wales."

"That puts a different complexion on things," said Markham grudgingly. "How do you think Quaggy got hold of them?"

Vance shrugged.

"Ah! Who knows? Pertinent question. We might ask the gentleman sometime. . . ."

We continued downtown in silence.

CHAPTER 8

Ultimatum
Thursday, July 21; 10 a.m.

The next morning, shortly before ten o'clock, Markham telephoned Vance at his apartment, and I answered.

"Tell Vance," came the District Attorney's peremptory voice, "I
think he'd better come down to my office at once. Fleel is here, and
I'll keep him engaged till Vance arrives."

I repeated the message to Vance while I still held the receiver to my
ear, and he nodded his head in agreement.

A few minutes later, as we were about to leave the house, he became unduly serious.

"Van, it may have happened already," he murmured, "though I really didn't expect it so soon. Thought we'd have at least a day or two
before the next move was made. However, we shall soon know."

We arrived at Markham's office a half-hour later. Vance did not go
to the secretary in the reception-room of the District Attorney's suite
in the old Criminal Courts Building, but through the private side
door which led from the corridor into Markham's spacious *sanctum*.

Markham was seated at his desk, looking decidedly troubled; and
in a large upholstered chair before him sat Fleel.

After casual greetings Markham announced: "The instructions promised in the ransom note have been received. A note came in Mr. Fleel's
mail this morning, and he brought it directly to me. I hardly know what
to make of it, or how to advise him. But you seemed to have ideas about
the case which you would not divulge. And I think, therefore, you ought
to see this note immediately, as it is obvious something must be done
about it at once." He picked up the small sheet of paper before him and
held it out to Vance. It was a piece of ruled note-paper, folded twice. The
quality was of a very cheap, coarse nature, such as comes in thick tablets

which can be bought for a trifle at any stationer's. The writing on it was in pencil, in an obviously disguised handwriting. Half of the letters were printed, and whether it was the composition of an illiterate person, or purposely designed to give the impression of ignorance on the writer's part, I could not tell as I looked at it over Vance's shoulder.

"I say, let's see the envelope," Vance requested. "That's rather important, don't y' know."

Markham shot him a shrewd look and handed him a stamped envelope, of no better quality than the paper, which had been slit neatly across the top. The postmark showed that the note had passed through the post-office the previous afternoon at five o'clock from the Westchester Station.

"And where might the Westchester Station be?" asked Vance, sinking lazily into a chair and taking out a cigarette.

"I had it looked up as soon as Mr. Fleel showed me the note," responded Markham. "It's in the upper Bronx."

"Interestin'," murmured Vance. "'East Side, West Side, All Around the Town,' so to speak. . . . And what are the bound'ries of the district it serves?"

Markham glanced down at the yellow pad on his desk.

"It takes in a section of nine or ten square miles on the upper east side of the Bronx, between the Hutchinson and Bronx Rivers and a zigzag line on the west boundary.[1] A lot of it is pretty desolate territory, and can probably be eliminated without consideration. As a matter of fact, it's the toughest district in New York in which to trace any one by a postmark."

Vance nodded casually and, opening the note, adjusted his monocle and read the pencil-scrawled communication carefully. It ran:

Sir. I no you and family have money and unless 50 thousand $ is placed in hole of oke tree 200 foot west of Southeast corner of old resivore in central park thursday at leven oclock at nite we will kill Casper Kenton. This is finel. If you tell police deel is off and we will no it. We are watching every move you make.

---

1. The Westchester Station of the Post-Office Department, situated at 1436 Williamsbridge Road, at the intersection of East Tremont Avenue, collects and delivers mail in the following territory, starting from Paulding Avenue and Pelham Parkway: South side of Pelham Parkway to Kingsland Avenue; to Mace Avenue; to Wickham Avenue; to Gunhill Road; to Bushnell Avenue; to Hutchinson River; west side of Hutchinson River to Givans Creek; to Eastchester Bay; to Long Island Sound; to Bronx River; to Ludlow Avenue (now known as Eastern Boulevard); to Pugsley Avenue; to McGraw Avenue; to Storrow Street; to Unionport Road; to East Tremont Avenue; to Bronxdale Avenue; to Van Nest Avenue; to Paulding Avenue; to Pelham Parkway.

The ominous message was signed with interlocking squares made with brush strokes, like those we had already seen on the ransom note found pinned to the window-sill of the Kenting house.

"No more original than the first communication," commented Vance dryly. "And it strikes me, offhand, that the person who worded this threatening epistle is not as unschooled as he would have us believe. . . ."

He looked up at the lawyer, who was watching him intently.

"Just what are your ideas on the situation, Mr. Fleel?" he asked.

"Personally," the man said, "I am willing to leave the whole matter to Mr. Markham here, and his advisors. I—I don't know exactly what to say—I'd rather not offer any suggestions. The ransom demands can't possibly be met out of the estate, as what funds were entrusted to me are largely in long-term bonds. However, I feel sure that Mr. Kenyon Kenting will be able to get the necessary amount together and take care of the situation—if that is his wish. The decision, naturally, must be left entirely up to him."

"Does he know of this note?" asked Vance.

Fleel shook his head in negation.

"Not yet," he said, "unless he, too, received a copy. I brought this one immediately to Mr. Markham. But my opinion is that Kenyon should know about it, and it was my intention to go to the Kenting house from here and inform Kenyon of this new development. He is not at his office this morning, and I imagine he is spending the day with Mrs. Kenting. I'll do nothing, however, without the consent of Mr. Markham." He looked toward the District Attorney as if he expected an answer to his remark.

Markham had risen, and now moved toward one of the windows which looked out into Franklin Street and over the grey walls of the Tombs. His hands were clasped behind him, and an unlighted cigar hung listlessly from his lips. It was Markham's characteristic attitude when he was making an important decision. After a while he turned, came back to the desk, and reseated himself.

"Mr. Fleel," he said slowly, "I think you should go to Kenyon Kenting at once, and tell him the exact circumstances." There was a hesitant note in his words, as if he had reached a decision but was uncertain as to the feasibility of its logical application.

"I'm glad you feel that way, Mr. Markham," the lawyer said, "for I certainly believe that he is entitled to know. After all, if a decision is to be made regarding the money, he must be the one to make it." He rose as he spoke, taking his hat from the floor beside him. With ponderous steps he moved toward the door.

"I quite agree with you both," murmured Vance, who was drawing vigorously on his cigarette and looking straight before him into space. "Only, I would ask you, Mr. Fleel, to remain at the Kenting house until Mr. Markham and I arrive there. We will be joining you very soon."

"I'll wait," mumbled Fleel as he passed through the swinging leather door out to the reception-room.

Vance settled back in his chair, stretched out his long legs, and gazed dreamily through the window. Markham watched him expectantly for some time without speaking. At last it seemed that he could bear the silence no longer, and he asked anxiously:

"Well, Vance, what do you think?"

"So many things," Vance told him, "that I couldn't begin to enumerate them. All probably frivolous and worthless."

"Well, to be more specific," Markham went on, endeavouring to control his rising anger, "what do you think of that note you have there?"

"Quite authentic—oh, quite," Vance returned without hesitation. "As I said, the money is passionately desired. Hasty business is afoot. A bit too precipitate for my liking, however. But there's no overlooking the earnestness of the request. I've a feelin' something must be done without loss of time."

"The instructions seem somewhat vague."

"No. Oh, no, Markham. On the contr'ry. Quite explicit. I know the tree well. Romantic lovers leave *billets-doux* there. No difficulties in that quarter. Quiet spot. All approaches visible. As good a crossroads as any for the transaction of dirty work. However, it could be adequately covered by the police. I wonder...."

Markham was silent for a long time, smoking intently, his brow deeply corrugated.

"This situation upsets me," he rumbled at length. "The newspapers were full of it this morning, as you may have noticed. The police are being condemned for refusing information to the federal boys. Maybe it would have been best if I had washed my hands of it all in the first place. I don't like it—it's poison. And there's nothing to go on. I was trusting, as usual, to your impressions."

"Let us not repine, Markham old dear," Vance encouraged him. "It was only yesterday the bally thing happened."

"But I must get some action," Markham asserted, striking his clenched fist on the desk. "This new note changes the whole complexion of things."

"Tut, tut." Vance's admonition was almost frivolous. "Really, y' know, it changes nothing. *It was precisely what I was waitin' for.*"

266

"Well," snapped Markham, "now that you have it, what do you intend to do?"

Vance looked at the District Attorney in mock surprise.

"Why, I intend to go to the Purple House," he said calmly. "I'm not psychic, but something tells me we shall find a hand pointin' to our future activities when we arrive there."

"Well, if that's your idea," demanded Markham, "why didn't you go with Fleel?"

"Merely wished to give him sufficient time to break the news to the others and to discuss the matter with brother Kenyon." Vance expelled a series of smoke rings toward the chandelier. "Nothing like letting every one know the details of the case. We'll get forrader that way."

Markham half closed his eyes and regarded Vance appraisingly.

"You think, perhaps," he asked, "that Kenyon Kenting is going to try to raise the money and meet the demands of that outrageous note?"

"It's quite possible, don't y' know. And I rather think he'll want the police to give him a free hand. Anyway, it's time we were toddlin' out and ascertainin'." Vance struggled to his feet and adjusted his Bangkok hat carefully. "Could you bear to come along, Markham?"

Markham pressed a buzzer under the ledge of his desk and gave various instructions to the secretary who answered his call.

"This thing is too important," he said as he turned back to Vance. "I'm joining you." He glanced at his watch. "My car is downstairs."

And we went out through the private office and judges' chambers and descended in the special elevator.

CHAPTER 9

Decisions Are Reached
Thursday, July 21; 11:15 a.m.

At the Kenting residence we found Kenyon Kenting, Fleel, young Falloway, and Porter Quaggy assembled in the drawing-room. They all seemed solemn and tense, and greeted us with grave restraint that suited the occasion.

"Did you bring the note with you, gentlemen?" Kenting asked immediately, with frightened eagerness. "Fleel told me just what's in it, but I'd like to see the message itself."

Vance nodded and took the note from his pocket, placing it on the small desk near him.

"It's the usual thing," he said. "I doubt if you'll find any more in it than Mr. Fleel has reported to you."

Kenting, without a word, bustled across the room, took the folded piece of paper from its envelope, and read it carefully as he smoothed it out on the green blotting pad.

"What do you think should be done about it?" Markham asked him. "Personally, I'm not inclined to have you meet that demand just yet."

Kenting shook his head in perturbed silence. At last he said:

"I'd always feel guilty and selfish if I did anything else. If I didn't comply with this request and anything should really happen to Kaspar—"

He left the sentence unfinished as he turned and rested against the edge of the desk, looking dolefully down at the floor.

"But I've no idea exactly how I'm going to raise that much money—and at such short notice. It'll pretty well break me, even if I can manage to get it together."

"I can help contribute to the fund," offered Quaggy, in a hard tone, looking up from his chair in the shadows of the room.

"And I'd like to do something, too," put in Fleel, "but, as you know, my personal funds are pretty well depleted at this time. As a trustee of the Kenting estate I couldn't use that money for such a purpose without a court order. And I couldn't get one in such a limited time."

Fraim Falloway stood back against the wall, listening intently. A half-smoked cigarette drooped limply between his thick, colourless lips.

"Why don't you let it go?" he suggested, with malicious querulousness. "Kaspar's not worth that much money to any one, if you ask me. And how do you know you're going to save his life, anyway?"

"Shut up, Fraim!" snapped Kenting. "Your opinion hasn't been asked for."

Young Falloway shrugged indifferently and said nothing. The ashes from his cigarette fell over his shiny black suit, but he did not take the trouble to brush them off.

"I say, Mr. Fleel," put in Vance, "just what would be the financial standing of Mrs. Kenting in the hypothetical case that Kaspar Kenting should die? Would she benefit by his demise—that is, to whom would Kaspar Kenting's share in the estate go?"

"To his wife," answered Fleel. "It was so stipulated in Karl Kenting's will, although he did not know Mrs. Kenting at the time, as Kaspar was not yet married. But the will clearly states that his share of the inheritance should go to his wife if he were married and she survived him."

"Sure," said Fraim Falloway sulkily, "my sister gets everything, and there are no strings attached to it. Kaspar has never done the right thing by Sis, anyway, and it's about time she was coming in for something. That's why I say it's rank nonsense to give up all this money to get Kaspar back. Nobody here thinks he's worth fifty cents, if they'll be frank."

"A sweet and lovable point of view," murmured Vance. "I suppose your sister is very lenient with you whenever possible?"

It was Kenyon Kenting who answered.

"That's it exactly, Mr. Vance. She's the kind that would sacrifice everything for her brother and her mother. That's natural, perhaps. But, after all, Kaspar is my brother, and I think something ought to be done about it, even on the mere chance it may save him, if it *does* take practically every cent I've got in the world. But I'm willing to go through with it, if you gentlemen and the police will agree to keep entirely out of it, until I have found out what I can do without any official assistance which might frighten off the kidnappers."

He looked at Markham apologetically and then added:

"You see, I discussed the point with Mr. Fleel just before you gentlemen arrived. We are agreed that the police should allow me a clear field in handling this matter in exact accordance with the instructions in the note; for if it is true, don't you see, that the kidnappers are watching my moves, and if they so much as suspect that the police are waiting for them, they may not act at all, and Kaspar would still remain in jeopardy."

Markham nodded thoughtfully.

"I can understand your attitude in the matter, Mr. Kenting," he said reassuringly. "And therefore,"—he made a suave gesture—"the decision on that point must rest solely with you. The police will turn their backs, as it were, for the time being, if that is what you wish."

Fleel nodded his approval of Markham's words.

"If Kenyon is financially able to go through with it," he said, "I feel that that course is the wisest one to follow. Even if it means shutting our eyes momentarily to the legal issues of the situation, he may have a better chance of having his brother safely returned. And that, after all, I am sure you will all agree, is the prime consideration in the present instance."

Vance had, to all appearances, been ignoring this brief discussion, but I knew, from the slow and deliberate movement of his hand as he smoked, that he was absorbing with interest every word spoken. At this point he rose to his feet and entered the conversation with a curious finality.

"I think," he began, "both of you gentlemen are in error, and I am definitely opposed to the withdrawal of the authorities, even temporarily, at this time in such a vital situation. It would amount to the compounding of a felony. Moreover, the reference in the note regarding the police is, I believe, merely an attempt at intimidation. I can see no valid reason why the police should not be permitted a certain discreet activity in the matter." His voice was firm and bitter and carried a stinging rebuke to both Kenting and Fleel.

Markham remained silent when Vance had finished, for I am convinced he felt, as I did, that Vance's remarks were based on a subtle and definite motivation. They had their effect on Kenting as well, for it was obvious that he was definitely wavering. And even Fleel seemed to be considering the point anew.

"You may be right, Mr. Vance," Kenting admitted finally in a hesitant tone. "On second thought, I am inclined to follow your suggestion."

"You're all stupid," mumbled Falloway. Then he leaned forward. His eyes opened wide, his jowls sagged and he burst forth hysterically:

"It's Kaspar, Kaspar, *Kaspar!* He's no good anyway, and he's the only one that gets a break around here. Nobody thinks of any one else but Kaspar. . . ." His voice was high-pitched and ended in a scream.

"Shut up, you ninny," ordered Kenting. "What are you doing down here, anyway? Go on up to your room."

Falloway sneered without replying, walked across the room, and threw himself into a large upholstered chair by the window.

"Well, what's the decision, gentlemen?" asked Markham, in a calm, quiet tone. "Are we to go ahead on the basis of your paying the ransom alone, or shall I turn the case over to the Police Department to handle as they see fit?"

Kenting stood up and took a deep breath.

"I think I'll go down to my office now," he said wearily, "and try to raise the cash." Then he added to Markham, "And I think the police had better go ahead with the case." He turned quickly to Fleel with an interrogative look.

"I'm sorry I can't advise you, Kenyon," the lawyer said in answer to Kenting's unstated question. "It's a damned difficult problem on which to offer positive advice. But if you decide to take this step, I think I should leave the details in the hands of Mr. Markham. If I can be of any help—"

"Oh, don't worry, Fleel, I'll get in touch with you." Kenting turned to the dark corner of the room. "And thank you, Quaggy, for your kindness; but I think I can handle the situation without your assistance, though we all appreciate your generous offer."

Markham was evidently becoming impatient.

"I will be at my office," he said, "until five o'clock this afternoon. I'll expect you to communicate with me before that time, Mr. Kenting."

"Oh, I will—without fail," returned Kenting, with a mirthless laugh. "I'll be there in person, if I can possibly manage it." With a listless wave of the hand, he went from the room and out the front door.

Fleel followed a few moments later, but Fraim Falloway still sat brooding sneeringly by the window.

Quaggy rose from his chair and confronted Markham.

"I think I'll remain a while," he said, "and speak to Mrs. Kenting."

"Oh, by all means," agreed Vance. "I'm sure the young woman needs cheering up." He went to the desk, refolded the note carefully, and, placing it in its envelope, slipped it into an inside pocket. Then he motioned to Markham, and we went out into the sultry summer noon.

When we were back at the District Attorney's office, Markham sent immediately for Heath. As soon as the Sergeant arrived from

Centre Street, a short time later, the situation was outlined to him, and he was shown the letter which Fleel had received. He read the note hastily and looked up.

"If you ask me, I wouldn't give those babies a nickel," he commented gruffly. "But if this fellow Kenyon Kenting insists, I suppose we'll have to let him do it. Too much responsibility in tryin' to stop him."

"Exactly," assented Markham emphatically. "Do you know where this particular tree is in Central Park, Sergeant?"

"Hah!" Heath said explosively. "I've seen it so often, I'm sick of lookin' at it. But it's not a bad location, at that. It's near the traffic lanes, and you can see in all directions from there."

"Could you and the boys cover it," asked Markham, "in case Mr. Kenting does go through with this and we decide it would be best to have the spot under surveillance?"

"Leave that to me, Chief," the Sergeant returned confidently. "There's lots of ways of doing it. Searchlights from the houses along Fifth Avenue could light up the place like daytime when we're ready. And some of the boys hiding in taxicabs, or even up the tree itself, could catch the baby who takes the money and tie him up in bow-knots."

"On the other hand, Sergeant," Markham demurred, "it might be better to let the ransom money go, so we can get young Kenting back—that is, if the abductors are playing straight."

"Playing straight!" Heath repeated with contempt. "Say, Chief, did you ever know any of these palookas to be on the level? I says, let's catch the guy who comes after the money, and we'll give him the works at Headquarters and turn him inside out. There won't be nothing we won't know when the boys get through shellacin' him. Then we can save the money and get this no-good Kaspar back for 'em, and round up the sweet little darlings who done it—all at the same time."

Vance was smiling musingly during this optimistic prophecy of future events. In the pause that followed Heath's last words he spoke.

"Really, y' know, Sergeant, I think you're going to be disappointed. This case isn't as simple as you and Mr. Markham think. . . ." The Sergeant started to protest, but Vance continued. "Oh, yes. Quite. You may round up somebody, but I doubt if you will ever be able to connect your victim with the kidnapping. Somehow, don't y' know, I can't take this illiterate note too seriously. I have an idea it is designed to throw us off the track. Still, the experiment may be interestin'. Fact is, I'd be overjoyed to participate in it myself."

Heath looked at Vance humorously.

"You like to climb trees, maybe, Mr. Vance?" he asked.

"I adore it, Sergeant," Vance told him. "But I simply must change my clothes."

Heath chuckled and then became more serious.

"That's all right with me, Mr. Vance," he said. "There'll be plenty of time for that."

(I knew that the Sergeant wished Vance to take this strategic position in the tree, for despite Vance's constant good-natured spoofing and his undisguised contempt for Heath's routine procedure, the Sergeant had a great admiration and fondness for, not to say a profound faith in, the debonair man before him.)

"That's bully, Sergeant," commented Vance. "What would you suggest as an appropriate costume?"

"Try rompers!" retorted Heath. "But make 'em a dark colour." With a snort he turned to Markham. "When will we know about the final decision, Chief?"

"Kenting is going to communicate with me sometime before I leave the office today."

"Swell," said Heath heartily. "That'll give us plenty of time to make our arrangements."

It was four o'clock that afternoon when Kenyon Kenting arrived. Vance, eager to be on hand for anything new that might develop, had waited in Markham's office, and I stayed with him. Kenting had a large bundle of $100 bills with him, and threw it down on Markham's desk with a disgruntled air of finality.

"There's the money, Mr. Markham," he said. "Fifty thousand good American dollars. It has completely impoverished me. It took everything I owned. . . . How do you suggest we go about it?"

Markham took the money and placed it in one of the drawers of his steel filing cabinet.

"I'll give the matter careful consideration," he answered. "And I'll get in touch with you later."

"I'm willing to leave everything to you," Kenting said with relief.

There was little more talk of any importance, and finally Kenting left the office with Markham's promise to communicate with him within two or three hours.

Heath, who had gone out earlier in the afternoon, came in shortly, and the matter was discussed pro and con. The plan eventually agreed on was that Heath should have his searchlights focused on the tree and ready to be flashed on at a given signal; and that three or four men of the Homicide Bureau should be on the ground and available at a moment's notice. Vance and I, fully armed, were to perch in the upper branches of the tree.

Vance remained silent during the discussion, but at length he said in his lazy drawl:

"I think your plans are admirable, Sergeant, but I really see no necessity of actually plantin' the money. Any package of the same size would answer the purpose just as well, don't y' know. And notify Fleel: I think he would be the best man to place the package in the tree for us."

Heath nodded.

"That's the idea, sir. Exactly what I was thinking. . . . And now I think I'd better be running along—or toddlin', as you would say—and get busy."

CHAPTER 10

The Tree in the Park
Thursday, July 21; 9:45 p.m.

Vance and Markham and I had dinner at the Stuyvesant Club that night. I had accompanied Vance home where he changed to a rough tweed suit. He had had little to say after we had left Markham's office at five o'clock. All the details for the night's project had been arranged.

Vance was in a peculiar mood. I felt he ought to be taking the matter more seriously, but he appeared only a little puzzled, as if the situation was not clear in his mind. He did not exhibit the slightest apprehension, however, although as we were about to leave the apartment he handed me a .45-automatic. When I put it in my outside coat pocket, where it would be handy, he shook his head whimsically and smiled.

"No call for so much precaution, Van. Put it in your trousers pocket and forget it. As a matter of fact, I'm not even sure it's loaded. I'm taking one myself, but only to humour the Sergeant. I haven't the groggiest notion what's goin' to happen, but I can assure you there will be no necessity for a display of fireworks. The doughty Sergeant's pre-arranged melodrama is bally nonsense."

I protested that kidnappers were dangerous people, and that ransom notes with orders of the kind that Fleel had brought to the District Attorney's office were not to be taken too lightly.

Vance smiled cryptically.

"Oh, I'm not takin' it lightly," he said. "But I'm quite sure that note need not be taken at its face value. And sittin' on the limb of a tree indefinitely is not what I should call a jolly evening's sport. . . . However," he added, "we may learn something enlightenin', even if we don't have the opportunity to embrace the person accountable for Kaspar's disappearance."

275

He slipped the gun in his pocket, buttoned the flap, and arranged his clothes more comfortably. Then he donned a soft, black Homburg hat and went to the door.

"*Allons-y!*"

At eight o'clock we found Markham waiting at the Stuyvesant Club. He seemed perturbed and nervous, and Vance attempted to cheer him. In the dining-room Vance had some difficulties with his order. He asked for the most exotic dishes, none of which was available, and finally compromised on *tournedos de boeuf* and *pommes de terre soufflées*. He had a long discussion with the *sommelier* regarding the wine, and he lingered over his *crêpes suzettes* after having explained elaborately to the waiter just how he wished them made. During the meal he was in a gay humour and refused to react to Markham's sombre mood. As a matter of fact, his conversation was limited almost entirely to the types and qualities of the two-year-old horses that year had produced and of their chances in the Hopeful Stakes.

We had finished our dinner and were having our coffee in the lounge, shortly before ten o'clock, when Sergeant Heath joined us and reported the arrangements he had made.

"Well, everything's been fixed, Chief," he announced proudly. "I got four powerful searchlights in the apartment house on Fifth Avenue, just opposite the tree. They'll all go on when I give the signal."

"What signal, Sergeant?" asked Markham anxiously.

"That was easy, Chief," Heath explained with satisfaction. "I had a red electric flood-light put on a traffic-light post on the north-bound road near the tree, and when I switch that on, with a travelling switch I'll have in my pocket, that will be the signal."

"What else, Sergeant?"

"Well, sir, I got three guys in taxicabs stationed along Fifth Avenue, all dressed up like chauffeurs, and they'll swing into the park at the same time the searchlights go on. I got a couple of taxicabs at every entrance on the east side of the park that'll plug up the place good and tight; and I also got a bunch of innocent-looking family cars running along the east and west roads every two or three minutes. On top of that, you can't stop people strolling in the park—there's always a bunch of lovers moving around in the evening—but this time it ain't gonna be only lovers on the path by that tree—there's gonna be some tough babies too. We'll stroll back and forth down the east lane ourselves where we can see the tree; and Mr. Vance and Mr. Van Dine will be up in the branches—which are pretty thick at this time of year, and will make good cover. . . . I don't see how the guys can get away from us, unless they're mighty slick." He chuckled and turned to Vance. "I don't think there'll be much for you two to do, sir, except lookin' on from a ringside seat."

"I'm sure we won't be annoyed," answered Vance good-naturedly. "You're so thorough, Sergeant—and so trustin'."

"What about the package?" Markham asked of Heath.

"Don't worry about that, sir. I got that all fixed too." The Sergeant's voice, though serious and earnest, exuded pride. "I had a talk with Fleel, like Mr. Vance suggested, and he's gonna put it in the tree a little while before eleven. And it's a swell package. Exactly the size and weight of that bunch of greenbacks Kenting brought to your office this afternoon."

"What about Kenting himself?"

"He's meeting us at half-past ten, and so is Fleel, in the superintendent's room at the new yellow brick apartment house on Fifth Avenue. I gave 'em both the number, and you can bet your sweet life they'll be there. . . . Don't you think Mr. Vance and Mr. Van Dine had better be gettin' themselves fixed in the tree pretty *pronto*?"

"Oh, quite, Sergeant. Bully idea. I think we'll be staggerin' along now." Vance rose and stretched himself in mock weariness. "Good luck, and cheerio."

It seemed to me that he was still treating the matter like an unnecessary farce.

Vance dismissed our taxicab at the corner of 83rd Street and Fifth Avenue, and we continued northward on foot to the pedestrians' entrance to the park. As we walked along without undue haste, a chauffeur from a near-by taxi jumped to the sidewalk with alacrity and, overtaking us, stepped leisurely in front of us across our path. I immediately recognized Snitkin in the old tan duster and chauffeur's cap. He apparently took no notice of us but must have recognized Vance, for he turned back, and when I looked over my shoulder a moment later, he had returned to the cab and taken his place again at the wheel.

It was a warm, sultry night, and I confess I felt a certain tinge of excitement as we walked slowly down the winding flagged pathway southward. There were several couples seated in the dark benches along the pathway, and an occasional shambling pedestrian. I looked at all of them closely, trying to determine their status, and wondering if they were sinister figures who might have some connection with the kidnapping. Vance paid no attention to them. His eyebrows were lifted cynically, and his surroundings seemed not to interest him at all.

"What a silly adventure," he murmured as he took my arm and led me due west into a narrow footpath toward a clump of oak trees, silhouetted against the silvered waters of the reservoir beyond. "Still, who can prophesy? One can never tell what may happen in this fickle world. One never knows, y' know. Maybe when you get atop your favourite limb in the tree you'd better shift your automatic. And I think I'll unbutton the flap on my hip pocket."

This was the first indication Vance had given that he attached any importance to the matter.

Far across the park the gaunt structures on Central Park West loomed against the dark blue western sky, and the lights in the windows suddenly seemed unusually friendly to me.

Vance led the way across a wide stretch of lawn to a large oak tree whose size set it apart from the others. It stood in comparative darkness, at least fifty feet from the nearest dimly flickering electric light.

"Well, here we are, Van," he announced in a low voice. "Now for the fun—if you regard emulating the sparrow as fun. . . . I'll go up first. Find yourself a limb where you won't be exposed, but where you can see pretty well all around you through the leaves."

He paused a moment, and then reaching upward to one of the lower branches of the tree, he pulled himself up easily. I saw him stand up on the branch, reach over his head to the next one, and draw himself up again. In a moment he had disappeared among the black foliage.

I followed at once, although I had not the skill he displayed—in fact, I had to sit down astride the lower limb for a moment or two before I could work myself upward into the outspreading branches. It was very dark, and I had difficulty keeping a sure foothold while I gave my attention to climbing higher. At last I found a fork-shaped limb on which I could establish myself with more or less comfort, and from which I could see, through various narrow openings in the leaves, in nearly all directions. After a few moments I heard Vance's voice at my left—he was evidently on the other side of the broad trunk.

"Well, well," he drawled. "What an experience! I thought my boyhood days were over. And there's not an apple on the tree. No, not so much as a cherry. A pillow would be most comfortin'."

We had been sitting in silence in our precarious seclusion for about ten minutes when a corpulent figure, which I recognized as Fleel, came into sight on the pathway to the left. He stood irresolutely opposite the tree for several moments and looked about him. Then he strolled along the footpath, across the greensward, and approached the tree. If any one had been watching, Fleel must certainly have been observed, for he chose a moment when there was no other person visible within a considerable radius of him.

He paused beneath where I sat twelve or fourteen feet above him, and ran his hand around the trunk of the tree until he found the large irregular hole on the east side; then he took a package from under his coat. The package was about ten inches long and four inches square, and he inserted it slowly and carefully into the hole. Backing away, he ostentatiously relighted his cigar, tossed the burnt match-end aside, and walked slowly toward the west, to another pathway at least a hundred yards away.

At that moment I happened to glance toward the narrow path by which we had entered the park and, by the light from a passing car, I suddenly noticed a shabbily dressed man leaning lazily against a bench in the shadows and evidently watching Fleel as he moved away in the distance. After a few moments I saw the same man step out from the darkness, stretch his arms, and move along the pathway to the north.

"My word!" muttered Vance in the darkness, in a low, guarded tone, "the assiduous Fleel has been observed—which is probably what the Sergeant wished. If everything moves according to schedule we shouldn't have to cling here precariously for more than fifteen minutes longer. I do hope the abductor or his agent is a prompt chappie. I'm gettin' jolly well worn out."

It was, in fact, less than ten minutes later that I saw a figure moving toward us from the north. No one had passed along that little-known, illy-lighted pathway since we had taken our places in the tree. At each succeeding light I picked out an additional detail of the approaching figure: a long dark cape which seemed to trail on the ground; a curious toque-shaped, dark hat, with a turned-down visor extending far over the eyes; and a slim walking-stick.

I felt an involuntary tightening of my muscles: I was not only expectant, but half frightened. Holding tightly with my left hand to the branch on which I was sitting, I reached into my coat pocket and fingered the butt of the automatic, to make sure that it was handy.

"How positively thrillin'!" I heard Vance whisper, though his voice did not sound in the least excited. "This may be the culprit we're waitin' for. But what in the world will we do with him when we catch him? If only he wouldn't walk so deuced slowly."

As a matter of fact, the dark-caped figure was moving at a most deliberate gait, pausing frequently to look right and left, as if sizing up the situation in all directions. It was impossible to tell whether the figure was stout or thin, because of the flowing cape. It was a sinister-looking form, moving along in the semidarkness, and cast a grotesque shadow on the path as it proceeded toward us. Its gait was so dilatory and cautious that a chill ran over me as I watched—it was like a mysterious nemesis, imperceptibly but inevitably creeping up on us.

"A purely fictional character," murmured Vance. "Only Eugène Sue could have thought of it. I do hope this tree is its destination. That would be most fittin'—eh, what?"

The shapeless form was now opposite us and, halting ominously, looked in our direction. Then it peered forward up the narrow winding path and backward along the route it had come. After a few moments the black form turned and approached the cluster of oak trees. Its progress over the lawn was even slower than on the cement walk. It seemed an interminable time before the dim shape reached the tree in which Vance and I were perched, and I could feel cold chills running up and down my spine. The figure was there beneath the branches, and stood several feet from the trunk, turning and gazing in all directions.

Then, as if with a burst of vigour, the cloaked form stepped toward the natural cache on the east side of the trunk and, fumbling round a moment or two, withdrew the package that Fleel had placed there a quarter of an hour earlier.

I glanced apprehensively at the red flood-light on the lamppost Heath had described to us, and saw it flash on and off like a grotesquely winking monster. Suddenly there were wide shafts of white light from the direction of Fifth Avenue splitting the gloom; and the whole tree and its immediate environs were flooded with brilliant illumination. For a moment I was blinded by the glare, but I could hear a bustle of activity all about us. Then came Vance's startled and awestruck voice somewhere at my left.

"Oh, my word!" he exclaimed over and over again; and there was the sound of his scrambling down the tree. At length I saw him swing from the lower limb and drop gracefully to the ground, like a well balanced pole-vaulter.

Everything seemed to happen simultaneously. Markham and Fleel and Kenyon Kenting came rushing across the eastern lawn, preceded by Heath and Sullivan.[1] The two detectives were the first to reach the spot, and they grasped the black-clad figure just as it straightened up to move away from the tree. Each man had an arm tight in his clasp, and escape was impossible.

---

1. A detective of the Homicide Bureau who participated in nearly all of Vance's criminal investigations.

"Pretty nice work," Heath sang out with satisfaction, just as I reached the ground and took a tighter hold on my automatic. Vance brushed by me from around the tree and stood directly in front of Heath.

"My dear fellow—oh, my dear fellow!" he said with quick sternness. "Don't be too precipitate."

As he spoke, two taxicabs swung crazily along the pedestrian walk on the left with a continuous shrill blowing of horns. They came to a jerky stop with a tremendous clatter and squeaking of brakes. Then the two chauffeurs leaped out of the cabs and came rushing to the scene with sub-machine guns poised ominously before them.

Heath and Sullivan looked at Vance in angry amazement.

"Step back, Sergeant," Vance commanded. "You're far too rough. I'll handle this situation." Something in his voice overrode Heath's zeal—there was no ignoring the authority his words carried. Both Heath and Sullivan released their hold on the silent figure between them and took a backward step, bumping unseeingly into the startled group formed by Markham, Fleel and Kenting behind them.

The apprehended culprit did not move, except to reach up and push back the visor of the toque cap, revealing the face in the glare of the searchlights.

There before us, leaning weakly and shakily on a straight snakewood stick, the package of false bank notes still clutched tightly in the left hand, was the benign, yet cynical, Mrs. Andrews Falloway. Her face showed no trace of fear or of agitation. In fact, there was an air of calm satisfaction in her somewhat triumphant gaze.

In her deep, cultured voice she said, as if exchanging pleasantries with some one at an afternoon tea:

"How are you, Mr. Vance?" A slight smile played over her features.

"I am quite well, thank you, Mrs. Falloway," Vance returned suavely, with a courteous bow; "although I must admit the rough limb which I chose in the dark was a bit sharp and uncomfortable."

"Truly I am desolated, Mr. Vance." The woman was still smiling.

Just then a slender form skulked swiftly across the lawn from the near-by path and, without a word, joined the group directly behind the woman. It was Fraim Falloway. His expression was both puzzled and downcast. Vance threw him a quick glance, but took no more notice of him. His mother must have seen him out of the corner of her eye, but she showed no indication that she was aware of her son's presence.

"You're out late tonight, Mrs. Falloway," Vance was saying graciously. "Did you enjoy your evening stroll?"

"I at least found it very profitable," the woman answered with a hardening voice. As she spoke she held out the package. "Here's the bundle—containing money, I believe—which I found in the hole of the tree. You know," she added lightly, "I'm getting rather old for lovers' trysts. Don't you think so?"

Vance took the package and threw it to Heath who caught it with automatic dexterity. The Sergeant, as well as the rest of the group, was looking on in stupefied astonishment at the strange and unexpected little drama.

"I am sure you will never be too old for lovers' trysts," murmured Vance gallantly.

"You're an outrageous flatterer, Mr. Vance," smiled the woman. "Tell me, what do you really think of me after this little—what shall we call it?—escapade tonight?"

Vance looked at her, and his light cynical expression quickly changed to one of solemnity.

"I think you're a very loyal mother," he said in a low voice, his eyes fixed on the woman. Quickly his mood changed again. "But, really, y' know, it's dampish, and far too late for you to walk home." Then he looked at the gaping Heath. "Sergeant, can either of your pseudo-chauffeurs drive his taxi with a modicum of safety?"

"Sure they can," stammered Heath. "Snitkin was a private chauffeur for years before he took up police work." (I now noticed that one of the two men who had dashed across the lawn with the sub-machine guns, which they had now lowered in utter astonishment, was the same driver who had crossed in front of us as we entered the park.)

"That's bully—what?" said Vance. He moved to Mrs. Falloway's side and offered her his arm. "May I have the pleasure of taking you home?"

The woman took his arm without hesitation.

"You're very chivalrous, Mr. Vance, and I would appreciate the courtesy."

Vance started across the lawn with the woman.

"Come, Snitkin," he called peremptorily, and the detective walked swiftly to his cab and opened the door. A moment later they were headed toward the main traffic artery which leads to Central Park West.

Another Empty Room

Thursday, July 21; 11:10 p.m.

It was but a short time before the rest of us started for the Kenting house. As soon as Snitkin had driven off with Vance and Mrs. Falloway, Heath began to dash around excitedly, giving innumerable brusque orders to Burke,[1] who came ambling toward us across the narrow path from the east. When he had made all his arrangements, he walked to the wide lane where the second taxicab still stood. This cab, I noticed, was manned by the diminutive Guilfoyle,[2] one of the two "chauffeurs" who came to the tree with sub-machine guns, ready for action.

"I guess we'd better follow Mr. Vance," Heath growled. "There's something mighty phoney about this whole business."

Markham, Fleel and young Falloway got into the back seat of the cab; Kenting and I took our places on the two small folding seats forward in the tonneau; and the Sergeant crowded into the front of the cab with Guilfoyle. When the doors were shut Guilfoyle drove off rapidly toward the main roadway on the west side of the park. Nothing was said on that short ride. Every one, it seemed, was too dumbfounded to make any comment on the unexpected outcome of the night's adventure.

Markham sat stiffly upright, looking out of the window, a dark frown on his face. Fleel leaned back more comfortably against the cushions in silence, staring straight ahead but apparently seeing nothing. Fraim Falloway crouched morosely in the corner of the seat, with his hat pulled far down over his eyes, his face a puzzled mask; and when I offered him

---

1. Burke was a detective from the Homicide Bureau, who, as a rule, acted as Sergeant Heath's right-hand man.
2. Guilfoyle was another detective from the Homicide Bureau, and had helped with the investigation of the "Canary" murder case.

a cigarette he seemed utterly oblivious to my gesture. Once or twice on the way to his home he uttered a cackling, breathless chuckle, as if at some thought that had flashed through his mind. Kenyon Kenting, sitting at my left, seemed weary and distressed, and bent forward with his elbows on his knees, his head bowed in his hands.

Through the plate-glass panel in front of me, I could see the Sergeant bobbing up and down with the motion of the cab, and shifting his cigar angrily from one side of his mouth to the other. Occasionally he turned to Guilfoyle, and I could see his lips move, but I could hear nothing over the hum of the motor; then he would resume his dour and bitter silence. It was obvious he was deeply disappointed and believed all his plans had gone awry for some reason he could not figure out.

After all, the whole incident that night had been unexpected and amazing. I tried to reason out what had happened, but could not fit any of the known factors together, and finally gave the matter up. The climax of the episode was the last thing I could possibly have dreamed of, and I am sure the others felt the same way about it. If no one had come to the tree for the package of supposed bank notes, it would have been easily understandable, but the fact that a crippled old woman had turned out to be the collector of the money was as astonishing as it was incredible. And, to add to every one's perplexity, there was Vance's attitude toward her—which was perhaps the most astounding thing of all.

Where had been the person who sent the note? And then I suddenly remembered the shabby man who had been leaning against the bench on the pathway, watching Fleel. Could this have been the person?—had he seen us at the tree and known that the spot was under observation?—had he lost his courage and gone off without attempting to secure the package of bills?—or was my imagination keyed up to a pitch where I was ready to suspect every stray figure? The problem was far too confusing, and I could not arrive at even a tentative solution.

When we pulled up in front of the Kenting house, which suddenly seemed black and sinister in the semi-dark, we all quickly jumped to the sidewalk and hastened in a body to the front door. Only Guilfoyle did not move; he relaxed a little in his narrow seat and remained there, his hands still at the wheel.

Weem, in a dark *pongee* dressing-robe, opened the door for us and made a superfluous gesture toward the drawing-room. Through the wide-open sliding doors we could see Vance and Mrs. Falloway seated. Vance, without rising, greeted us whimsically as we entered.

"Mrs. Falloway," he explained to us, "wished to remain here a short while to rest before going upstairs. Beastly ascent, y' know."

"I really feel exhausted," the woman supplemented in her low, cultured voice, looking at Markham and ignoring the rest of us. "I simply had to rest a while before climbing those long flights of stairs. I do wish old Karl Kenting hadn't put such unnecessarily high ceilings in this old house, or else that he had added a lift. It's very tiring, you know, to walk from one floor to another. And I'm so fatigued just now, after my long walk in the park." She smiled cryptically and adjusted the pillow behind her back.

At that moment there was a ring at the front door, and Heath went out quickly to answer it. As he swung the ponderous door back, I could easily see, from where I stood, the figure of Porter Quaggy outside.

"What do you want?" Heath demanded bluntly, barring the way with his thick body.

"I don't want anything," Quaggy returned in a cold, unfriendly voice; "—if that answer will benefit you in any way—except to ask how Mrs. Kenting is and if you know anything more about Kaspar. I saw you drive past my hotel just now and get off here. . . . Do you want to tell me, or don't you?"

"Let the johnnie come in, Sergeant," Vance called out in a low, commanding voice. "I'll tell him what he wants to know. And I also desire to ask him a question or two."

"All right," Heath grumbled in a modified tone to the man waiting on the threshold. "Come on in and get an earful."

Quaggy stepped inside briskly and joined us in the drawing-room. He glanced round the room with narrowed eyes and then asked of no one in particular: "Well, what happened tonight?"

"Nothing—really nothing," Vance answered casually, without looking up. "Positively nothing. Quite a fizzle, don't y' know. Very sad. . . . But I am rather glad you decided to pay us this impromptu visit, Mr. Quaggy. Would you mind telling us where you were tonight?"

The man's eyelids drooped still lower, till they were almost entirely shut, and he looked down at Vance for several moments with a passive and expressionless face.

"I was at home," he said finally, in an arctic, aggressive tone, "fretting about Kaspar." Then he suddenly shot forth, "Where were *you*?"

Vance smiled and sighed.

"Not that it should concern you in the slightest, sir," he said in his most dulcet voice, "but—since you ask—I was climbing a tree. Silly pastime—what?"

Quaggy swung about to Kenting.

"You raised the money, Kenyon, and complied with the instructions in the follow-up note?" he asked.

Kenting inclined his head: he was still solemn and perturbed.

"Yes," he said in a low voice, "but it did no good."

"A swell bunch of cheap dicks," Quaggy sneered, flashing Heath a contemptuous glance. "Didn't any one show up to collect?"

"Oh, yes, Mr. Quaggy." It was Vance who answered. "Some one called for the money at the appointed hour, and actually took it."

"And I suppose he got away from the police—as usual. Is that it?" Quaggy had turned again and was contemplating Vance's bland features.

"Oh, no. No. We saw to that." Vance took a long puff on his cigarette. "The culprit is here with us in this room."

Quaggy straightened with a start.

"The fact is," went on Vance, "I escorted the guilty person home myself. It was Mrs. Falloway."

Quaggy's expression did not change—he was as unemotional and noncommittal as a veteran poker player; but I had a feeling the news had shocked him considerably.

Before the man had time to say anything Vance continued lackadaisically.

"By the by, Mr. Quaggy, are you particularly interested in black opals? I noticed a jolly good pair of them on your desk yesterday."

Quaggy hesitated for several moments.

"And if I am, what then?" His lips barely moved as he spoke, and there was no change in the intonation of his voice.

"Queer, don't y' know," Vance went on, "that there are no representative black opals in Karl Kenting's collection. Blank spaces in the case where they should be. I can't imagine, really, how an expert collector of semiprecious stones should have overlooked so important an item as the rarer black opal."

"I get the implication. Anything else?" Quaggy was standing relaxed but motionless in front of Vance. Slowly he moved one foot forward, as if shifting the burden of his weight from an overtired leg. By an almost imperceptible movement his foot came to within a few inches of Vance's shoe.

"Really, y' know," Vance said with a cold smile, lifting his eyes to the man, "I shouldn't try that if I were you—unless, of course, you wish to have me break your leg and dislocate your hip. I'm quite familiar with the trick. Picked it up in Japan."

Quaggy abruptly withdrew his foot, but said nothing.

"I found a balas-ruby in Kaspar Kenting's dinner jacket yesterday morning," Vance proceeded calmly. "A balas-ruby is also missing from the collection across the hall. Interestin' mathematical item—eh?"

"What the hell's interesting about it?" retorted the other with a sneer.

Vance looked at him mildly.

"I was only wonderin'," he said, "if there might be some connection between that imitation ruby and the black opals in your apartment. . . . By the by, do you care to mention where you obtained such valuable gem specimens?"

Quaggy made a noise in his throat which sounded to me like a contemptuous laugh, but the expression on his face did not change. He did not answer, and Vance turned to the District Attorney.

"I think, in view of the gentleman's attitude, Markham, and the fact that he is the last person known to have been with the missing Kaspar, it would be advisable to hold him as a material witness."

Quaggy drew himself erect with a jerk.

"I came by those opals legitimately," he said quickly. "I bought them from Kaspar last night, as he said he needed some immediate cash for the evening."

"You knew, perhaps, that the stones were part of the Kenting collection?" asked Vance coldly.

"I didn't inquire where they came from," the man returned sullenly. "I naturally trusted him."

"'Naturally,'" murmured Vance.

Mrs. Falloway struggled to her feet, leaning heavily on her stick.

"I've suspected for a long time," she said, "that Kaspar had been resorting to that collection of gems for gambling money. I've come down occasionally and gone over the exhibits, and it seemed to me each time there were a few more missing. . . . But I'm very tired, and I'm sufficiently rested now to return to my room. . . ."

"But, Mrs. Falloway," blurted Kenting—I had noticed that he had been staring at the woman incredulously ever since we had returned to the house, and he could not, apparently, restrain his curiosity any longer; "I—I don't understand your being in the park tonight. Why—why—?"

The woman gave him a withering look.

"Mr. Vance understands," she answered curtly. "That, I think, is quite sufficient." Her gaze shifted from Kenting and she seemed to take us all in with a gracious glance. "Good night, gentlemen. . . ."

She started unsteadily toward the door, and Vance sprang to her side.

"Permit me, madam, to accompany you. It's a long climb to your room."

The woman bowed a courteous acknowledgment and, for the second time that evening, took his arm. Fraim Falloway did not rise to assist his mother; he seemed oblivious to everything that was going on. Markham, with a significant look at the Sergeant, left his chair and took the woman's free arm. Heath moved closer to Quaggy who remained standing. Mrs. Falloway, with her two escorts, went slowly from the drawing-room, and I followed them.

It was with considerable effort that the woman mounted the stairs. She found it necessary to pause momentarily at each step, and when we reached her room she sank into the large wicker armchair with the air of a person wholly exhausted.

Vance took her stick and placed it on the floor beside the chair. Then he said in a kindly voice:

"I should like to ask one or two questions, if you are not too weary."

The woman nodded and smiled faintly.

"A question or two won't do any harm, Mr. Vance," she said. "Please go ahead."

"Why did you make the tremendous effort," Vance began, "of walking in the park tonight?"

"Why, to get all that money, of course," the old woman answered in mock surprise. "Anyway, I didn't attempt to walk all the way: I took a cab to within a few hundred feet of the tree. Think how rich I would have been had I not been caught in the disgraceful act. And," she added with a sigh, "you have spoiled everything for me."

"I'm frightfully sorry," said Vance in a bantering manner. "But really, there wasn't a dollar in that package." He paused and looked down earnestly at the woman. "Tell me, Mrs. Falloway, how you knew your son intended to go to the tree for that ransom package."

For a moment Mrs. Falloway's face was a mask. Then she said in a deep, clear voice:

"It is very difficult to fool a mother, Mr. Vance. Fraim knew of the ransom note and the instructions in it. He knew also that Kenyon would raise the money somehow. The boy came upstairs and told me about it after you had left the house this afternoon. Then, when he came to my room a little before ten o'clock tonight, after having spent the evening with his sister and Kenyon, and said he was going out, I knew what was in his mind—although he very often does go out late of an evening. He invented an important engagement—I always know when Fraim isn't telling the truth, although he doesn't realize that I do. I knew well enough where he was going and what he was going for. I could read it in his eyes. And I—I wished to save him from that infamy."[3]

Vance was silent for a moment as he regarded the weary old woman with pity and admiration, and Markham nodded sympathetically.

"But Fraim is a good boy at heart—please believe that," the woman added. "He merely lacks something—strength of body and spirit, perhaps."

Vance bowed.

"Quite. He's not well, Mrs. Falloway. He needs medical attention. Have you ever had a basal metabolism test made on him?"

The woman shook her head.

"A blood sugar?" proceeded Vance.

"No." Mrs. Falloway's voice was barely audible.

"A blood count?"

Again the woman shook her head.

"A Wassermann?"

"The truth is, Mr. Vance," the woman said, "he has never been examined." Then she asked quickly: "What do you think it is?"

"I wouldn't dare to venture an opinion, don't y' know," Vance returned, "though I'd say there was an endocrine insufficiency somewhere—an inadequacy of some internal secretion, a definite and prolonged hormone disturbance. It may be thyroid, parathyroid, or pituitary, or adrenal. Or maybe neuro-circulatory asthenia. It is deplorable how little science knows as yet about the ductless glands. A great work, however, is being done along those lines, and progress is constantly being made. I think you should have your son checked up. It may be something that can be remedied."

He scribbled something on a page from a small note-book and, tearing it out, handed it to Mrs. Falloway.

"Here is the name and address of one of the country's greatest endocrinologists. Look him up, for your son's sake."

The woman took the slip of paper, folded it, and put it in one of the large pockets of her skirt.

---

3. Vance's immediate knowledge regarding the exact truth of the situation, when he recognized Mrs. Falloway beneath the tree that night, was another instance of his uncanny ability to read human nature. I myself was startled by the simplicity and accuracy of his logic as the woman confessed the facts; for Vance had reasoned, almost in a flash, that the crippled old woman, who obviously was not guilty of the crime of kidnapping, could not have summoned sufficient strength for so heroic an act, unless it was on behalf of some one very dear to her and whose welfare and protection were foremost in her mind.

"You are very good—and very understanding, Mr. Vance," she said. "The moment I saw you in the park tonight, I knew you would understand. A mother's love—"

"Yes, yes—of course," murmured Vance. "And now I think we'll return to the drawing-room. And may you have a well-earned night's rest."

The woman looked at him gratefully and held out her hand. He took it and, bowing, raised it to his lips.

"My eternal admiration, madam," he said.

When we re-entered the drawing-room we found the group just as we had left it. Fleel and Kenyon Kenting still sat stiffly in their chairs near the front window, like awed wooden figures. Quaggy stood smoking thoughtfully before the chair where Vance had sat; and Heath, his sturdy legs spread, was at his side, glowering at him morosely. On the sofa, his head drooping forward, his mouth slightly open, and his arms hanging listlessly, lounged Fraim Falloway. He did not even look up as we entered; and the thought flashed through my mind that he might not be a glandular case at all, but that he was merely suffering from the early stages of *encephalitis lethargica*.

Vance glanced about him sharply and then strolled to his chair. Re-seating himself with unconcern, he lighted a fresh cigarette. Markham and I remained standing in the doorway.

"There are one or two matters—" drawled Vance and stopped abruptly. Then he said: "But I think Mrs. Kenting should be here with us for this discussion. After all, it is her husband who has disappeared, and her suggestions might be dashed helpful."

Kenyon Kenting stood up, nodding his head vigorously in approval.

"I think you're right, Mr. Vance," he said, going toward the door. "I'll get Madelaine myself."

"I trust it is not too late to disturb her," said Vance.

"Oh, no, no," Kenting assured him. "She almost never retires so early. She has not been able to sleep well for a long time, and reads far into the night. And tonight I was with her till after half-past nine, and she was terribly keyed up; I know she wouldn't think of retiring till she heard the outcome of our plans tonight."

He bustled from the room as he finished speaking, and we heard him going up the stairs. A few moments later we could hear his sharp, repeated knocking on a door. Then there was a long silence, and the sound of a door being opened hurriedly. Vance leaned forward in his chair and seemed to be waiting expectantly.

A few minutes later Kenting came rushing down the stairs. He stopped in the doorway, glaring at us with wide-open eyes. He looked breathless and horror-stricken as he leaned for support against the door-frame.

"She's not there!" he exclaimed in an awed voice. He took a deep breath. "I knocked on her door several times, but I got no answer—and a chill went through me. I tried the door, but it was locked. So I went through Kaspar's room, into Madelaine's. The lights are all on, but she isn't there. . . ."

He sucked in his breath again excitedly and stammered as if with tremendous effort:

"The window—over the yard—is wide open, and—and the ladder is standing against it!"

Emerald Perfume
Thursday, July 21; 11:30 p.m.

Kenyon Kenting's announcement that his sister-in-law was gone from her room and that the portentous ladder was standing below the open window had an instantaneous effect upon the gathering in the drawing-room. Markham and I had stepped into the room, and instinctively both of us turned to Heath who was, after all, technically in charge of the routine end of the Kenting kidnapping case. The wordless feud which had been going on between Heath and Porter Quaggy was immediately forgotten, and Heath was now directing his fierce glance to Kenting as he stood dejectedly in the doorway.

Quaggy's cigarette fell from his lips to the rug, where he stepped on it with automatic quickness, without even looking down.

"Good God, Kenyon!" he exclaimed, half under his breath. The man seemed deeply moved.

Fleel rose to his feet and, as he jerked down his waistcoat with both hands, appeared dazed and inarticulate. Even Fraim Falloway raised himself suddenly out of his stupor and, glowering at Kenting, began babbling hysterically.

"The hell you say! The hell you say!" he cried out in a high-pitched voice. "That's some more of Kaspar's dirty work. He's playing a game to get money, I tell you. I don't believe he was kidnapped at all—"

The Sergeant swung about and grabbed the youth roughly by the shoulder.

"Pipe down, young fella," he ordered. "Makin' fool statements like that ain't gonna help anything."

Falloway subsided and made a nervous search through his pockets till he found a crumpled cigarette.

I myself was shocked and dumbfounded by this startling turn of events. As a matter of fact, I hadn't yet recovered from the strange adventure in the park, and I was totally unprepared for this new blow.

Only Vance seemed unruffled and composed. He always had astounding control of his nerves, and it was difficult to judge just what was his reaction to the news of Mrs. Kenting's disappearance.

Markham, I noticed, was watching Vance closely, and as Vance slowly crushed out his cigarette and got indolently to his feet, Markham blurted out angrily:

"This doesn't seem to surprise you, Vance. You're taking it too damned calmly to suit me. Had you any idea of this—this new outrage when you suggested that Mrs. Kenting be called?"

"Oh, I rather expected something of the kind, but, frankly, I didn't think it would happen so soon."

"If you expected this thing," Markham snapped, "why didn't you let me know, so that we could do something about it?"

"My dear Markham!" Vance spoke with pacifying coolness. "There was nothing any one could do. The predicament was far from simple; and it's still a difficult one."

Heath had gone to the telephone, and I could hear him, with one ear, as it were, calling the Homicide Bureau and giving officious instructions. Then he slammed down the receiver and stalked toward the stairs.

"I want to look at that room," he announced. "Two of the boys from the Bureau are coming up right away. This is a hell of a night . . . ." His voice trailed off as he went up the steps two at a time. Vance and Markham and I had left the drawing-room and were immediately behind him.

Heath first tried the door-knob of Mrs. Kenting's room, but, as Kenting had informed us, the door was locked. He went up the hall to Kaspar Kenting's room. The door here was standing ajar, and at the far end of the room we could see into Mrs. Kenting's brightly lighted boudoir. Stepping through the first chamber, we entered the lighted bedroom. As Kenting had said, the window facing on the court was wide open, and not only was the Venetian blind raised to the top, but the heavy drapes were drawn apart. Cautiously avoiding any contact with the window-sill, Heath leaned out at the window, and then turned quickly back.

"The ladder's there, all right," he asserted. "The same like it was at the other window yesterday."

Vance was apparently not listening. He had adjusted his monocle and was looking round the room without any apparent show of interest. Leisurely he walked to the dressing-table opposite the window and looked down at it for a moment. A round cut-glass powder jar stood uncovered at one side; the tinted glass top was resting on its side several inches away. A large powder puff lay on the floor beneath the table. Vance reached down, picked it up, fitted it back into the jar, and replaced the cover.

Then he lifted up a small perfume atomizer which was resting perilously near the edge of the dressing-table, and pressed the bulb slightly. He sniffed at the spray, and set the bottle down at the rear of the table, on the crystal tray where it evidently belonged.

"Courtet's Emerald," he murmured. "I'm sure this was not the lady's personal preference in perfumes. Blondes know better, don't y' know. Emerald is suitable only for brunettes, especially those with olive complexions and abundant hair. . . . Very interestin'."

Heath was eyeing Vance with obvious annoyance. He could not understand Vance's actions. But he said nothing and merely watched impatiently.

Vance then went to the door and inspected it briefly.

"The night latch isn't on," he murmured, as if to himself. "And the turn-bolt hasn't been thrown. Door locked with a key. And no key in the keyhole."

"What are you getting at, Vance?" demanded Markham. "What if there is no key there? The door could have been locked and the key removed."

"Quite so—theoretically," returned Vance. "But rather an unusual procedure just the same—eh, what? When one locks oneself in a bed-room with a key, one usually leaves the key in the lock. Just what would be the object in removing it? Dashed if I know. . . . It could be, however. . . ."

He went across the room and into the bathroom. This room too was brightly lit. He glanced at the long metal cord hanging from the electric fixture, and with his hand tested the weight of the painted glass cylindrical ornament attached to the end of the chain. He re-leased it and watched it swing back and forth. He looked into the tumbler which stood on the wide rim of the washbowl and, setting it down again, examined the washbowl itself, and around the edges. He then bent over the soap dish. Markham, standing in the bathroom doorway, followed his movements with a puzzled frown.

"What in the name of God—" he began irritably.

"Tut, tut, my dear fellow," Vance interrupted, turning to him with a contemplative look. "I was merely attemptin' to ascertain at just what time the lady departed. . . . I would surmise, don't y' know, that it was round ten o'clock this evening."

Markham still looked perplexed.

"How do you figure that out?" he asked sceptically.

"Indications may be entirely misleadin'." Vance sighed slightly. "Nothing certain, nothing accurate in this world. One may only venture an opinion. I'm no oracle, Delphic or otherwise. Merely strugglin' toward the light." He pointed with his cigarette to the pull-chain of the electric fixture overhead. It was still swinging back and forth like a pendulum, but with a slight rotary motion, and its to-and-fro movement had not perceptibly abated.

"When I came into the bathroom," Vance explained, "yon polished brass chain was at rest—oh, quite—and I opined that its movement, with that heavy and abominable solid glass cylinder to control it, would discernibly continue, once it was pulled and released, for at least an hour. And it's just half-past eleven now. . . . Moreover, the glass here is quite dry, showing that it has not been used for an hour or two. Also, there's not a drop of water, either in the washbowl or on the edge; and a certain number of drops and a little dampness always remain after the washbowl has been used. And, by the by, the rubber stopper is dry. That process, I believe, would take in the neighbourhood of an hour and a half. Even the small amount of lather left on the cake of soap is dry and crumbly, which would point to the fact that it had not been used for at least an hour or so."

He took several puffs on his cigarette.

"And I cannot imagine Mrs. Kenting, with her habit of remaining up late, performing her nightly toilet as early as these matters would indicate. And yet the light was on in the bathroom, and there is a certain amount of evidence that she had been powdering her nose and spraying herself with perfume some time during the evening. Moreover, my dear Markham, there are indications of haste in the performance of these feminine rites, for she did not put the perfume atomizer back where it belongs, nor did she stop to retrieve the powder puff from where it had fallen on the floor."

Markham nodded glumly.

"I begin to see what you are trying to get at, Vance," he mumbled.

"And all these little details, taken in connection with the open latch and the unthrown bolt and the missing key in the hall door, lead me—rather vaguely and shakily, I admit—to the theory that she had a rendezvous elsewhere, for which she was a wee bit late, at some time around the far-from-witching hour of ten o'clock."

Markham thought a moment. Then he said slowly:

"But that's only a theory, Vance. It might have been at any time earlier in the evening after the dusk was sufficiently advanced to make artificial light necessary."

"Quite true," agreed Vance, "on the mere visible evidence hereabouts. But don't you recall that Kenting informed us only a few minutes ago that he was here at the house with Mrs. Kaspar Kenting until half-past nine this evening? And have you forgot already, my dear Markham, that Mrs. Falloway mentioned that young Fraim had been with his sister until a short time before he had his important engagement at ten o'clock?—which may have accounted for the lady's flustered state in preparing herself for the rendezvous, provided the assignation was made for ten o'clock. You see how nicely it all dovetails."

Markham nodded comprehendingly.

"All right," he said. "But what follows from all that?"

Without answering the question, Vance turned to Heath.

"What time, Sergeant," he asked, "did you notify Fleel and Kenyon Kenting about the arrangements for tonight?"

"Oh,—I should say—" Heath thought a moment. "Round six o'clock. Maybe a little after."

"And where did you find these gentlemen?"

"Well, I called Fleel at his home and he wasn't there yet. But I left word for him and he called me back in a little while. But I didn't think to ask him where he was. And Kenting was here."

Vance smoked a moment and said nothing, but he seemed satisfied with the answer. He glanced about him and again addressed Heath.

"I'm afraid, Sergeant, your finger-print men and your photographers and your busy boys from the Homicide Bureau are going to draw a blank here. But I'm sure you'd be horribly disappointed if they didn't clutter this room up with insufflators and tripods and what not."

"I still want to know," persisted Markham, "what all this time-table hocus-pocus means."

Vance looked at him with unwonted seriousness.

"It means deviltry, Markham." His voice was unusually low and resonant. "It means something damnable. I don't like this case.—I don't at all like it. It infuriates me because it leaves us so helpless. Again, I fear, we must wait."

"But we can't just sit back," said Markham in a dispirited voice. "Isn't there some step you can suggest?"

"Well, yes. But it won't help much. I propose that first we ask one or two questions of the gentlemen downstairs. And then I propose that we go into the yard and take a look at the ladder." Vance turned to Heath. "Have you your flashlight, Sergeant?"

"Sure I have," the other answered.

"And after that," Vance went on, resuming his reply to Markham, "I propose that we go home and bide our time. The Sergeant will carry on with his prescribed but futile activities while we slumber."

Heath grunted and started toward Kaspar Kenting's room, headed for the hallway.

When we reached the drawing-room we found all four of its occupants anxious and alert. Even Fraim Falloway seemed excited and expectant. They were all standing in a small group, talking to each other in short jerky sentences the gist of which I did not catch, for the conversation stopped abruptly, and they turned to us eagerly the moment we entered the room.

"Have you learned anything?" asked Fraim Falloway, in a semi-hysterical falsetto.

"We're not through looking round yet," Vance returned placatingly. "We hope to know something definite very soon. Just now, however, I wish to ask each of you gentlemen a question."

He did not seem particularly concerned and sat down as he spoke, crossing his knees leisurely. When he had selected a cigarette from his platinum-and-jet case he turned suddenly to the lawyer.

"What is your favourite perfume, Mr. Fleel?" he asked unexpectedly.

The man stared at him in blank astonishment, and I am sure that had he been in a courtroom, he would have appealed instantly to the judge with the usual incompetent-irrelevant-and-immaterial objection. However, he managed a condescending smile and replied:

"I have no favourite perfume—I know nothing about such things. It's true, I send bottles of perfume to my women clients at Christmas, instead of the conventional flower-baskets, but I always leave the selection to my secretary."

"Do you regard Mrs. Kenting as one of your women clients?" Vance continued.

"Naturally," answered the lawyer.

"By the by, Mr. Fleel, is your secret'ry blond or brunette?"

The man seemed more disconcerted than ever, but answered immediately.

"I don't know. I suppose you'd call her brunette. Her hair certainly doesn't look anything like Jean Harlow's or like Peggy Hopkins Joyce's—if that's what you mean."

"Many thanks," said Vance curtly, and shifted his gaze to Fraim Fallo-way who stood a few feet away, gaping before him with unseeing eyes.

"What is your favourite scent, Mr. Falloway?" Vance asked, watching the youth closely and appraisingly.

"I—I don't know," Falloway stammered. "I'm not familiar with such feminine matters. But I think Emerald is wonderful—so mysteri-ous—so exotic—so subtle." He raised his eyes almost rapturously, like a young poet reciting his own verses.

"You're quite right," murmured Vance; and then he focused his gaze on Kenyon Kenting.

"All perfumes smell alike to me," was the man's annoyed assertion before Vance could frame the question again. "I can't tell one from another—except Gardenia. Whenever I give any woman perfume, I give her Gardenia."

A faint smile appeared at the corners of Vance's mouth.

"Really, y' know," he said, "I shouldn't do it, if I were you."

As he spoke he turned his head to Porter Quaggy.

"And how about you, Mr. Quaggy?" he asked lightly. "If you were giving a lady perfume, what scent would you select?"

Quaggy gave a mirthless chuckle.

"I haven't yet been guilty of such foolishness," he replied. "I stick to flowers. They're easier. But if I were compelled to present a fair creature with perfume, I'd first find out what she liked."

"Quite a sensible point of view," murmured Vance, rising as if with great effort and turning. "And now, I say, Sergeant, let's have a curs'ry look at that ladder."

As we walked down the front steps I saw Guilfoyle still sitting at the wheel of his cab, with the motor humming gently.

Heath flashed on his powerful pocket light, and for the second time we went through the street gate leading into the yard, and ap-proached the ladder leaning against the side of the house.

The short grass was entirely dry, and the ground had completely hardened since the rain two nights ago. Vance again bent over at the foot of the ladder while Heath held the flashlight.

"There's no need to fear my spoiling your adored footprints to-night, Sergeant,—the ground is much too hard. Not even Sweet Alice Cherry[1] could have made an impression on this sod." Vance straight-ened up after a moment and moved the ladder slightly to the right, as he had done the previous morning. "And don't get jittery about

---

1. A famous side-show "fat woman" of the time.

finger-prints, Sergeant," he went on. "I'm quite convinced you'll find none. This ladder, I opine, is merely a stage-prop, as it were; and the person who set it here was clever enough to have used gloves."

He bent over again and inspected the lawn, but rose almost immediately.

"Not the slightest depression—only a few blades of grass crushed. . . . I say, *sergente mio*, it's your turn to step on the ladder—I'm frightfully tired."

Heath immediately clambered up five or six rungs and then descended; and Vance again moved the ladder a few inches. Both he and Heath now knelt down and scrutinized the ground.

"Observe," said Vance as he rose to his feet, "that the uprights make a slight depression in the soil, even with the weight of only one person pressing upon the ladder. . . . Let's go inside again and dispense our *adieux*."

On re-entering the house Vance immediately joined Kenting at the entrance to the drawing-room and announced to him, as well as to the others inside, that we were going, and that the house would be taken over very shortly by the police. There was a general silent acquiescence to his announcement.

"I might as well be going along myself," said Kenting despondently. "There is obviously nothing I can do here. But I hope you gentlemen will let me know the moment you learn anything. I'll be at home all night, and in my office tomorrow."

"Oh, quite," returned Vance, without looking at the man. "Go home, by all means. This has been a trying night, and you can help us better tomorrow if you are able to get any rest now."

The man seemed grateful: it was obvious he was much discouraged by the shock he had just received. Taking his hat from the hall bench, he hurried out the front door.

Quaggy's eyes followed the departing man. Then he rose and began pacing up and down the drawing-room.

"I guess I'll be getting along too," he said finally, with a note of interrogation in his voice. "I may go, I suppose?" There was a suggestion of sneering belligerence in his tone.

"That's quite all right," Vance told him pleasantly. "You probably need a bit of extra sleep, don't y' know, after your recent all-night vigil."

"Thanks," muttered Quaggy sarcastically, keeping his eyes down. And he too left the house.

When the front door had closed after him, Fleel looked up rather apologetically.

"I trust you gentlemen will not misunderstand my seeming right-about-face this morning regarding the assistance of the Police Department. The fact is, I was entirely sincere in telling you in the District Attorney's office that I was inclined to leave everything in your hands regarding the payment of the fifty thousand dollars. But on my way to the house here to see Kenting, I weighed the matter more carefully, and when I saw how eager Kenting was to follow the thing through alone, I decided it might be better, after all, to agree with him regarding the elimination of the police tonight. I see now that I was mistaken, and that my first instinct was correct. I feel, after what happened in the park tonight—"

"Pray don't worry on that score, Mr. Fleel," Vance returned negligently. "We quite understand your advis'ry attitude in the matter. Difficult position—eh, what? After all, one can only make guesses, subject to change."

Fleel was now on his feet, looking down meditatively at his half-smoked cigar.

"Yes," he muttered; "it is, as you say, a most difficult situation. . . ." He glanced up swiftly. "What do you make of this second terrible episode tonight?"

"Really, y' know,"—Vance was covertly watching the man—"it is far too early to arrive at any definite conclusions. Perhaps tomorrow. . . ." His voice faded away.

Fleel shook himself slightly, as with an involuntary tremor.

"I feel that we have not reached the end of this atrocious business yet. There appears to be a malicious desperation back of these happenings. . . . I wish I had never been brought into the case—I'm actually beginning to harbour fears for my own safety."

"We appreciate just how you feel," Vance returned.

Fleel straightened up with an effort and moved forward resolutely.

"I think I too will be going." He spoke in a weary tone, and I noticed that his hand trembled slightly as he picked up his hat and adjusted it.

"Cheerio," said Vance as the lawyer turned at the front door and bowed stiffly to us.

Meanwhile Fraim Falloway had risen from his place on the davenport. He now moved silently past us, with a drawn look on his face, and trudged heavily up the stairs.

Falloway had barely time to reach the first landing when the telephone resting on a small wobbly stand in the hall began ringing. Weem suddenly appeared from the dimness of the rear hall and picked up the receiver with a blunt "hello." He listened for a moment; then laying down the receiver, turned sullenly in our direction.

"It's a call for Sergeant Heath," he announced, as if his privacy had been needlessly invaded.

The Sergeant went quickly to the telephone and put the receiver to his ear.

"Well, what is it?" he started belligerently. ". . . . Sure it's the Sarge—shoot! . . . Well, for the love of—Hold it a minute." He clapped his hand over the mouthpiece and swung about quickly.

"Where'll we be in half an hour, Chief?"

"We'll be at Mr. Vance's apartment," Markham answered after one glance at Heath's expression.

"Oh, my word!" sighed Vance. "I had hoped to be reposing. . . ."

The Sergeant turned back to the instrument.

"Listen, you," he fairly bawled; "we'll be at Mr. Vance's apartment in East 38th Street. Know where it is? . . . That's right—and make it snappy." He banged down the receiver.

"Important, is it, Sergeant?" asked Markham.

"I'll say it is." Heath stepped quickly away from the telephone table. "Let's get going, sir. I'll tell you about it on the way down. Snitkin's meeting us at Mr. Vance's apartment. And Sullivan and Hennessey will be here any minute to take over."

The butler was still in the hall, half standing and half leaning against one of the large newel posts at the foot of the stairs, and Heath now addressed him peremptorily.

"Some of my men will be here pretty soon, Weem. And then you can go to bed. This house is in the hands of the police from now on—understand?"

The butler nodded his head dourly, and shuffled away toward the rear of the house.

"Just a moment, Weem," called Vance.

The man turned and approached us again, sulky and antagonistic.

"Weem, did you or your wife hear any one go out or enter this house around ten o'clock tonight?" Vance asked.

"No, I didn't hear anything. Neither did Gertrude. Mrs. Kenting told both of us that we wouldn't be needed and could do as we pleased after dinner. We had a long day and were tired, and we were both asleep from nine o'clock till you and Mrs. Falloway rang and I had to let you in. After the others came I got dressed and came down to see if there was anything I could do."

"Most admirable of you, Weem," Vance commended him, turning to the front door. "That's all I wanted to ask just now."

CHAPTER 13

The Green Coupé
Thursday, July 21; midnight

Just as Markham and Heath and I turned to follow Vance, there came, from somewhere outside, a startling and ominous rattle that sounded like the staccato and rapid sputtering of a machine-gun. So keyed up were my nerves that the reports went through me with a sickening horror, almost as if it had been the bullets themselves.

"God Almighty!" came the explosive exclamation of the Sergeant, who was at my side; and he stopped abruptly, as if he, too, had been struck by a bombardment of bullets. Then he suddenly sprang forward past Vance and, jerking the front door open, hurried out into the warm summer night without a word to any one. The rest of us followed close behind him. The Sergeant had halted at the edge of the stone pathway to the sidewalk and was looking confusedly up and down the street, uncertain which way to turn. Guilfoyle had jumped down from his seat in the cab as we came out of the vestibule, and was gesticulating excitedly in front of Heath.

"The shots came from up that way," he told Heath, waving his arm toward Central Park West. "What do you want me to do, Sarge?"

"Stay here and keep your eyes open," Heath ordered in clipped accents, "until Sullivan and Hennessey arrive. . . . And," he added as he started off toward the park, "stick around after that, in case of any emergency."

"I'm wise," Guilfoyle called after him.

Guilfoyle saluted half-heartedly, as Markham and Vance appeared on the sidewalk, and again he waved his arm to indicate, I presume, which way Heath had gone. He leaned reluctantly against his cab as we followed the Sergeant up the street.

"No," murmured Vance as we hurried along, "not a pleasant case—

and if my intuition is correct, these shots are another manifestation of its complexity."

Heath was now breaking into a run ahead of us; and Markham and I had difficulty keeping pace with Vance as he, too, lengthened his stride.

Just this side of the Nottingham Hotel at the corner, a small group of excited men were gathered under the bright light of the lamppost set between two trees along the curb. As Heath came abreast of the cluster of onlookers we could hear his gruff voice ordering them to disperse, and one by one they reluctantly moved off. Some continued on whatever business they had been about, while others remained to look on from the opposite side of the street. In the few moments it took us to reach the lamppost, the Sergeant had succeeded in clearing the scene.

There, leaning in a crouching attitude against the iron lamppost, was Fleel. His face was deathly pale. I have yet to see so unmistakable a picture of collapse from fright as he presented. His nerves were completely shattered. He was as pitiful a figure as I have ever looked at, huddled beneath the unflattering glare of the large electric light overhead, as he leaned weakly for support against the lamppost. In front of the lawyer stood Quaggy, looking at him with a curious hard-faced serenity.

Heath was staring at Fleel with a startled, inquisitive look in his eyes; but before he could speak to Fleel, Vance took the man under the arms and, knocking his feet from under him, set him down gently on the narrow strip of lawn which bordered the sidewalk, with his back against the lamppost.

"Breathe deeply," Vance advised the lawyer, when he had settled him on the ground. "And pull yourself together. Then see if you can tell us what happened."

Fleel looked up, his chest rising and falling as he sucked in the stagnant air of that humid July night. Slowly he struggled to his feet again and leaned heavily against the post, his eyes fixed before him.

Quaggy put a hand on the man's shoulder, as if to steady him, and shook him gently as he did so.

Fleel managed a sickly grimace intended for a smile, and turned his head weakly back and forth, blinking his eyes as if to clear his vision.

"That was a close call," he muttered. "They almost got me."

"Who almost got you, Mr. Fleel?" asked Vance.

"Why—why—" the man stammered, and paused for breath. "The men in the car, of course. I—didn't see—who they were—"

"Try to tell us, Mr. Fleel," came Vance's steadying voice, "just what happened."

Fleel took another deep breath and, with an obvious effort, straightened up a little more.

"Didn't you see it all?" he asked, his voice high and unnatural. "I was on my way to the corner, to get a taxicab, when a car drove up from behind me. I naturally paid no attention to it until it suddenly swerved toward the curb and stopped with a screeching of brakes, just as I reached this street light. As I turned round to see what it was, a small machine-gun was thrust over the ledge of the open window of the car and the firing began. I instinctively grasped this iron post and crouched down. After a number of shots the car jerked forward. I admit I was too frightened to notice which way it turned."

"But at least you were not hit, Mr. Fleel."

The man moved his hands over his body.

"No, thank Heaven for that," he muttered.

"And," Vance continued, "the car couldn't have been over ten feet away from you. A very poor shot, I should say. You were lucky, sir, this time." He spun round quickly to Quaggy, who had taken a step or two backward from the frightened man. "I don't quite understand your being here, Mr. Quaggy. Surely, you've had more than ample time to ensconce yourself safely in your *boudoir*."

Quaggy stepped forward resentfully.

"I *was* in my apartment. As you can see,"—he pointed indignantly to his two open front windows in the near-by hotel—"my lights are on. When I got to my rooms I didn't go directly to bed—I hope it wasn't a crime. I went to the front window and stood there for a few minutes, trying to get a breath of fresh air. Then I caught sight of Mr. Fleel coming up the street—he had apparently just left the Kenting house—and behind him came a car. Not that I paid any particular attention to it, but I did notice it. Only, when it turned in to the curb and stopped directly opposite Mr. Fleel as he reached the light post my curiosity was naturally aroused. And when I heard the machine-gun and saw the spits of fire coming through the window, and also saw Mr. Fleel grasp the lamppost and sink down, I thought he had been shot. I naturally dashed down—so here I am. . . . Anything illegal in that procedure?" he asked with cold sarcasm.

"No—oh, no," smiled Vance. "Quite normal. Far more normal, in fact, than if you had gone immediately to bed without a bit of airin' by the open window." He glanced at Quaggy with an enigmatical smile. "By the by," he went on, "did you, by any chance, note what type of car it was that attacked Mr. Fleel?"

"No, I didn't get a very good look at it," Quaggy returned in a chilly tone. "At first I didn't pay much attention to it, as I said; and when the shooting began I was too excited to get any vivid impression. But I think it was a coupé of some kind—not a very large car, and certainly not a new model."

"And the colour?" prompted Vance.

"It was a dingy, nondescript colour." Quaggy narrowed his eyes, as if trying to recall a definite picture. "It might have been a faded green—it was hard to be certain from the window. In fact, I think it was green."

Heath was watching Quaggy shrewdly.

"Yeah?" he said sceptically. "Which way did it go?"

Quaggy turned to the Sergeant.

"I really didn't notice," he replied none too cordially. "I caught only a glimpse of it as it started toward the park."

"A fine bunch of spectators," Heath snorted. "I'll see about that car myself." And he started running toward Central Park West.

As he neared the corner, a burly figure in uniform turned suddenly into 86th Street from the south, and almost collided with the Sergeant. By the bright corner light I could see that the newcomer was McLaughlin, the night officer on duty in that section, who had reported to us the morning of Kaspar Kenting's disappearance. He drew up quickly and saluted with a jerk.

"What was it, Sergeant?" His breathless, excited query carried down to us. "I heard the shots, and been trying to locate 'em. Did they come outa this street?"

"You're damn tootin', McLaughlin," replied Heath, and, grasping the officer by the arm, he swung him about, and the two started off again.

"Did you see any car come out of this street, into Central Park West?" demanded Heath.

I could not now hear what the officer answered, but when the two had reached the curb at the corner McLaughlin was waving his arm uptown, and I assumed that he was pointing in the direction that the green coupé had taken.

Heath looked up and down the avenue for a moment, no doubt trying to find a car he could requisition for the chase; but there was apparently none in sight, and he started diagonally across the street uptown, with McLaughlin at his heels. In the middle of the crossing the Sergeant turned his head and called out over his shoulder to us:

"Wait here at the corner for me." Then he and McLaughlin disappeared past the building on the north corner of Central Park West.

"My word, such energy!" sighed Vance when Heath and the officer were out of sight. "The coupé could be at 110th Street by this time—and thus the mad search would end. Heath is all action and no mentation. Sad, sad. . . . Vital ingredient of the police routine, I imagine—eh, what, Markham?"

Markham was in a solemn mood, and took no offence at Vance's levity.

"There's a taxicab stand just a block up on Central Park West," he explained patiently. "The Sergeant is probably headed for that in order to commandeer a cab for the chase."

"Marvellous," murmured Vance. "But I imagine even the green coupé could outrun a nocturnal taxi-cab if they both started from scratch."

"Not if the Sergeant were to puncture one of its rear tires with a bullet or two," retorted Markham angrily.

"I doubt if the Sergeant will have the opportunity, by this time." Vance smiled despondently. Then he turned to Fleel. "Feeling better?" he asked pleasantly.

"I'm all right now," the lawyer returned, taking a wobbly step or two forward and biting the end from a cigar he took from his pocket.

"That's bully," Vance said consolingly. "Do you want an escort home?"

"No, thanks," said Fleel, in a voice that was still dazed. "I'll make it all right." And when he had his cigar going he turned shakily toward Central Park West. "I'll pick up a taxicab." He held out his hand to Quaggy, who took it with surprising cordiality. "Many thanks, Mr. Quaggy," he said weakly and, I thought, a little shamefacedly. Then he bowed somewhat stiffly and haughtily to us and moved away out of the ring of light.

"Queer episode," commented Vance, as if to himself. "Fits in rather nicely, though. Lucky for your lawyer friend, Markham, that the gentleman in the green coupé wasn't a better shot. . . . Ah, well, we might as well toddle to the corner and await the energetic Sergeant. Really, y' know, Markham, there's no use gazing at the lamppost any longer."

Markham silently followed Vance toward the park.

Quaggy turned too and walked with us the short distance to the entrance of his apartment-hotel, where he took leave of us. At the great iron-grilled door he turned and said tauntingly: "Many thanks for not arresting me."

"Oh, that's quite all right, Mr. Quaggy," Vance returned, halting momentarily and smiling. "The case isn't over yet, don't y' know. . . . Cheerio."

At the corner Vance very deliberately lighted a cigarette and seated himself indolently on the wide stone balustrade extending along the east wall of the Nottingham Hotel.

"I'm not bloodthirsty at all, Markham," he said, looking quizzically at the District Attorney; "but I rather wish the gentleman with the machine-gun had potted Mr. Fleel. And he was at such short range. I've never wielded a machine-gun myself, but I'm quite sure I could have done better than that. . . . And the poor Sergeant, dashing madly around at this hour. My heart goes out to him. The whole explanation of this evening's little *contretemps* lies elsewhere than with the mysterious green coupé."

Markham was annoyed. He was standing at the curb, straining his eyes up the avenue to the north. "Sometimes, Vance," he said, without taking his eyes from the wide macadamized roadway, "you infuriate me with your babble. A lot of good it would have done us to have Fleel shot a few feet away from myself and the police."

Vance joined Markham at the edge of the sidewalk and followed his intense gaze northward to the quiet blocks in the distance.

"Lovely night," murmured Vance tantalizingly. "So quiet and lonely. But much too warm."

"I'll warrant the Sergeant and McLaughlin overhaul that car somewhere." Markham was apparently following his own trend of thought.

"Oh, I dare say," sighed Vance. "But I doubt if it will get us forrader. One can't send a green coupé to the electric chair. Silly notion—what?"

There were several moments of silence, and then a taxicab came at a perilous rate out of the transverse in the park, swung south, and drew up directly in front of us.

Simultaneously with the car's abrupt stop the door swung open, and Heath and McLaughlin stepped down.

"We got the car all right," announced Heath triumphantly. "The same dirty-green coupé McLaughlin here saw outside the Kenting house Wednesday morning."

The officer nodded his head enthusiastically.

"It's the same, all right," he asserted. "I'd swear to it. Jeez, what a break!"

"Where did you find it, Sergeant?" asked Markham. (Vance was unimpressed and was blowing smoke-rings playfully into the still summer air.)

"Right up there in the transverse leading through the park." The Sergeant waved his arm with an impatient backward flourish, and barely missed striking McLaughlin who stood beside him. "It was half-way up on the curb. Abandoned. After the guys in it ditched the car they musta come out and hopped a taxicab up the street, because shortly after the green coupé turned into the transverse two guys walked out and, according to the driver here, took the cab in front of his."

Without waiting for a reply from either Markham or Vance, Heath swung about and beckoned imperiously to the chauffeur of the cab from which he had just alighted. A short rotund man of perhaps thirty, with a flat cap and a duster too long for him, struggled out of the front seat and joined us.

"Look here, you," bawled Heath, "do you know the name of the man who was running the cab ahead of you on the stand tonight who took the two guys what come out of the transverse?"

"Sure I know him," returned the chauffeur. "He's a buddy of mine."

"Know where he lives?"

"Sure I know where he lives. Up on Kelly Street, in the Bronx. He's got a wife and three kids."

"The hell with his family!" snapped Heath. "Get hold of that baby as soon as you can, and tell him to beat it down to the Homicide Bureau *pronto*. I wanta know where he took those two guys that came out of the transverse."

"I can tell ya that right now, officer," came the chauffeur's respectful answer. "I was standin' talkin' to Abe when the fares came over from the park. I opened the door for 'em myself. An' they told Abe to drive like hell to the uptown station of the Lexington Avenue subway at 86th Street."

"Ah!" It was Vance who spoke. "That's very interestin'. Uptown— eh, what?"

"Anyway, I wanta see this buddy of yours," Heath went on to the chauffeur, ignoring Vance's interpolated comment. "Get me, fella?"

"Sure I getcha, officer," the chauffeur returned subserviently. "Abe ought to be back on the stand in half an hour."

"That's O.K.," growled Heath, turning to Markham. "Gosh, Chief, I gotta get to a telephone quick and get the boys lookin' for these guys."

"Why rush the matter, Sergeant?" Vance spoke casually. "We really ought not to keep Snitkin waiting too long at the apartment, don't y' know. I say, let's take this taxi and we'll be home in a few minutes. You can then use my phone to your heart's content. And this gentleman here"—indicating the chauffeur—"can return at once to his stand and await the arrival of his friend, Mr. Abraham."

Heath hesitated, and Markham nodded after a quick look at Vance.

"I think that will be the best course, Sergeant," the District Attorney said, and opened the door of the taxicab.

We all got inside, leaving McLaughlin standing on the curb, and Heath gave Vance's address to the driver. As we pulled away, Heath put his head out of the window.

"Report that empty car," he called out to McLaughlin. "And then keep your eye on it till the boys come up for it. Also watch for Abie till this fellow gets back—then get to the Kenting house and stand by with Guilfoyle."

Chapter 14

Kaspar is Found
Friday, July 22; 12:30 a.m.

As we drove rapidly down Central Park West, Markham nervously lighted a cigar and asked Heath, who was sitting on the seat in front of him:

"Well, what about that telephone call you got at the Kenting house, Sergeant?"

Heath turned his head and spoke out of the corner of his mouth.

"Kaspar Kenting's body has been found in the East River, around 150th Street. The report came in right after Snitkin got back to Headquarters. He's got all the details. . . . I thought I'd better not say anything about it up at the Kentings' place with that snoopy butler hanging around."

Markham did not speak for a few seconds. Then he asked:

"Is that all you know, Sergeant?"

"My God, Chief!" Heath exclaimed. "Ain't that enough?" And he settled down in the narrow, cramped quarters of his seat.

Again there was silence in the cab. Though I could not see Markham's face, I could well imagine his mixed reactions to this disturbing piece of news.

"Then you were right, Vance," he commented at length, in a strained, barely audible tone.

"The East River—eh?" Vance spoke quietly and without emotion. "Yes, it could easily be. Very distressin'. . . ." He said no more; nor was there any further talk until we reached Vance's apartment.

Snitkin was already waiting in the upper hallway, just outside the library. Heath merely grunted to him as he brushed by and picked up the telephone. He talked for five minutes or more, making innumerable reports relating to the night's happenings and giving various instructions. When he had the routine police ball rolling he beck-oned to Snitkin, and entered the library where Vance, Markham, and I were waiting.

"Go ahead, Snitkin," ordered Heath, before the man was barely in the room. "Tell us what you know."

"Oh, I say, Sergeant," put in Vance, "let Snitkin have a bit of this brandy first." And he poured a copious drink of his rare Napoléon into a whiskey glass on the end of the library table. "The gruesome particulars will keep a moment."

Snitkin hesitated and glanced sheepishly at the District Attorney. Markham merely nodded his head, and the detective gulped down the cognac. "Much obliged, Mr. Vance," he said. "And here's all I know about it:"—It is interesting to note that Snitkin addressed himself to Vance and not to either Markham or Heath, although Vance had no official standing in the Police Department.—"There's a small inlet up there in the river, which isn't over three feet deep, and the fellow on the beat—Nelson, I think it was—saw this baby lying on the bank, with his legs sticking out of the water, along about nine o'clock to-night. So he called in and reported it right away, and they sent over a buggy from the local station. The Medical Examiner of the Bronx gave the body the once-over, and it seems the fellow didn't even die from drowning. He was already dead when he was dumped into the water. His head was bashed in with—"

"With the usual blunt instrument," broke in Vance, finishing the sentence. "That's what the medicos always call it when they are not sure just how a johnnie was laid low by violence."

"That's right, Mr. Vance," resumed Snitkin with a grin. "The fel-low's head was bashed in with a blunt instrument—that's just what the report said. . . . Well, the doc guessed the guy had been dead twelve hours maybe. There's no telling how long he'd been lying there in the inlet. It's not a place that's likely to be seen by anybody, and it was only by accident that Nelson ran across the body."

"What about identification?" asked Heath officiously.

"Oh, there was plenty identification, Sarge," Snitkin answered. "The guy not only fit the description like a glove, but his clothes and his pockets was full of identification. Looked almost like whoever threw him there wanted him to be identified quick. He had his name on a label on the inside of his coat pocket, and another one under the strap of his vest, and still another one sewed into the watch pocket of his pants. And that ain't all: his name was written on the inside of his shoes—though I don't get that exactly. . . ."

"That's quite correct, Snitkin," remarked Vance. "It's the practice of all custom boot-makers. And the three labels in his clothes merely mean that they were made to order by a custom tailor. Quite custom'ry and understandable."

"Anyhow," Snitkin went on, "I'm simply tellin' you how we know the body is Kenting's. There was a wallet with initials in his inside coat pocket, with a couple of letters addressed to him, and a bunch of callin' cards. . . ."

"I do wish you'd call them visitin' cards," murmured Vance.

"Hell, I'll call 'em anything you want," grinned Snitkin. "Anyhow, they was there. And there was a pocket comb with his initials on it—"

"A pocket comb—eh?" Vance nodded with satisfaction. "Very interestin', Markham. When a gentleman carries a pocket comb—not a particularly popular practice these days, since beards went out of fashion—he would certainly not add a toilet comb to his equipment. . . . Forgive the interruption, Snitkin. Go ahead."

"Well, there was monograms on damn-near everything else he had in his pockets, like his cigarette case and lighter and knife and key-ring and handkerchiefs; and there was even monograms on his underwear. According to the boys at the local station, he was either the Kaspar Kenting we're looking for, or he wasn't nobody. And that was a pretty complete description of him we sent out this morning to all the local precincts."

"No pyjamas and no toothbrush in his pocket, Snitkin?" Vance asked.

"Pyjamas—a toothbrush?" Snitkin was as much surprised as he was puzzled. "Nothing was said about 'em, Mr. Vance, so I guess they wasn't there. Are they needed for identification?"

"Oh, no—no," Vance returned quickly. "Just a bit of curiosity on my part. Oh, I don't question the identification for a moment, Snitkin. It needs far less proof than you've given us."

"Who gave you all this dope, Snitkin?" asked the Sergeant in a somewhat mollified tone.

"The desk sergeant uptown," Snitkin told him. "He telephoned the Bureau as soon as he got the report from the doc. I had just come in, and took the call myself. Then I phoned you."

Heath nodded as if satisfied.

"That's all right, Snitkin. You'd better go home now and hit the hay,—you been wearin' out your dogs all day. But get down to the Bureau early tomorrow—I'll be needin' you. I'll see about getting some members of the family for official identification of the body in the morning—probably the fellow's brother will be enough. This is a hell of a case."

"But ain't you gonna tear off some rest yourself, Sergeant?" Snitkin asked solicitously.

"I'm a young fellow," retorted Heath with good-natured contempt. "I can take it. You old guys need a lot of beauty sleep."

Snitkin grinned again and looked at the Sergeant admiringly.

"Have another little spot, Snitkin, before you go," suggested Vance. And, without waiting for a response, he refilled the whiskey glass.

As before, Snitkin hesitated.

"You know, I'm not officially on duty now, Chief," he said, looking toward Markham almost coyly.

Markham did not glance up—he seemed depressed and worried.

"Go ahead," he barked, but not without a certain kindliness. "And don't talk so much. We all need a little support right now."

Snitkin picked up the whiskey glass and emptied it with alacrity. As he set the glass down he drew his coat sleeve across his mouth.

"Chief, you're a swell—" he began. But Heath cut him short.

"Get the hell out of here," he bawled at his subordinate. The Sergeant knew only too well Markham's aversion for any compliments and the curious reticence of the District Attorney's nature.[1]

Snitkin went out—somewhat meekly and wonderingly, but, withal, gratefully—and ten minutes later Heath followed. When we were alone Markham asked: "What do you think of it, Vance?"

"Thinkin' is an awful bore, Markham," Vance answered with irritating nonchalance. "And it's growing frightfully late, especially considerin' how early I dragged myself into consciousness this morning."

"Never mind all that." Markham spoke with exasperation. "How did you know Kaspar Kenting was dead when I spoke to you on the stairway yesterday morning?"

"You flatter me," said Vance. "I didn't really know. I merely surmised it—basin' my conclusion on the indications."

"So that's your mood," snorted Markham hopelessly. "I'm telling you, you outrageous fop, that this is a damned serious situation—what happened to Fleel tonight ought to prove that."

Vance smoked a moment in silence, and his brow clouded: his whole expression, in fact, changed.

---

1. It is interesting to note that in the entire association between Markham and Vance I had never heard either of them pay the other a compliment of any kind. When one of them so much as bordered on a compliment, the other always broke in sharply with a remark which made any further outward display of sentiment impossible. To me it seemed as if both of them had a deep-rooted instinct to keep the intimate and personal side of their affection for each other disguised and unspoken.

"I know only too well, Markham, how serious the situation is," he said in a grave and curiously subdued voice. "But there's really nothing we can do. We must wait—please believe me. Our hands and feet are tied." He looked at Markham and continued with unwonted earnestness. "The most serious part of the whole affair is that this is not a kidnapping case at all, in the conventional sense. It goes deeper than that. It's cold-blooded, diabolical murder. But I can't quite see my way yet to proving it. I'm far more worried than you, Markham. The whole thing is unspeakably horrible. There are subtle and abnormal elements mixed up in the situation. It's an abominable affair, but as we sit here tonight, I want to tell you that I don't know—I don't know. . . . I'm afraid to make a move until we learn more."

I had rarely heard Vance speak in this tone, and a curious sensation of fear, so potent as to be almost a physical reaction, ran through me.

I am certain that Vance's words had a similar effect on Markham, who made no comment: he sat silent for several minutes. Then he took his leave, without again referring to the case. Vance bade him good night absent-mindedly and remained in his chair, gazing before him into the empty grate.

I myself went immediately to bed and—I am a little loath to admit it—slept fairly well: I was somewhat exhausted, and a physical relaxation had come over me, despite my mental tension. But had I known what terrible and heart-paralyzing events the following day held in store, I doubt if I could have slept a wink that night.

CHAPTER 15

Alexandrite and Amethyst
Friday, July 22; 8:40 a.m.

I shall never forget the following day. It will ever remain in my memory as one of the great horrors of my life. It was the day when Vance and Heath and I came nearer to death than ever before or since. I still remember the scene in the private office of the now closed Kinkaid Casino;[1] and the report of Vance's hideous death in the course of the Garden murder case will never be erased from my mind. But as I look back upon these and other frightful episodes which froze my blood and filled my heart with cold fear, not one of them looms as appalling as do the events of that memorable Friday in the blistering heat of this particular summer.

It was, in a way, the outcome of Vance's own decision. He deliberately sought it as the result of some strange and unusual emotional reaction. He staked his own life in the attempt to prevent something which he considered diabolical. Vance was a man whose cold mental processes generally governed his every action; but in this emergency he impulsively followed his instincts. I frankly admit that it was, to me, a new phase of the man's many-sided character—a phase with which I was unfamiliar, and which I would not have believed was actually part of his make-up.

The day began conventionally enough, except that Vance rose at eight. I did not know how much sleep he actually got after Markham departed the night before. I know only that I myself woke up for a brief interval, hours after I had retired, and could hear his footsteps as if he were pacing up and down in the library. But when I joined him for breakfast at half-past eight that morning, there was no indication either in his eyes or in his manner—which was as nonchalant and disinterested as ever—that he had been deprived of his rest.

---

1. *The Casino Murder Case*, 1934.

He was dressed in a dark grey herring-bone suit, a pair of soft black leather oxfords, and a dark green cravat with white polka-dots. He greeted me with his customarily cynical but pleasant ease. But he made no comment to explain his early (for him) rising. He seemed altogether natural and unconcerned about the happenings of the day before. When he had finished his Turkish coffee and lighted a second *Régie* he settled back in his chair and spoke, quite casually, about the Kenting case.

"An amazin' and complicated affair—eh, what, Van? There are far too many facets to it—same like those stones in old Karl Kenting's collection—to leave one entirely comfortable. Dashed elusive—and deuced tangled. I naturally have certain suspicions, but I am by no means sure of my ground. I don't like those missin' gems—they tie up too consistently with the rest of the incidents. I don't like that unused ladder—so subtly and uselessly moved from one window to another. I don't like that abortive attempt on Fleel's life last night, or Quaggy's fortuitous appearance on the scene—Fleel was undoubtedly in a jittery state when we found him and actually incredulous at finding himself still alive. And I don't at all like the general situation in that old high-ceilinged purple house—it's not a wholesome place and has too many sinister possibilities.... There has already been one murder that we know of, and there may be another which we haven't yet heard about."

He looked up with a troubled glance and drew in a deep breath.

"No—oh, no; it's not a nice case," he went on as if to himself. "But what are we to do about it? Today may bring an answer. Haste on our part might spoil everything. But haste—oh, tremendous haste—is now of the utmost importance to the killer. That is why I think something will happen before very long. I'm hopin', Van. I'm also countin' on the anxiety of the person who has plotted and carried out this beastly affair to this point...."

He smoked a while in silence. I offered no comment or opinion, for I knew he had been thinking aloud rather than addressing me personally. When the lighted tip of his cigarette had almost reached the platinum rim of his slender ivory holder he got up slowly, moved to the front window, and stood gazing out at the sunlit street. Despite the sunshine, a humid mist fell over the city and presaged a stagnant, airless day. When Vance turned back to me he seemed to have made a decision.

"I think we'll take a spin down to Markham's office, Van," he said. "There's nothing to do here, and there may be some news which

Markham naively regards as too trivial to telephone me about. But it's the little obscure things that are goin' to solve this case."[2]

Vance walked energetically across the room and, ringing for Currie, ordered his car.

Vance drove swiftly down Madison Avenue in a curiously abstracted mood. We arrived at Markham's office a few minutes before ten o'clock.

"Glad you came, Vance," was Markham's greeting. "I was about to call you on the phone."

"Ah!" Vance sat down lazily. "Any tidin's, glad or otherwise?"

"I'm afraid not," Markham returned dispiritedly, "although things have been going ahead. A great deal of the necessary police work has been done, but we haven't come upon any promising lead as yet."

"Oh, yes. Of course." Vance smiled mildly. "Jolly old Police Department simply must imitate the whirling dervish before they feel entitled to settle down to the serious business in hand. I suppose you mean finger-prints, photographs, and the futile search for possible lookers-on, and the grilling—as you call it—of perfectly innocent and harmless people, and a careful search of the spot where Kaspar was found, as well as a thorough overhauling of the abandoned car."

Markham responded with a contemptuous snort.

"Those things simply have to be done. Very often they lead us to vital facts in the case. All criminals are not super-geniuses—they make mistakes occasionally."

"Oh, to be sure," Vance sighed. "Concatenation of circumstances impossible of duplication. Reconstruction from two points of view—and so on ad infinitum. I think I know all the catch phrases by this time. . . . However, proceed to unburden thyself."

"Well," said Markham in a hard, practical voice, ignoring Vance's frivolous interlude, "Kenyon Kenting was taken to the uptown morgue this morning and he identified his brother's body beyond a doubt. And I saw no need to put any other members of the family through the harrowing experience."

"Most considerate of you," murmured Vance—and it was difficult to know whether his remark was intended to convey a tinge of sarcasm or was merely a conventional retort. In any event, Markham's statement left him utterly indifferent.

"Mrs. Kenting's room," continued Markham, "as well as the window-sill and the ladder, was gone over thoroughly for finger-prints—"

---

2. Vance was greatly mistaken on this point, as I now have reason to know. It turned out to be no less than a matter of life and death.

"And none was found, of course, except the Sergeant's and mine."

"You're right," conceded Markham. "The person, or persons, must have worn gloves."

"Assumin' there was a person—or persons."

"All right, all right." Markham was beginning to be annoyed. "You're so damned cryptic about everything, and so reticent, that I have no way of knowing what prompted that last remark of yours. But, whatever you think, there must have been some one somewhere, or Mrs. Kenting could not have disappeared as she did."

"Quite true," returned Vance. "We can quite safely eliminate *a capella* accidents or amnesia or such things, in view of all the circumstances. I suppose all the hospitals have been checked as part of the pirouetting activities of Centre Street's master minds?"

"Naturally. And we drew a blank at every step. But if we failed in that respect we have, at least, disposed of the possibility."

"Amazin' progress," commented Vance. "There'll be finger-prints somewhere, so don't be downcast, old dear. But the signs-manual will be found, if at all, somewhere far removed from the Kenting house. Personally, I'd say you wouldn't find them till you have located the car in which Mrs. Kenting was probably driven away last night."

"What do you mean—what car?" demanded Markham.

"I haven't the slightest idea," said Vance laconically. "But I hardly think the lady walked out of sight. . . . And, by the by, Markham, speakin' of cars, what enormous array of information did you marshal about the green coupé that the energetic Sergeant found so conveniently waiting for him in the transverse? . . . Doubtless stolen—eh, what?"

Markham nodded glumly.

"Yes, Vance, that's just it. Belongs to a perfectly respectable spinster on upper West End Avenue. And a careful search of the car itself produced only the fact that there was a small sub-machine gun thrown into the tool chest under the seat."

"And the license plates?" asked Vance casually.

"Oh, those were stolen too." Markham spoke disgustedly.

"Plates didn't belong to the car, eh?" Vance smoked meditatively without stirring. "Very interestin'. Stolen car and stolen license plates. A car that doesn't belong to the fleeing occupants, and plates that don't belong to the car—well, well. Implies two cars, don't you know. Maybe it was the second car in which Mrs. Kenting was spirited away. Merely hazardin' a guess, don't y' know." He now uncrossed his knees and drew himself up slightly in his chair. "I rather imagine the dirty-green coupé was following Fleel around last night when Mrs. Kenting sallied forth to her assignation, and it was left to the other car to take care of the lady, as it were. Fairly well equipped gang."

"I don't follow you, Vance," Markham returned; "although I have a vague notion of the theory you're working out. But many other things might have happened last night."

"Oh, quite," agreed Vance. "As I said, I was merely hazardin' a guess. . . . What about Abe, the buddy of the chauffeur who drove us home last night? I suppose Heath or some of the Torquemadas in Centre Street put the poor devil through the requisite torture?"

"You read too many trashy books, Vance." Markham was indignant. "Heath talked to the driver of the number one cab at Headquarters within an hour of the time he left here last night. He merely corroborated what our chauffeur told us—namely, that he dropped the two men who came out of the transverse at the uptown entrance of the Lexington Avenue subway. Incidentally, they didn't wait for change but hurried down the stairs—they were probably just in time to catch the last express."

Vance again sighed lightly. "Most helpful. . . . Any other coruscatin' discoveries?"

"I spoke to the doctor who went over Kaspar's body," Markham went on. "And there's little or nothing to add to Snitkin's report of last night. The exact location of the spot where he was found was determined, and the ground was gone over carefully. But there were no footprints or suggestive indications of any kind. McLaughlin heard and saw nothing last night around the Kenting house; Weem and the cook both stick to the story that they were asleep during that whole time; and two taxicab drivers who were at the Columbus Avenue corner did not remember seeing Mrs. Kenting, whom they know by sight, come down that way."

"Well, your information seems to be typically thorough and typically useless," said Vance. "Did any one do a bit of checkin' up to ascertain whether there were any unaccounted-for semiprecious stones round town?"

Markham gave him a look of mild surprise and mock pity.

"Good heavens, no! What have your semiprecious stones to do with a case of kidnapping?"

"My dear Markham!" protested Vance. "I have told you—and I thought, in my naive way, that it had even been demonstrated to you—that this is *not* a case of kidnapping. Won't you even permit a subtle killer to set the stage for himself—to indulge in a bit of spectacular *décor*, so to speak? That collection of old Karl Kenting's gems has a dashed lot to do with the case. . . ."

319

"Well, suppose those pieces of coloured glass do have something to do with the disappearances, what of it?" Markham interrupted aggressively. "I'm not worried as much about such vague factors in the case as I am about that attack on Fleel."

"Oh, that."Vance shrugged. "A mere bit of technique. And the operator of the sub-machine gun was kind enough to miss his target. As I told Fleel, he was very lucky."

"But whether Fleel survived or not," muttered Markham, "it was a dastardly affair."

"I quite agree with you there, Markham," said Vance approvingly.

At this moment Markham's secretary, coming swiftly through the swinging leather door, interrupted the conversation.

"Chief," he announced, "there's a young fellow outside who's terribly excited and insists on seeing you at once. Says it's about the Kenting case. Gives his name as Falloway."

"Oh, send him in, by all means," said Vance, before Markham had time to answer.

The secretary looked interrogatingly at the District Attorney. Markham hesitated only a moment and then nodded. A few moments later Fraim Falloway was shown into the office. He came into the room with a frightened air, and bade Markham good morning. His eyes seemed larger and his face paler than when I had last seen him.

"Tell us what's on your mind, Mr. Falloway."Vance spoke softly.

The youth turned and noticed him for the first time.

"I'll tell you, all right," he said in quick, tremulous accents. "That— that beautiful alexandrite stone is gone from the collection. I'm sure it's been stolen."

"Stolen?" Vance looked at the youth closely. "Why do you say stolen?"

"I—I don't know," was the flustered reply. "All I know is that it is gone—how else could it have disappeared unless it was stolen? It was there two days ago."

Even I remembered the stone—an unusually large and beautifully cut octagonal stone of perhaps forty carats, which was in a place of honour, in the most conspicuous case, surrounded by other specimens of chrysoberyl. I had taken particular notice of it the morning of Kaspar Kenting's disappearance when Vance and I had looked over the various glass cases before ascending the stairs to Kaspar's room.

"I don't know anything about those stones in the collection," Falloway went on excitedly, "but I do know about this magnificent alexandrite. It always fascinated me—it was the only gem in the collection

320

I cared anything about. It was a wonderful and beautiful thing. I used to go into the room often just to look at that stone. I could lose myself before it for an hour at a time. In the daytime it was the most marvellous green, like dark jade, with only touches of red in it; but at night, in the artificial light, it changed its colour completely and became a thrilling red, like wine."

As Markham threw him a look of incredulity, Falloway hastened on.

"Oh, it was no miracle.—I looked it up in a book; I read about it. It had some strange and mystic quality which made it absorb and refract and reflect the light upon it in different ways. But I haven't feasted my eyes on it for two days—we've all been so upset—until last night—but that was in the yellow artificial light—and it was a beautiful red then."

Falloway paused and then hurried on ecstatically.

"But I like it most in the daylight when it turns green and mysterious—that's when it recalls to me Swinburne's great poem, *The Triumph of Time*: 'I will go back to the great sweet mother, mother and lover of men, the sea.'—Oh, I hope you see what I mean. . . ." He looked at each of us in turn. "So this morning—a little while ago—I went downstairs to look at it: I needed something—something . . . But it wasn't green at all. It was still red, almost purple. And after I had looked at it a while in amazement, I realized that even the cutting was different. It was the same size and shape—but that was all. Oh, I know every facet of that alexandrite. It was not the same stone. It had been taken away and another stone left in its place! . . ."

He fumbled nervously in his outside pocket and finally drew out a large deep-coloured gem, which can best be described as deep red but with a very decided purple cast. He held it out to Vance on the palm of his shaking hand.

"That's what was left in the place of my beloved alexandrite!"

Vance took the stone and looked at it a moment. Still holding the gem he let his hand fall to his lap, and looked up at Falloway with a comprehending nod.

"Yes, I see what you mean—quite," he said. "As good a substitution as possible. This is merely amethyst. Of comparatively little value. Similar to alexandrite, however, and often mistaken for it by amateurs. Any one would trade an amethyst for an alexandrite, the price of which has recently begun to soar. Can you say with any accuracy when the exchange was made?"

Falloway shook his head vaguely and sat down heavily.

"No," he said phlegmatically. "As I told you, I haven't seen it in

321

daylight for two days, and last night I looked at it for just a second and didn't realize that it wasn't the alexandrite. I discovered the truth this morning. The exchange might have been made at any time since I last saw the real stone in daylight."

Vance again looked at the stone and handed it back to Falloway.

"Return it to the case as soon as you reach home. And say nothing about it to any one till I speak to you again." He turned to the District Attorney. "Y' know, Markham, fine alexandrite is a very rare and valuable variety of chrysoberyl. It was discovered less than a hundred years ago, in the Urals, and it was named after the czarevitch who later became the conservative and reformative Alexander II, Czar of Russia, for it first came to light on his birthday. As Mr. Falloway rightly says, it is a curious *dichroic* gem. The light of the spectrum is reflected, absorbed and refracted in such a way that in the daylight it is quite green, and in artificial light, especially gas-light, it is a pronounced deep and scintillating red, slightly on the blue, or short wavelength end of the spectrum. A fine specimen of alexandrite the size of that stone would now be worth a small fortune. Such a specimen is the dream of every collector. I saw the stone when I glanced through the cases Wednesday morning and marvelled at old Karl's good luck. The other indifferent items in the collection were anything but consistent with that alexandrite; and when I spoke to Kenyon Kenting that morning, I entirely omitted any mention of that particular stone, for it takes more than one exceptional piece of chrysoberyl, no matter how beautiful, to constitute a well-rounded collection."

Vance paused a moment with a reflective look, and then continued.

"Amethyst, a variety of quartz, which likewise comes from Russia, although somewhat similar in shade to alexandrite, does not have that peculiar *dichroic* characteristic. Amethyst, d' ye see, has a structural dissimilarity from alexandrite. At times we find in the crystals a right-angular formation to the edge of the prism, shaped in sectoral triangles. This accounts for its bi-colouration—the so-called white and purple tints, making it resemble two separate, fused stones. The fractural ripples and the feather-like effects—so apparent in amethyst—result from this peculiar laterality of structure. On the other hand, Markham, alexandrite—"

"Thanks for the lecture, but forgive me if I am not interested." Markham was irritated. "What I'd like to know is whether you see anything significant in the disappearance of the alexandrite and the substitution of the amethyst."

"Oh, yes—decidedly. You'd be amazed if you knew how highly

significant it is." He turned quickly to Fraim Falloway, who had been listening with an eagerness of interest I had not seen him display at any previous time. "I think, Mr. Falloway, you would better return to your home at once and do exactly as I told you. We are grateful no end for your coming here and telling us about the missin' stone."

Falloway rose heavily.

"I'll put the stone back in place right away."

"Oh, by the by, Mr. Falloway." Vance drew himself up sharply. "If, as you have intimated, your favourite cutting of alexandrite was stolen, could you suggest the possible thief? Could it, for instance, have been any one you know?"

"You mean some one in the house?—or Mr. Quaggy or Mr. Fleel?" retorted Falloway with a show of indignation. "What would they want with my alexandrite?" He shook his head shrewdly. "But I have an idea who did take it."

"Ah!"

"Yes! I know more than you think I do." Falloway made a pitiful effort to thrust forward his narrow chest. "It was Kaspar—that's who it was!"

Vance nodded indulgently.

"But Kaspar is dead. His body was found last night."

"A damned good riddance!" Vance's announcement left Falloway unruffled. "I was hoping he wouldn't come back."

"He won't," interjected Markham laconically, staring at the youth with unmistakable disgust.

I doubt if Falloway even heard the District Attorney's remark: his attention was concentrated on Vance.

"But do you think you can ever find my beautiful alexandrite?" he asked. He seemed to regard the disappearance of the alexandrite as a personal loss.

"Oh, yes—I'm quite sanguine we shall recover it," Vance assured him.

The youth, greatly relieved, went toward the door with heavy, dragging feet.

Markham's secretary came again through the leather door, just before Falloway reached it, and announced Kenyon Kenting.

"Send him in," said Markham.

Kenting and Falloway passed each other on the threshold. I was forcibly struck by the wordless exchange of hostility which passed between the elder and the younger man. Kenting bowed stiffly and muttered a word of greeting as he passed the other, with a stiff, elderly dignity in his manner. But Falloway did not respond as he went through to the outer office.

CHAPTER 16

"This Year of Our Lord"
Friday, July 22; 11 a.m.

As Kenting stepped into the office it was obvious that he was in a perturbed state of mind. He nodded to Vance and to me, and, going to Markham's desk, dejectedly placed an envelope before the District Attorney.

"That came in the second mail this morning, to my office," Kenting said, controlling his excitement with considerable effort. "It's another one of those damn notes."

Markham had already picked up the envelope and was carefully extracting the folded sheet of paper from inside.

"And Fleel," added Kenting, "got a similar one in the same mail—at his office. He phoned me about it, just as I was leaving to come here. He sounded very much upset and asked me if I also had received a note from the kidnappers. I told him I had, and I read it to him over the phone. I added I was bringing it immediately to you; and Fleel said he would meet me here shortly and bring his own note with him. He hasn't, by any chance, come already?"

"Not yet," Markham answered, glancing up from the note. His face was unusually grave, and there was a deep, hopeless frown round his eyes. When he had finished his perusal of the note he picked up the envelope and handed them both to Vance.

"I suppose you'll want to see these, Vance," the District Attorney muttered distractedly.

"Oh, quite—by all means."

Vance, with his monocle already adjusted, took the note and the envelope with suppressed eagerness, glancing first at the envelope and then at the single sheet of paper. I had risen and was standing behind him, leaning over his chair.

The paper on which the note was written in lead pencil was exactly like that of the first note Fleel had received in the mail the day before. The disguised, deliberately clumsy chirography was also similar, but there was a distinct difference in the way it was worded. The spelling was correct, and the sentences grammatically constructed. Nor was there any pretence here in the means of expression. It was as if whoever wrote it had purposely abandoned such tactics so that there might be no mistake or misunderstanding of any kind regarding the import of the message. Vance merely read it through once—he did not seem greatly interested in it. But it was obvious that something about it annoyed and puzzled him.

The note read:

You did not obey instructions. You called in the police. We saw everything. That is why we took his wife. If you fail us again, the same thing will happen to her that happened to him. This is your last warning. Have the $50,000 ready at five o'clock today (Friday). You will get instructions at that time. And if you notify the police this time it is no dice. We mean business. Beware!

For signature there was the interlocking-squares symbol that had come to have such a sinister portent for us all.

"Very interestin' and illuminatin'," murmured Vance, as he carefully refolded the note, replaced it in the envelope, and tossed it back on Markham's desk.

"The money is quite obviously wanted immediately. But I am not at all convinced that it was only the presence of the police that turned last night's episode in the park into a fiasco. However . . ."

"What shall I do—what shall I do?" Kenting asked, glancing distractedly from Vance to the District Attorney and back again.

"Really, y' know," said Vance in a kindly tone, "you can't do anything at present. You must wait for the forthcoming instructions. And then there's Mr. Fleel's *billet-doux* which we hope to see anon."

"I know, I know," mumbled Kenting hopelessly. "But it would be horrible if anything should happen to Madelaine."

Vance was silent a moment, and his eyes clouded. He showed more concern than he had since he had entered the Kenting case.

"One never knows, of course," he murmured. "But we can hope for the best. I realize that this waiting is abominable. But we are at a loss at present even as to where to begin. . . . By the by, Mr. Kenting, I don't suppose you heard the shots that were fired at Mr. Fleel shortly after you left your brother's house last night?"

"No, I didn't." Kenting seemed greatly perturbed. "I was frightfully shocked on hearing about it this morning. When I left you last night I was lucky enough to catch a taxicab just as I reached the corner, and I went directly home. How long after I left the house did Fleel go?"

"Just a few minutes," Vance returned. "But no doubt you had time to have got a taxi and have been well on your way."

Kenting considered the matter for a minute; then he looked up sharply with a frightened expression.

"Perhaps—perhaps—" he began in an awed voice which seemed to tremble with a sudden and uncontrollable emotion. "Perhaps those shots were intended for me! . . ."

"Oh, no, no—nothing like that," Vance assured him. "I'm quite sure the shots were not intended for you, sir. The fact is, I am not convinced that the shots were intended even for Mr. Fleel."

"What's that you say!" Kenting sat up quickly. "What do you mean by that? . . ."

Before Vance could answer, a buzzer sounded on Markham's desk. As the District Attorney pressed a key on the inter-communicating callbox a voice from the outer office announced that Fleel had just arrived. Markham had barely given instructions that Fleel be sent in when the lawyer came impatiently through the swinging door and joined us. He, too, looked pale and drawn and showed unmistakable traces of lack of rest,—he appeared to have lost much of his earlier self-confidence. He greeted all of us formally with the exception of Kenyon Kenting, with whom he shook hands with a silent, expressive grasp.

"A difficult situation," he said with a formal effort at condolence. "My deepest sympathy goes to you, Kenyon."

Kenting shrugged despondently.

"You yourself had a pretty close call last night."

"Oh, well," the other muttered, "at least I'm safe and sound enough now. But I can't understand that attack. Can't imagine who would want to shoot me, or what good it would do any one. It's the most incredible thing."

Kenting threw a sharp look at Vance, but Vance was busying himself with a fresh cigarette and seemed oblivious to the conventional interchange between the two men.

Fleel moved toward the District Attorney's desk.

"I brought the note I received in the mail this morning," he said, fumbling in his pocket. "There's no reason whatever why I should be getting anything like this—unless the kidnappers imagine that I control all the Kenting money and have it on deposit. . . . You can understand that I am greatly disturbed by this communication, and I thought it would be best to show it to you without delay, at the same time explaining to you that there's absolutely nothing I can do in the matter."

"There's no need for an explanation," said Markham abruptly. "We are wholly cognizant of that phase of the situation. Let's see the note."

Fleel had drawn an envelope from his inside coat pocket and held it out to Markham. As he did so his eyes fell on the note that Kenting had brought and which lay on the District Attorney's desk.

"Do you mind if I take a look at this?" he asked.

"Go right ahead," answered Markham as he opened the envelope Fleel had given him.

The note that Fleel turned over to Markham was not as long as the one received by Kenting. It was, however, written on the same kind of paper; and it was written in pencil and in the same handwriting. The few brief sentences struck me as highly ominous:

You have double-crossed us. You have control of the money. Get busy. And don't try any more foolishness again. You are a good lawyer and can handle everything if you want to. And you had better want to. We expect to see you according to instructions in our letter to Kenting today in this year of our Lord, 1936, or else it will be too bad.[1]

The interlocking, ink-brushed squares completed the message.

When Markham had finished reading it and handed it to Vance, Vance went through it quickly but carefully and, sliding it into the envelope, laid it on Markham's desk beside the note which Kenting had brought in, and which Fleel had read and replaced without comment.

"I can say to you, Mr. Fleel," Vance told him, "only what I have already said to Mr. Kenting—that there is nothing to be done at the

---

1. I have made one small and wholly immaterial change in transcribing this note. I have used the year in which I am actually writing the record of that memorable case, instead of stating the exact year in which it occurred (which, naturally, was the year given in the note); for I regard it as both unimportant and unnecessary to identify specifically the time at which the events herewith enumerated occurred. If that date has been forgotten, or if it is of any particular interest to the reader of this chronicle, it will not be difficult to find the year by referring to the back files of newspapers, for what has come to be known as the Kenting kidnap case received nation-wide publicity at the time.

present moment. A rational decision is quite impossible just now. You must wait for the next communication—by whatever method it may come—before you can decide on a course of action."

He rose and confronted the two unstrung men.

"There is much to be done yet," he said. "And we are most sympathetic and eager to be helpful. Please believe that we are doing everything possible. I would advise that you both remain in your offices until you have heard something further. We will certainly communicate with you later, and we appreciate the cooperation you are giving us. . . . By the by,"—he spoke somewhat offhand to Kenting—"has your money been returned to you?"

"Yes, yes, Vance." It was Markham's impatient voice that answered. "Mr. Kenting received the money the first thing this morning. Two of the men in the Detective Division across the hall delivered it to him."

Kenting nodded in confirmation of the District Attorney's statement.

"Most efficient," sighed Vance. "After all, y' know, Markham, Mr. Kenting couldn't give the money out unless he had it again in his possession. . . . Most grateful for the information."

Vance addressed Fleel and Kenting again.

"We will, of course, expect to hear immediately when you receive any further communication, or if any new angle develops." His tone was one of polite dismissal.

"Don't worry on that score, Mr. Vance." Kenting was reaching for his hat. "As soon as either one of us gets the instructions promised in my note, you'll hear all about it."

A few moments later he and Fleel left the office together.

As the door closed behind them Vance swung swiftly about and went to Markham's desk.

"That note to Fleel!" he exclaimed. "I don't like it, Markham. I don't at all like it. It is the most curious concoction. I must see it again."

As he spoke he picked up the note once more and, resuming his chair, studied the paper with far more interest and care than he had shown when the lawyer and Kenting had been present.

"You notice, of course, that both notes were cancelled in the same post-office station as was yesterday's communication—the Westchester Station."

"Certainly I noticed it," Markham returned almost angrily. "But what is there significant about the postmark?"

"I don't know, Markham,—I really don't know. It's probably a minor point."

Vance did not look up: he was earnestly engaged with the note. He

328

read it through several times, lingering with a troubled frown at the last two or three lines.

"I cannot understand the reference to 'this year of our Lord.' It doesn't belong here. It's out of key. My eyes go back to it every time I finish reading the note. It bothers me frightfully. Something was in the writer's mind—he had a strange thought at that time. It may be entirely meaningless, or it may have been written down inadvertently, like an instinctive or submerged thought which had struggled through in expression, or it could have been written into the note with some very subtle significance for some one who was expected to see it."

"I noticed that phrase, too," said Markham. "It is curious; but, in my opinion, it means nothing at all."

"I wonder...."Vance raised his hand and brushed it lightly over his forehead. Then he got to his feet. "I'd like to be alone a while with this note. Where can I go—are the judges' chambers unoccupied?"

Markham looked at him in puzzled amazement.

"I don't know." His perturbed, questioning scrutiny of Vance continued. "By the way, Sergeant Heath should be here any minute now."

"Stout fella, Heath,"Vance murmured. "I may want to see him.... But where can I go?"

"You can go into my private office, you damned *prima donna*." Markham pointed to a narrow door in the west wall of the room. "You'll be alone in there. Shall I let you know when Heath gets here?"

"No—no."Vance shook his head as he crossed the room. "Just tell him to wait for me." And, carrying the note before him, he opened the side door and went out of the room.

Markham looked after him in bewildered silence. Then he turned half-heartedly to a pile of papers and documents neatly arranged at one side of his desk blotter. He worked for some time on extraneous matters.

It was fully ten minutes before Vance emerged from the private office. In the meantime Heath had arrived and was waiting impatiently in one of the leather lounging chairs near the steel letter files in one corner of the room. When the Sergeant had stepped into the office Markham greeted him with simulated annoyance.

"Our pet orchid is communing with his soul in my private office," he explained. "He said he may want to see you; so you'd better take a chair in the corner and wait to see what his profound contemplation will produce. Meanwhile, you might look at the note Kenting received this morning." Markham handed it to the Sergeant. "Another note, received by Fleel, is being submitted to the searching monocle, as it were."

Heath had grinned at Markham's sarcastic, but good-natured, comments and sat down as the District Attorney returned to his work.

When Vance re-entered the room he threw a quick glance in Heath's direction. It was obvious he was in an unusually serious mood and seemed unmindful of his surroundings.

"Cheerio, Sergeant," he greeted Heath as he became fully aware of his presence. "I'm glad you came in. Thanks awfully for waitin', and all that. . . . I'm sure you've already read the note Kenting received. Here's the one Fleel brought in."

And he tossed it negligently to me with a nod of his head toward Heath. His eyes, a little strained and with an unwonted intensity in them, were still on Markham as I stepped across the room to Heath with the paper.

Vance now stood in the centre of the room, gazing down at the floor, deep in thought as he smoked. After a moment he raised his head slowly and let his eyes rest meditatively on Markham again.

"It could be—it could be," he murmured. And I felt that he was making an effort to control himself. "I want to see a detailed map of New York right away."

"On that wall—over there." Markham was watching him closely. "In the wooden frame. Just pull it down—it's on a roller."

Vance unrolled the black-and-white chart, with its red lines, and smoothed it against the wall. After a few minutes' search of the intersecting lines he turned back to Markham with a curious look on his face and heaved a sigh of relief.

"Let me see that yellow slip you had yesterday, with the official bound'ries of the Westchester Station post-office district."

Markham, still patiently silent, handed him the paper. Vance took it back to the map with him, glanced from the slip of paper to the chart and back again, and began to trace an imaginary zigzag line with his finger. I heard him enumerating, half to himself: "Pelham, Kingsland, Mace, Gunhill, Bushnell, Hutchinson River . . ."

Then his finger came to a stop, and he turned triumphantly.

"That's it! That's it!" His voice had a peculiar pitch. "I think I have found the meaning of that phrase."

"What in the name of Heaven do you mean?" Markham had half risen from his chair and was leaning forward with his hands on the desk.

"'This year of our Lord,' and the numerals. There's a Lord Street in that outlined section—up near Givans Basin—a section of open spaces and undeveloped highways. And the year 19—" and he gave the other two digits. "That's the house number—they run in the nineteen-hundreds over near the water on Lord Street. And, incidentally, I note that the only logical way to reach there is to take the Lexington Avenue subway uptown."

Markham sank slowly back into his chair without taking his eyes from Vance.

"I see what you mean," he said. "But—" He hesitated a moment. "That's merely a wild guess. A groundless assumption. It's too specious, too vague. It may not be an address at all. . . ." Then he added: "You may merely have stumbled on a coincidence—" He stopped abruptly. "Do you think we ought to send some men out there—on a chance?"

"My word, no!" Vance returned emphatically. "That might wreck everything, providin' we've really got something here. Your myrmidons would be sure to give warning and bungle things; and only a moment would be needed for a strategic move fatal to our plans. This matter must be handled differently."

His face darkened; his eyelids drooped menacingly; and I knew that some new and overpowering emotion had taken hold of him.

"I'm going myself," he said. "It may be a wild-goose chase, but it must be done, don't y' know. We can't leave any possible avenue of approach untried just now. There's something frightful and sinister going on. And I'm not at all certain as to what will be found there. I'm a helpless babe, cryin' for the light."

Markham was impressed and, I believe, a little concerned at his manner.

"I don't like it, Vance. I think you should have protection, in case of an emergency—"

Heath had come forward and stood solemnly at one end of the desk.

"I'm going with you, Mr. Vance," he said, in a voice that was both stolid and final. "I got a feeling you may be needin' me. An' I sorta like the idea of that address you figured out. Anyhow, I'll have something to tell my grandchildren about learnin' how wrong you were."

Vance looked at the man a while seriously, and then slowly nodded.

"That will be quite all right, Sergeant," he said calmly. "I may need your help. And as for finding me wrong: I'm willin', don't y' know—like Barkis. But how are you going to have grandchildren when you're not even a benedick?[2] . . . In the meantime, Sergeant," he went on, dropping his jocular manner, and jotting down some-

---

2. Sergeant Ernest Heath was what is popularly known as a confirmed bachelor. Even when he retired from the Homicide Bureau at fifty, he devoted himself not to a wife, but to raising wyandottes on his farm in the Mohawk valley.

thing on a small piece of yellow paper he had torn from the scratch-pad on Markham's desk, "have this carefully attended to—constant observation. You understand?"

Heath took the yellow slip, looked at it in utter amazement, and then stuffed it into his pocket. His eyes were wide and a look of scepticism and incredulity came into them.

"I don't like to say so, Mr. Vance, but I think you're daffy, sir."

"I don't in the least mind, Sergeant." Vance spoke almost affectionately. "But I want you to see to it, nevertheless." And he met the other's gaze coldly and steadily.

Heath moved his head up and down, his lips hanging open in disbelief.

"If you say so, sir," he mumbled. "But I still think—"

"Never mind making the effort, Sergeant." There was an irresistibly imperious note in Vance's tone. "But if you disobey that order—which, incidentally, is the first I've ever given you—I cannot proceed with the case."

Heath tried to grin but failed.

"I'll take care of it," he said. Though he was still awestricken, his tone was subdued. "When do we go?"

"After dark, of course," Vance replied, relaxing perceptibly. "It's misty and somewhat overcast today. . . . Be at my apartment at half-past eight. We'll drive up in my car."

Again the Sergeant moved his head up and down slowly.

"God Almighty!" he said. "I can't believe it: it don't make sense. Anyway," he added, "I'll string along with you, Mr. Vance. I'll be there at eight-thirty—heeled plenty."

"So you really believe I may be right," said Vance with a smile.

"Well, I ain't taking any chances—come what may."

CHAPTER 17

Shots in the Dark
Friday, July 22; noon

Vance remained in Markham's office only a short time after his enigmatic talk with Heath. (I did not regard that brief conversation as particularly momentous at the time, but within a few hours I learned that it was actually one of the most important conversations that had ever passed between these two widely disparate, but mutually sympathetic, men.)

Markham attempted repeatedly, with both cajolery and brusqueness, to draw Vance out. The District Attorney wished particularly to hear what significance Vance attached to the missing alexandrite, and what import he had sensed in the two notes which Kenting and Fleel had brought in. Vance, however, was unusually grave and adamant. He would give no excuse for not expressing freely his theory regarding the case; but his manner was such that Markham realized, as did I, that Vance had an excellent reason for temporarily withholding his suspicions from the District Attorney—and, I might add, from me as well.

In the end Markham was highly annoyed and, I think, somewhat resentful.

"I trust you know, Vance," he said in a tone intended to be coldly formal, but which did not entirely disguise his deep-rooted respect for the peculiar methods Vance followed in his investigation of a case, "that, as official head of the Police Department, I can compel Sergeant Heath here to show me that slip of paper you handed him."

"I fully appreciate that fact," Vance replied in a tone equally as frigid as Markham's. "But I also know you will not do it." Only once, during the investigation of the Bishop murder case, had I seen so serious an expression in Vance's eyes. "I know I can trust you to do nothing of the kind, and to forgo your technical rights in this instance." His voice suddenly softened and a look of genuine affection overspread his face as he added: "I want your confidence until tonight—I want you to believe that I have good and specific reasons for my seemingly boorish obstinacy."

Markham kept his eyes on Vance for several moments and then glanced away as he busied himself a little ostentatiously with a cigar.

"You're a damned nuisance," he mumbled, with simulated anger. "I wish I had never seen you."

"Do you flatter yourself, for one minute, Markham," retorted Vance, "that I have particularly enjoyed your acquaintance during the past fifteen years?"

And then Vance did something I had never seen him do before. He took a step toward Markham and held out his hand. Markham turned to him without any show of surprise and grasped his hand with sincere cordiality.

"After all," said Vance lightly, "you're only a District Attorney, don't y' know. I'll make due allowances." And he went from the room without another word, leaving the Sergeant and Markham in the room together.

Vance and I had luncheon at the Caviar Restaurant, and he lingered unconscionably long over his favourite brandy, which they always kept for him and brought out ceremoniously when he appeared at that restaurant. During the meal he spoke but infrequently—and then about subjects far removed from the Kenting case.

We went directly home after he had finished sipping his cognac, and Vance spent the entire afternoon in desultory reading in the library. I went into the room for some papers around four o'clock and noticed that he was engrossed in Erasmus' *Encomium Moriae*.

As I stood for a moment behind him, looking discreetly over his shoulder, he looked up with a serious expression: he had settled into a studious mood.

"After all, Van," he commented, "what would the world be without folly? Nothing matters vitally—does it? Listen to this comfortin' thought:"—he ran his finger along the Erasmus passage before him and translated the words slowly—"'*So likewise all this life of mortal man, what is it but a certain kind of stage play?*' . . . Same like Shakespeare wrote in *As You Like It*, which came a century later—what?"

Vance was in a peculiar humour, and I knew he was endeavouring to cover up what was actually in his mind; and for some reason, which I could not understand, I was prompted to quote to him, in answer, the famous line from Horace's Epistles: *Nec lusisse pudet, sed non incidere ludum.* However, I refrained, and went on about my work as Vance took up his book again.

A little before six o'clock Markham came in unexpectedly.

"Well, Vance," he said banteringly, "I suppose you're still indulging your flair for melodramatic reticence, and are still playing the part of *l'homme de mystère*. However, I'll respect your idiosyncrasies—with tongue in cheek, of course."

"Most generous of you," murmured Vance. "I'm overwhelmed. . . . What do you wish to tell me? I know full well you didn't come all the way to my humble diggin's without some sad message for me."

Markham sobered and sat down near Vance.

"I haven't heard yet from either Fleel or Kenting. . . ." he began.

"I rather expected that bit of news." Vance rose and, ringing for Currie, ordered Dubonnet. Then, as he resumed his seat, he went on. "Really, there's nothing to worry about. They have probably decided to proceed without the bunglin' assistance of the police this time—those last notes were pretty insistent on that point. Kenting undoubtedly has received his instructions. . . . By the by, have you tried to communicate with him?"

Markham nodded gravely.

"I tried to reach him at his office an hour ago, and was told he had gone home. I called him there, but the butler told me he had come in and had just gone out without leaving any instructions except that he would not be home for dinner."

"Not what you'd call a highly cooperative johnnie—what?"

The Dubonnet was served, and Vance sipped the wine placidly.

"Of course, you tried to reach him at the Purple House?"

"Of course I did," Markham answered. "But he wasn't there either and wasn't expected there."

"Very interestin'," murmured Vance. "Elusive chap. Food for thought, Markham. Think it over."

"I also tried to get in touch with Fleel," Markham continued doggedly. "But he, like Kenting it seems, had left his office earlier than usual today; nor was I able to reach him at his home."

"Two missin' men," commented Vance. "Very sad. But no need to be upset. Just a private matter being handled privately, I fear. District Attorney's office and the police not bein' trusted. Not entirely unintelligent." He set down his Dubonnet glass. "But there's business afoot, or else I'm horribly mistaken. And what can you do? The actors in the tragic drama refuse to make an appearance. Most disconcertin', from the official point of view. The only thing left for you is to ring down

335

the curtain temporarily, and bide your time. *C'est la fin de la pauvre Manon*—or words to that effect. Abominable opera. Incidentally, what are your plans for the evening?"

"I have to get dressed and attend a damned silly banquet tonight," grumbled Markham.

"It'll probably do you good," said Vance. "And when you make your speech, you can solemnly assure your bored listeners that the situation is under control, and that developments are expected very soon—or golden words to that effect."

Markham remained a short time longer and then went out. Vance resumed his interrupted reading.

Shortly after seven we had a simple home dinner which Currie served to us in the library, consisting of *gigot*, *rissoulées potatoes*, fresh mint jelly, asparagus *hollandaise*, and *savarins à la Medicis*.

Promptly at half-past eight the Sergeant arrived.

"I still think you're daffy, Mr. Vance," he said good-naturedly, as he took a long drink of Bourbon. "However, everything is being attended to."

"If I'm wrong, Sergeant," said Vance with pretended entreaty, "you must never divulge our little secret. The humiliation would be far too great. And I'm waxin' old and sensitive."

Heath chuckled and poured himself another glass of Bourbon. As he did so Vance went to the centre-table and, opening the drawer, brought out an automatic. He inspected it carefully, made sure the magazine was full, and then slipped it into his pocket.

I had risen and was now standing beside him. I reached out my hand for the other automatic in the drawer—the one I had carried in Central Park the night before—but Vance quickly closed the drawer and, turning to me, shook his head in negation.

"Sorry, Van," he said, "but I think you'd better bide at home to-night. This may be a very dangerous mission—or it may be an erroneous guess on my part. However, I rather anticipate trouble, and you'll be safer in your *boudoir*. . . ."

I became indignant and insisted that I go with him and share whatever danger the night might hold.

Again Vance shook his head.

"I think not, Van." He spoke in a strangely gentle tone. "No need whatever for you to take the risk. I'll tell you all about it when the Sergeant and I return."

He smiled with finality, but I became more insistent and more indignant, and told him frankly that, whether he gave me the gun or not, I intended to go along with him and Heath.

Vance studied me for several moments.

"All right, Van," he said at length. "But don't forget that I warned you." Without saying any more he swung about to the table, opened the drawer, and brought out the other automatic. "I suggest you keep it in your outside pocket this time," he advised, as he handed me the gun. "It's rather difficult to prophesy, don't y' know—though I'm hopin' you won't need the bally thing." Then, going to the window, he looked out for a moment. "It'll be dark by the time we get there." He turned slowly from the window and crossed the room to ring for Currie.

When the butler came into the room Vance looked at him for a while in silence, with a kindly smile.

"If you don't hear from me by eleven," he said, "go to bed. And *schlafen Sie wohl!* If I am not back in the morning, you will find some interesting legal documents in a blue envelope with your name on it, in the upper right-hand drawer of the secret'ry. And notify Mr. Markham." He turned round to Heath with an air of exaggerated nonchalance. "Come along, Sergeant," he said. "Let's be on our way. Duty calls, as the sayin' goes. *Ich dien*, and all that sort of twaddle."

We went down to the street in silence—Vance's instructions to Currie had struck me as curiously portentous. We got into Vance's car, which was waiting outside, Heath and I in the tonneau and Vance at the wheel.

Vance was an expert driver, and he handled the Hispano-Suiza with a quiet efficiency and care that made the long, low-slung car seem almost something animate. There was never the slightest sound of enmeshing gears, never the slightest jerk, as he stopped and started the car in the flow of traffic.

We drove up Fifth Avenue to its northern end, and there crossed the Harlem River into the Bronx. At the far side of the bridge Vance stopped the car and drew a folded map from his pocket.

"No need to lose ourselves in this maze of crisscrossing avenues," he remarked to us over his shoulder. "Since we know where we're going, we might as well mark the route." He had unfolded the map and was tracing an itinerary at one side of it. "Westchester Avenue will take us at least half of the way to our destination; and then if I can work my way through to Bassett Avenue we should have no further difficulties."

He placed the map on the seat beside him and drove on. At the intersection of East 177th Street he made a sharp turn to the left, and we skirted the grounds of the New York Catholic Protectory. After a few more turns a street sign showed that we were on Bassett Avenue, and Vance continued to the north. At its upper end we found ourselves at a small stretch of water,[1] and Vance again stopped the car to consult his map.

"I've gone a little too far," he informed us, as he took the wheel again and turned the car sharply to the left, at right angles with Bassett Avenue. "But I'll go through to the next avenue—Waring, I think it is—turn south there, and park the car just round the corner from Lord Street. The number we're looking for should be there or thereabouts."

It took a few minutes to make the detour, for the roadway was unsuitable for automobile traffic. Vance shut off all his lights as we approached the corner, and we drove the last half block in complete darkness, as the nearest street light was far down Waring Avenue. The gliding Hispano-Suiza made no sound under Vance's efficient handling; even the closing of the doors, as we got out, could not be heard more than a few feet away.

We proceeded on foot into Lord Street, a narrow thoroughfare and sparsely inhabited. Here and there was an old wooden shack, standing out, in the darkness of the night, as a black patch against the overcast sky.

"It would be on this side of the street," Vance said, in a low, vibrant voice. "This is the even-number side. My guess is it's that next two-story structure, just beyond this vacant lot."

"I think you're right at that," Heath returned, *sotto voce*.

When we stood in front of the small frame dwelling, it seemed particularly black. There was no light showing at any of the windows. Until we accustomed our eyes to the darkness it looked as if the place had no windows at all.

Heath tiptoed up the three sagging wooden steps that led to the narrow front porch and flashed his light close to the door. Crudely painted on the lintel was the number we sought. The Sergeant beckoned to us with a sweeping gesture of his arm, and Vance and I joined him silently before the wooden-panelled front door with its nondescript peeling paint. At one side of the door was an old-fashioned bell-pull with a white knob, and Vance gave it a tentative jerk.

There was a faint tinkle inside, and we stood waiting, filled with misgivings and not knowing what to expect. I saw Heath slip his hand into the pocket where he carried his gun; and I too—by instinct or imitation—dropped my hand into my right outside coat pocket and, grasping my automatic, shifted the safety release.

---

1. This, I later learned, was Givans Basin.

After a long delay, during which we remained there without a sound, we heard a leisurely shifting of the bolts. The door then opened a few inches, and the pinched yellow face of an undersized Chinaman peered out cautiously at us.

As I stood there, straining my eyes through the partly open door at the yellow face that looked inquisitively out at us, the significance of the imprint of the Chinese sandals at the foot of the ladder, as well as of the Sinological nature of the signatures of the various ransom notes, flashed through my mind. I knew in that brief moment that Vance had interpreted the address correctly, and that we had come to the right house. Although I had not doubted the accuracy of Vance's prognostication, a chill swept over me as I stared at the flat yellow features of the small man on the other side of the door.

Vance immediately wedged his foot in the slight aperture and forced the door inward with his shoulder. Before us, in the dingy light of a gas jet which hung from the ceiling far back in the hall, was a Chinaman, clad in black pyjamas and a pair of sandals. He was barely five feet tall.

"What you want?" he asked, in an antagonistic, falsetto voice, backing away quickly against the wall to the right of the door.

"We want to speak to Mrs. Kenting," said Vance, scarcely above a whisper.

"She not here," the Chinaman answered. "Me no know Missy Kenting. Nobody here. You have wrong house. Go away."

Vance had already stepped inside, and in a flash he drew a large handkerchief from his outer breast pocket and crushed it against the Chinaman's mouth, pinioning him against the wall. Then I noticed the reason for Vance's act:—only a foot or so away was an old-fashioned push-bell toward which the Chinaman had been slyly reaching. The man stood back against the wall under Vance's firm pressure, as if he felt that any effort to escape would be futile.

Then, with the most amazing quickness and dexterity, he forced his head upward and leaped on Vance, like a wrestler executing a flying tackle, and twined his legs about Vance's waist, at the same time throwing his arms round Vance's neck. It was an astonishing feat of nimble accuracy.

But, with a movement almost as quick as the Chinaman's, Heath, who was standing close to Vance, brought the butt of his revolver down on the yellow man's head with terrific force. The Chinaman's legs disentangled themselves; his arms relaxed; his head fell back; and he began slipping limply to the floor. Vance caught him and eased him down noiselessly. Leaning over for a moment, he looked at the China-man by the flame of his cigarette lighter, and then straightened up.

"He's good for an hour, at least, Sergeant," he said in a hoarse whisper. "My word! You're so brutal. . . . He was trying to reach that bell signal. The others must be upstairs." He moved silently toward the narrow carpeted stairway that led above. "This is a damnable situation. Keep your guns handy, both of you, and don't touch the banister—it may creak."

As we filed noiselessly up the dimly-lit stairs, Vance leading the way, Heath just behind him, and I bringing up the rear, I was assailed by a terrifying premonition of disaster. There was something sinister in the atmosphere of that house; and I imagined that grave danger lurked in the deep shadows above us. I grasped my automatic more firmly, and a sensation of alertness seized me as if my brain had sud-denly been swept clear of everything but the apprehension of what might lie ahead. . . .

It seemed an unreasonably long time before we reached the upper landing—a sensation like a crazy hashish distortion—and I felt myself struggling to regain a sense of reality.

As Vance stepped into the hallway above, which was narrower and dingier than the one downstairs, he stood tensely still for a moment, looking about him. There was only one small lighted gas jet at the rear of the hall. Luckily, the floor was covered with an old worn run-ner which deadened our footsteps as we followed Vance up the hall. Suddenly the muffled sound of voices came to us, but we could not distinguish any words. Vance moved stealthily toward the front of the house and stood before the only door on the left of the corridor. A line of faint light outlined the threshold, and it was now evident that the voices came from within that room.

After listening a moment Vance tried the doorknob with extreme care. To our surprise the door was not locked, but swung back eas-ily into a long, narrow, squalid room in the centre of which stood a plain deal table. At one end of the table, by the light of an oil lamp, two illy dressed men sat playing casino, judging by the distribution of the cards.

Though the room was filled with cigarette smoke, I immediately recognized one of the men as the shabby figure I had seen leaning against the bench in Central Park the night before. The lamp fur-nished the only illumination in the room, and dark grey blankets, hanging in full folds from over the window-frames, let no ray of light escape either at the front or side window.

340

The two men sprang to their feet instantaneously, turning in our direction.

"Down, Van!" ordered Vance; and his call was submerged under two deafening detonations accompanied by two flashes from a revolver in the hand of the man nearest us. The bullets must have gone over us, for both Heath and I had dropped quickly to the floor at Vance's order. Almost immediately—so quickly as to be practically simultaneous—there came two reports from Vance's automatic, and I saw the man who had shot at us pitch forward. The thud of his body on the floor coincided with the crash of the lamp, knocked over by the second man. The room was plunged in complete darkness.

"Stay down, Van!" came the commanding voice of Vance.

Almost as he spoke there was a *staccato* exchange of shots. All I could see were the brilliant flashes from the automatics. To this day I cannot determine the number of shots fired that night, for they overlapped each other in such rapid succession that it was impossible to make an accurate count. I lay flat on my stomach across the door-sill, my head spinning dizzily, my muscles paralyzed with fear for Vance.

There was a brief respite of black silence, so poignant as to be almost palpable, and then came the crash of an upset chair and the dull heavy sound of a human body striking the floor. I was afraid to move. Heath's laboured breathing made a welcome noise at my side. I could not tell, in the blackness of the room, who had fallen. A terrifying dread assailed me.

Then I heard Vance's voice—the cynical, nonchalant voice I knew so well—and my intensity of fright gave way to a feeling of relief and overpowering weakness. I felt like a drowning man, who, coming up for the third time, suddenly feels strong arms beneath his shoulders.

"Really, y' know," his voice came from somewhere in the darkness, "there should be electric lights in this house. I saw the wires as we entered."

He was fumbling around somewhere above me, and suddenly the Sergeant's flashlight swept over the room. I staggered to my feet and leaned limply against the casing of the door.

"The idiot!" Vance was murmuring. "He kept his lighted cigarette in his mouth, and I was able to follow every move he made. . . . There must be a switch or a fixture somewhere. The lamp and the blankets at the window were only to give the house the appearance of being untenanted."

The ray from Heath's pocket flash moved about the walls and ceiling, but I could see neither him nor Vance. Then the light came to a halt, and Heath's triumphant voice rang out.

"Here it is, sir,—a socket beside the window." And as he spoke a weak, yellowed bulb dimly lit up the room.

Heath was at the front window, his hand still on the switch of a small electric light socket; and Vance stood near-by, to all appearances cool and unconcerned. On the floor lay two motionless bodies.

"Pleasant evening, Sergeant." Vance spoke in his usual steady, whimsical voice. "My sincerest apologies, and all that." Then he caught sight of me, and his face sobered. "Are you all right, Van?" he asked.

I assured him I had escaped the mêlée unscathed, and added that I had not used my automatic because I was afraid I might have hit him in the dark.

"I quite understand," he murmured and, nodding his head, he went quickly to the two prostrate bodies. After a momentary inspection, he stood up and said:

"Quite dead, Sergeant. Really, y' know, I seem to be a fairly accurate shot."

"I'll say!" breathed Heath with admiration. "I wasn't a hell of a lot of help, was I, Mr. Vance?" he added a bit shamefacedly.

"Really nothing for you to do, Sergeant."

Vance looked about him. Through a wide alcove at the far end of the room a white iron bed was clearly visible. This adjoining chamber was like a small bedroom, with only dirty red rep curtains dividing it from the main room. Vance stepped quickly between the curtains, and switched on a light just over the wooden mantel near the bed. At the rear of the room, near the foot of the bed, was a door standing half ajar. Between the mantel and the bed with its uncovered mattress, was a small bureau with a large mirror swung between two supports rising from the bureau itself.

Heath had followed Vance into the room, and I trailed weakly after them. Vance stood before the bureau for a moment or so, looking down at the few cigarette-burnt toilet articles scattered about it. He opened the top drawer and looked into it. Then he opened the second drawer.

"Ah!" he murmured half aloud, and reached inside.

When he withdrew his hand he was holding a neatly rolled pair of thin Shantung-silk pyjamas. He inspected them for a moment and smiled slightly.

"The missin' pyjamas," he said as if to himself, though both Heath and I heard every word he spoke. "Never been worn. Very interestin'." He unrolled them on the top of the bureau and drew forth a small green-handled toothbrush. "And the missin' toothbrush," he added. He ran his thumb over the bristles. "And quite dry. . . . The pyjamas, I opine, were rolled quickly round the toothbrush and the comb, brought here, and thrown into the drawer. The comb, of course, slipped out into the hedge as the Chinaman now prostrate below descended the ladder from Kaspar Kenting's room." He re-rolled the pyjamas, placed them back into the drawer, and resumed his inspection of the toilet articles on the bureau top.

Heath and I were both near the archway, our eyes on Vance, when he suddenly called out, "Look out, Sergeant!"

The last word had been only half completed when there came two shots from the rear door. The slim, crouching figure of a man, somewhat scholarly looking and well dressed, had suddenly appeared there.

Vance had swung about simultaneously with his warning to Heath, and there were two more shots in rapid succession, this time from Vance's gun.

I saw the poised revolver of blue steel drop from the raised hand of the man at the rear door: he looked round him, dazed, and both his hands went to his abdomen. He remained upright for a moment; then he doubled up and sank to the floor where he lay in an awkward crumpled heap.

Heath's revolver too dropped from his grip. When the first shot had been fired, he had pivoted round as if some powerful unseen hand had pushed him: he staggered backward a few feet and slid heavily into a chair. Vance looked a moment at the contorted figure of the man on the floor, and then hastened to Heath.

"The baby winged me," Heath said with an effort. "My gun jammed."

Vance gave him a cursory examination and then smiled encouragingly.

"Frightfully sorry, Sergeant,—it was all the fault of my trustin' nature. McLaughlin told us there were only two men in that green car, and I foolishly concluded that two gentlemen and the Chinaman would be all we should have to contend with. I should have been more far-seein'. Most humiliatin'. . . . You'll have a sore arm for a couple of weeks," he added. "Lucky it's only a flesh wound. You'll probably lose a lot of gore; but really, y' know, you're far too full of blood as it is." And he expertly bound up Heath's right arm, using a handkerchief for a bandage.

The Sergeant struggled to his feet.

"You're treating me like a damn baby." He stepped to the mantel

343

and leaned against it. "There's nothing the matter with me. Where do we go from here?" His face was unusually white, and I could see that the mantel behind him was a most welcome prop.

"Glad I had that mirror in front of me," murmured Vance. "Very useful devices, mirrors."

He had barely finished speaking when we heard a repeated ringing near us.

"By Jove, a telephone!" commented Vance. "Now we'll have to find the instrument."

Heath straightened up.

"The thing's right here on the mantel," he said. "I've been standing in front of it."

Vance made a sudden move forward, but Heath stood in the way.

"You'd better let me answer it, Mr. Vance. You're too refined." He picked up the receiver with his left hand.

"What d' you want?" he asked, in a gruff, officious tone. There was a short pause. "Oh, yeah? O.K., go ahead." A longer pause followed, as Heath listened. "Don't know nothing about it," he shot back, in a heavy, resentful voice. Then he added: "You got the wrong number." And he slammed down the receiver.

"Who was it, do you know, Sergeant?" Vance spoke quietly as he lighted a cigarette.

Heath turned slowly and looked at Vance. His eyes were narrowed, and there was an expression of awe on his face as he answered.

"Sure I know," he said significantly. He shook his head as if he did not trust himself to speak. "There ain't no mistaking *that* voice."

"Well, who was it, Sergeant?" asked Vance mildly, without looking up from his cigarette.

The Sergeant seemed stronger: he stood away from the mantelpiece, his legs wide apart and firmly planted. Rivulets of blood were running down over his right hand which hung limply at his side.

"It was—" he began, and then he was suddenly aware of my presence in the room. "Mother o' God!" he breathed. "I don't have to tell you, Mr. Vance. You knew this morning."

CHAPTER 18

The Windowless Room
Friday, July 22; 10:30 p.m.

Vance looked at the Sergeant a moment and shook his head.

"Y' know," he said, in a curiously repressed voice, "I was almost hoping I was wrong. I hate to think—" He came suddenly forward to Heath who had fallen back weakly against the mantel and was blindly reaching for the wall, in an effort to hold himself upright. Vance put his arm around Heath and led him to a chair.

"Here, Sergeant," he said in a kindly tone, handing him an etched silver flask, "take a drink of this—and don't be a sissy."

"Go to hell," grumbled Heath, and inverted the flask to his lips. Then he handed it back to Vance. "That's potent juice," he said, standing up and pushing Vance away from him. "Let's get going."

"Right-o, Sergeant. We've only begun." As he spoke he walked toward the rear door and stepped over the dead man, into the next room. Heath and I were at his heels.

The room was in darkness, but with the aid of his flashlight the Sergeant quickly found the electric light. We were in a small box-like room, without windows. Opposite us, against the wall, stood a narrow army cot. Vance rushed forward and leaned over the cot. The motionless form of a woman lay stretched out on it. Despite her dishevelled hair and her deathlike pallor, I recognized Madelaine Kenting. Strips of adhesive tape bound her lips together, and both her arms were tied securely with pieces of heavy clothes-line to the iron rods at either side of the cot.

Vance dexterously removed the tape from her mouth, and the woman sucked in a deep breath, as if she had been partly suffocated. There was a low rumbling in her throat, expressive of agony and fear, like that of a person coming out of an anaesthetic after a serious operation.

Vance busied himself with the cruel cords binding her wrists. When he had released them he laid his ear against her heart for a moment, and poured a little of the cognac from his flask between her lips. She swallowed automatically and coughed. Then Vance lifted her in his arms and started from the room.

Just as he reached the door the telephone rang again, and Heath went toward it.

"Don't bother to answer it, Sergeant," said Vance. "It's probably the same person calling back." And he continued on his way, with the woman in his arms.

I preceded him as he carried his inert burden down the dingy stairway.

"We must get her to a hospital at once, Van," he said when we had reached the lower hallway.

I held the front door open for him, my automatic extended before me, ready for instant use, should the occasion arise. Vance went down the shaky steps without a word, just as Heath joined me at the door. The Chinaman still lay where we had left him, on the floor against the wall.

"Drag him up to that pipe in the corner, Mr. Van Dine," the Sergeant told me in a strained voice. "My arm is sorta numb."

For the first time I noticed that a two-inch water pipe, corroding for lack of paint, rose through the front hall, behind the door, a few inches from the wall. I moved the limp form of the Chinaman until his head came in contact with the pipe; and Heath, with one hand, drew out a pair of handcuffs. Clamping one of the manacles on the unconscious man's right wrist, he pulled it around the pipe and with his foot manipulated the Chinaman's left arm upward till he could close the second iron around it. Then he reached into his pocket and drew out a piece of clothes-line which he had obviously brought from the windowless room upstairs.

"Tie his ankles together, will you, Mr. Van Dine?" he said. "I can't quite make it."

I slipped my gun back into my coat pocket and did as Heath directed.

Then we both went out into the murky night, Heath slamming the door behind him. Vance, with his burden, was perhaps a hundred yards ahead of us, and we came up with him just as he reached the car. He placed Mrs. Kenting on the rear seat of the tonneau and arranged the cushions under her head.

"You can both sit in front with me," he suggested over his shoul-

346

der, as he took his place at the wheel; and before Heath and I were actually seated he had started the engine, shifted the gear, and got the car in motion with a sudden but smooth roll. He continued straight down Waring Avenue.

As we approached a lone patrolman after two or three blocks, Heath requested that we stop. Vance threw on his brakes, and honked his horn to attract the patrolman's attention.

"Have I got a minute, Mr. Vance?" asked Heath.

"Certainly, Sergeant," Vance told him, as he drew up to the curb beside the officer. "Mrs. Kenting is fairly comfortable and in no immediate danger. A few minutes more or less in arrivin' at a hospital will make no material difference."

Heath spoke to the officer through the open window, identified himself, and then asked the man, "Where's your call-box?"

"On the next corner, Sergeant, at Gunhill Road," answered the officer, saluting.

"All right," returned Heath brusquely. "Hop on the running-board." He leaned back in the seat again and we went on for another block, stopping at the direction of the officer.

The Sergeant slid out of the car, and the patrolman unlocked the box for him. Heath's back was to us, and I could not hear what he was saying over the telephone, but when he turned he addressed the officer peremptorily:

"Get up to Lord Street"—he gave the number, and added: "The second house from the corner of Waring—and stay on duty. Some of the boys from the 47th Precinct station will join you in a few minutes, and a couple of men from the Homicide Bureau will be coming up a little later—as soon as they can get here. I'll be returning myself inside of an hour or so. You'll find three stiffs in the joint and a Chink chained up to a water pipe in the front hall. There'll be an ambulance up before long."

"Right, sir," the officer answered, and started on the run up Waring Avenue.

Heath had climbed into the car as he spoke, and Vance drove off without delay.

"I'm heading for the Doran Hospital, just this side of Bronx Park, Sergeant," Vance said, as we sped along. In about fifteen minutes, ignoring all traffic lights and driving at a rate far exceeding the city speed limit, we drew up in front of the hospital.

Vance jumped from the car, took Mrs. Kenting in his arms again, and carried her up the wide marble steps. He returned to the car in less than ten minutes.

"Everything's all right, Sergeant," he said as he approached the car. "The lady has regained consciousness. Fresh air did it. Her mind is a bit misty. Nothing fundamentally wrong, however."

Heath had stepped out of the car and was standing on the sidewalk. "So long, Mr. Vance," he said. "I'm getting in that taxi up ahead. I gotta get back to that damn house. I got work to do." He moved away as he spoke.

But Vance rushed forward and took him by the arm.

"Stay right here, Sergeant, and get that arm properly dressed first." He led Heath back, and accompanied him up the hospital steps.

A few minutes later Vance came out alone.

"The noble Sergeant is all right, Van," he said, as he took his place at the wheel again. "He'll be out before long. But he insists on going back to Lord Street." And Vance started the car once more, and headed downtown.

When we reached Vance's apartment Currie opened the door for us. There was relief written in every line of the old butler's face.

"Good heavens, Currie!" said Vance, as we stepped inside. "I told you, you might tuck yourself in at eleven o'clock if you hadn't heard from me—and here it is nearing midnight, and you're still up."

The old man looked away with embarrassment as he closed the door.

"I'm sorry, sir," he said in a voice which, for all its formality, had an emotional tremolo in it. "I—I couldn't go to bed, sir, until you returned. I understood, sir,—if you will pardon my saying so—your reference to the documents in the drawer of the secretary. And I've taken the liberty this evening of worrying about you. I'm very glad you have come home, sir."

"You're a sentimental old fossil, Currie," Vance complained, handing the butler his hat.

"Mr. Markham is waiting in the library," said Currie, like an old faithful soldier reporting to his superior officer.

"I rather imagined he would be," murmured Vance as he went up the stairs. "Good old Markham. Always fretting about me."

As we entered the library, we found Markham pacing up and down. He stopped suddenly at sight of Vance.

"Well, thank God!" he said. And, though he attempted to sound trivial, his relief was as evident as old Currie's had been. He crossed the room and sank into a chair; and I got the impression, from the way he relaxed, that he had been on his feet for a long time.

"Greetings, old dear," said Vance. "Why this unexpected pleasure of your presence at such an hour?"

"I was merely interested, officially, in what you might have found on Lord Street," returned Markham. "I suppose you found a vast vacant space with a real estate sign saying 'Suitable for factory site.'"

Vance smiled.

"Not exactly that, don't y' know. I had a jolly good time—which will probably make you very angry and envious."

He turned round and came to where I had seated myself. I felt weak and shaky. I was only then beginning to feel the reaction from the excitement of the evening. I realized now that in the brief space of time we had spent on Lord Street, I had become too keyed up physically to apprehend completely the dread possibilities of the situation. In the quiet and safety of familiar surroundings, the flood of reality suddenly overwhelmed me, and it was only with great effort that I managed to maintain a normal attitude.

"Let's have your gun, Van," said Vance, in his cool, steadying voice, holding out his hand. "Glad you didn't have to use it. . . . Horrible mess—what? Sorry I let you come along. But really, y' know, I myself was rather surprised and shocked by the turn of affairs."

A little abashed, I took the unused automatic from my pocket and handed it over to him: it was he who had assumed the entire brunt of the danger, and I had been unable to be of any assistance. He stepped to the centre-table and pulled open the drawer. Then he tossed my automatic into it, laid his own beside it, and, closing the drawer meditatively, rang the bell for Currie.

Markham was watching him closely but restrained his curiosity as the old butler entered with a service of brandy. Currie had sensed Vance's wish and had not waited for an order. When he had set down the tray and left the room, Markham leaned forward in his chair.

"Well, what the hell *did* happen?" he demanded irritably.

Vance sipped his cognac slowly, lighted a *Régie*, took several deep inhalations, and sat down leisurely in his favourite chair.

"I'm frightfully sorry, Markham," he said, "but I fear I have made you a bit of trouble. . . . The fact is," he added carelessly, "I killed three men."

Markham leaped to his feet as if he had been shot upward by the sudden release of a powerful steel spring. He glared at Vance, in doubt whether the other was jesting or in earnest. Simultaneously he exploded:

"What do you mean, Vance?"

Vance drew deeply again on his cigarette before answering. Then he said with a tantalizing smile:

"J'ai tué trois hommes—Ich habe drei Männer getötet—Ho ucciso tre uomini—He matado tres hombres—Három embert megöltem—Haragti sheloshah anashim. Meanin', I killed three men."

"Are you serious?" blurted Markham.

"Oh, quite," answered Vance. "Do you think you can save me from the dire consequences? . . . Incidentally, I found Mrs. Kenting. I took her to the Doran Hospital. Not a matter of life and death, but she required immediate and competent attention. Rather upset, I should imagine, by her detention. A bit out of her mind, in fact. Frightful experience she went through. Doin' nicely, however. Under excellent care. Should be quite herself in a few days. Can't co-ordinate just yet. . . . Oh, I say, Markham, do sit down again and take your cognac. You look positively perturbed."

Markham obeyed automatically, like a frightened child submitting to his parent. He swallowed the brandy in one gulp.

"For the love of God, Vance," he pleaded, "drop this silly ring-around-the-rosy stuff and talk to me like a sane human being."

"Sorry, Markham, and all that sort of thing," murmured Vance contritely. And then he told Markham in detail everything that had happened that night. But I thought he too greatly minimized his own part in the tragic drama. When he had finished his recital he asked somewhat coyly:

"Am I a doomed culprit, or were there what you would call extenuatin' circumstances?—I'm horribly weak on the intricacies of the law, don't y' know."

"Damn it! forget everything," said Markham. "If you're really worried, I'll get you a brass medal as big as Columbus Circle."

"My word, what a fate!" sighed Vance.

"Have you any idea who these three men were?" Markham went on, in tense seriousness.

"Not the groggiest notion," admitted Vance sadly. "One of them, Van Dine tells me, was watchin' us from the footpath in the park last night. Two of the three were probably the lads McLaughlin saw in the green coupé outside the Kenting domicile Wednesday morning. The other one I have never had the exquisite pleasure of meetin' before. I'd say, however, he had a gift for tradin' in doubtful securities on the sly: I've seen bucket-shop operators who resembled him. Anyhow, Markham old dear, why fret about it tonight? They were not nice persons, not nice at all. The geniuses at Headquarters will check up on their identities. . . ."

The front door-bell rang, and a minute later Heath entered

the library. His ordinarily ruddy face was a little pale and drawn, and his right arm was in a sling. He saluted Markham and turned sheepishly to Vance.

"Your old saw-bones at the hospital told me I had to go home," he complained. "And there's nothing in God's world the matter with me," he added disgustedly. "Imagine him puttin' this arm in a sling!—said I had to take the weight offen it, that it would heal quicker that way. And then had to go and make my other arm sore by stickin' a needle in it! . . . What was the needle for, Mr. Vance?"

"Tetanus antitoxin, Sergeant," Vance told him, smiling. "Simply has to be done, don't y' know, with all gun-shot wounds. Nothing to cause you any discomfort, though. Reaction in a week—that's all."

Heath snorted. "Hell! If my gun hadn't jammed—"

"Yes, that was a bad break, Sergeant," nodded Markham.

"The doc wouldn't even let me go back to the house," grumbled Heath. "Anyway, I got the report from the local station up there. They took the three stiffs over to the morgue. The Chink'll live. Maybe we can—"

"You'll never wangle anything out of him," put in Vance quietly. "Your beloved hose-pipes and water-cures and telephone directories will get you nowhere. I know Chinamen. But Mrs. Kenting will have an interestin' story to tell as soon as she's rational again. . . . Cheer up, Sergeant, and have some more medicine." He poured Heath a liberal drink of his rare brandy.

"I'll be on the job tomorrow all right, Chief," the Sergeant asserted as he put down the glass on a small table at his side. "Just imagine that young whipper-snapper of an intern at the Doran Hospital tryin' to make a Little Lord Fauntleroy outa me! A sling!"

Vance and Markham and Heath discussed the case from various angles for perhaps a half hour longer. Markham was getting impatient.

"I'm going home," he said finally, as he rose. "We'll get this thing straightened out in the morning."

Vance left his chair reluctantly.

"I sincerely hope so, Markham," he said. "It's not at all a particularly nice case, and the sooner you're free of it, the better."

"Is there anything you want me to do, Mr. Vance?" Heath's tone was respectful, but a little weary.

Vance looked at him with commiseration.

"I want you to go home and have a good sleep. . . . And, by the by, Sergeant, how about rounding everybody up and invitin' them to the Purple House tomorrow, around noon?" he asked. "I'm speakin' of

Fleel, Kenyon Kenting, and Quaggy. Mrs. Falloway and her son will, I'm sure, be there, in any event."

Heath got to his feet and grinned confidently.

"Don't you worry, Mr. Vance," he said. "I'll have 'em there for you." He went toward the door, then suddenly turned round and held out his left hand to Vance. "Much obliged, sir, for tonight—"

"Oh, please ignore it, my good Sergeant,—it was merely a slight nuisance, after all," returned Vance, though he grasped the Sergeant's hand warmly.

Markham and Heath departed together, and Vance again pressed the bell for Currie.

When the old man had entered the room Vance said:

"I'm turning in, Currie. That will be all for tonight."

The butler bowed, and picked up the tray and the empty cognac glasses.

"Very good, sir. Thank you, sir. Good night, sir."

CHAPTER 19

The Final Scene
Saturday, July 23; 9 a.m.

Vance was up and dressed in good season the next morning. He seemed fairly cheerful but somewhat distrait. Before he sat down to his typical meagre breakfast he went into the anteroom and telephoned to Heath. It was rather a long conversation, but no word of it reached me where I sat at the desk in the library.

As he returned to the room he said to me: "I think, Van, we're in a position now to get somewhere with this case. The poor Sergeant!—he's practically a ravin' maniac this morning, with the reporters houndin' him every minute. The news of last night's altercation did not break soon enough for the morning editions of the papers. But the mere thought of reading of our escapade in the noon editions fills me with horror." He sipped his Turkish coffee. "I had hoped we could clear up the beastly matter before the news vendors began giving tongue. The best place to conclude the case is in the Purple House. It's a family gathering-place, as it were. Every one connected with the family, don't y' know, is rather intimately concerned, and hopin' for illumination. . . ."

Late in the forenoon Markham, haggard and drawn, joined us at the apartment. He did not ask Vance any questions, for he knew it would be futile in the mood Vance was in. He did, however, greet him cordially.

"I think you're going to get that medal, whether you like it or not," he said, lighting a cigar and leaning against the mantel. "All three men have been definitely identified, and they have all been on the police books for years. They've been urgently wanted at Headquarters for a long time. Two of them have served terms: one for extortion, and the other for manslaughter. They're Goodley Franks and Austria Rentwick—no, he didn't come from Austria. The third man was none other than our old elusive friend, Gilt-Edge Lamarne, with a dozen aliases—a very shrewd crook. He's been arrested nine times, but we've never been able to make the charges stick. He's kept the local boys, as well as the federal men, awake nights for years. We've had the goods on him for eight months now, but we couldn't find him."

Markham smiled at Vance with solemn satisfaction.

"It was a very fortunate affair last night, from every point of view. Everybody's happy; only, I fear you're about to become a hero and will have ticker-tape rained on you from the windows whenever you go down Broadway."

"Oh, my Markham, my Markham!" wailed Vance. "I won't have it. I'm about to sail to South America, or Alaska, or the Malay Peninsula. . . ." He got to his feet and went to the table where he finished his old port. "Come along, Markham," he said as he put his glass down. "Let's get uptown and conclude this bally case before I sail for foreign parts where ticker-tape is unknown."

He went toward the door, with Markham and me following him.

"You think we can finish the case today?" Markham looked sceptical.

"Oh, quite. It was, in fact, finished long ago." Vance stopped with his hand on the knob and smiled cheerfully. "But, knowin' your passionate adoration for legal evidence, I have waited till now."

Markham studied Vance for a moment, and said nothing. In silence we went out and descended the stairs to the street.

We arrived at the Kenting residence, Vance driving us there in his car, fifteen minutes before noon. Weem took our hats and made a surly gesture toward the drawing-room. Sergeant Heath and Snitkin were already there.

A little later Fleel and Kenyon Kenting arrived together, followed almost immediately by Porter Quaggy. They had barely seated themselves when old Mrs. Falloway, supported by her son Fraim, came down the front stairs and joined us.

"I'm so anxious about Madelaine," Mrs. Falloway said. "How is she, Mr. Vance?"

"I received a telephone call from the hospital shortly before I came here," he replied, addressing himself to the others in the room, as well as to the old woman who, with Fraim's help, had now seated herself comfortably at one end of the small sofa. "Mrs. Kenting is doing even better today than I would have expected. She is still somewhat irrational—which is quite natural, considering the frightful experience she has been through—but I can assure you that she will be home in two or three days, fully recovered and in her normal mind."

He sat down by the window leisurely, and lighted a cigarette.

"And I imagine she will have a most interestin' tale to unfold," he went on. "Y' know, it was not intended that she return."

He moved slightly in his chair.

"The truth is, this was not a kidnapping case at all. The authorities were expected to accept it in that light, but the murderer made too many errors—his fault lay in trying to be excessively clever. I think I can reconstruct most of the events in their chronological order. Some one wanted money—wanted it rather desperately, in fact,—and all the means for an easy acquisition were at hand. The plot was as simple as it was cowardly. But the plotter met a snag when some of the early steps failed rather dismally, and a new and bolder procedure and technique became necess'ry. A damnable new technique, but one that was equally encumbered by the grave possibility of error. The errors developed almost inevitably, for the human brain, however clever, has its limitations. But the person who mapped out the plot was blinded and confused by a passionate desire for the money. Everything was sordid. . . ."

Again Vance shifted his position slightly and drew deeply on his cigarette, expelling the smoke in curling ribbons, as he went on.

"There is no doubt whatever that Kaspar Kenting made an appointment for the early morning hours, after he had returned from his evening's entertainment at the casino with Mr. Quaggy. He came in and went to his room, changed his suit and his shoes, and kept that appointment. It was a vital matter to him, as he was deeply in debt and undoubtedly expected some sort of practical solution of his problem to result from this meeting. The two mysterious and objectionable gentlemen whom Mrs. Kenting described to us as callers here earlier in the week, were quite harmless creatures, but avid for the money Kaspar owed them. One of them was a book-maker, the other a shady fellow who ran a *sub-rosa* gambling house—I rather suspected their identity from the first, and verified it this morning: I happened to recognize one of the men through Mrs. Kenting's description.

"When Kaspar left this house early Wednesday morning, he was met at the appointed place not by the person with whom he had made his appointment, but by others whom he had never seen before. They struck him over the head before he so much as realized that anything was amiss, threw him into a coupé, and then drove off with him to the East River and disposed of him, hoping he would not be found too soon. It was straight, brutal murder. And the persons who committed that murder had been hired for that purpose and had been instructed accordingly. You will understand that the plotter at the source never intended anything less than murder for the victim—since there was grave risk in letting him live to point an accusing finger later. . . . The slender Chinaman—the *lobby-gow* of the gang, who now has concussion of the brain from the Sergeant's blow last night—then returned to the house here, placed the ladder against the window—it had been left here previously for just that purpose—entered the room through the window, and set the stage according to instructions, taking the toothbrush, the comb, and the pyjamas, and pinning the note to the window-sill, generally leaving mute but spurious indications that Kaspar Kenting had kidnapped himself in order to collect the money he needed to straighten out his debts. Kaspar's keeping of the appointment at such an hour naturally implied that the rendezvous was with some one he thought could help him. I found the pyjamas and toothbrush, unused, in the Lord-Street house last night. It was the Chinaman that Mrs. Kenting heard moving about in her husband's room at dawn Wednesday. He was arranging the details in which he had been instructed."

Vance continued in a matter-of-fact voice.

"So far the plot was working nicely. The first set-back occurred after the arrival in the mail of the ransom note with the instructions to take the money to the tree. The scheme of the murderer to collect the money from the tree was thwarted, makin' necess'ry further steps. The same day Mrs. Kenting was approached for an appointment, perhaps with a promise of news of her husband—obviously by some one she trusted, for she went out alone at ten o'clock that night to keep the appointment. She was awaited—possibly just inside Central Park—by the same hard gentlemen who had done away with her husband. But instead of meeting with the same fate as Kaspar Kenting, she was taken to the house on Lord Street I visited last night, and held there as a sort of hostage. I rather imagine, don't y' know, that the perpetrator of this fiendish scheme had not yet been able to pay the price demanded for the neat performance of Kaspar's killing, thereby irking the hired assassins. The lady still alive was a very definite menace to the schemer, since she would be able, if released, to tell with whom she had made the appointment. She was, so to speak, a threat held over one criminal by another criminal who was a bit more clever.

"Mrs. Kenting undoubtedly used, that evening, a certain kind of perfume—Emerald—because it had been given to her by the person with whom she had the rendezvous. Surely, being a blonde, she knew better than to use it as her personal choice. That will explain to you gentlemen why I asked you so seemingly irrelevant a question the night before last. . . . Incidentally," he added calmly, "I happen to know who gave Mrs. Kenting that Courtet's Emerald."

There was a slight stir, but Vance went on without a pause:

"Poor Kaspar! He was a weak chappie, and the price for his own murder was being wangled out of him without his realizing it. Through the gem collection of old Karl Kenting, of course. He was depleting that collection regularly at the subtle instigation of some one else, some one who took the gems and gave him practically nothing compared to what they were actually worth, hopin' to turn them over at an outrageous profit. But semiprecious stones are not so easy to dispose of through illegitimate channels. They really need a collector to appreciate them—and collectors have grown rather exactin' regarding the origin of their purchases. A shady transaction of this nature would naturally require time, and the now-defunct henchmen who were waiting for settlement were becoming annoyed. Most of the really valuable stones, which I am sure the collection contained originally, were no longer there when I glanced over the cases the other morning. I am quite certain that the balas-ruby I found in the poor fellow's dinner coat was brought back because the purchaser would not give him what he thought it was worth—Kaspar probably mistook the stone for a real ruby. There were black opals missing from the collection, also exhibits of jade, which Karl Kenting must undoubtedly have included in the collection; and yesterday morning the absence of a large piece of alexandrite was discovered—"

Fraim Falloway suddenly leaped to his feet, glaring at Vance with the eyes of a maniac. There was an abnormal colour in the young man's face, and he was shaking from head to foot.

"I didn't do it!" he screamed hysterically. "I didn't have Kaspar killed! I tell you I didn't—*I didn't!* And you think I'd hurt Madelaine! You're a devil. I didn't do it, I say! You have no right to accuse me." He reached down quickly and picked up a small, but heavy, bronze statue of Antinoüs on the table beside him. But Heath, who was standing at his side, was even quicker than Falloway. He grasped the youth's shoulder with his free arm, just as the other lifted the statue to hurl at Vance. The figurine fell harmlessly to the floor, and Heath forced young Falloway back into his chair.

"Put your pulse-warmers on him, Snitkin," he ordered.

Snitkin, standing just behind Fraim Falloway's chair, leaned over and deftly manacled the youth, who sank back limply in his chair, breathing heavily.

Mrs. Falloway, who had sat stoically throughout the entire unexpected scene in the drawing-room, now looked up quickly as Snitkin placed the handcuffs on her son. She leaned forward with horror in her eyes. I thought for a moment she was going to speak, but she made no comment.

"Really, Mr. Falloway," Vance admonished in a soothing voice, "you shouldn't handle heavy objects when you're in that frame of mind. Frightfully sorry. But just sit still and relax." He drew on his cigarette again and, apparently ignoring the incident, went on in his unemotional drawl:

"As I was sayin', the disappearance of the stones from the collection was an indication of the identity of the murderer, for the simple reason that the hirin' of thugs and the underground disposal of these gems quite obviously suggested that the same type of person was involved in both endeavours: to wit, both procedures implied a connection with undercover characters—fences and assassins. Not that the reasonin' was final, you understand, but most suggestive. The two notes yesterday were highly enlightenin'. One of them was obviously concocted for effect; the other was quite genuine. But boldness—usually a good technique—was, in this case, seen through."

"But who," asked Quaggy, "could possibly have fulfilled the requirements, so to speak, of your vague and amusing theory?" The smile on his lips was without mirth—it was cold and self-satisfied. "Just because you saw two black opals in my possession—"

"My theory, Mr. Quaggy, is not nearly so vague as you may think," Vance interrupted quickly. "And if it amuses you, I am delighted." Vance looked at the man with steady, indifferent eyes. "But, to answer your question, I should say that it was some one with an opportunity to render legal service, with legal protection, to members of the underworld...."

Fleel, who was sitting at the small desk at the front of the room, quickly addressed Vance.

"There is a definite implication in your words, sir," he said, with his customary judicial air. (I could not resist the impression that he was pleading for a client in a court of law.) "I'm a lawyer," he went on, with ostentatious bitterness, "and I naturally have certain contacts with the type of men you imply were at the bottom of this outrage." Then he chuckled sarcastically. "However," he added, "I shall not hold the insult against you. The fact is, your amateurish ratiocinations are highly amusing." And, leaning back in his chair, he smirked.

Vance barely glanced at the man, and continued speaking as if there had been no interruption.

"Referrin' again to the various ransom notes, they were dictated by the plotter of Kaspar's murder—that is, all but the one received by Mr. Fleel yesterday—, and they were couched in such language that they could be shown to the authorities in order to side-track suspicion from the actual culprit and at the same time impress Mr. Kenyon Kenting with the urgent necessity of raising the fifty thousand dollars. I had two statements as to the amount of money which Kaspar himself was demanding for his debts—one, an honest report of fifty thousand dollars; the other, no doubt a stupidly concocted tale of thirty thousand dollars—again obviously for the purpose of diverting suspicion from the person connected with the crime."

Vance looked thoughtfully at Fleel and continued.

"Of course, it is possible that Kaspar asked you for only thirty thousand dollars, whereas he had just asked his brother for fifty thousand. But it is highly significant that he first asked his brother for fifty thousand dollars and then asked you for a different amount, whereas the ransom note called for the fifty thousand. This discrepancy between Mr. Kenting's report and your report of the amount would certainly have a tendency to point toward the brother and not toward you—which could easily be interpreted, in view of everything, as another clever means of your pointing suspicion away from yourself in case you were suspected. Certainly Mr. Kenyon Kenting was not lying about the amount, and there could be little or no reason to think that Kaspar's brother was guilty of the crime, for in such a case the money would have had to come from him—and people, don't y' know, do not ordinarily commit crimes in order to impoverish themselves—eh, what? Summing it up, there was no reason for Mr. Kenyon Kenting to lie about the amount demanded by Kaspar, whereas there was a definite reason for you to lie about it."

Vance moved his eyes slowly round the startled group.

"The second note received by Mr. Fleel, was not, as I have already intimated, one of the series written at the instructions of the guilty man—it was a genuine document addressed to him; and the recipient felt that he not only could use it to have the ransom money paid over to him, but to disarm once more any suspicion that might be springing up in the minds of the authorities. It did not occur to him that the address, cryptically written in for his eyes alone, could be interpreted by another. Oh, yes, it was a genuine message from the unpaid minions, demanding the money they had earned by disposing of Kaspar."

He turned slowly to Fleel again and met the other's smirk with a cold smile.

"When I suspected you, Mr. Fleel," he said, "I sent you from the District Attorney's office Thursday before Mr. Markham and I came here, in order to verify my expectation that you would urge Mr. Kenyon Kenting to request that all police interference be eliminated. This you did, and when I learned of it, after arriving here with Mr. Markham, I definitely objected to the proposal and counteracted your influence on Mr. Kenting so that you could not get the money safely that night. Seeing that part of your plan hopelessly failing, you cleverly changed your attitude and agreed to act for us—at my request through Sergeant Heath—as the person to place the money in the tree, and went through with the farce in order to prove that no connection existed between you and the demand for money. One of your henchmen had come to Central Park to pick up the package if everything went according to your prearranged schedule. Mr. Van Dine and I both saw the man. When he learned that you had not been successful with your plans, he undoubtedly reported your failure, thereby throwing fear into your hirelings that they might not be paid—which accounts for their keeping Mrs. Kenting alive as an effective threat to hold over you till payment was forthcoming."

Fleel looked up slowly with a patronizing grin.

"Aren't you overlooking the possibility, Mr. Vance, that young Kaspar kidnapped himself—as I maintained from the beginning—and was murdered by thugs later, for reasons and under circumstances unknown to us? Certainly all the evidence points to his self-abduction for the purpose of acquiring the money he needed."

"Ah! I've been expecting that observation," Vance returned, meeting the other's cynical stare. "The self-kidnapping setup was very clever. Much too clever. Overdone, in fact. As I see it, it was to have been your—what shall we call it?—your emergency escape, let us say, if your innocence in the matter should at any time be in doubt. In that event how easy it would have been for you to say just what you have said regarding the implications of a self-motivated pseudo-crime. And I am not overlooking the significant fact that you have consistently advised Mr. Kenyon Kenting to pay over the money in spite of the glaring evidence that Kaspar had planned the kidnapping himself."

Fleel's expression did not change. His grin became even more marked; in fact, when Vance paused and looked at him keenly, Fleel began to shake with mirth.

"A very pretty theory, Mr. Vance," he commented. "It shows remarkable ingenuity, but it entirely fails to take into consideration the fact that I myself was attacked by a sub-machine gunner on the very night of Mrs. Kenting's disappearance. You have conveniently forgotten that little episode since it would knock the entire foundation from under your amusing little house of cards."

Vance shook his head slowly, and though his smile seemed to broaden, it grew even chillier.

"No. Oh, no, Mr. Fleel. Not conveniently forgot—conveniently remembered. Most vivid recollection, don't y' know. And you were jolly well frightened by the attack. Surely, you don't believe your escape from any casualty was the result of a miracle. All quite simple, really. The gentleman with the machine-gun had no intention whatever of perforating you. His only object was to frighten you and warn you of exactly what to expect if you did not raise the money instanter to pay for the dastardly services rendered you. You were never safer in your life than when that machine-gun was sputtering away in your general direction."

The smirk slowly faded from Fleel's lips; his face flushed, and he stood up, glowering resentfully at Vance.

"Your theory, Mr. Vance," he said angrily, "no longer has even the merit of humour. Up to this point I have been amused by it and have been able to laugh at it. But you are carrying a joke too far, sir. And I wish you to know that I greatly resent your remarks." He remained standing.

"I don't regard that fact as disconcertin' in the least," Vance returned with a cold smile. "The fact is, Mr. Fleel, you will be infinitely more resentful when I inform you that at this very minute certified public accountants are at work on your books and that the police are scrutinizing most carefully the contents of your safe." Vance glanced indifferently at the cigarette in his hand.

For two seconds Fleel looked at him with a serious frown. Then he took a swift backward step and, thrusting his hand into his pocket, drew forth a large, ugly looking automatic. Both Heath and Snitkin had been watching him steadily, and as Fleel made this movement Heath, with lightning-like speed, produced an automatic from beneath the black sling of his wounded arm. The movements of the two men were almost concurrent.

But there was no need for Heath to fire his gun, for in that fraction of a second Fleel raised his automatic to his own temple and pulled the trigger. The weapon fell from his hand immediately, and his body slumped down against the edge of the desk and fell to the floor out of sight.

Vance, apparently, was little moved by the tragedy. However, after a deep sigh, he rose listlessly and stepped behind the desk. The others in the room were, I think, like myself, too paralyzed at the sudden termination of the case to make any move. Vance bent down.

"Dead, Markham,—quite," he announced as he rose, a moment or so later. "Consid'rate chappie—what? Has saved you legal worry no end. Most gratifyin'."

He was leaning now against the corner of the desk, and, nodding to Snitkin, who had rushed forward with an automatic in his hand, jerked his head significantly toward Fraim Falloway.

Snitkin hesitated but a moment. He slipped the gun back into his pocket and unlocked the handcuffs on young Falloway.

"Sorry, Mr. Falloway," murmured Vance. "But you lost your self-control and became a bit annoyin'. . . . Feelin' better?"

The youth stammered: "I'm all right." He was alert and apparently his normal self now. "And Sis will be home in a couple of days!" He found a cigarette, after much effort, and lighted it nervously.

"By the by, Mr. Kenting," Vance resumed, without moving from the desk, "there's a little point I want cleared up. I know that the District Attorney is aching to ask you a few questions about what happened yesterday evening. He had not heard from you and was unable to reach you. Did you, by any chance, give that fifty thousand dollars to Fleel?"

"Yes!" Kenting stood up excitedly. "I gave it to him a little after nine o'clock last night. We got the final instructions all right—that is, Fleel got them. He called me up right away and we arranged to meet. He said some one had telephoned to him and told him that the money had to be at a certain place—far up in the Bronx somewhere—at ten o'clock that night. He convinced me that this person on the telephone had said he would not deal with any one but Fleel."

He hesitated a moment.

"I was afraid to act through the police again, after that night in the park. So I took Fleel's urgent advice to leave the police out of it, and let him handle the matter. I was desperate! And I trusted him—God help me! I didn't telephone to Mr. Markham, and I wouldn't speak to him when he called. I was afraid. I wanted Madelaine back safe. And I gave the money to Fleel—and thought he could arrange everything. . . ."[1]

---

1. The practice of turning over ransom money to outsiders, in the hopes of settling kidnap cases, is not an unusual one. There have been several famous instances of this in recent years.

"I quite understand, Mr. Kenting." Vance spoke softly, in a tone which was not without pity. "I was pretty sure you had given him the money last night, for he telephoned to the Lord-Street house while we were there, obviously to make immediate arrangements to pay off his commissions, as it were. Sergeant Heath here recognized his voice over the wire. . . . But, really, y' know, Mr. Kenting, you should have trusted the police. Of course, Fleel received no message of instructions last night. It was part of his stupid technique, however, to tell you he had, for he needed the money and was at his wit's end. He too was desperate, I think. When Mr. Markham told me he was unable to get in touch with you, I rather thought, don't y' know, you had done just what you have stated. . . . Fleel was far too bold in showing us that note yesterday. Really, y' know, he shouldn't have done it. There were references in it which he thought only he himself could understand. Luckily, I saw through them. That note, in fact, verified my theory regarding him. But he showed it to us because he wished to make an impression on you. He needed that money. I rather think he had gambled away, in one way or another, the money he held in trust for the Kenting estate. We sha'n't know definitely till we get the report from Stitt and McCoy,[2] the accountants who are goin' over Fleel's books. It is quite immaterial, however."

Vance suddenly yawned and glanced at his watch.

"My word, Markham!" he exclaimed, turning to the District Attorney, who had sat stolidly and nonplussed through the amazing drama. "It's still rather early, don't y' know. If I hasten, old dear, I'll be able to catch the second act of Tristan and Isolde."

Vance went swiftly across the room to Mrs. Falloway and bowed over her hand solicitously with a murmured *adieu*. Then he hurried out to his car waiting at the curb.

* * * * * * * *

When the reports from the accountants and the police came in at the end of the day on which Fleel had shot himself, Vance's theory and suppositions were wholly substantiated. The accountants found that Fleel had been speculating heavily on his own behalf with the funds he held in trust for the Kenting estate. His bank had already called upon him to cover the legitimate investments permitted him

---

2. This was the same firm of certified public accountants whom Markham had called in to inspect the books of the firm of Benson and Benson in the investigation of the Benson murder case.

by law as the trustee of the estate. The amount he had embezzled was approximately fifty thousand dollars, and as he had long since lost his own money in the same kind of precarious bucket-shop transactions, it would have been but a matter of days before the shortage caused by his extra-legal operations would have been discovered.

In his safe were found practically all the gem-stones missing from the Kenting collection, including the large and valuable alexandrite. (How or when he had acquired this last item was never definitely determined.) The package of bills which Kenyon Kenting had so trustingly given him was also found in the safe.

All this happened years before the actual account of the case was set down here. Since then, Kenyon Kenting has married his sister-in-law, Madelaine, who returned to the Purple House the second day after Fleel's suicide.

Less than a year later Vance and I had tea with Mrs. Falloway. Vance had a genuine affection for the crippled old woman. As we were about to go, Fraim Falloway entered the room. He was a different man from the one we had known during the investigation of what the papers persisted in calling the Kenting kidnap case (perhaps the alliteration of the nomenclature was largely the reason for it). Fraim Falloway's face had noticeably filled in, and his colour was healthy and normal; there was a vitality in his eyes, and he moved with ease and determined alacrity. His whole manner had changed. I learned later that old Mrs. Falloway had called in the endocrinologist whose name Vance had given her, and that the youth had been under observation and treatment for many months.

After our greetings that day Vance asked Falloway casually how his stamp collecting was going. The youth seemed almost scornful and replied he had no time for such matters any more—that he was too busy with his new work at the Museum of Natural History to devote any of his time to so futile a pursuit as philately.

It might be interesting to note, in closing, that Kenyon Kenting's first act, after his marriage to Madelaine Kenting, was to have the exterior of the Purple House thoroughly scraped and sand-blasted, so that the natural colour of the bricks and stones was restored. It ceased to be the "purple house," and took on a more domestic and *gemütlich* appearance, and has so remained to the present day.

LEONAUR

ALSO FROM LEONAUR
AVAILABLE IN SOFTCOVER OR HARDCOVER WITH DUST JACKET

THE LONG PATROL *by George Berrie*—A Novel of Light Horsemen from Gallipoli to the Palestine campaign of the First World War.

NAPOLEONIC WAR STORIES *by Arthur Quiller-Couch*—Tales of soldiers, spies, battles & sieges from the Peninsular & Waterloo campaingns.

THE FIRST DETECTIVE *by Edgar Allan Poe*—The Complete Auguste Dupin Stories—The Murders in the Rue Morgue, The Mystery of Marie Rogêt & The Purloined Letter.

THE COMPLETE DR NIKOLA—MAN OF MYSTERY: 1 *by Guy Boothby*—*A Bid for Fortune & Dr Nikola Returns*—Guy Boothby's Dr.Nikola adventures continue to fascinate readers and enthusiasts of crime and mystery fiction because—in the manner of Raffles, the gentleman cracksman—here is character far removed from the uncompromising goodness of Holmes and Watson or the uncompromising evil of Professor Moriarty.

THE COMPLETE DR NIKOLA—MAN OF MYSTERY: 2 *by Guy Boothby*—*The Lust of Hate, Dr Nikola's Experiment & Farewell, Nikola*—Guy Boothby's Dr.Nikola adventures continue to fascinate readers and enthusiasts of crime and mystery fiction because—in the manner of Raffles, the gentleman cracksman—here is character far removed from the uncompromising goodness of Holmes and Watson or the uncompromising evil of Professor Moriarty.

THE CASEBOOKS OF MR J. G. REEDER: BOOK 1 *by Edgar Wallace*—*Room 13, The Mind of Mr J. G. Reeder* and *Terror Keep*—Edgar Wallace's sleuth—whose territory is the London of the 1920s—is an unlikely figure, more bank clerk than detective in appearance, ever wearing his square topped bowler, frock coat, cravat and muffler, Mr Reeder is usually inseparable from his umbrella.

THE CASEBOOKS OF MR J. G. REEDER: BOOK 2 *by Edgar Wallace*—*Red Aces, Mr J. G. Reeder Returns, The Guv'nor* and *The Man Who Passed*—Edgar Wallace's sleuth—whose territory is the London of the 1920s—is an unlikely figure, more bank clerk than detective in appearance, ever wearing his square topped bowler, frock coat, cravat and muffler, Mr Reeder is usually inseparable from his umbrella.

THE COMPLETE FOUR JUST MEN: VOLUME 1 *by Edgar Wallace*—*The Four Just Men, The Council of Justice & The Just Men of Cordova*—disillusioned with a world where the wicked and the abusers of power perpetually go unpunished, the Just Men set about to rectify matters according to their own standards, and retribution is dispensed on swift and deadly wings.